THE LAST
SECRET
OF
GALILEO

ARISTIDE BERGAMASCO

PRESS

VULPINE
PRESS

First published in Italian as *L'ultimo Segreto di Galileo* by Leone Editore in 2015
Published by Vulpine Press in the United Kingdom in 2020

Translated by Julia Gabrielle Barnes and Giuseppe Sofo

Cover by Claire Wood

ISBN: 978-1-83919-024-7

www.vulpine-press.com

To Simona, my wife
and to my daughters, Sara and Marta.

PROLOGUE

Pisa, 1631

The woman's heartrending cries still rang in his ears, although more than six hours had passed. The doctor Cristofano Galotti had set the long beak-shaped mask against the table mirror, while the fragrant herbs that filled its papier-mâché nostrils fell scattered on the furniture. The man prayed that those substances had protected him from infection that day, but he was increasingly doubtful of this. He sighed, shaken, leaning his hands on the wooden ledge. The woman blamed him for the death of her two children, tormented by purple and festering boils that he had not been able to cure, despite all his medication, his bloodlettings, his purges, despite the "theriac," made from opium and viper poison that came from Venice and had cost him two weeks of preparation. While she railed against him and struck him with her nearly skeletal hands, causing his mask to fall off, dark blood began to drip from her mouth and nostrils. She had died two hours later, cursing him with her last breath. Without knowing why, the doctor's thoughts returned to the ship that, walking in the port, he had seen drifting, full of sick people who were barred from landing. Cristofano felt that his city was like this too: a great ship, full of the dead and those few who had still not resigned themselves to the inevitable, lost in the sea of despair.

To return home he had to use a stick to drive off a pack of dogs that were feeding on the flesh of a corpse. The gravediggers, convicts snatched from the galleys specifically to remove the dead and throw them in mass graves, had not yet passed by that way. Or maybe they had already gone by and the Grim Reaper had continued his trade behind them, indifferent. He felt weak. Cristofano attributed it to the fact that he had not gotten anything to eat throughout the day; in the city food was scarce because the crops were drying up in the fields and the animals were dying in the stables or wandering in the woods with no one to take care of them.

A purplish drop fell onto his tired hand, leaning on the table mirror. The doctor looked at his reflection and paled: rivulets of dark lymph flowed from his nose, and with a sudden coughing fit he sprayed the metallic mirror with blood.

It was the plague.

Ancona, a few months earlier

MURDER ON THE RIVER.

VICTIM FOUND HANGED FROM A BRIDGE, but doctors rule out suicide.

According to investigators the death of Antonio Martone happened by homicide; 45-year-old alcoholic mason whose body was found hanged from a bridge on the Esino river, in the province of Ancona. The position of the body had initially looked like suicide, but the doctor who arrived at the scene immediately denied that hypothesis, making the investigators spring into action. The man had worked sporadically with the Terenzi brothers construction company and was already known by the police for a record of theft and alcohol-related problems. The motive however remains unclear and the investigators are not excluding any hypothesis.

1

Dr. Rebecca De Cardinale gazed, satisfied, at the monitor of her computer in the middle of her office desk, on the second floor of the Zooprophylactic Institute of the Triveneto in Legnaro, province of Padua. Sipping hot tea, she made sure that the corrections she had requested on her personal profile had been respected. Since a minister had mandated that the résumés of all civil servants and their salaries be published online, she had had to waste a lot of working time to fill out questionnaires that the secretary had then released on the web, though incorrect. She was born in Padua and proud of it; her profile, however, after a week read that her hometown was Cittadella. Cute, but not her Padua. As soon as she read it, she had furiously phoned the secretary, burying the elderly lady who was responsible for it in curses and demands for immediate modification. "Immediate" was not exactly the most appropriate term to describe the rate at which the offending data had been changed, but in early March, after one month, her profile was finally corrected. However, although three months had now passed since the clarification, she returned to the site periodically to ensure that her profile was in order. The profile which, however, did not matter much to her, and which she was sure that no one was going to read.

After her break, she put on her white coat, arranging her long auburn curls and heading towards the lab. Wielding the Petri dish under the exhaust hood and wearing gloves to protect herself from contact,

3

she could not help but consider the exaggeration of that alarm: in Germany and France, several cases of contamination by Escherichia coli had been confirmed, a bacteria residing in the intestine which in the past was only rarely associated with some form of sickness: in most cases, trivial cystitis. The cases in Germany and France that summer, however, had been caused by a strain of bacteria hitherto unknown, which could cause the death of red blood cells and kidney failure and, in a few tens of cases, turn out to be fatal. The bacterium had proved resistant to most known antibiotics. She had been given the critical task of finding out which combination of antibiotics the superbug, sent by German laboratories, was sensitive to. In any case, a solution to the modest epidemic that had caused extensive damage to the European food industry was welcomed, and the director had instructed her to find it, as she was the brightest among all microbiologists in his service.

Rebecca prepared the sample in the capsule, closed it again sterilely and put it back carefully, following the protocol, in the temperature-controlled cabinet that had been dedicated to the investigation of just that kind of artifact. She closed the heavy, tempered-glass door of the cabinet holding her breath and quickly ridded herself of the double pair of sterile gloves that she had taken, throwing them in a special airtight container. If the fear of the bacterium had affected her, too, as author-ized personnel, she was not surprised that the phobia of contamination was taking hold of the population; already the newspapers dedicated pages and pages to estimations of the economic damages caused by the bromatotoxism and by the paranoia that it was causing through all the old continent. At times globalization and the immediate availability of news could be detrimental, she reflected. The doctor left the laboratory and returned to her computer station, with the intent of resuming the data collection begun that morning when the intercom on her desk made her jump. Rebecca automatically responded: "De Cardinale?"

"Rebecca, the professor wants you in his office right away," said the voice of the secretary. The doctor hung up, curious. The woman's tone had been far from her usual apathy; she could have defined it as almost...excited. She stood up from her desk and walked down the long corridor that separated her from the office of Professor Benatti.

The professor was an elderly instructor at the University of Padua, perhaps one of the oldest. Having had to give up his position at the Institute of Microbiology because of his advanced age, he had managed to take over direction of the Zooprophylactic Institute. His office was a spacious one with a real leather chair and a root-wood desk, preceded by a small antechamber of which Miss Carli was the uncontested owner. When Rebecca passed in front of her, she was meticulously coloring her lips with a scarlet red that now was out of fashion. *Another strange one,* the doctor thought to herself. When she opened the door she understood the reason for such excitement. Professor Benatti welcomed her with a smile, indicating the other two people present in his office: "Rebecca, I'd like to introduce you to Professor Spinelli and Doctor Vinci."

The professor was a man in his fifties, with thick gray hair, like Richard Gere in *Shall We Dance.* Rebecca was almost immediately struck by his equally noble and relaxed bearing, without any trace of haughtiness. The real reason behind Miss Carli's lipstick, however, was his assistant, Dr. Vinci: around thirty-five years old, six feet tall, dark hair cut short, perfectly sculpted chin. Not so much as his torso, barely concealed by his large, nearly shapeless dark shirt. Now he smiled at her cordially, but the gaze with which he had scrutinized her upon her entrance into the room did not escape the doctor. In a fraction of a second his dark eyes had weighed her up and stripped her; a glacial sensation that had almost frozen her in the door.

A luxurious leather portfolio was lain on the desk, whose contents, judging by the gazes of all those present, must be delicate or precious or both. Professor Benatti was handling a yellowed page, just lifting the edges of the glass frame that protected it, while the apprehensive eyes of the other teacher followed his movements attentively.

"The professor and his assistant are from the Department of Literature and Philosophy," explained the microbiologist, adjusting his vision while exerting himself to read the words handwritten on the folio. "They want to know from us if another professor of this university had an intuition that could literally change our understanding of history or just anticipated the delirium of countless science-fiction writers." It was at that point that Spinelli intervened; his voice was confident and warm, pleasantly coordinated with his appearance.

"I'm sure that you will have heard of him; he was a famous mathematics professor..." He waited for the expression of curiosity that he expected to appear on the doctor's face. "I'm talking about Galileo Galilei."

The literature professor rose to his feet: he was taller than her by almost a whole head, a bit less than his intimidating assistant who wore an elegant jacket, tailored to his size. He delicately took the document from Benatti's hands and presented it for the attention of the doctor. What Rebecca saw was a yellowed, diligently sealed document in a frame of transparent glass, which rendered both the front and the back legible.

"This document, which came into my possession a short time ago," explained the professor without taking his eyes off his interlocutor, "is an authentic letter by Galileo."

"Fascinating," she replied, sincere and intrigued. She waited for the follow-up and opened her eyes wide in search of understanding— between those words penned hundreds of years before with faded ink and incomprehensible handwriting—of the importance of the missive.

Professor Spinelli smiled, imitated by his assistant, then decided to move with the help of the two others present.

"In order to be met by your irreverent eyes," he teased affably, "I prepared a draft of the letter in Arial," he concluded, signaling to his assistant who, with a few finger strokes on his laptop keyboard, arranged for it to be sent to Professor Benatti's email address. *Obviously they agreed on this little show before leaving,* Rebecca thought while observing the elegant movement with which Spinelli had passed from the other side of the desk to help his elderly colleague open the electronic document and print it out. It was the host who took the first sheet from the printer, while Rebecca had to hierarchically wait for the second copy.

"Are you sure of its authenticity?" the director of the institute asked seriously. Professor Benatti was an adept researcher whose reflexes had slowed a bit with age, but now his attention had focused on the document and it seemed those years had never passed.

"I can guarantee it to you," Spinelli confirmed, impatient.

Rebecca, lost in the antiquated syntax, had not yet finished reading, but interrupted herself to follow the dialogue between the two instructors. In raising her gaze she met the eyes of Spinelli's assistant and, in that precise moment, she knew how prey might feel when it met the eyes of the predator, an instant before being seized inexorably in the fatal attack. She froze as though paralyzed, incapable of thought, but the man's features immediately relaxed, assuming a serene and relaxed expression; the exact opposite of the one prior.

"So you're saying that Galileo Galilei was convinced that the plague was brought on by…a shooting star?" Benatti asked.

"A meteorite," intervened Dr. Vinci, speaking up for the first time. His voice was clear and sure, his tone dry and precise. *Almost militaristic,* thought Rebecca. Spinelli continued: "In the letter Galileo makes reference to a book: *Stella Novissima.* The two microbiologists nodded,

7

searching for the words that had just been cited in the text that they still clutched in their fingers, as though the act of locating them would clarify their interlocutor's point. He, picking up on their uncertainty, continued: "It's a 'mythical book' like William Shakespeare's *The History of Cardenio* or most of Aeschylus's tragedies…" Spinelli's eyes shone with excitement.

The scholar sighed, looking towards his assistant, who returned the look of commiseration and intervened to help: "They are all books whose titles were preserved though history, but lost to us; several citations survive, when we're lucky, a few lines repeated by other authors. The Holy Grail of literature, *Stella Novissima* is among the most sought-after—"

"It is believed to have been written by Galileo," Spinelli intervened, reclaiming control over the situation. "Even if he obviously could not print it in Italy."

"Why?" asked Rebecca.

"Otherwise he would have been burned at the stake!" Spinelli shot at her with a malicious look. Rebecca stayed silent, intimidated; the treatment suffered by the scientist four hundred years previously was certainly not her fault.

Dr. Vinci spoke again, as if to soften the bitter comment: "Galileo had already been tried and convicted by the Inquisition for his astro-nomical writings and had avoided the death penalty only by abjuring his own postulates. Obviously, he had been forbidden from writing, teaching, or even thinking beyond the widespread geocentric theory."

"Indeed," recalled Professor Benatti. "But Galileo maintained, and rightly so, the heliocentric theory of Copernicus, which placed the sun almost to its correct position in the center of our system. It is said that, forced to recant, he muttered the famous phrase 'And yet it moves,' referring to the earth."

"This is just part of the legend," corrected Spinelli. "Galileo never uttered those words. Forced by the Inquisition, he spent a short time in Rome, confined to the residence of the Signoria of Florence, until he was permitted to return to his city, still under 'house arrest,' a condition in which he spent the last years of his existence. *Stella Novissima* would be the proof that not only did the scientist not observe the interdiction of the Inquisition, but that he made further discoveries and tried to make them public."

"Well," concluded Benatti, tired of the digression and clearly resentful of being treated by his colleague like a student who had shown up for an exam unprepared. "How can two microbiologists help the Department of Literature? Certainly not by establishing the paternity of the disappeared book, much less by finding it…"

Spinelli's expression softened: "I'm afraid that this is beyond even our means," he admitted, "but I intend to publish the most comprehensive scientific work on this subject and I can assure you that it will cause a racket; and your contribution will be crucial," he coaxed. "I ask you to assess the scientific consistency of Galilei's theory…"

"Meaning, if an infectious disease can be carried by a meteorite?" Benatti repeated incredulously. "Absurd!" was his immediate judgment.

"Actually, there are studies that claim to have demonstrated the presence of some archaeobacteria on meteorites," contradicted Dr. De Cardinale.

Benatti snorted again and then smiled, pleased to see on the two scholars' faces the same perplexed expression that he had displayed a bit earlier, when they were discussing literature. "The archaea are extremely primitive and ancient life forms: they date back to over three point five billion years ago," he explained to them. Then turning to his assistant: "Their presence on meteoric bodies is at the very least controversial; according to most, they may simply be terrestrial bacteria that contaminated the meteorites after they entered the atmosphere…" Then he fell silent, realizing that he had just found to a way to satisfy the request of his illustrious colleague without any effort on his own part: "Dear Spinelli, I think you've found a collaborator for your research," he concluded mischievously, without giving her time to reply.

Returning to her office, Rebecca sloppily threw the notes she had just received on Galileo's book down onto the desk. An umpteenth scientific article to prepare – just what she needed, with the long-overdue vacation that awaited her! Moreover, she knew she would still be working for others, one of the motives for which she had left the university Department of Microbiology. Rebecca knew from experience that in this case too, although the bulk of the work had fallen on her shoulders, the credit would go to the two professors; if she was lucky her name would be cited third, and thus beyond the point where, according to the new norms, she would be able to cite the work on her résumé. Provided that the imposing Dr. Vinci did not outdo her, since the topic was more literary than scientific.

As though materializing from her thoughts, Vinci appeared in her office. Rebecca rose from her chair, immediately on the defensive. Since the door was open, she could not even reproach him for failing to knock. The microbiologist immediately sought the eyes of Valentina, the chemical engineer who was working in the office to the left, beyond the glass wall that formed the border of their respective stations. Despite seeming engaged in something, Rebecca realized that her eyes were wandering; more probably, her eyes kept wandering back to the muscular back of her uninvited guest. The doctor relaxed a little. She looked at the man questioningly and tried not to appear too annoyed by the intrusion. After all, they would be working together for who knew how long, which seemed to her like too much time anyway.

"The professor wants you to have these too," he said cordially. His black eyes were framed by long lashes and thick eyebrows: she was sure

10

that the expression he was directing at her had found him a way into many female hearts, or at least into their panties. This knowledge irritated her.

"Thank you," she replied laconically, hoping that he had not noticed the way she had mistreated the rest of the entrusted documentations; but the man's eyes were fixed instead on the scattered papers on the opposite corner of the table.

"Do you already have my number?" he asked her, pulling a business card from his pocket. "It could be useful…for work," he hurriedly clarified, pointing a finger at the papers he had just delivered.

"That's an idea," she said, but her tone worked instead to convey, *If you think I'm going to give you my number you can just wait for Galileo to give you his…* This did not seem to upset the doctoral candidate, who went back on the attack: "You seem very taken by your work," he said, sounding sincere.

"Yeah," she admitted, satisfied, convinced that the perfect opportunity to get rid of him had just been handed to her on a silver platter. But he surprised her instead: "I would like to take some photographs of you," he blurted. Seeing her reaction, somewhere between surprised and scandalized, he corrected the slip: "At work, I mean. I loved your intent expression while you read the letter a little while ago."

"Look, Doctor Vinci…" Rebecca began, with chills running down her spine while she thought back to his eyes on her just before.

"Alessandro."

"Doctor Vinci," she responded, as if she had not heard. "I think that our relationship should stay as professional as possible…" she said, letting his business card that she still clutched in her fingers drop to the desk. Then she turned to her computer, flushed with anger, hoping that he had gotten the message and would liberate her of his presence. On her screen she watched the reflection of the doctoral student's back as

11

her desire was fulfilled and she finally breathed a sigh of relief. As soon as she was gone, Valentina swooped into her office.

"Tell me that he gave you his number," implored the young chemist, while another colleague joined her.

"No," Rebecca lied, fearing that their interest could give her another reason to get back in contact with him, and she threw the business card he had given her into the trash. "He wanted…to photograph me," she then confessed, still upset by his proposal.

"And you agreed to it, right?" demanded Rita, the newcomer.

"Of course not!" she replied, doubly offended. "What kind of approach was that?" she asked aloud.

"Did you see those shoulders?"

"His shoulders?" shot Nicoletta, appearing at the door. The curly haired and stick-thin janitor was famous throughout the department for her frivolity and congeniality, which were both abundant. "But didn't you hear? He's a photographer! God, how I'd like to see his telephoto lens!" A salvo of laughter resounded at the janitor's words and she cheekily continued: "Tell me that Miss Rottermeier took down his address…" she closed, alluding to the grim Miss Carli.

"I don't think so," Valentina said, disappointing her. Then her face brightened. "But I think Rebecca could get it…"

The doctor shot her a dirty look, but Rita joined the attack: "Of course! Do you still have the password?"

Rebecca resumed cursing the day that she had let it slip that she was still in possession of the account credentials reserved for university employees. When she had left, she had been certain that no one would ever take up the hassle of revoking them, so she was still in possession of privileged access to confidential information about the academic world. The three women insisted until she capitulated; she typed quickly on her keyboard and found the name they were looking for. Behind her, three pairs of hungry eyes made her feel guilty about her breach of privacy, even if the unknowing victim was the unpleasant Dr Vinci. On the site page his picture appeared almost drab, and certainly did not do him justice. Rebecca thought it was strange; she would have expected from that obvious exhibitionist that even his official profile would say, "Look how beautiful and muscular I am." She got lost in his personal details.

"He's also a bit slow on the uptake," she said after a while, overwhelmed by the criticisms of the other women. "Look here: he looks my age but he graduated a while after me, and a degree in Literature takes less time than medicine, even without counting the residency. I'm not surprised that he's still completing his doctorate…"

"Maybe he did something else, before enrolling at the university," defended Rita.

Rebecca started to look for his date of registration but was interrupted by Nicoletta, quivering: "Search for his address, I'll give him some private lessons…"

Just then one of her colleagues, another janitor, poked her head in. She looked into the office and conspiratorially warned, "Ceccottin's in the hallway!"

At those words, Nicoletta ran to her cleaning cart and rapidly left the room, pretending to empty the dustpan. Ceccottin was her supervisor and did not look upon her favorably; if he had surprised her wasting time again during working hours she would have certainly been in trouble. Once, Rebecca had literally hidden her under her desk: that day the supervisor had been in a fury and had he caught her talking with them instead of working, he certainly would have fired her. Having escaped the danger, Nicoletta had promised her that she would always remember the kindness that had saved her job.

"The address!" she mumbled in Rebecca's direction, leaving the office.

The doctor, groaning over the childish waste of time, gave in and wrote it down on a sticky note that she then slipped into her purse, promising herself to deliver it at the end of the shift.

One morning Rebecca was examining an email containing encouraging results from a German hospital that confirmed the efficacy of the antibiotics she had tested when she was interrupted by the phone ringing.

"De Cardinale," she answered, while her eyes continued reading the data.

"Doctor," said a warm and strong voice, which she recognized immediately and which commanded her full attention. "This is Professor Spinelli. Do you have a free moment for me?"

Her heart began to beat hard, and not only because of her sense of guilt; exactly one week had passed since she had been assigned the project and she had not yet begun the bibliographical research for the scientific article that she would collaborate on with him. "I...I just began the work—" she stammered in justification.

But the man interrupted her: "Of course, don't worry; but there is something I must speak to you about, even more pressing than the scientific article we are writing, although we might say it's closely related to that."

"Of course," she agreed. "Would you like me to alert Professor Benatti?"

"No!" he exclaimed, almost alarmed. "Can I count on your discretion?"

They met in a bar off the beaten track, chosen by Professor Spinelli half an hour prior. The man was already seated and wearing a brand-name polo shirt, carefully ironed, whose dark blue color set off the man's tanned complexion and pale blue eyes perfectly. A match that was undoubtedly the result of a careful selection. He stood up in a gallant gesture when she approached.

"Good morning, Professor…" the woman began, amazed at herself for using the same deferential tone as when she was a student.

"Doctor… May I order something for you?" he asked, holding in his hand a glass half-full of tonic water. Rebecca stared at the slender, manicured fingers that were gripping it.

"No, thank you, I'm all right," she declined, taking a place at the secluded table. Spinelli looked around warily, as if the retirees who spent the early morning hours ordering the "*ombre*," the traditional small glasses of wine, were interested in what a literature professor would confide in a microbiologist.

"I'm not satisfied with just publishing a new article on *Stella Novissima*," he said conspiratorially with his blue eyes blazing. "I want to find it!" Rebecca felt a chill run down her spine. She did not know if it came from the look on his face or what he was implying.

"But…Doctor Vinci?"

Spinelli smiled sardonically, leaning against the back of the chair. "Vinci? Like good old Benatti, he's too cautious; he doesn't believe in the manuscript's existence, he doesn't believe in its author. But I am convinced that Galilei left us clues to find his book. And the first…" The man furtively brought his leather portfolio out on the table and extracted a folio from the manuscript, very similar to the framed one that he had exhibited to them a few days ago, in Professor Benatti's office. He gently handed it to Rebecca.

Two hours later, on the desk of the Zooprophylactic Institute's secretary, Dr. De Cardinale's overdue vacation request appeared.

2

The Tuscan-Emilian Apennines extended around them, breathtakingly beautiful in spite of the circuitous slap of asphalt and exhaust gas that was the A1 motorway.

She had agreed on the spot to the proposal that the man had made to her only the day before and he had not wasted any time. Spinelli's dark gray Mercedes rounded the steep curves of that section of highway with care and silence, except for the music coming from the car. The notes of the Pink Floyd concert in Venice, chosen by Spinelli in honor of his guest, had been the trip's soundtrack from Padua to Florence. "I have to admit that I don't know much about Galileo Galilei," confessed the doctor, who had not even had time to brush up on her remote knowledge of history.

Spinelli smiled condescendingly. "To understand him, you need to understand his historical period," he began, as if expecting her cue. "Around the seventeenth century, Italy did not exist as a political entity. The head of house was Spain, which ruled Sicily, Sardinia, Naples and the Duchy of Milan. A perfect description of this period can be found in *The Betrothed*," he told her, while Rebecca thought back to what she remembered of Manzoni's work. "The era of Lorenzo the Magnificent had ended, as well as Italian monetary superiority, overtaken by the far more aggressive economies of the Protestant countries."

"And the Church?" Rebecca intervened, calling upon all her memories of high school.

"The Papal States," corrected the professor, "thanks to the Spanish, had extended their dominion even over most of central Italy. In previous centuries it had given rise to Humanism, filling the streets of Rome with pictorial, architectural, and sculptural splendors which still today mark the pinnacle of human creativity. To do this, however, they indebted themselves to the marrow and sold the most valuable things they had, just to compete: the sacraments. It was also for this reason, the so-called "sale of indulgences," that Luther railed against the worldliness of the Roman Church, giving rise to the Protestant schism. In order to decorate their capital, the popes lost half of their Christians. In order to react to the schism and reiterate its moral, intellectual and political superiority, the Church of Rome called for the Council of Trent. If Luther proposed a reform, the Church retaliated with a counter-reform, barricading themselves within the infallibility of the precepts of its own doctrine. The popes that followed during and after the Council were busy creating an apparatus of control, especially doctrinal, founded on congregations, which were owned by the Holy Office, headed directly by the pope himself. It is against this backdrop that Galileo Galilei moved, under the watchful eye of the Catholic Church and the Inquisition."

The car swept gracefully up the stretch of highway and the short section of bypass that separated it from the Tuscan capital, crept through the suburb streets, and finally made its way with difficulty among the tourists who trod enchanted along the paths of the city center. Rebecca, who had even visited it a number of times, let her gaze be captured by the magnificent basilica of Brunelleschi. The car stopped a few feet from Piazza della Repubblica. For a moment it seemed that Professor Spinelli had stopped someone to ask for directions, but instead he turned the car engine off and with a nod of his head signaled a valet, who immediately took the keys to the Mercedes from his hands.

"We're here," he confirmed, dedicating a benevolent smile to the stunned expression of his assistant. Rebecca got out and looked up: the hotel Savoy, as indicated by its elegant insignia, boasted two stars more than the places where she could afford to spend the holidays. "Obviously you will be my guest," the professor assured her, gallantly offering her an arm as he guessed her thoughts. Rebecca breathed a sigh of relief as the professor withdrew the keys to the two superior deluxe rooms booked under his name; she did not know how she would have reacted had she discovered that there was only room booked…and why should she?

Shortly after, having reached her room on the top floor, she opened the elegant French doors that led to the balcony. The view of the city was a breathtaking one. Florence spread out magnificently, sensual and noisy at her feet; its perfumes intoxicated her almost until her head spun. She was in the most elegant room that she had ever seen, in quest of a "mythical book" and in the company of an interesting university professor. A charming university professor, she admitted. Trying to contain her excitement, she decided to unpack her suitcase, reprimanding herself for having thought to bring only casual clothing. She could not present herself at the restaurant wearing what she had in her suitcase, but even if she wanted to spend a small fortune buying something suitable in the city center boutiques, it was too late now. They would already be closed. Struck by the most atavistic complex of feminine inadequacy, she cursed the Cinderella in her and let her excitement vanish well before the last stroke of midnight by opting for a tormented, but dignified, empty stomach.

"Good morning." His voice was warm and deep as ever.

"Good morning, Professor," said Rebecca.

The breakfast room was richly illuminated by crystal chandeliers in the expectation that the rays of the morning sun would strengthen considerably, cutting an intricate path through the tall building surrounding the square.

"Michele."

"What?" asked Rebecca.

"It's better if we set aside the formalities, don't you think?"

"As you like," she forced herself to say, pleasantly uncomfortable.

"You didn't come down to dinner last night," he ascertained.

"No, I was very tired," Rebecca lied and, hesitating in front of the wide variety of delicacies at the buffet, she tried to ignore the pangs of hunger that clutched her. She looked at the single cup of coffee that the server had just brought to her companion and she was about to abandon any hope of filling her stomach: she really did not want to look bad. But Spinelli saved her; bearing the largest plate available, he approached the lavish buffet tables and began to fill it. Rebecca smiled and, reassured, managed to satisfy her hunger. "So, what's the plan?" she asked, curious.

"A visit to Count Gianfranco Zacchia," he replied. "According to my research he is in possession of a letter attributed to Galilei in which his new book is mentioned between the lines. It may contain some clues as to where to seek it out."

"All right." She nodded, rising from the table.

After receiving the car from a valet, they left Florence to go along the winding roads of the Tuscan Apennines. After a good hour of travel they arrived at an old country house built on top of a hill, in an elevated position with respect to the surrounding countryside and not far from the main road. They parked and walked to the main entrance; Spinelli rang the bell. The door opened without a creak, but it was perhaps the last efficient part of what must have once been a magnificent villa. The wrinkled hands clutching the door handle did not, in fact, belong to a servant, but to the last descendant of the family. The signs of decay that consumed what must have once been a wealthy dynasty were evident in every corner, even in the slightly stale air, despite the open windows. While their host welcomed them and bade them sit in the worn-out living room, Rebecca noticed an attitude of arrogance on his part, or almost discomfort at their entrance within those noble walls. She was glad that Michele was talking. Caught in his unnatural haughtiness, he had not even removed the lightweight leather gloves that complemented his refined look.

In the minutes that followed, their recalcitrant host's air of superiority dissolved more and more as Professor Spinelli performed an extraordinary demonstration of culture and barely perceptible flattery which stroked the impoverished nobleman's ego. Rebecca was admiring of the effect of the man's charm on the elderly count and the nonchalance with which he pulled a white envelope from the inside pocket of his coat, waving it before the eyes of his interlocutor like a bone before the eyes of a hungry dog, and then quietly disappearing it back where it came from.

Rebecca could have sworn that she saw Gianfranco Zacchia swallow his drool. She struggled to hold back a smile. He stood in silence watching Spinelli who, in turn, did not take his eyes off him while he rose and slowly disappeared from the room, reappearing shortly thereafter carrying several binders. He deposited them on the table before them and began to leaf through the contents with agonizing slowness; they were all ancient documents of various origins. The woman thought that, were this intentional, that seller's tactic was working; even Spinelli showed signs of impatience as he watched the man's uncertain fingers flip through the yellowed folios in their protective envelopes. At last they came to the relevant one and here Zacchia's voice became more certain: "It's a fond family memory," he began cryptically. "A letter from Galileo Galilei to Evangelista Torricelli."

His eyes fell to Rebecca's, questioning. Seeing the signs of an embarrassed ignorance, he smiled maliciously. "Certainly, you know who this is," he teased her treacherously. Spinelli stood up to examine the letter, leaning on a table of antiques standing a short way from the couch, on which their host had prepared three glasses and a carafe of fruit juice. Rebecca blushed like a schoolgirl caught unprepared for an exam. Perhaps to participate in this research she should really have better acquainted herself with the details of the scientist's life, but on the other hand she simply had not had the time. If she had expected Michele's solidarity, she was disappointed; the man remained aloof, absorbed in his analysis and only deigning to give her a smile, an accomplice of their host. "Of course, the presence of beauty is important," Zacchia conceded magnanimously, giving a long, sarcastic look. Rebecca was about to testily reply but Spinelli gently rested a hand on her arm, quieting her. Obviously he wanted to exploit any possible advantage on the sale born from the collusion he had just established with the ruined nobleman. Smiling captivatingly, he looked disdainfully at the woman, pointing to the letter that interested him: "Where were we?" he asked, urging towards the conclusion of the deal.

"Indeed," conceded the other, "we must go study."

"The letter," Rebecca exploded, pale with rage. "We're here for the letter."

"A family heirloom," the man repeated, again barricading himself cunningly behind the comfortable guise of the enthusiast who must surrender a valuable piece in spite of himself.

"Certainly," granted Spinelli, retrieving the white envelope and depositing it on the table. "It's a pity that its authenticity has not been confirmed, otherwise it might be displayed in a museum along with the other letters."

"If you came here from Padua that means that its authenticity is confirmed enough for you," the man retorted, nearly offended, but his

21

gaze broke away from the envelope. "You know, I received another offer for the letters recently."

"For this particular one?" asked Spinelli, stiffening in disbelief.

"No, for all of them. A…generous offer."

"How generous?" the man snapped.

With an elegant gesture the old man wrote a figure in pencil on a block of high-quality paper, turning it towards the professor. Rebecca watched his jaw twitch, his willingness clearly surpassed by that amount, true or professed as it was.

"Why did you have us come all the way here?" hissed Spinelli, grabbing his envelope and placing it in his jacket. He stood up, as if to conclude the meeting.

The old man leaned back in his vintage chair, smirking. "The offer is for all the letters in my possession," he explained. "If I were to sell one before concluding with the other party, I would no longer be the owner of it…Of course, we still have to take another look at the figure you proposed," he finished triumphantly.

Spinelli sat down, only marginally calmer. "Who's offering?" he asked, grabbing his pencil and writing a counteroffer.

"I'm afraid I am not at liberty to answer that. They specifically demanded absolute secrecy."

The professor stiffened again, but Rebecca thought this time it was for the new proposal, a higher one, that the man was writing underneath his. She saw him take the paper back into his hands, writing another number, a bit lower. "Final offer," he declared, standing up, immediately imitated by her.

Zacchia realized he had pushed his luck too far and with an accommodating smile, pulled the folio from its container along with its protection and laid it on the table. Spinelli took the envelope from his pocket for the last time and added more bills from his wallet until he reached the agreed amount. Making the best of a bad job, he picked up the juice-filled glass and proposed a toast, which Zacchia reacted to contentedly.

They left the house shortly after. The doctor waited for him to speak first.

"The Count wasn't very naïve, was he?" the scholar finally sighed with a smile, holding tight to the leather portfolio where he had placed his purchase. She shot back a half-smile still seething with the humiliation suffered at the hands of the unpleasant old man. She was especially stung by the bad impression she had made next to Spinelli. She was a bit upset that he had not come to her defense; but she justified him by considering that, in the end, that little show had had the effect of facilitating the sale.

"I wonder who the other buyer was?" she asked, forcing herself to take her mind off the desire for revenge against Zacchia. But Spinelli gave no sign of having heard. The man was staring with apprehension at the winding road that led them to the state highway.

"He spoke in the plural," he said finally, watching a dark car speed down the road and disappear almost instantly behind the first corner. Rebecca did not know much about them, but it seemed like a Mercedes or a BMW. She shrugged, trying to ignore the shiver that ran down her spine.

As soon as they arrived back in Florence, Michele retired to his room to examine the letter, hardly giving Rebecca more than a courteous smile. They spent the rest of what remained of the afternoon and the evening like this, each in their own room. Once dinnertime had passed, Rebecca approached Spinelli's door, uncertain of what to do. She was just about to knock and ask the man to reemerge from the letters to go with her and grab some food but then, intimidated, she gave up. Disappointedly, she took the opportunity to leave the hotel and get a bite to eat. Finally, she headed toward one of the best bookstores in Florence, quite close to the hotel and the cathedral of Santa Maria del Fiore. She had decided that she would never again tolerate humiliation like what she had borne that afternoon.

Out of the corner of her eye she noticed a dark car that started the engine and drove away in a hurry when she moved. Thoughtful, she stood watching it for a while, then became convinced that it had to have been a coincidence and walked briskly into the bookshop. It took her a little time to get oriented. Reading had always been one of her favorite pastimes and she had to strain to focus her attention on what was closest to her heart in that moment, without being distracted by the dozens of volumes on display. She found numerous works on Galileo Galilei and after careful consideration she bought an annotated summary of the main events in the scientists' life, and a denser work which also described in detail all of his works. While leafing through them, sitting at the bookstore café, her thoughts brought her back to the embarrassing encounter with Zacchia that afternoon. That man had insulted her gratuitously. How she would have liked to retaliate...

3

The next morning, dark and menacing clouds amassed in the sky promising rain. While the car climbed on along the main road between the Tuscan hills, Rebecca could not help but notice the change in her companion's mood with respect to the previous day and also reflected on his driving, which was decidedly nervous that morning. Catching her breath after one last screech that had brought the wheels beneath her a bit too close to the edge of the road, she decided to end his solitary brooding: "You said that they're expecting us?"

"Yeah," he answered laconically. Then, almost angrily, he added, "Let's hope that the short notice I gave won't leave time for them to increase their demands, as the 'nice' Count did yesterday." He almost smiled and held back a yawn. The examination of the letter recovered at a high price the day before must have kept him busy throughout the night; his eyes were marked by fatigue. Perhaps that explained his nervousness.

They left the main road to take the small dirt road that would lead them to their destination: a well-kept farmstead, perhaps freshly painted with a dark brown that complemented the surrounding landscape which consisted of vineyards, olive groves and small farms with their characteristic red soil. Although it had none of the pretentiousness of the house they had visited the day before, it certainly did not share its sense of decadence. They parked almost directly opposite the entrance and were immediately greeted by Antonio Simoni, the owner, who seated them in a bright living room. The floor was marble, the wide light-colored leather sofa illuminated the center of the room, while on the walls numerous framed prizes for the vineyard's wine production stuck out alongside newspaper clippings that extolled the company's qualities.

Antonio Simoni was a middle-aged man, as revealed by the considerable wrinkles in the skin around his eyes, accustomed to squinting in the sunlight of the vineyards, but the rest of his person emanated an almost surprising vigor. He invited the two guests to choose a chair and sat down in front of them. Shortly thereafter, in a slight, studied lateness, a lady who had to be his wife appeared. The woman, obviously coiffed to welcome the professor of the University of Padua, wore a white dress that brought out her tanned skin and her black eyes. She was younger than her husband, but despite her appearance, at the moment of introductions she demonstrated an intelligence and wit that hardly suited the first impression that Rebecca had gotten of her. She did not seem like a "trophy wife," one of those buxom, brainless women that successful men bought to exhibit as if they were sports cars.

"Maddalena," she introduced herself in a soothing voice.

If she was aware of the effect that she had on the newcomers, she did not let it show. She semi-seriously scolded her husband for not having offered anything to their guests and went away briefly to reappear carrying a silver tray with a crystal decanter containing iced tea, a few cups of steaming coffee and some cookies. Rebecca did not resist and quenched her thirst with the fragrant peach tea, not followed by her companion, who remained in dignified silence as he waited for the pleasantries to end. Only watching him closely could you see any sign of impatience. But their host was in no hurry.

"So, Professor," she began, after fulfilling the duties of hospitality. "Why this interest in the letters? They were already examined in the past and scholars concluded that they were likely mere counterfeits; or at least testimonials of such marginal interest that they did not deserve to be part of the official collection."

Rebecca knew from having her personal studies in recent days that there was a museum in Florence dedicated to Galileo, which also collected most of his epistolary material that had not gotten lost. Moreover, it was scanned electronically and freely available to anyone with an internet connection.

"If you always look in the same direction," Spinelli replied enigmatically, paraphrasing Albert Einstein, "you will always find the same things."

"True," she conceded, not satisfied by the response. "But we're talking about a letter written to Vincenzo Viviani, containing only a few service notices. It isn't even signed."

Rebecca was floored; she really was not in the company of a trophy wife. She felt a twinge of jealousy in observing Spinelli's smug expression; but she did not even know who Vincenzo Viviani was. She partially consoled herself by reading her same ignorance on her host's face. She swore to herself; despite studying the night before, she had once again managed to look like a fool in Michele's eyes and because of that woman who was making sweet eyes at him, on top of everything!

The professor, seeing the non-experts' embarrassment, explained: "Vincenzo Viviani was a young apprentice of Galileo during his final years. He was beside him and assisted him during his house arrest—"

"House arrest?" the woman interrupted him. "I thought that after his sentencing he was allowed to retire himself near his city."

Spinelli almost attacked her: "The Inquisition forced him into house arrest," he contradicted heatedly. "He could only see a few people, priests and Jesuits. The same people who condemned him. Even ambassadors of more enlightened countries that his fame had reached couldn't converse with him!" A glacial atmosphere descended on the living room.

Once again it was the woman, only partially intimidated by the professor's outburst, who broke the silence: "It has still not been explained to us why you want that letter," she replied.

Spinelli, perhaps realizing that he had overdone it in the heat of his contradiction, smiled back, visibly anxious not to further annoy the potential seller.

"I am preparing a book about the 'private' Galileo, the more intimate one," he replied soothingly. "One side of his personality that was not sufficiently revealed." What surprised Rebecca was not so much the sudden change in her companion's mood, but the skill with which he told the lie. Not only did his words sound convincing but the tone of his voice, the posture of his body were so in harmony that she, who was aware of the true purpose of their quest, almost believed it.

This time it was Antonio Simoni who moved away. He returned a few minutes later, exhibiting a shiny binder. He placed it in the elegant, gloved hands of the scholar, who did not hesitate to open it. Enclosed in a transparent folder a handwritten letter was visible. ARCHIVE QUALITY PVC FREE was written on the envelope, to indicate the high-quality casing used to protect the ancient paper.

"This is the one I'm looking for," confirmed Spinelli after having briefly examined it. It was time for negotiations. Unlike Zacchia, Antonio seemed strangely calm, smiling. As if, after all, he was not really interested in the transaction. Rebecca could not help but wonder if he really needed the money Spinelli had promised.

It was once again his wife who appeared more interested: "It is truly worth something to you, Professor?"

Here it is, thought Rebecca. That was the moment to raise the price. This time, having learned his lesson, Spinelli did not try to bluff: "It is worth exactly what we agreed upon," he replied decidedly. "Not a Euro more!"

"If it were the money that we were interested in, we would have accepted the generous offers of other people interested in the letter," Antonio Simoni interrupted candidly, sounding almost offended.

Spinelli looked at him, amazed.

"I want something different," explained the other man. "I would like your book to contain a specific reference to my wife for the literary value. You know, she is a scholar too; we hope that soon she'll earn her doctorate in the Classics and this could help her…The collection of documents is a legacy of her family; it is only right for her to benefit from that."

The woman, singled out, reddened and explained: "After all, Professor, we prefer to give the letter to you, rather than a pharmaceutical company."

Rebecca winced, but Spinelli remained calm, almost seraphic, flashing her a candid smile that did not fail to arouse a new twinge of jealousy in Rebecca.

"It can be done," he declared triumphantly. "I assure you that if my book on the private Galileo sees the light of day, your wife will be mentioned."

The return to Florence was quiet; evidently Michele's mood affected his driving because, as jerky as he had been that morning, when he was evidently tense about the coming meeting, he was just as relaxed that afternoon, now that he had gotten what he wanted. Even his expression was relaxed, almost sly. Rebecca was convinced that it was from the manner in which he had deceived the couple who had just handed him a fragment of their family's memory almost for free. She did not know if the professor's promise constituted a scam in itself; the book on the private life of Galileo would never see daylight, as it was certainly not their quest's true objective. She temporarily silenced her scruples considering that, surely, the woman would have a citation in the book

29

that would be published if their efforts were successful and they found the hidden manuscript.

They dined in a restaurant which served excellent local specialties. The promised storm finally broke violently, trapping them in the building for a long time, but they departed after it passed and left a clear blue sky in its wake. They undertook the return trip without any hurry.

Once in Florence, which shone like a jewel in the afternoon sun, Rebecca hoped that Spinelli would involve her in studying the second letter, but was once again disappointed: after a quick farewell, he locked himself in his room again. The doctor took refuge in the shower and then sat bored in her bathrobe, imagining that every footstep she heard in the hallway was him coming to call her. Annoyed, she decided to dress and, passing the silent doorway of Michele's room, she directed herself towards the city center. A walk would calm her spirit.

While she walked, she reflected on the fact that her presence there, up to that point, had been totally unnecessary; she wondered why the scholar had involved her. Maybe it was not yet her moment; her microbiological expertise would probably be helpful at a later time, she told herself. She smiled as she passed a news vendor who was flagrantly exhibiting a poster for the *Vernacoliere,* the popular satirical newspaper. Emblazoned on the front page was the drawing of a man bent over his knees, or rather, of his rear in full view. The bold-type headline jeered at some poor sap who was evidently discovered in an act of sodomy...Yes, "dis-covered" was the most appropriate term, thought Rebecca, passing the newsstand without paying it further heed.

She was immediately brought back to reality by the passing of a black car with tinted windows, which almost slammed into her as it swept away after cutting off an old woman on a bike. The doctor was swift to support her, as she would otherwise have certainly fallen. Reassuring the woman, Rebecca cursed because she had not been able to get a better look at the car. She had to talk about it with Spinelli. Maybe it was time to notify the police.

Fortunately, Michele was free that evening. He had managed to book the last available table at the crowded trattoria *I Pazzi,* near the Basilica of Santa Croce. Rebecca had finally decided not to inform him of her concerns; in retrospect, it just seemed like silly fears fueled by her own imagination. The man was beaming—it seemed that the letters had proved important to the investigations.

"Here, see?" he said to her, opening the usual leather portfolio and exhibiting them on the table like a hunter who was proud of his catch. Rebecca did her best to brush some crumbs from under the folder, amazed by the apparent nonchalance with which the man was treating those pieces of evidence, so different from the religious meticulousness she had seen in Professor Benatti's study. Perhaps the fever of research had infected Spinelli, bringing him to abandon his caution; insofar as he was explaining to her, his examination of the last two letters had given important clues as to where the missing volume could be kept. "I'm sure that the next letter, along with these two, will direct us to the book…"

"Why did the other people who examined these not think of this?" she asked, losing herself again between the twisted handwriting and the archaic diction with which the letters had been penned centuries before.

"They didn't know what they were looking for," the man promptly replied, "and above all they didn't imagine that there was anything to look for; they didn't have the first letter, and that's where Galilei mentions his book!" The woman did not share his enthusiasm and the professor, basking in his successes up to that point, could not help but notice. "Is something bothering you?" he asked, taking another sip of Chianti.

"No," she lied at first. But then she decided: "It's just that I wonder why you asked me to accompany you on these errands. I was nothing but a pretty ornament while you retrieved the documents you needed and then you closed yourself in your room to study them. I thought you needed some of my expertise, but I think I'm just a burden to you. I think tomorrow I will return to Padua," she concluded, looking him straight in the face.

"I hope you're joking," said the man, his expression changing. "You can't go now, you really can't!" Rebecca watched closely and saw genuine concern spread across his face. "All I have…we have found so far is just the tip of the iceberg, mere clues that will lead us to our prize. *Stella Novissima* is still hidden, but I feel it is getting closer. It is then that I will need all your skill."

Rebecca remained deep in thought, wondering if those words hid some deception, like those he spoke at the Simonis' home. However, in the bright blue eyes of the man before her she read a sincere interest, a desire that inadvertently she hoped would harmonize with her own. In fact, for the rest of the evening, and for the first time since they had set out on that trip, Michele paid her all his attention. Once they finished eating, he accompanied her along the oldest and most charming streets of Florence. When they crossed the Piazza della Signoria, Michele pointed out a stone coat of arms, close to the palace: "Know what this is?"

"The coat of arms of a Florentine family?"

"Not of just any family," he coaxed her. "Those are the six balls of the Medici coat of arms." He paused, his eyes lit by the fire of admiration. "If there is an Italian dynasty that deserves a place in history it is precisely that of the Medici. For about two hundred years, from the fifteenth to the seventeenth century, they influenced Italian politics, art, thought. They actually created the banking system. They gave two popes to the Church, cultivated the likes of Leonardo da Vinci, Giorgio

Vasari, Michelangelo. Wives and mothers of French kings were part of the Medici. They nurtured and cultivated Humanism, making Western culture flourish after the dark years of the Middle Ages. The Medici were Italy—or rather, Italy did not even exist. They were Europe: they were the best of what Western civilization was capable of."

Rebecca did not know if it was the magical feel of the evening, the fact of being swept up in that quest somewhere between reality and fiction, if it was the hypnotic tone of his voice or the Chianti's haze, but she had felt this way few times in her simple life: almost impalpable, a nut shell swept along by the current of centuries of history and by the voice of the person who was unveiling them to her for the first time, as if they were unfolding before her eyes. She heard the cries of the Pazzi conspiracy, saw the industrious hands of Leonardo, Michelangelo, Brunelleschi. Without realizing it, she walked closer and closer to Michele. Strolling, their hands often grazed one another's. The smell she caught of his sophisticated cologne contributed to the daze of that evening. Spinelli seemed to have noticed, because he never missed an opportunity to support her amicably by the arm, gently encircling her waist with the excuse of pointing out a particular piece of architecture. Until, arriving under a dimly lit archway not far from their hotel, he took her delicately by the waist and pulled her towards him. Rebecca did not resist, and let the current drag her into the harbor of his arms, his lips. They kissed long, deeply, until she drew away, freeing herself from his embrace. He smiled slyly and encircled her again, kissing her more.

The beams of a car's headlights hit them, violating the pedestrian zone and their fleeting moment of intimacy. Spinelli broke their embrace and Rebecca, blushing, stepped back, raising her eyes to Michele. "It's late," he said, looking at his watch and finally breaking the spell.

They climbed slowly back up to their own rooms, their parting words almost formal. Closing the door behind her, Rebecca let herself be a silly, immature high school girl. She slipped into the shower, smiling at herself and her silly crush on the professor, blaming the wine and praying that she had not ruined everything. The jet of hot, soapy water caressed her sensually, so she achieved the opposite of the result she had hoped for; coming out from the water she was still eager for the man, his lips and even more. She threw herself onto the bed, tried to read, squirmed between the sheets, but the only thing on her mind was what Spinelli was doing in that moment. Finally she could not take it anymore: she threw off the linens and put on the hotel robe, then, barefoot, she walked to his room. She took a deep breath, steeled herself and then knocked. No reply. She started to knock again, but then stopped; whether Michele was sleeping or not, the fact remained that he had not opened the door showed that he did not desire her as much as she did him. For no reason, in that moment the memory of Simoni's wife came back to her mind, her gentle eyes and the smile that Spinelli had given in return. Her blood boiled; returning to her room, she dressed in a hurry and left the hotel.

She asked the concierge to call a taxi and asked the driver to take her to any bar he liked. After some protest, the bewildered driver was convinced and chose a place for the woman, who was clearly angry for some reason. The place he took her, Yab, was a few minutes from her hotel and was one of the hottest clubs around; the kind of place where the bouncers chose who could enter and who could not. Evidently her auburn hair and her miniskirt had a shot, because she soon cut ahead of some teenagers, who did not fail to voice their grievances in colorful Florentine slang. Rebecca paid the entrance fee with her credit card and approached the bar. The loud music began to distract her, but for the first time in her life she decided that she needed something alcoholic, something really strong, to clear her mind. She ordered a cocktail with an unpronounceable name, hoping that it would suit the case, but it was only after the third glass that the anger and frustration left her and made room for a rhythmic slumber, lulled by the music's low tones.

The memory of Maddalena Simoni's smiling face hit her like a slap. Again, she felt overwhelmed by anger.

4

The next morning Rebecca got up early. Rather, she was not even sure that she had gone to bed. She could not recall clearly the details of the night before; just alcohol, torpor, and music at full volume. And now she had the worst headache since the days of university drunkenness. She was among the first to come downstairs to the breakfast room, also to ensure that she would not find herself at the same table as Michele. It was not so much her own appearance that worried her, as much as the memory of what had happened between them the night before. God, how stupid she felt! Like a teenager with her first crush. It did not seem to her that it was really she who behaved that way. Normally she tried to remain very restrained in her dealings with men, very careful not to expose herself to pain, to sentimental wounding. Many of her relationships had ended for that very reason, because they were going deeper than she was prepared to allow, closer to where they could hurt her. And now she found herself with sweating hands and a dry mouth at the thought of a man whom she had practically just met. She convinced herself that she was in love with the situation, not the person of Michele Spinelli. That her infatuation was all mental, her own construction. She felt like the heroine of her favorite book, *The Da Vinci Code,* with the addition of the one thing that was, in her opinion, lacking in Dan Brown's work: sex. The rationalization, however, only partly helped: just as Michele appeared in the doorway of the restaurant, impeccable in suit and tie, perfectly groomed, as if going to a ceremony or conference, her heart started to beat hard in her chest. So hard that she feared he could hear it even from far away. She breathed deeply.

"I didn't find you in your room," Spinelli greeted her with a broad smile; only the two deep bags under his eyes were in disagreement with his fresh and rested appearance. He must have been working on the letters all night.

"I was hungry," she lied, pointing to the almost-full cappuccino cup before her, grateful that the waitress had already cleared the two coffee cups that she had drunk to clear her mind. She had not managed to consume anything else, despite the delicious buffet. Michele ordered a coffee from the attentive waitress who, seeing him arrive, had come straight to their table.

"One more letter and then I'm sure that, combining all the information, we'll eventually get to the book," he said then, making sure that there was nobody around who could overhear them. He made no mention of the kiss the night before and Rebecca was grateful, although she could not help but notice that his expression with her had changed a little bit.

Maybe it was another mental construction of hers, but it did not seem to her like the air of intimacy that usually binds two people at the beginning of a relationship, nor did it seem like the embarrassment of someone who wakes up regretful after a night of excessive drinking. Perhaps, the expression of satisfaction that seemed painted onto Spinelli's face was his way of reacting to what had happened. In spite of herself, Rebecca felt intrigued by that mischievous air.

"I'm ready," she said, rising from the table with her cup half full, fearing that her thoughts were all-too obvious. "Where are we going today?"

"Latium," responded Spinelli, rising in turn.

Again their car left the city of Florence to be funneled onto the A1 highway, following the two-lane route along almost all of Tuscany and part of Latium. According to Spinelli's research, the owner of the last letter lived almost at the gate of the Great Ring Road of Rome. After several kilometers, Rebecca looked for a way to break the awkward silence that had been created between them, filled only by the notes of one of Bach's arias on the radio. "Is Galileo really that important in the history of science?" she asked, hoping he would answer.

Spinelli's expression changed immediately, his eyes lit with the fire of his passion. "In the history of thought there is a 'before' and an 'after' Galileo Galilei," he affirmed. "No single person has been as influential in thinking and in scientific advancement as him. He was a versatile genius; maybe you aren't aware that he is considered one of the greatest Italian authors; Italo Calvino places him on the same level as Leopardi. Among his works are studies of Dante and Ariosto. His work on the movement of a pendulum was the basis for the exact measurement of time, and thus for the realization of modern chronometers. He anticipated the laws of physics of motion, erecting the foundations of modern physics. If today space flights are possible it is because his studies were analyzed and perfected; indeed, the whole concept of space as we understand it today depends on his findings; Kepler's calculations on the orbits of the planets and the Copernican theory were only theoretical hypotheses and they would have stayed that way, nothing more than intellectual playthings for some philosopher afraid to raise his head from under the gaze of the Inquisition. If Galileo had not confirmed the new cosmology with his own observations, we might still be thinking in terms of fixed stars and celestial spheres and if their research had any weight, it was because it was published by Galileo Galilei; only his fame gave the discoveries the authority they needed to be considered, studied and submitted to the scrutiny of the greatest thinkers of that time. Even Urban VIII, the pope whose turnaround delivered the scientist to the Inquisition, initially defined him: 'This great man, whose fame shines in the sky and continues on Earth.' Of course, the most obtuse found no better than to appeal to the Bible, the verse from the Book of Joshua, where God orders the sun to stop to give more time for the Israelites to get the better of their enemy: if God himself had ordered the sun to stop, and not the earth, for recalcitrant fundamentalist Christians it was incontestable that the earth was not the one that moved."

Spinelli's fascinating voice accompanied them for the whole trip and it was almost noon when they neared their destination. Rebecca, grateful and a little bit intimidated by that intense presentation, was a bit sad to leave refined, picturesque Tuscany to be caught in the traffic and hectic bustle that surrounded the city. The house they were looking for was on the outskirts of a town in the hinterland of the capital. The trip had been quite long and now, because of her meager breakfast, her stomach was rumbling with hunger. She hoped that their host had prepared at least a welcome drink. Following the directions given by the navigation system's monotonous voice, they finally parked in a ruined courtyard. They looked at one another doubtfully. Could it actually be the house they were looking for? A filthy and disheveled dog welcomed them with his hoarse, insistent barking, while the worn chain that attached him to the only tree in the courtyard crawled on the dusty gravel. They got out of the car. A strange odor lingered in the courtyard. Michele went first, ringing the bell. The faded name sticker read: CARMELA GEROSPI.

"I'd heard that she is a…peculiar person," he whispered in Rebecca's direction, while a voice from inside the house yelled, "Come in!"

"Peculiar," was not exactly the right definition for the woman. As soon as the door was opened it was clear that the source of the stench they smelled was not coming from outside, but from inside the house itself, if it could be called a "house." It was…indescribable: furniture, decorations, rags, carpets, boxes containing unrecognizable objects, clothing of all shapes and colors, even in tatters, were amassed everywhere; shoes, slippers, sandals, boots for men and for women were piled up here and there, while leftover food in various stages of decay peeked out from all sides, much of it covered in bluish mold. Rebecca was happy that her stomach was empty, otherwise the impulse to vomit that had surprised her as soon as they entered the hovel would have come to a more severe result than simply discombobulating her. Trying to hold their noses to avoid being overcome by the stench, she wondered if whoever lived there would ever notice if she vomited somewhere. The hostess was clearly a hoarder, a person with a personality disorder that compels the afflicted to obsessively preserve hundreds, thousands of items of which they are unable to rid themselves, until they take up all areas of their existence. What they had before them was a case well beyond something that social services, if they ever took it upon themselves, could solve. It was a case for psychiatry.

"If you don't like it you can get out!" snapped the home owner in Roman dialect, emerging suddenly in front of them; or perhaps she had been there the whole time, indistinguishable from the waste that surrounded her, and had noticed the expression of disgust that disfigured Rebecca's face. The doctor, reeling from the surprise, made no attempt to conceal it. Before she could reply, however, she was preceded by Michele Spinelli. Demonstrating remarkable self-control, he introduced himself to the woman, even extending a gloved hand to her. Their host was a woman in her fifties, very obese, with her lank, thinning hair so dirty and greasy that it seemed wet. She was covered by a large robe that fell to mid-leg with an unusual pattern, embellished here and there with patches of unknown age and origin. She was barefoot and her long toenails were so filthy that they were indistinguishable from the brown floor, soiled in its turn to the point that she could not have determined what its original color was.

"We had spoken about a book, you remember?" inquired Spinelli, maintaining a professional and courteous manner.

"It's there," replied the woman in a guttural voice, nodding her head towards the wall on their left. In what had once been a library there were piled notebooks, newspapers and magazines, all mixed together on curved shelves sagging with their own weight and buried under a thick layer of dust. Rebecca was the closest of the three to the shelf and Spinelli looked at her as though prompting her to move.

In response, she snapped, "I'm not putting my hands in there without a pair of gloves." Just as she uttered these words her shoulder was hit with a greasy, blackened pot, flung by their host, who was suddenly and threateningly coming nearer. Michele was quick to interpose himself between the two, preventing the virago from reaching her astonished guest.

"Hey princess why don't you just go—" but the man cut her off before she could finish her colorful imprecation.

"Rebecca, why don't you wait in the car?" he asked aloud, trying to hold back the woman who ceaselessly abused her, displaying her horribly decayed teeth.

"Get out of my house!" she thundered hysterically, almost overwhelming Michele to push her towards the exit.

"Go!" he urged her, and Rebecca did not need telling twice.

As she left the hovel, she was finally able to breathe deeply. From outside she could still hear Spinelli's voice as he tried to calm the psychopath and her agitated screams, more and more guttural, almost desperate in their fury. She mentally prepared herself to intervene in Michele's defense, although she shuddered at the thought of a confrontation with the huge, disgusting woman. She pulled her phone from her pocket, ready to call the police. She approached the door and tried to peek inside; she was reassured to see that the two had not come to blows. The tone of the woman's screams had dropped a little but was vehemently rekindled when she saw her peeking back into her home.

"Wait in the car, please," Spinelli exasperatedly urged her, still trying to calm the woman down. Rebecca hesitantly walked to the car as she was asked, at once straining her ears and keeping her cell phone within reach.

The screams, however, ceased suddenly. Another miracle of Spinelli's charm. Smirking maliciously to herself, she prayed that he had not had to kiss her, and that thought brought her back painfully to the previous evening, to her own embarrassment. She, too, wondered if she were a victim of Michele Spinelli's charm? Evidently, yes, if she had gone so far as kissing him; only she had not yet figured out his intentions…

She looked around, brought back to the present by a new whiff of that horrible stench that seemed to permeate the air. The dog had begun barking like crazy; how long would Michele take? After a while, impatient and annoyed, she concluded that if not the police, then at least health services should be notified of the woman's condition; she needed help. She dialed 118, but with dismay realized that the line cut in and out; there was very little reception. When she finally managed to establish a choppy connection with an operator, after listening to a long, automated message that the call was recorded, she was just able to introduce herself before Spinelli, appearing behind her, frightened her.

"Michele!" she said, jumping. "I didn't hear you coming. I'm alerting social workers…"

"Hang up!" he commanded, nearly shouting. When the startled doctor followed his order, his expression seemed to relax. "Excuse me, but I'm still a bit shaken by what's in there," the man explained. "Let her call the social services herself; if she wants to live in a pigsty that's her business, is it not?" he concluded, pointing to the hovel. He held a book in his hands, bound as best possible. "Can you believe it?" he asked her, indicating his prey. "She got the letter we're looking for bound together with dozens of flyers and sheets of paper…And don't even ask me where I had to retrieve the book from!" he concluded reluctantly, tucking it into his fine leather briefcase, but not before wrapping it in a clean-looking newspaper.

When they set out again, Rebecca could no longer restrain herself: "Look, I've decided; tomorrow I'm going back to Padua."

"What?" asked Spinelli, sincerely upset.

"This research…it's not for me, I have done nothing but embarrass you, like with old Zacchia and that Maddalena. Had it been up to me, today that woman would have thrown us out of the house and you wouldn't have gotten the letter. I'm just an obstacle…"

"I've already explained to you that your time is coming; just give me the time to examine the letters, then we'll find the book and I will need you."

"But in the meantime I'm just dead weight to you," she replied, because she did not want to mention the real motive for which she wanted to go away—in other words, all that had happened the previous evening. "Let's do this: when you've found the book you can contact me and if you really need my skills in microbiology, I will be even more useful from my laboratory than from here."

"At least spend the weekend here," Spinelli proposed with a smile. "The room is already paid for."

Again Rebecca felt herself the prey of those seductive eyes and accepted: "Only until Sunday," she closed. "Monday, I go back to Padua." In that moment, a whiff of the stench from the house they had just fled reached her; it must have saturated their clothes. She struggled to contain another bout of retching. *Disgusting tramp…*

5

Once they were back at the hotel, Rebecca needed an interminable, scalding shower to remove every last remnant of the stench which she had found herself sneaking around in that morning. While the hot water and fragrant foam relieved her nostrils and her spirits, she went back to wondering if leaving Florence, abandoning Spinelli to his research, was really the best choice. She got out of the shower and wrapped herself in the soft cotton of the white hotel robe. She looked around, admiring the luxury that surrounded her and the warm light that heralded sunset reverberating on the roofs and the streets of Florence, just outside her open window. She took off the robe to fully enjoy the gentle touch of the breeze on her skin. *But yes, why leave all this so quickly?* she mused. Then she thought back to Michele's words that afternoon, their tone, the effect that they seemed to elicit from her, the bewitching smile that, she now understood, he used as his real weapon…Someone knocked at the door.

"Room service," said a flat voice. She put her robe back on and opened the door, letting in a hotel valet in uniform. In his hands he held a box and…a dress? "Compliments of Professor Spinelli," said the valet, handing her the gift.

Bewildered, Rebecca tipped him and sent him away, stretching the dress on the bed. It was a beautiful dress made of red silk, embellished with lace embroidery. After removing it from its transparent cover, she touched the fabric and, recognizing the one-of-a-kind brand, she could not help but wonder how many salaries it would have cost had she paid for it. She did not resist and put it on; it fit like a glove, as if it had been sewn just for her. Admiring herself in the mirror she could not help but be impressed by Michele's sharp eye, as he had been able to guess her size perfectly. Only the neckline made her a bit uncomfortable; the wide V that it drew on her chest left no room for undergarments and showed off her breasts in a way that was not vulgar, but certainly very showy. She was not used to wearing such low-cut dresses, but that one really suited her well; and she was neither made up nor groomed yet. On the bed, inside the package, there was a message written in pen on watermarked Florentine paper: "Tonight at nine." In the box there were super high-heeled shoes, red as well, in exactly her size. Rebecca put them on and turned to gaze at herself in the mirror. Satisfied, she looked at the image reflected and tilted her head back, giving way to a sensual laugh.

Dinner that night was just perfect. Michele had chosen a luxury restaurant in the hills, from whose terrace one could enjoy a splendid view of the illuminated city. He hypnotized her with his perfect smile and entertained her with tales of bandits and cursed painters, marveling the maître d' with his knowledge of the most valuable and sought-after wines. Rebecca tasted those fine, flavorful nectars, won over by the warm insistence of her host and the lights of the evening, the atmosphere of the ancient city that stretched below them and the audacious gown that concealed so little of her. She abandoned all her reservations about him.

She did not remember how they got back to Florence, how much time had passed nor how she wound up in Spinelli's room. The only thing she felt in that moment was Michele's mouth on hers, his tongue intertwined with her own, while the man's anxious hands played eagerly with her breasts. She smelled his sophisticated cologne in her nostrils, his excited panting on her neck, as his hands, his lips, ran down her chest and then lower still. She felt her skin respond to him, but her mind was confused, captivated by the situation and at once incredulous. His fingers strayed down to her navel and then lower still, freeing her of her dress. The glare of the headlights of a car that was passing in the street lit up the room for a moment and Rebecca was thus able to perceive more than the blurred outlines of the shadows. She saw Spinelli leaning over her, saw the sheets rolled beneath them, the large mirror next to the bed. On the rococo style bedside table were scattered several items that seemed familiar, but which at first she could not recognize. The man was still focusing on her clothes. Arching her back to help him liberate her of the expensive garments, she felt his lips, his tongue, on her bare skin.

She did not know if she really wanted to go through with it, or perhaps she wanted it, but something still made her hesitate, a last shred of rational thought in the tsunami of sensation that was overwhelming her. When the man's fingers slipped into her underwear she relented and prepared to welcome him, but in that instant a flash of understanding crossed her mind, suddenly freeing her from that strange pall of sensuality that clouded her mind. She had recognized one of those boxes on the bedside table: it was one of those blue and white boxes that contained the blue pills to ensure outstanding performance in lifeless male organs…Perplexed, she looked down and saw him. She saw Spinelli who…was looking at himself in the mirror, gazing at his slim reflection with the same bewitching look that had captured her too, but directing the gaze at himself.

"No," she said weakly. "No!" she cried louder, confusedly, stopping Spinelli's hands with her own before he could undress her completely.

"Let yourself go…" he said in his warm voice, tempting her.

"No," she insisted, trying to break free from the weight that until then had consensually captivated her. "You let me go!"

"Rebecca..." he tried to soothe her, but she had become hysterical. She felt overwhelmed by the ebb of the tide, by the guilt she felt for what was happening, the way she had succumbed to his elaborate staging, for not knowing how to explain how she had wound up in that bed, practically naked and willing. She picked her dress up off the ground and walked away from Michele who, completely nude and aroused before her, attempted to hold her back with his arms.

"Let me go!" she repeated, almost shouting, writhing and reeling into the door. In a hurry she recovered her clutch with the key card and did not even make sure that the corridor was empty before going out; she ran away barely covering herself with the dress in her arms, barefoot, praying that the door to her room would open without any difficulty. As soon as she got in, she slammed the door behind her and collapsed to the ground crying, confused, sobbing so hard that she eventually vomited. The smell of her stomach brought back the woman from that afternoon: the hoarder, her hovel. She vowed to do something about her the next day.

The next morning she woke up late with a headache and all the trimmings—nausea and discomfort as she had never felt before, not even in the worst hangover of her college years. She hoped to recover by slipping into the shower, but not even that had the desired effect. She put on some sportswear, throwing just a glance at the scarlet dress from the night before, still crumpled next to the sink where she had thrown it. With the memory of that evening returned the shame and anger with herself. But how had she drunk so much? Damn! It seemed to her that she had had three, maybe four glasses of wine, but had been careful to just sip as much as was poured by her host. Maybe it had been just that: the mixture of different types of wine...there was no other explanation. So to avoid passing in front of Michele's door to take the elevator, she walked to the other end of the hall and down the stairs from the fifth floor of the hotel. Nearing the dining room, though it was now close to eleven o' clock, she savored the fragrant scents of coffee and the last croissants available for the latecomers among the guests, but her stomach was churning and she could not manage to eat anything. In the hopes that a little movement would make her feel better, she went out to walk through the streets of Florence; the cloudy sky did not discourage her. Now more than ever she was determined to go home— or rather, she would take the train that afternoon.

Immersed in the multiethnic crowd of tourists, local workers and beggars of the most disparate backgrounds, all seemingly occupied by their affairs, she was able to gradually calm down. In the shadow of Palazzo Vecchio and its centuries of history, she even managed to detach her mind from the last few days' events, to think twice about their quest and its value; because her contribution was utterly negligible, she felt like the last wheel of a chariot driven by the lone Magnificent Professor Spinelli. In that story, she had no role other than that of the foolish, saucy lass who winds up in the protagonist's bed. Now she understood why there was no hint of sex in *The Da Vinci Code,* because the female lead was not an imbecile like her! She retraced her steps back to the hotel.

"Doctor De Cardinale," said a voice behind her, tearing her from her ruminations. Rebecca turned, both curious and alarmed. She looked at the man in front of her and, after an initial impression of familiarity, she was certain of it: she had never seen him before. She would certainly have remembered the scar that disfigured his forehead and half his face. He hastened to reassure her: "Don't worry," he said in a conciliatory tone, handing her an elegant business card. The doctor took it between her fingers and read it quickly: "Doctor A. Krupp," and a mobile phone number were the only printed words, with the logo of Pegasus Pharmaceutics as the backdrop. Rebecca did not know what the man wanted from her, but that it had something to do with their research seemed the only possible explanation. Where the hell was Spinelli when she needed him? "I'd like to offer you a drink," he suggested with a faint German accent, indicating an establishment right around the corner from them. Rebecca looked around, startled. "If you prefer, we can sit in this outdoor cafe," he changed his mind, gesturing towards a crowded cafe with tables outside, exposed to the gaze of hundreds of passers-by.

"I'm not in the habit of sitting down with the first stranger I meet," she said, looking around and trying to buy time.

"I'm alone," he assured her again, "and now that we've been introduced, I'm no longer a stranger," he replied, indicating the business card still clutched between Rebecca's fingers. Then, before she could protest, he pulled a tablet from his inside jacket pocket, turned the screen towards her and promised, "I ask only two minutes: if what I say does not interest you, I will not insist."

Struggling against the sun's reflection on the screen, Rebecca tried to focus on the image and her heart leaped in her chest. It looked like a letter, much like the one that Professor Spinelli had brought into Professor Benatti's office. A letter from Galileo Galilei. She immediately accepted Krupp's invitation and they sat at a table in the bar first suggested by the man, very close to the hotel. The automatic cover was raised, since the sun's rays were filtered by clouds and did not bother the tables' occupants. Rebecca settled herself so she could look towards the window of Spinelli's room, hoping that the professor would look over and see them.

"How did you get this letter?" asked Rebecca, trying to buy time, glancing ever more frequently at the hotel window.

"Of course you realize that the resources available to my company are…remarkable," he said.

"I mean how did you hear about it," she said coldly, remembering all too well the interference in the sale of the other letters.

"Let's say it was a little bird who told us," he teased. "A little bird very close to you."

Rebecca wondered who it could be. Besides Michele and herself, the only ones aware of their research were the people present at the meeting held in Professor Benatti's office. Excluding Benatti, she supposed it had to be Michele's graduate student, Dr. Vinci. She remembered the feeling of unease that had been aroused the first time she met him, his strange proposal to photograph her. Looking back to what had happened the night before, she wondered if erotomania were a prerequisite for admission to the Department of Literature...or that of Medicine, judging by how she herself was behaving with Spinelli.

"What do you want from me?" she finally asked abruptly.

"You see, our letter is only one part of a far more complete correspondence. We believe that the missing part is in your possession." Spinelli's letter, the first letter! Rebecca did not respond, waiting. "We know that you are looking for a book by Galileo Galilei," the man finally said, the tone of his voice far too high. Rebecca came closer to him, unwittingly revealing her own interest.

"Even if that were true," she prevaricated, "how might that interest you?"

"It wouldn't, actually," Krupp confirmed. "I told you this just to let you know that the cards are on the table. My company's interest is not in the book, don't worry. We are interested in much more than the contents of the letters you have already recovered."

"The letters?" she asked, not understanding. "You should speak with Professor Spinelli for this. Even I have not seen them."

"We have already had contact with the professor, but without luck." The doctor looked at him impassively; if they had already gotten a response, why were they involving her? "You see," Krupp went on, "we believe that you can better understand the need to involve the resources of a major pharmaceutical company in this research. From analyzing what we have, it seems that Galilei had had notice of a meteorite that caused the plague of 1630."

"The…plague?" the doctor asked incredulously. "The plague was caused by a bacterium, Yersinia pestis, which is spread through fleas carried—"

"By black rats from Asia, of course, we know," Krupp interrupted her.

"There are no recorded cases of plague since the—"

"Since 2009, in Libya," he interrupted her again. "In a village near Tobruk."

"Okay," the doctor conceded, admitting that she was not so up to date on the state of modern pestilence. Of Yersinia, at least. Her thoughts brought her back to Escherichia coli. "They are very small epidemics, sporadic cases."

"With three thousand victims a year," the man corrected her.

"Less than the seasonal flu," she said, still not understanding what he was getting at.

"Indeed," Krupp murmured, leaning closer to her still. "Three thousand victims. Not thirty thousand. Not three million. Don't you wonder why these outbreaks don't have the same virulence of historical plagues?"

"Well…we have to consider modern treatments available today, the improvement of nutrition and sanitary conditions…"

"In the desert of Libya or in some remote region of Mongolia?" The man quieted for a moment, letting her reflect. "No, the response is different," he continued. "These are different diseases. The possibility exists that those epidemics were transmitted by a different agent, potentially a virus, considering modality and diffusion rate. And we have a great witness, the first scientist worth his salt, convinced that they were linked to meteorites."

"Truly ahead of his time," she said sarcastically, referring to the most recent debates on panspermia, that controversial theory—which she had never taken seriously—according to which life on Earth could have originated from bacteria of extraterrestrial origin.

"I would not be so quick to laugh, Doctor," he replied, his tone of voice suddenly changing. It seemed as though he were almost personally offended. "Don't forget that we are talking about Galileo Galilei. Don't do what the Inquisition did…"

"What do you want from me?" Rebecca asked again, increasingly confused and worried, throwing one more impatient look at the hotel window.

"We need to examine the letter in your possession. If you help us, we might even consider hiring you at Pegasus."

"I already have a job."

"We know—at the Zooprophylactic Institute of the Triveneto. Two thousand, seven hundred euro a month, career opportunities, let's say…lacking?" Rebecca reddened, surprised by the accuracy with which they had read up on her and her own depressing reality. "At Pegasus your salary would be at least ten times as much. We might even make you head of the project."

"What project?"

"Have you not yet figured it out, Doctor? Galileo had linked the plague with a specific meteorite. The epidemics of 1347 and 1630 had almost halved the world's population whose given density was a tenth of what it is today; one has to wonder what would happen if another infected meteorite fell today in the densely populated regions of Asia and Europe, with the current facility of travel. Remember the bird flu a few years ago: if mortality was significantly lower than expected, its diffusion was virtually immediate. Imagine what would happen if that came about with a form of pneumonic plague! It is our duty to find a vaccine at all costs. We must prevent the disease from hitting an area of high population density and unleashing the worst epidemic the world has ever seen."

"And the whole world's salvation will be owed to Pegasus, correct?"

"Certainly." Krupp nodded.

"For free, I imagine."

The man burst into a loud laugh, catching the eye of another café customer.

"Pegasus'…resources are considerable, but not unlimited," he pointed out.

"It's all quite clear," said Rebecca, rising from her chair.

"Can we count on your cooperation?" Krupp asked.

"I'll think about it," she conceded, "but I cannot promise anything."

"Think fast," he hissed, sounding intimidating. "Professor Spinelli didn't want to accept our proposal…a major error on his part. Don't you commit it too; my company has grown tired of waiting."

Rebecca paled at the threat and anger, then decidedly distanced herself and crossed the square, heading straight for the hotel entrance. She knew that the man from Pegasus was watching her, but did not care. Her mind was fully occupied by deciding how to act with Michele. She had been thinking about it for hours but had still not decided, not knowing how to overcome the embarrassment for what had happened the night before. She had even thought of returning to Padua without telling him, but now her shame had been pushed to the back burner; if there was some truth in what Krupp had said, it was essential to work with the pharmaceutical company. While the man was speaking she had been struck by a flash of intuition; she did not want to reveal it to the slippery emissary with whom she had just spoken, but by connecting what Krupp had told her with her own research, there was a possibility even more terrifying than the one he had proposed, something that went far beyond any imaginings. Crossing the threshold of the hotel, she could not wait for the arrival of the elegant but slow elevator and followed the steps that separated her from the floor Spinelli's room was on, almost running, so once she arrived in front of his door she was breathing hard. She did not want him to think it was from embarrassment, so she forced herself to catch her breath and knocked on the door. No reply. She knocked louder. Still nothing.

She pulled her iPhone from her pocket but the phone wound up on the ground, slipping out of its case. Damn it! But how had the case come off? She wondered, cursing her trembling hands. She quickly put it back together and dialed, waiting for a response to the call. His phone, however, proved unreachable. Flustered, she returned to her room, undecided about what to do. She phoned reception a short while later, but she was told that the professor had not been seen leaving and had not left her any message. Rebecca resigned herself against her will to wait for his return. Following the line of her intuition, she turned on her laptop and began to consider the documents she had collected in the preparatory stages of what was to be a simple scientific article in collaboration with the Literature Department, to look for new pieces on the internet while continually throwing nervous glances at the clock and the phone. As she worked, her attention was drawn to a white envelope on the floor in the hallway. It must have been slipped under her door and she, entering, had trodden on it and moved it. She picked it up with trepidation; the writing on the envelope was in Spinelli's handwriting. Her heart pounding, she hastened to open it. Inside she found a piece of paper with the printed copy of an email. There were a few lines, and then, just below, was a forwarded copy of another original message, to which the lines above referred.

Here was how Pegasus had had information about their research! In the first message they were notified of the first letter's discovery and their objectives. The second sender was Krupp; the leader of Pegasus was trying to secure Spinelli's cooperation, to whom the email was addressed, and revealed that the company was aware of his findings.

What shocked her was the first sender, the original author of the letter, which was forwarded as evidence. She knew that email by heart, she had used it many times. It had not been Vinci to betray them: it was Professor Benatti. In her rage she tore the paper and ripped it up into pieces. While she threw it into the trashcan, she noticed that there was another small paper in the envelope, which she had thrown away before. She picked it up. Penned in Spinelli's handwriting, there was a message that chilled her to the bone: "*Trust no one.*"

6

Rebecca spent all that day and the next studying the documentation and desperately searching for Michele. As she proceeded, she realized more and more the urgency of the situation. She desperately needed to talk to Spinelli but the man was still untraceable. The professor's words, *Trust no one,* ran through her mind along with Krupp's veiled threat. After another sleepless night, just as the lights of day illuminated her unmade bed, Rebecca made a decision and positioned herself close to her slightly ajar door to spy on the hallway, waiting for the service personnel. When the attendant opened Spinelli's door she followed her and entered, waving her own key card as if she were the legitimate occupant of the room. Faced with the maid's embarrassed look and ceaseless apologizing in a strong accent for what she believed to be an importunate intrusion, Rebecca politely downplayed it. She waited until the woman left with the promise of returning again later, then locked the door.

The room was in perfect order, the bed still made. There was nothing that seemed out of place. Even the stylish clothes in the closet were hung diligently. She started opening the drawers too, then remembered what she had seen on the night when she had literally slipped out of his bed, and paused; she had no intention of revealing other sordid details of Spinelli's private life. In a corner, she spotted the fine leather portfolio. She opened it and was amazed to see that all the letters retrieved until then, including the one he had showed her in Padua, were still there. She impulsively grabbed them all, tucked them in her purse and slipped out of the room. She left the hotel in a hurry, without even allowing the usher in livery to open the glass door for her. It was raining heavily outside but she did not even take the large umbrella provided by the hotel and went running out in the rain in search of a taxi.

A little while later, the taxi dropped her off in front of the police station, and she hurried towards the information desk. When she declared that she needed to file a missing persons report, she was reluctantly directed to a special office on the ground floor, where an agent proceeded to gather the necessary information.

"Obviously you have tried to call the professor on his cell phone," the man asked.

"Of course!" Rebecca confirmed, impatient with the obvious lack of interest that the man was showing. "But I can never reach him. Here, listen," she said, making him listen to the telephone service provider's recorded message.

"Could you repeat for me the nature of your…relationship?"

"No relationship," said Rebecca, not very sure of her answer. She reddened a little and this did not escape the man who was questioning her, whose lips curled into a slight smile.

"And he allegedly disappeared how long ago?"

Allegedly? she thought with dismay, certain that the man was taking her for a compulsive liar or a disappointed lover. "He has been missing for at least two days," she said more severely, exaggerating the verbs.

"His wife was informed?"

"I don't think he's married," she admitted, realizing that she did not even know this detail; she had never even doubted. Oh God, let him be unmarried, she prayed to herself.

"Had you two argued, by chance?" the man insisted. Rebecca flushed, recalling the incident the last night she had seen him.

"No," she replied, unconvinced.

"Look…" the agent said with a condescending tone, handing back the missing persons report. "Why don't you go back to the hotel and wait for him to call you? Maybe he's just returned to Padua—"

The woman sprang up and slammed her hands on the table. "Can you cut it out?! I'm saying that a man, a university professor, has disappeared and you treat me like a—"

"Calm down," the man ordered, almost threateningly.

"What's happening here?" an authoritative voice interrupted.

Rebecca turned toward the newcomer who, judging by the deference that the agent showed him, must have outranked his position.

"Nothing, Inspector, this lady came because she can't find a friend of hers and I was advising her to consider all the possibilities."

"Doctor," Rebecca corrected him. "Doctor De Cardinale, and I wish to report the disappearance of Professor Michele Spinelli." The officer asked her to sit down and settled in the agent's chair, who was now standing next to him smugly. With greater professionalism, the man began repeating the conventional questions, but without a trace of malice or arrogance. The woman felt relieved.

"The professor has a car?"

"Yes, but I already checked; it's still parked in the hotel lot."

"And you two were in the city for the whole length of your stay?"

"No," she replied, and told him of the visits to the count Zacchia, the Simoni estate and Latium. She mentioned the book they were looking for and the meeting with Krupp and Pegasus' intentions but without going into detail; she was about to do so, but she remembered Spinelli's warning: *Trust no one.* If the man picked up on her reticence, he did not show it; he seemed far more interested in what she was saying than in what she was not. The more she talked, the more his eyes seemed to light up. He wanted to know the details of their movements, the times, what happened during the meetings. Put at ease by the consideration that was now being shown her by the attentive inspector, Rebecca also reported her resentment for the humiliation suffered at the hands of Count Zacchia, and the obvious personal antipathy with regards to Maddalena Simoni. Finally, the man got up showing a slight, barely perceptible excitement.

"Mioni, you are to remain at the doctor's disposal," he ordered, articulating his words with great emphasis. The agent, who had stood hostile at his side until then, replied with a smile that was more like a sneer; she could almost foretaste a vendetta against him. An insistent pulsing began to drum in her head and she was overcome by a feeling of unease. She thought of the interests of the other man, of the details he had requested, of the way he let her talk... *Trust no one.* She looked towards the agent, who had slowly positioned himself between her and the door, as though to bar the way out, and her anxiety turned into fear. They were closing her off.

"I need to use the bathroom," she said, trying to sound natural.

"You can go, in a moment," the man replied, but his eyes gave him away.

Rebecca almost blushed: "I have to change...you know...my tampon..." she stammered, counting on the most atavistic male embarrassment. It worked; the man directed her to go to the public restrooms located near the entrance. Rebecca had glimpsed them when entering the building and knew that they faced the street. Left alone in the bathroom, she opened its small window and was relieved to see that it was not barred. She prayed that there were no cameras and that no one around there was looking her way. She leaned out and, regardless of the passage of several foreign tourists, she almost leisurely lowered herself from the windowsill. She set off in the rain at a brisk pace and as soon as she could, turned the corner and walked briskly towards the city center, fighting the temptation to break into a run, as that would immediately attract attention. She tossed away the idea of returning to the hotel; it was the first place they would come looking for her, but she needed to sit down and think. Once she had put one city block's distance between herself and the police, she went into a bar and sat at a small table.

She ordered a caffè lungo and a focaccia to soothe the hypoglycemia headache that gripped her. What was going on? Maybe it was all in her head and now all the agents were laughing at her; surely they had ripped up the report, branding her a mythomaniac. Their behavior, however, had seemed too strange, almost threatening. And now what was she to do? Spinelli, after all, was still missing. She tried to call him on his cell phone once more, to no avail. After she finished eating and sipping her coffee her attention was drawn to the display boards in front of the newsstand outside. The cup almost fell from her hands. In a whirl she left a few coins on the table and rushed out. Dark headlines peeked out from all the local newspapers. She picked one up at random.

MASSACRE AT THE SIMONI ESTATE.

The murderer (or murderers) in the massacre three days ago at the Simoni winery are still unknown. The bodies of the two victims, owner Antonio Simoni and his wife Maddalena Centini, were found dead in horrific conditions. Internal police sources reveal that the man was killed by a single gunshot to the forehead, while his wife suffered torture and numerous beatings. Centini in fact did not receive a quick death: she was first tied to the bed, raped with a bottle, and ultimately quartered. Her entrails were removed and arranged around the corpse like a macabre ritual. Not satisfied, the murderer also beat her mercilessly. Her faced displayed countless bruises and blunt trauma, conceivably by the same bottle found in her vagina. Investigators are not giving anything away but, partly in light of the brutal attack suffered by the elderly Count Gianfranco Zacchia, they are not ruling out the trail of a serial killer. The man had been assaulted and sodomized with a carrot and is now hospitalized, fighting for his life after an overdose of GHB, a nightclub drug that is very popular among rapists, fed to him by his attacker to subdue him. Although official confirmations have not been issued, the suspicion is that a new monster is acting in Tuscany. The manner of the two brutal assaults unfortunately does not leave much doubt...

Rebecca stopped reading; her vision clouded over. She remembered Count Zacchia's arrogance and the almost-perfect features of Maddalena, and reading the description of what had been done to her, she almost vomited. Her heart pounded so hard in her chest that she feared she was going to faint and hurried to slump against the wall of the kiosk. This explained all of the interest in her; she had virtually confessed to the police that she was connected to both crimes! And the hoarder? Had something happened to her? She hoped that the police were also checking in her hovel. The piercing shriek of a siren brought her painfully back to reality. Two squad cars sped out of the police station towards the city center. Rebecca was just about to give herself up. After all, she had done nothing wrong; it would all be cleared up. She imagined herself explaining the whole thing to the policemen and, with growing terror, she realized how the whole story would appear from the outside. Without Spinelli to confirm his version, she was probably the only person to link all three attacks. Maybe four, if the professor had become a victim. She prayed that it was not so.

Still undecided about what to do, she walked aimlessly westward, avoiding the main roads. She could not wind up in prison, she did not want that! The very idea terrified her. And then she could not forget Pegasus' research. The corporation would not have stopped looking for Galileo's book, it was critical and had she incriminated them, they would have just pretended not to know her since the only point of contact with them, from the email in her possession, was Spinelli, and he was missing. And if somebody working for them had committed the murders? What had Krupp said? That his company was tired of waiting. It was a threat, of course. Perhaps Spinelli had been kidnapped by them. If what she had been told was true, she absolutely needed to get there first! Especially in light of her intuition, which was even more compelling considering the research she had done over the past two days. She looked around for a taxi so as not to be visible from the street in case they were looking for her. She forced herself to walk slowly, trying to calm her frenzy, dipping the umbrella almost all the way over her face so as not to be easily identifiable. Finally, she found an available one.

"Santa Maria Novella," she told the driver, hoping to beat the cops to it. She was almost certain that in that moment they would be at the hotel to ask about her and Spinelli; perhaps those few moments would be sufficient to enable her to reach the station and leave Florence. Once she arrived at her destination she ran out of the taxi without even waiting for the driver to give her change. But there was a queue at the ticket booth. The doctor forced herself to wait; what the hell did they need to ask about? And how long would it have taken to pocket that change? She was tempted to board a train without a ticket, but she feared that if she were fined, she would be tracked down even faster. She heard the sirens from afar and felt faint. *Already here! Damn it!* she thought like panicked prey.

"Miss, are you going to move up?" shot the sullen voice behind her. Committed to scrutinizing the station's entrance, she had not realized that it was her turn. The agents were approaching, she saw them enter the soaring atrium, patrolling in twos, hands on the holsters of their guns.

"One ticket to Rome. The first train," she said to the ticket officer, handing over her credit card.

"There's a Frecciarossa train leaving in two minutes."

"All right, all right!" she said excitedly.

The police were separating; some were on the platforms, a couple were heading towards the ticket booth. The ticket printer seemed to her the slowest machine ever created since the invention of binary code, but finally the man handed her the ticket and receipt of payment under the glass. Rebecca signed it casually so as not to attract attention and slipped away from the line, grabbing the ticket voucher on the fly.

"Miss, you forgot your credit card!" the ticket officer called in vain. Rebecca gave no sign that she had heard and walked quickly towards the platform while several guys, out of kindness, tried in vain to call her back. The scene attracted the two policemen who were walking that way. Rebecca turned towards them just slightly; they had missed her by a hair's breadth!

"What's going on?" one of the two asked distractedly, while the other continued to scour the ticket booth with his gaze.

"A young lady left her credit card here," replied the ticket officer. "Can I give it to you?" he asked, lifting it against the glass to show it to him. The man started to tell him that he could deliver it to their office at the station but just before opening his mouth he froze: the name on the card! It was just the woman they were looking for!

"What ticket did she buy?" he asked urgently.

"Rome," the ticket officer promptly responded. "Platform three; it's leaving right now!" The policeman immediately circulated the news on the radio, but it was too late; the agents ran like mad along the platform, but the conductor did not see them. The Frecciarossa quickly picked up speed and left them behind, helpless.

With her heart pounding, Rebecca saw the policemen run beside the tracks and then turn back, defeated, along the platform. At the last second she had decided that the risk of being fined was certainly less than that of being captured and she had gotten on a Frecciargento train to Milan, departing from the platform alongside the train to Rome. After a seemingly endless time, her train too finally left the station. She barricaded herself in the tiny bathroom, making sure to close the door. Tears of desperation began to roll down her face but, after a few minutes of giving vent to her emotions, she forced herself to regain composure. She washed her face, assumed the most natural-looking expression she could, and searched for an unoccupied seat at the back of the carriage, hoping that no one—least of all the ticket-checker—would notice her. She was lucky; all the way up to the capital of Emilia Romagna, nobody asked for her ticket. She alighted from the train in Bologna and jumped at the chance to take the regional fast train connection to Padua, nearly certain that no ticket checker would stop her because in all the years she had taken that train she had never seen a trace of one.

Once she had arrived at the station in Padua, she found no patrol awaiting her on the platform. Spirits raised, she made sure to immerse herself in the crush of commuters, without ever looking up at the surveillance cameras, hoping that this would throw anyone who tried to track her movements off her trail. During the course of the trip she had drawn up a plan; she would go towards the Institute, in Legnaro, and would force Professor Benatti to disclose to the police the tip-off he had given to Pegasus. Whatever is sent via the Internet is forever; he could not deny the evidence. She was certain that this would be enough not only to show that she was not a psychopath, but to exonerate her. Immediately after that she would resume the quest Spinelli had begun. If her fear was well-founded, the survival of thousands, perhaps millions of lives, was at stake. She could not be arrested right now! Surely, however, she could not show up at the laboratory in her state; she would stop at home and take a shower. Then, with new, dry clothes, she would confront the professor.

Cocky now from the success of her train stratagem, she got on the bus going in the direction of her home and relaxed; the police were waiting for her in Rome; she still had a bit of time to spare. But her confidence was shaken after a few minutes when the bus neared her stop; two police cars surpassed them, sirens wailing, to screech to a halt right in front of her apartment building. They were looking for her! How could she have been so naïve? It was clear that even if the train to Rome had not already been stopped and searched, someone had informed the local police of her address and now they had come to search her apartment. As the bus continued on its journey, the woman shrank inside it, away from the huge windows, to avoid the risk of being identified by the police. At that point there was no choice other than to go on to the Institute. Rebecca pulled her phone from her bag and dialed the director's number. The phone rang incessantly with no response. But where the hell was the secretary? After more rings, someone picked up the phone on the other side.

"About time!" the woman roared.

"Doctor…" an unsteady voice greeted her.

"Nicoletta?" she asked, recognizing the janitor. There was probably no one nearby and she had decided to pick up in the secretary's stead. "Hi, Nicoletta, is Professor Benatti there? I need to speak with him urgently," she said, not skirting the issue.

"Uh…no," the voice hesitated. "Did you not hear?"

"What?"

"Professor Benatti is dead," she whispered. "This morning he was hit by a car, a hit-and-run, while he got off the bus, right here in front of the Institute." Rebecca nearly dropped the phone. Her head began to spin and she staggered so much that a worried gentleman promptly offered her his seat. White-faced, she refused with a wave of her hand and resumed the conversation.

"What…how?"

"Ah, Mr. Dinozzo is here looking for you," the janitor said in a barely perceptible voice, ending the call. Rebecca looked at her phone's screen, incredulous. She thought of Nicoletta's last words. She did not know any Dinozzo, about that she was certain. The only time that she had heard that name, she was watching television. There was an

65

investigator with that name… she felt faint. The fact that Nicoletta had used that name could only mean one thing: the police had already arrived at the Institute and were looking for her. Perhaps they had even been right there while she had spoken to her. The cell phone! Surely that too was under surveillance. She turned it off right away, resigned. In the meantime, the bus was slowly nearing a shopping mall and she, considering it appropriate for the time to stay in a crowd as much as possible, got off the bus, almost dragged by the rest of the passengers. Professor Benatti dead, killed by a hit-and-run driver. She hoped that he had not suffered, at least.

And now she had no alibi; of course, the mail was still traceable, but without Benatti's confession, its value was minimal. Someone could even instill suspicions that she had sent it because, like others among his closest associates, she knew his credentials. But in this case no one could accuse her of murder! She was in Florence while it was happening. No, wait; if the accident had happened that morning, theoretically she would have had time to return to Florence after hitting him…She put her hands in her hair, increasingly desperate, and only then realized that she was completely drenched. Her purse, hidden under her arm, seemed in slightly better condition than the rest, but she could not help but think of Galileo's letters, the only physical evidence that everything going on was not just the product of a sick mind. She had to protect them at all costs. She thought back to all the espionage films she had seen in her life and an idea that seemed decent came to her. A bit less desperate than before, she walked determinedly into the supermarket.

She left the supermarket shortly thereafter and began to wander aimlessly. She was tired, wet, hungry and terrified. The heavy summer rain had soaked through all of her pores down to the bone and her body, not having eaten for hours, was periodically shaken by chills. She walked away from the city center towards the periphery. While she walked, Rebecca contemplated surrendering to the police; sooner or later they would find her. What she had said to the agent at the police station made her the prime suspect in a series of terrible murders and maybe a kidnapping and her fingerprints confirmed her presence at the scene of all those crimes. Spinelli could not confirm her non-involvement; indeed, if he ever resurfaced, she wondered if he would be able to do so. There had been many times when they remained apart, and he certainly would not be able to give assurance as to her movements; provided that in the meantime he had not disappeared underwater or into a concrete cast, in classic Mafia fashion. But he could not reveal himself now! Professor Benatti's murder merely confirmed the importance of his quest. Perhaps her flight, her very life was the only guarantee of Michele's survival; the people from Pegasus would probably not have dared to harm him, knowing that she could lead the police in their direction…or not?

Angered with herself, she slapped herself full in the face as hard as she could. *Damn it, Rebecca, focus! Stop thinking about everything you don't know. Think about what you know!* Momentarily revitalized by the pain, she took a deep breath and forced herself to discipline her mind. One question at a time. *What do I do now?* She could not go back home; her office was off-limits. She slipped her hands into her shoulder bag, her favorite, the only lifeline to her normal life. She sought out her wallet and looked disconsolately into the banknote compartment; sadly empty, only one slip of paper prevented the leather sides of the compartment from touching one another. A ticket? Rebecca unfolded it and read: an address and a phone number scribbled on Institute letterhead. When she remembered why she had made that note, several days before, she could not help but smile briefly, a bitter smile that smacked of defeat. She had really fallen far if she had nothing left to do but knock on that door. She took a deep breath, swallowed a mouthful of rain and what was left of her pride, and proceeded along the outskirts of Padua.

7

She struggled greatly to find the address; only on the third attempt did she realize that the apartment must be above the workshop that she had passed several times. At that hour nothing around that was open: not a bar, not a single shop in sight. If you scream no one will hear you, she thought instinctually, but she was tired, wet, and increasingly cold and it did not take her long to decide that it was worth taking the risk. She took a deep breath and rang the bell with conviction. No response. Desperate, she tried again. She had not even considered the possibility that there was no one home. And now? She took a step back, resigned to turn herself in, when the door opened and she found herself face to face with the pure astonishment of Alessandro Vinci. He wore a pair of shorts and a T-shirt that, judging by the look of it, must have been slipped on at the last minute to answer the bell and he was barefoot, his forehead and arms beaded with sweat, like someone who had just been interrupted during a sporting activity. While registering this information Rebecca realized that Vinci in his turn was scrutinizing her, noting her hair dripping on the doormat, her completely waterlogged clothes and filthy shoes. She blushed violently. She had never felt more miserable.

"I never thought I'd see the Ice Queen in person at my door," Dr. Vinci welcomed her sarcastically.

"I knew it!" she snapped at the height of tension, her face streaked with tears and rain. She angrily ran a hand through her hair with an air of despair, turning to leave.

"Rebecca!" the young man called, following her.

"Doctor, come in before you drown, would you?"

The young woman's sense of pride seethed, but the cold and the rain convinced her to retrace her steps. Vinci brought her back to the door of the building and led her inside. She followed him up a metal staircase that only appeared shaky for a good two flights. She did not count any other doors, besides the one that the academic was now indicating. When she was inside, Rebecca realized that the apartment was actually a kind of penthouse which, by square footage, had to cover roughly the entire workshop. High above their heads, the rain bounced off sloping glass that made up the entire ceiling. Hanging along the wall of the L-shaped corridor were some photos, mostly in black and white.

Passing next to them, Rebecca could not help but stare. The portraits were equally of men and women, children and the elderly. It did not take her long to grasp the common thread linking all the subjects; they had all been caught in a salient moment: the dancer during a pirouette, the wood carver in the stillness of a masterful hand gesture. There were rugby players in the act of scoring a goal and even a baby crying over breaking his toy. Rebecca was no photography expert, but she was enchanted to observe those expressions hung on the walls, admiring the work of their author. *Vinci, without a doubt.* Understood. So his proposal, on the day they met, was not an excuse to pick her up! *You're an idiot*, she said to herself, feeling guilty. The next instant, looking at the collection of photos, she was seized by the same feeling of cold and danger that had frozen her the first time her gaze had met that of the author. The uneasiness she felt at this brought her straight back to reality. Where was Vinci?

"Here you are," he said, reappearing from nowhere, holding a large, red towel and a shirt. He pointed to the puddle that had formed at the woman's feet. "You can wear these clothes," he explained to her, pulling a pair of shorts out of the bundle of clothes. He showed her to the bathroom. She took the clothes and the towel in her arms and, once she was alone, was dismayed to see that the key was missing from the lock. Apart from this particular, the bathroom was otherwise clean and friendly, being that of a single male, and it had a Plexiglas shower stall. Rebecca decided that she would run the risk of being seen naked; she could not stay in that condition a moment longer. She ran the hot water and began to undress, throwing her soaked clothes and undergarments in the sink. She stayed in the shower for a long time, letting the near-boiling water warm her and trying to decide what she would do once she left the bathroom. If just one day ago someone had told her that she would find herself taking a shower in Alessandro Vinci's bathroom, she would have taken them for a fool. On the other hand, so many things had happened in the interim that being half naked in the disquieting graduate student's home, wearing his clothing, was certainly neither the strangest nor the most dangerous.

When she had decided to take refuge in the last place that remained to her, she had even taken into account the possibility of having to sleep with him. That possibility is not ruled out yet, she said to herself, resigned to that chance. Sex or jail, that's what the alternatives seemed to be at the moment. She sought out a hair dryer and brush and used them both; finally, there was really no excuse to stay in the bathroom and she reluctantly joined her host. She opened the door almost with circumspection and immediately heard the rhythmic thuds coming from another room. Barefoot on the tile floor, she tried to follow the sound, her curiosity piqued. The plasterboard walls created four rooms: a kitchen, a living room, a bedroom and what looked like a small study. The noise, however, came from farther away. Rebecca silently approached and discovered a fifth room, larger than the others. It was…a gym. Rebecca saw a number of apparatuses—which she did not recognize—some weights, a pommel horse and a punching bag; and it was upon precisely this that the owner was unleashing himself. The woman could not help but notice the agility and power with which his mass of muscles, clearly visible on his naked torso, railed against the powerless apparatus. She did not have the opportunity to admire long, however, because almost immediately Alessandro stopped hitting the bag and turned towards her, somehow aware of her presence, although Rebecca was certain that she had made no noise. In that moment the doctor noticed, on his left shoulder, a long scar that extended all the way to his pectoral muscle.

"Are you hungry?" he asked her, putting his T-shirt back on. If he had noticed that she was not wearing undergarments beneath his shirt, he did not show it.

"I'm so hungry I can't see straight," she admitted, smiling a little and remembering that she had not put anything in her stomach since that morning.

"Come, then," he said and led her to the kitchen. There was already a pot full of water on the stove; he lit the fire and handed her a pack of spaghetti with a gesture almost of camaraderie. "Can you throw them in when it's boiling? I really need a shower," he justified himself. Neither his ways nor the opportunity to be alone for a little longer to gather her thoughts were displeasing to Rebecca, and she gladly agreed with a nod. "If you're hungry, take whatever you want in the fridge!" he shouted from the hallway. Out of politeness she tried to resist her hunger but finally relented; she found cheese, a bit of bread and devoured them while cooking the pasta. Alessandro returned just as she was draining the spaghetti. He wore clean clothes, but his hair was still wet and the aroma of his bubble bath teased her as he approached to pass her a jar of prepared sauce to dress the pasta. Despite the snack from just earlier,

Rebecca scarfed down her portion and Vinci pulled two steaks out of the fridge, which he cooked on the hot plate. During dinner they spoke little and her host never asked about the reason for the intrusion, but all the same Rebecca perceived his curiosity hovering in the air. After she had cleared the table, she set about addressing the issue: "Listen…" she began, trying to find the words to describe the situation in which she found herself. She had decided to be honest, to say everything; she did not know if he could—or would want—to help her, but he was giving refuge to a wanted person, risking trouble too, and as a result, she was indebted to him.

"Tomorrow," Alessandro interrupted her.

"What?"

"Explanations tomorrow. Let's go to bed now."

Rebecca unconsciously crossed her arms over her chest. She had considered that possibility and had concluded that she would accept having sex with the graduate student in exchange for hospitality if necessary, because her mission was truly too important. However, Vinci's manner up to that point had not hinted that he wanted to go that far. "You must be tired," he conceded. "Come." She followed him hesitantly into the bedroom. Divided, she watched Vinci as he removed the sheets and pillowcases and replaced them with clean ones taken from the dresser. Had she not been deeply disturbed she would even have admired the precision with which he handled the linens, making them fall perfectly on both sides. "There," he said, indicating the freshly made bed. "I'll sleep on the couch. Don't worry, you need not fear for your virtue," he teased her. Rebecca turned the same color as her hair.

"Was it so obvious?" she demurred, trying to make up for the fool she had made of herself by making a joke of it. In vain.

"Goodnight," he replied in utter seriousness, closing the door behind him. She waited until his footsteps became further away down the hall, then slowly turned the key in the lock while her other hand sought to deaden the sound. Shortly thereafter she slipped into the bed and sank into a fitful sleep.

When she reopened her eyes the next morning, at first she did not recognize anything of her surroundings; the morning light filtered through the sloping windows and, while she fully awakened, she gradually focused on the strange walls and remembered where she was. The bedside clock marked half past eight and the sun was high, as if to make amends for the previous days' merciless rain. Rebecca laughed to herself thinking that amongst her friends she was famous for only being able to sleep in places completely shrouded in darkness. On several occasions she had even changed hotel rooms just because a bit of light filtered through the shutters. Now however her bed had been inundated with sunbeams for…a couple of hours? And she had not noticed anything. She must have been exhausted, to say the least. She got up and retrieved her clothing from on top of the radiator, which Alessandro had turned on the previous evening for the occasion; they were dry now, unlike her shoes, which were still wet.

While she dressed she noticed for the first time the singular, gigantic photograph that leaned on a wall to the side of the bed. A female nude in black and white. The model was a girl with light-colored hair; her white skin was almost confused with the whiteness of the sheets that sensually encircled her, emphasizing her curves and masterfully veiling her most intimate parts. It was a delicate pose but in synchrony with the strong, almost indecent, erotic charge. One could not observe it without feeling unsettled, excited about it. Rebecca tried to connect it with the other pictures hanging in the entry, but try as she might she could not grasp the common thread. *Is this how he wanted to photograph me?* she wondered, without being able to give herself an answer. The chivalry with which he had treated her the night before prevented her from taking for granted any sexual interest on Vinci's part. On that note…*where is Vinci?* Rebeca wondered, noticing then that the apartment was totally silent.

"Vinci?" she called. No answer. "Alessandro?" she persisted, waiting for an answer that did not come. She walked as far as the kitchen barefoot, where she found a note in plain sight on the table: "I'm out running. Milk in the fridge, cookies, jam in the pantry. Alex." Who knows how long he's been gone, she thought to herself, regretting that she had not heard him leave. She had warm milk and cookies for breakfast and when she had finished, as she washed the mug and the bowl, she cast a sidelong glance out the window and quite nearly fainted; there was a police car in the street. She saw it slow down until it stopped under the workshop. With her heart in her throat, Rebecca suddenly moved away from the window, panicked. *He betrayed me!* She moved back to glance out the window and saw a figure standing next to the squad car, it looked like…yes, it was truly Vinci! That bastard! She ran to the bathroom and threw on her still-wet shoes in a rush and hurried down the stairs. As she descended she heard the sound of the building door close noisily. Vinci was coming back; maybe he was accompanied by the officers. *Shit!* She had no way out. Rebecca stood listening, expecting the agents, but she heard only the footsteps of a single person treading up the stairs that separated them from her. She looked behind her; fortunately she had not closed the apartment door and she managed to reenter unseen. She heard the key turning in the keyhole. Had Vinci wanted to betray her, he would have come up with the police, but…

"Good morning," he greeted her reentering, taken aback to find her there before him, waiting.

"Hi," she greeted him back, uncertain of what to do.

"Did you eat breakfast?"

"Yes, thank you," she replied laconically.

"Listen, I don't want to repeat myself, but…let me have a shower."

"I saw you in the street," she said, too tense to hold back.

"Ah," he replied, curious, and then his expression suddenly became serious. "You saw the police car. They're friends. They come by now and again to say hello." Rebecca relaxed a bit, but now he was the suspicious one. "The shower will wait. We have to talk."

"True," she admitted, throwing a glance at the door. Dr. Vinci stepped aside, freeing the way to the exit; had she wanted to, she could have left. It was this gesture that convinced her that she could trust him. Rebecca directed herself toward the kitchen, set her wet bag on a chair and took another for herself. "It would be better if you took a chair as well," she began, "because it's a long story."

She told him everything: from the day that she had been approached by Spinelli up until that moment, omitting nothing. Alessandro listened attentively, interrupting often to ask for clarifications. Meanwhile he fidgeted with his phone, turning it over in his hands like a toy; the one sign that revealed how distraught he was. Rebecca kept an eye on the phone keypad; if he decided to denounce her, his fingers would soon move to form the number 112, the police. How could she blame him? If he had told her the same story, she would not have believed him either.

"Spinelli?" he asked at the end, scrutinizing her.

"Missing. Maybe abducted."

The same concentrated, scrutinizing expression that struck her the day of their first meeting in Benatti's office painted itself across his face. Rebecca instinctively recoiled in her chair.

"And now what do you want from me?" he asked without a trace of warmth. The doctor realized just how much lower her chance of success was, if it had ever existed. How could she have hoped he would believe her? Her despair was about to overwhelm her, but that man was her last hope and she needed to convince him at any cost. There were millions of lives at stake.

"Help," she confessed, running a hand through her hair in a gesture of despair. "Whatever kind of help you can give me."

Alessandro looked again at the display on his cellphone. Rebecca was sure that within a few seconds his fingers would dial the fateful numbers. She cast a quick glance at the door, seized by the impulse to escape, but when she brought them back to him, again she met his unrelenting gaze and remained rooted to the spot.

"I want half," he said.

"What?"

"I want the credit for the possible discovery of that book and, if that plague bit turns out to be true, I want half of what any pharmaceutical company will offer to produce the vaccine or serum or who-knows-what other drug."

"Okay," said Rebecca, incredulous and relieved. "All right, that seems fair."

"And you will do as I say." Rebecca nodded. "Without debate or reluctance." The woman nodded quickly again, but this time with the terror that those words also included sexual intercourse in the list of things about which she would not be allowed to be "reluctant." Alessandro, however, seemed to have completely different thoughts in his head; he walked away from the kitchen and returned with a massive legal pad and some pens. Within a few minutes she watched him structure a precise and detailed working plan on the paper, with the hallmark casualness of someone who does a routine job. Everything to be done was arranged in boxes, sketched by pen, while the uncertainties were written in pencil and progressively revised as, discussing them with her, he obtained more precise information. More than a work plan, it seemed the planning of a military operation.

"We need the original document," he said finally. "Galilei's letter. Rather, we need all the letters you have found." Rebecca sat back, tentative, crossing her arms in front of her. "You still have them, right?" he urged. She was nearly going to lie to him, but Alessandro prevented her, stiffening in his chair. "Don't lie to me. Never. You want me to believe you, risking career and prison, and you don't trust me?" The letters were the only material that showed that everything had actually happened and it was no machination or figment of her mind…and he was asking her to give them to him. Rebecca felt like one who, after being pushed to the brink of a precipice, is then forced to choose whether to turn back and face certain death, or leap into the void, hoping for a miracle.

"Yes," she admitted, opting for the miracle. "Let's go get them."

8

"You're not coming," Alessandro said to her, preparing to go out; it was now midmorning. "If they're looking for you, they'll certainly have issued an identikit and description of the clothes you're wearing. The first thing to do will be to find something else to put on. You will also need to cut your hair and dye it."

"Not a chance!"

He quieted, staring at her with an eloquent expression. "What did we say earlier about reluctance?"

Rebecca looked puzzled and embarrassed. It would be hard for her. "Fine," she resigned herself grudgingly. "What else do I have to do? Change religion? Gain fifty pounds?"

"Another fifty?" Vinci shot back, his lips parting in an amused smile. "I think you've gained weight since the last time we met..." Rebecca hit his arm with her fist, irked. He burst out laughing. "I was just kidding, I swear I was just kidding. If anything you've lost weight, seriously!" he concluded, trying to mollify her. The woman could not manage to suppress a freeing laugh, and she massaged the fist with which she had struck him, sore. It had been like punching a wall. "There's something else," he continued. "No cell phone. They will already be trying to track it down."

"It's already off," she said. "Well, I thought I would keep it on, but without the sim card."

"And what do you use it for?" he demanded.

"A clock," she replied, without confessing that that object was the only familiar thing that remained to her; an electric security blanket to hang onto to avoid slipping into total psychological deterioration. She took out the sim card and handed it to him.

Alessandro seemed pleased and proceeded: "I need you to make me a list of what you need and you need to tell me how to recover the letters." Rebecca was again tempted to protest, but Alessandro stopped her dead with a withering look.

"How do I know that I can trust you? How can you expect me to stay at home waiting for you?" she asked with a note of desperation in her voice. Those letters were the only material object that showed all that had happened was no figment of her imagination; perhaps they could not have cleared her of the charges, but she could not bear to think of parting with them. He stared at her for a moment, then finally relented.

"Okay, we'll do it like this: I'll go out now and come back with new clothes for you and dye for your hair. We'll wait until you are sufficiently disguised and then we'll go together. The police are looking for a single woman, redheaded, on the run from central Italy. They won't pay attention to a couple of sweethearts walking together."

"All right, Captain," she said, relieved, smiling at her companion.

Three hours later, they went together to the mall where she had been the day before. With extreme regret, Rebecca had had to renounce her beloved auburn curls and she now sported a dark brown bob that she did not like at all but that would, she hoped, keep her safe from the eyes of the police. She knew that it was a necessary sacrifice, but she doubted that she would ever forgive Alessandro for compelling her to do so. For added security, in addition to two containers of dye—two different colors and both of them horrendous—Vinci had bought her some new clothes and a wide straw hat that overshadowed much of her face. A very useful accessory that day, which unlike the one before it, was clear, hot and sunny. Vinci had also lent her his sunglasses. Dressed up like so, she was really unrecognizable.

They parked his gray Ford Fiesta in the basement, near the exit. Along the escalator that carried them inside, she saw that Alessandro bent his head down every time they passed a camera. She did the same, with the help of the hat. Once they had reached the windows where customers deposit bags and purchases from other shops before entering the superstore, she pulled out the little key she had hidden until then. She slipped it into the corresponding little box and, holding her breath, she opened it. With incredible relief she found the drawing carrier-tube that she had bought for the occasion. She opened it immediately to check. She nodded her head to Alessandro, who was watching her with trepidation. Everything was there.

As agreed upon earlier, they entered the supermarket side by side, each carrying a red basket for purchases. Rebecca needed other under-garments and clothes, and Alessandro had taken the opportunity to do a bit of shopping in light of the trip they would need to make on the quest for *Stella Novissima*. Rebecca felt embarrassed to use his money— she had no more cash—but he had reassured her, telling her to consider it an advance on future earnings that would result from their discovery. Maybe they should have taken a cart, Rebecca thought while she arranged more underwear precariously in her basket. When she raised her eyes she froze. Two policemen, and they were coming her way. They had found her! It was over! A kiss on the lips roused her from her stupor, disorienting her even more.

"Cereal!" Alessandro said, pulling his mouth away from hers. He waved a big colored box in front of her face, and the noise had the effect of bringing her fully back to reality. The police stopped right in front of them. "Corrado!" he said, greeting the older of the two.

"Vinci!" the other replied, smiling. "How long…?" He was a stocky and sturdy man and all his body language expressed a sincere joy for this meeting, as well as a kind of respect for his interlocutor, who was at least fifteen years younger than him. "De Marchi!" he said, turning to his colleague. "This is Alessandro Vinci."

"A pleasure," said the young policeman, lifting his gaze from Rebecca's basket. Unlike his companion he was slender, muscular, and seemed alert. Alessandro could not help but to introduce her too. "This is Angela Colomba, my…friend." The two men gave her just a glance before they got caught up chatting with Vinci, taking their leave shortly thereafter. Rebecca resumed breathing and instinctively quickened her pace. She could not wait to leave. But the young man stopped her, continuing their tour through the shelves as though nothing had happened.

"Why the kiss?" she attacked him half-heartedly, still tense from the meeting.

"You were stock-still like a cat in car headlights. I imagine that for them that constitutes a more than suspicious reaction. When I kissed you, to them you changed from a suspect to a friend's companion."

"You're right," she admitted, thinking back to the younger cop's expression, and she was happy when they finally left the superstore. They drove back to Vinci's apartment. The normal bustle of the workshop had struck up again like every other day of the week, accompanied by the constant sounds of the equipment; nothing remained of the surreal calm of the night before. Climbing the stairs, Rebecca could not help but notice it. "They certainly make a big racket."

"Yeah, but usually they're not in at this hour and they don't work on the weekends. A good compromise, otherwise I couldn't afford all this space, with my salary." He continued, changing the subject, "We need to bring these letters to the department; we need a consultation. How about grabbing a bite before going?"

Rebecca agreed, thankful that he had proposed that she come with him and, for the first time, she was not afraid when she saw him pull out his phone and call a colleague at the university, announcing their visit.

To reach the Department of Cultural Heritage at the University of Padua, in Piazza Capitaniato, they first had to go through the much larger Piazza dei Signori, which at that hour of the afternoon was already packed with spritz-drinkers. Rebecca nervously scrutinized every officer, policeman and even the parking attendants, who did not fail to return her worried gaze.

"Relax," Alessandro murmured, smiling at her, as though the only thing they were looking for was some small table in an outdoor bar.

"Easy for you," she replied tartly. "It's not you who's risking jail…"

"You think?" he replied, reminding her that after all, after that morning, he was her accomplice. She sighed, releasing a little tension. The young man's smile was almost mocking.

"Now why are you laughing?" she reproached him, fearing that she was the cause of his mirth.

"You see the clock in front of us?" he continued, pointing to the restored monument that crowed the Piazza dei Signori. "Don't you see something strange?" he insisted. Rebecca had always lived in Padua. She had seen that clock hundreds, if not thousands of times. Only then did she realize that she had never really looked at it. "Look closely at the hands: what do you see?"

"The sun," she replied.

"Just that?"

Rebecca stood thoughtfully, studying the monument for a few more seconds, then her face lit up with triumph. "The earth!" she exclaimed aloud, inadvertently attracting the attention of a group of German tourists, who turned towards her. "The earth is in the center, the sun travels around it. It's a depiction of the Ptolemaic system!"

"Exactly!" he congratulated. "We're about to pass under one of the symbols rendered obsolete by Galileo…" Immediately brought back to reality by these words, Rebecca quickly put the sunglasses back on, holding the folder of old documents close to her. Alessandro rightly interpreted this as an invitation to get them back on their way, so they did. Rebecca followed the man inside the department, up to a glass door closed with an electronic lock that the young man unlocked with his university badge, identical to the one that Rebecca had used in the past. They walked down several corridors illuminated coldly by neon lights and cooled by noisy air-conditioning equipment. They went down some stairs and finally found themselves in another corridor, this one wider and brighter. They stopped in front of a closed wooden door, which bore no sign. Alessandro knocked and opened without waiting for an answer. Rebecca followed him and was amazed by what she saw.

It was not the dark, dusty room that she expected, but a well-lit laboratory full of machines in operation—all dedicated to the study of ancient texts. Some were kept in glass display cases in partial darkness. Others were simple sheets, some even illuminated. The only occupant of the laboratory, however, corresponded perfectly with the classic image the woman had of a bookworm. He was short, gray-haired and gray-skinned. He was wearing such thick lenses that Rebecca wondered if indeed he needed the microscope that was projecting onto a screen the results of his efforts at magnification. He had not noticed their presence, seemingly immersed in the study of a large letter L that, in its convoluted illumination, took up the full screen.

"Doctor Menin?" Alessandro called him. His narrow shoulders jumped under his white coat. He turned to the intruders and Rebecca could see that his eyes, magnified by lenses, seemed gray. His voice was high-pitched, almost feminine.

"Vinci!" the little man greeted him, recovering from the shock.

"Meet…Marina Gamba," he said, pointing to Rebecca.

"A pleasure," the little man replied, stammering. His embarrassed gaze immediately returned to his colleague.

"The letters I was talking to you about are hers," Alessandro continued, inviting Rebecca to hand them over to him with a nod of his head. The young woman sighed, pulled the folder from her bag and reluctantly delivered them into the man's dry hands. She marveled at the reverent skill with which those gray fingers extracted the folios, one by one, pushing his eyes so close that they almost touched them.

"When do you need the report?" he asked, without taking his eyes from the sheets.

"Soon," said Vinci, and his tone of voice conveyed their urgency so effectively that the man looked up one last time before turning around and setting to work already on their letters, oblivious to their presence.

"They are in good hands," Alessandro tried to reassure her while, a little later, they walked back along the corridors to the exit.

"I hope so," Rebecca restricted herself to replying, grumbling; she felt like an insecure trapeze artist forced to perform without a safety net. "Marina Gamba, huh?" she asked then. "Galileo's woman, the mother of his children. But your friend won't get that?"

"Don't worry, I don't think he registered your presence; when he saw the letters his concentration was all on them. You could have danced naked in front of him and he wouldn't have even noticed."

"Thank you for the consideration!" she said, stung. Then, thinking back to the figure of Marina Gamba, continued, "He really never married that woman? After he gave her three children, he just abandoned her?"

"At that time it wasn't so strange that prominent people, without giving up the pleasures of their company, refused to marry women of a much lower rank, and Marina Gamba is one of them. Nonetheless, Galileo behaved quite well towards her, both in Padua and after his departure for Florence; he paid her a monthly sum, though it wasn't required. A kind of 'alimony' before its time. He even had a falling out with his terrible mother over that."

"His mother?"

"Yeah," the student continued. "She was an unbearable woman: after having tormented her husband, throwing his professional failures in his face and squeezing money out of his purse for the expensive clothes she adored, she took out her dissatisfaction on her son Galileo. He called her a whore and she went all the way before the Inquisition of Florence to denounce him; first on charges that he did not regularly attend Mass, and then for magic. Fortunately, the government of the Serenissima, the Republic of Venice, of which Padua was an appendage, covered up the trials."

"For...magic?"

Alessandro smiled. "Yes, Galileo used to get paid, and handsomely, even, to write horoscopes. Even nobles and rulers demanded his prognostications. He also gave private lessons to many students, including one that would become a cardinal and would participate in his trial by voting for his condemnation: Guido Bentivoglio. For that matter he needed every penny: to support his family, but also to maintain his own vices. During the happy years spent in Padua he made his first astronomical observations and studies of physics, but he also let himself go to numerous excesses—real debauchery."

"I like him a lot more already," commented Rebecca.

"Maybe you'll like him less so once you hear what he did to his daughters," Alessandro said. Rebecca's expression darkened. "No, nothing shameful," he assured. "Simply put, not being able to or wanting to think about the dowries for their weddings, he put them both in the convent; it was established practice for those times. The youngest, Livia, took her vows at thirteen and turned her monastic life into a sickness, between frustration and hysteria. The older, however, who took the name Maria Celeste, always remained close to her father…I'm boring you, aren't I?"

"No," she assured him. "I swear I could listen for hours." The student looked into her eyes and, finding no trace of irony, smiled.

"Come on, then." The warm glow of the sunset gave way to a cool evening, lit by streetlamps and the electric signs of the city center. They walked down Via Dante, enveloped in the growing darkness, up to the mighty Roman tower that dominated the arched doorway of Torre Molino. In the silence broken only by their footsteps on stone pebbles, the young woman—immersed in thought—obliviously passed the ancient gate, but was called back by Alessandro. "What, didn't you notice?" he teased. But Rebecca was not in the mood to solve riddles; the more time passed, the more she felt the lack of the letters, the last foothold that could lend credibility to her story. And if she had made a mistake by entrusting the letters to that insignificant bookworm—and her freedom, her life in the hands of the doctoral students? She stood there, a few steps from the door, in the middle of the pathway that served as a parking area with a few parked cars. She raised her gaze impatiently, following Alessandro's. Her eyes caught sight of a white plaque on the left on the inside of the door. She read.

FROM THIS TOWER
GALILEO
MANY OF THE HEAVENS' WAYS REVEALED

Her heart skipped a beat. Was it possible that so much of her city spoke of Galilei? And that in all of the dozens, hundreds of times she had gone through the same door she had never paid attention? He came quickly to the rescue. "It's a plaque from the nineteenth century, I think," Vinci said. "It is said that it was at the top of this tower that Galileo, with the telescope that he perfected himself, discovered the satellites of Jupiter."

"The Galilean moons."

"Exactly," he agreed, smiling. "He dedicated them to the whole Medici family. He hoped to curry favor with the Grand Duke Cosimo, coveting the dream of a professorship in Florence. It was a perfectly successful move, since in a few years his dream would be realized."

Transported back centuries, Rebecca stood listening, stopped in the middle of the lane and smiling. Alessandro looked at her quizzically and she hastened to explain: "It just amazes me to find out how just a few hundred meters away the stone testimonials of this duel of the 'chief world systems,' as Galileo defined them, have coexisted," she said, pointing with her hand in the direction of the clock in Piazza dei Signori. "While the clock and its outdated theory triumph in the main square of the city, this here is almost hidden, forgotten."

"You forget that the geocentric cosmology has reigned for centuries, canonized by Aristotle and the vast ranks of his supporters. Galileo's discoveries are only four hundred years old."

"Only?" she echoed. At that precise moment, announced only by the imperceptible jolt of an engine, one of the parked cars behind Rebecca, a black sedan with tinted windows, moved suddenly without turning on the headlights. Out of the corner of her eye, the young woman saw the dark spot rush towards her and she did not even have time to realize she was going to die before she felt herself struck and hoisted up, but not by the metal bodywork. It was Alessandro's body that hit her, violently throwing her out of the car's trajectory, wrapping her in an embrace of solid flesh that protected her even when they hit the sidewalk. While rolling, she glimpsed the car that screeched, vanishing into the darkness behind them. A dark sedan. Like the one that had followed her and Spinelli in Tuscany! Another jolt and he had her rolling on the ground again; it was Alessandro who in urgency had slipped out from under her. Still stunned, she watched him stand up and stare after the car that had almost run them over while it raced away at full speed. When she was able to see his face she winced: from his head a trickle of blood was running down his forehead and from there, down his cheeks.

"You're hurt!" she shouted, drawing the attention of an elderly couple.

"We have to go," he rebuked her with a low voice, indicating the two people who were approaching them worriedly. "It's nothing!" he yelled in their direction, with a hint of a smile that was meant to be reassuring, but it turned into a snarl, so much so that the two stopped in their tracks, intimidated. Then he turned to Rebecca, still squatting on the ground and trembling: "Are you all right?" he asked worriedly.

"Yes, but if you hadn't thrown me to the ground…You saved my life," she realized, shaking even harder.

"Come on," he said curtly. He grabbed Rebecca by an arm, shaking her from her torpor, and he led her delicately towards his Fiesta, which was fortunately parked nearby. Once inside the car, he pulled a handkerchief from his pocket, pressing it firmly to his head to stem the bleeding slightly. Then he pulled several wet wipes from a compartment of the car and wiped his face. "Here," he said to the woman, still in shock. He urged her to take a few towelettes from the packet to clean her dirty hands of dust. Slowly obeying those simple commands, she abandoned her immobility and began to tremble. He placed one hand over her wrists, which were cold with fear, while keeping an eye on the road, on the alert for more surprises. He drove home trying to avoid further jolting.

Climbing the stairs that took them towards the relative safety of his home, Vinci stayed very close to Rebecca, ready to support her if her legs could not bear her; but she did not fall. At least not right away. She waited for him to open the door and close it behind them and only then did she begin trembling again, while thick tears streamed down her face. She struggled to restrain herself, cursed herself for that weakness…in vain. *What did I do to deserve this?* Alessandro was ready to support her and she, feeling the contact with his strong, warm body, immediately experienced a sensation of wellness, feeling protected and reassured by the spontaneous gesture. She savored his musky scent and closed her eyes, seeking his lips with hers. Alessandro returned the kiss for a brief moment, then he pulled away from their embrace, separating from her. He grasped her shoulders, staring straight into her eyes, and whispered four words. Four words that were taken for granted, but the tone in which he spoke them and the intensity of his gaze meant that she, against all logic, believed him: "Everything will be fine." And in that moment she understood that it did not matter how, and it did not matter when, but in the end everything would be resolved. Thanks to him.

"Let me have a look at that head," she said, shaking with embarrassment.

He drew back. "It's nothing; it already stopped bleeding."

"Hold still," she ordered him. "I'm the doctor here, and a microbiologist too. Wounds are never to be underestimated. Where do you keep the disinfectant?" she asked.

"In the bathroom," he sighed defeatedly, while Rebecca dragged him by the arm. He pointed to the medicine cabinet, from which she took out a bottle of purplish liquid and gauze. Once she removed a bit of coagulum she was able to make out the injured area: "It's just an abrasion," she ascertained, heartened. "I hope you're vaccinated against tetanus."

"I told you so," he replied, trying vainly to escape her attentions. "And I'm good on the tetanus front, thank you, Mom."

"Hold still!" she insisted, holding him back to complete the disinfection. Then she looked down and saw that his shirt was soaked with blood. "Take it off," she ordered. Alessandro tried to protest but she, oblivious, started to take it off herself.

"Okay…all right," he surrendered, flashing her a sly smile. "But if you wanted to see me naked you just had to ask."

Rebecca blushed, avoiding his gaze. "It's just blood that ran down from your hard head," she concluded after removing it with disinfectant. Her fingers lingered on the scars on his left shoulder. "What happened to you?"

"An accident," he replied sharply, dressing himself again.

He tried to leave the bathroom, but she stopped him.

"Thank you," she whispered, looking him straight in the eye. "And not just for saving my life tonight."

"I'm hungry," said Alessandro, quickly changing the subject.

"As you wish, my silent hero," Rebecca conceded. "It's up to the damsel in distress to prepare the meal, right?"

"Actually, it's up to you to wait," he told her. "I'd like to save what we have for the journey and, if you're up for it, I'll get a pizza to go that can sustain us for the night. There's a really good place two blocks from here."

"Can I come with you?"

"Better not." Alessandro's expression darkened and she knew he was still thinking about the incident. "Wait here: it won't take more than forty-five minutes. Just in case, I'll leave the car keys."

Rebecca shuddered at the thought of being forced to run fleeing from that apartment without him. She watched him walk away almost in a hurry, amazed at how quickly he had recovered from the shock of the failed collision. Did that man know fear?

"Indeed! Indeed!" squealed Dr. Vittorio Menin, swinging his shabby coat on his arms. "This will not please Vinci…" Satisfied, he looked up from his work, emerging from his investigation and returning to the real world as if disembarking from a spaceship, or better still, from a time machine. He was not surprised by the lateness of the hour as much as by the light that filtered through his office door from the main corridor. Resigned to his erratic schedule, the janitors had learned to turn everything off and leave him to his studies. He had never had any scruples about working all night on one document.

It was when he heard footsteps in the corridor that Menin was certain he was not alone. Intrigued, he started to open the door, but the handle lowered before his fingers could touch it. He was surprised and a little disappointed when he recognized the person, and he was also visibly irritated to hear his request: "I still do not have definitive results…" he said rudely. "Did you not see the email? You left me the papers just a few hours ago!" Then he turned to his instruments, as if to physically demonstrate his commitment up to that point, and that was how he did not notice the heavy metal bar that came down on his skull. The last image that filled his eyes was that of his beloved machines, silent and powerless witnesses of the massacre of their faithful guardian.

9

"Any idea of who might have been in that car?" Vinci asked late that evening, after both had made a clean sweep of the Chinese food that Alessandro had brought back. As he arrived in front of the workshop, he had seen Rebecca parking before him and running towards him in a panic. Not seeing him return, she was frightened and went out looking for him. Unfortunately, he had found that his trusty pizzeria was closed and he had to go looking for another place, going well beyond the promised forty-five minutes. Once the fact of his well-being had calmed Rebecca, he then reprimanded her harshly. First for not having the patience to wait for him; secondly, for not changing her bloodstained blouse before getting in the car. It was probably his, wound up all over her during treatment, even if he had not noticed it before. For a policeman, however, it would have been more than reason enough to pull her over. Exhausted, he finally swooped voraciously on his dinner, calming hunger pangs and waiting for her to follow suit.

"During our stay in Tuscany we often had the impression of being followed by a dark car," she said. "Spinelli believed it was people from Pegasus. They had preceded us on a couple of occasions, offering to buy the letters we were looking for." She opened her mouth again but closed it, awed by her own thoughts.

"No reluctance," he reminded her.

"I...think that it's them, behind the homicides," she confessed, hoping she would not be taken for a fool.

"Why should they get their hands dirty?" Alessandro objected. "Certainly they have more resources than Spinelli, or even the university."

"They're in a hurry and Michele…Professor Spinelli, was paying for everything out of pocket; he didn't want to share the glory with anyone else."

"That's obvious," Vinci replied coldly. Rebecca remembered that the scholar had passed up his own successor to propose the quest to her, with all the benefits that it would bring. He had reason to be angry! The ding of a cell phone came providentially to break the awkward silence that had descended.

"It's mine," Alessandro admitted, pulling the phone out from under the table. "It's Menin!" he reported excitedly. He immediately turned the phone off and headed to the running PC in the office: "We need the monitor. He sent us scans in high resolution," he explained. In the laconic message accompanying, Dr. Menin reported that the attached images showed, at ninety-nine percent, that three out of four letters were false. The paper was the right kind, even the handwriting was very similar, but the ink was not. That was visibly counterfeit, although its color was indistinguishable from the original. The expert declared that he was almost offended by how easy it was to analyze them. Only the first missive, the one brought to Professor Benatti's office by Spinelli, was real. His images, which were even attached, showed all the characteristics corresponding to the time when they were penned. Menin reserved the right to make a few last investigations before giving the final confirmation, but Vinci knew that he would not go too far if he was already sure of the preliminary results. Rebecca froze, reading those lines. She limited herself to staring into space without thinking about anything while Alessandro printed the images that had been sent.

"You don't seem surprised," she said feebly.

"Not entirely," Vinci admitted. "The first letter had already been examined and analyzed and, even if Spinelli was very possessive of it, I had read the results of the evaluation: almost no doubt that it was authentic. The others...I wouldn't have bet my paycheck, but the feeling they gave me was what Menin confirmed: fake."

"But Michele...Spinelli had examined them at length, he valued them!"

"Sometimes you see what you want to see," Vinci commented, and Rebecca realized why the professor had not chosen him to accompany him on his quest. She put her hands in her hair. She thought back to her own theory, which she had developed precisely based on those letters...to no avail. She had followed a soap bubble...And now the police were chasing her. "It's over. It's all over. We don't—I don't have any cards in hand. Even my four aces were fake. I'm going to the police," she concluded in tears, getting up and rubbing her hands from the nerves. "You're not involved; if your name gets out there somewhere I will say I never told you."

"Three," Vinci stopped her. "Three aces were fake." With his eyes, he indicated the monitor on which the processed images of the first letter were displayed. "Let's start with the real ace."

"Are you serious?" Rebecca was astonished.

"Yes. You have more than enough time to go to prison, but then we'd lose any hope of finding the book and, if Spinelli is still alive, maybe he owes it to the fact that you haven't been arrested yet."

"What?" asked Rebecca.

"The other victims were all found shortly after the homicide. Only Spinelli missed the headcount. Maybe they want something from him, perhaps even this letter. Or he or they don't know what you know and if you end up in prison, what you know becomes public domain. Maybe that's why they tried to eliminate you tonight."

"But I don't know anything!" she replied, shuddering at the memory of the peril recently escaped.

"But they don't know that," he concluded. "And this is another ace in our hands. The choice is yours," said Alessandro. "If you want to give up, I can take you to the police and testify about the attempted murder; or we can try to get to the bottom of this affair, right up to the end."

"You really still want to move forward?"

"Up to the end," he repeated, serious.

"Well, then. Where do we start?"

"From the authentic letter. Spinelli always refused to give me details about how they were obtained, but I remember that around the date of the discovery, he had taken an interest in a certain newspaper article, enough to cut it out," he said, pulling a heavy binder out from a bookshelf. "Seeing his interest, I procured a copy." Only then did Rebecca pay any attention to all the other binders kept in the office. She could not help but wonder if those too contained newspaper clippings. They must have been collected in chronological order, because that blurb occupied one of the last pages of the binder. "Here it is," said Alessandro, showing it to her.

AUTHENTIC WRITINGS OF GALILEO GALILEI: FROM DELICATESSEN TO OBLIVION

A series of disastrous coincidence seems to haunt the personal writings of Galileo Galilei. Many authentic letters and an unknowable number of other documents belonging to the illustrious Tuscan scientist were in fact sold by their heirs to a delicatessen as scrap paper for pennies and it is not difficult to guess what use was made of it. But that ink-smeared paper was not suitable for wrapping slices of Cinta Senese salami, because during the renovation of a villa near Florence many writings were rediscovered, mixed with lime, in the construction material of the perimeter walls of the villa itself. The irony is that what the delicatessen saved was probably destroyed by the unskilled laborers from Padua who, upon finding the ancient papers, unknowingly sent them for pulping. Had it not been for an elderly high school teacher passing nearby at the time, perhaps nothing would have been saved. What was not destroyed by unsuspecting construction workers is currently under examination by the Inspectorate of Fine Arts. S.C.

When she had finished reading the short article, Rebecca was puzzled: "Do you think that the letter comes from there?" she asked.

"I don't know, but it's a possibility that we can't ignore," said the young man, clearly annoyed.

"And where does that take us?" Rebecca asked, trying to interpret his change in mood.

"To the fair, tomorrow morning," he said. "And to a good dose of antacid," he concluded laconically, glancing at the initials printed at the end of the article and preparing to go back to sleep, on the sofa again. Later, alone in the bed of her host, Rebecca could not help but wonder if it would be fair that she invited him to take it back. He had saved her life; really, he deserved it. She was about to get up and take the first step, but then stopped, frozen by the memory of the embarrassing fiasco with Spinelli and decided that it was not appropriate to add further complications to her partnership with Alessandro. If she ruined that too, she would truly have nothing left. Before falling asleep she thought back to Vinci's chivalry; she was sure that it was not normal for a human being of the male sex to not hit on her, considering her absolute dependence on him at the time. She was grateful to him for it but, thinking back to the doctoral student's perfect body, she was a bit sorry for it. Damned chivalry, she concluded, falling asleep.

The police car arrived at the Department of Cultural Heritage shortly after dawn, not even twenty minutes after the janitors' gruesome discovery. The special agent De Marchi came running into the building, followed by the heavier Valente. They knew they had to act quickly, before the crime scene was contaminated by the paramedics, who were later than them for once. Their presence would only create problems given that it was more than obvious there was nothing more to do for the poor scientist.

While Valente awaited the arrival of the ambulance and kept curious eyes at bay, De Marchi slipped inside Menin's laboratory, eager to get busy and careful not to undermine the work of the forensic police. His eyes flashed to and fro, his nostrils dilated; he could almost follow a scent trail like a bloodhound. But that was not why he had been nicknamed Pitbull by his colleagues. That epithet that bothered him at the beginning now almost gave him pleasure, and it was due to another feature: like the dog the name came from, once he had bitten onto something, he never gave up.

10

The bulky, desolate sheds of the Padua fairgrounds faced Via Niccolò Tommaseo, the major thoroughfare that connects the populous and once notorious area of Stanga with the train station. The entrance to the editorial office of the *Corriere della Sera* was nearby in Via Venezia, and they managed to park almost in front of the door. At the entrance they were greeted by the receptionist's look of cold courtesy, as she looked at them quizzically.

"Good morning. I would like to see Silvia Canelli," Alessandro explained. The employee in a blue uniform quickly typed something on her keyboard, listening steadily through her headset.

"I'm sorry, she's in a meeting," the lady said after a few seconds.

"Tell her that Alessandro Vinci is here," he insisted. As he uttered those words, the clerk's expression became more attentive, a sign that on the other end of her headset someone was talking to her.

"She's coming," she said matter-of-factly. "If in the meantime you want to give me an identification for the passes…" Alessandro drew out his identity card, then met Rebecca's questioning gaze. "I told you we'd need our wallets," he shot out loud. Then, turning to the receptionist, went on: "She never listens to me. I had told her to take her purse, but she didn't, she never stops to listen to me… can I put both passes in my name?" he asked, shaking his head.

The embarrassed receptionist was about to reply when a woman poked her head out of the sliding door to her right and turned to her with authority: "I'll take care of it, Rosa," she said, swiping her badge over the appropriate sensor and opening the electronic gate. The two guests did not wait for her to ask and they entered despite the receptionist's weak protests. A brief introduction followed, in which Alessandro introduced his companion as Marina Gamba. Shaking her hand, Rebecca realized that the woman lingered in the contact, studying her. She stared back at her in turn and could not help but think that her appearance was perfectly suited for the image she had created for herself of a career woman: a perfect bob hairstyle, exquisite blonde hair—more the gift of nature than the work of a hairdresser—dark suit, designer shoes. The only oddities that granted femininity were a Venetian Murrina pendant and a very strong scent, maybe too much. *Maybe she chose it to hide the odor of smoke*, slightly perceptible despite the precaution, thought Rebecca who had a growing sensation of having seen her before the more she stared at her, although she could not remember where. Then she hugged Alessandro, but without warmth; it did not take a psychologist to realize that there was something personal between the two.

"Wow," he appraised, "you have come a long way!"

"To what do I owe your visit?" she said, getting straight to the point and gesturing for her guests to accommodate themselves in an office with three desks, packed in by the millimeter. Aside from the journalist and the two visitors, there were no other people at that time.

"Work," he replied. Rebecca was astonished to ascertain a trace of embarrassment in his words.

"Work?" the journalist asked, raising an eyebrow. Alessandro pulled from his pocket the newspaper clipping that he had read just before and showed it to her.

"I remember it well," she confirmed, recognizing one of her articles.

"I need to know the name of the curator of the recovered documents," Alessandro asked without preamble.

The woman's professional curiosity was piqued: "Surely the university has more access to this news than a journalist," she said.

"Let's say that, at least for the moment, this is a personal interest."

"You're asking me a favor?" Silvia's face expressed real surprise.

"Exactly," he replied firmly, but his jaw betrayed his tension. He did not want to do so, Rebecca realized.

"You're putting me in a difficult position with this," she temporized. "The newspaper's resources are not available to private individuals."

"Help me this once and we'll be even," said Alessandro. There was an expectant silence, in which the reporter did nothing but fix Alessandro with a dazed expression.

"Follow me," the woman concluded. Her body now expressed an evident tension. She seemed almost frightened. Amongst the indifferent glances of some editorial staff employees, they went down into the basement. Rebecca almost got lost among the catalogued shelves of the immense archive, but their escort led them assuredly to the chosen binder, and took out a red folder with the information they were looking for. "Here is everything I know," she said, holding the folder out to Vinci and showing him a copy machine a few feet away in a dimly lit corner. Without delay, he took it and started to copy all of the papers in the parcel, an operation that lasted only a few minutes since there was very little material. For the entire time, which to Rebecca seemed endless, the two women stared at one another. She immediately understood that the journalist knew that Marina Gamba was not her name. And had she guessed the true color of her hair? The thought made her tremble, but fortunately Alessandro finished and returned to them. Silvia escorted them to the exit and Rebecca could not help but notice the palpable embarrassment between the two at the moment of farewells. A few seconds later they were outside, heading for the car.

As the gray Fiesta grew further away Silvia watched almost enchantedly, then her eyes closed, assuming a harder expression. Only then did she remember that curious coincidence: that particular she had noticed for an instant when she had flipped rapidly through the documents before handing them to Alessandro. A mental link flashed for a moment in her subconscious, but the more she tried to focus on it the more it escaped her. She deposited the dossier in the red folder on the desk and decided to study it again, more carefully.

"Yes, yes, good." Dr. Vinci sighed, closing the conversation and snorting loudly. Apparently Professor Rastrini, from the Literature Department at the University of Florence, was not very willing to cooperate; Alessandro had had to call upon all his diplomatic skills to get a meeting to examine what had been recovered from the latest papers attributed to Galileo. It was clear that the professor wanted to be the first to sign a study on the new findings and had not the slightest intention of allowing a potential competitor near his little treasure. Vinci had torn a pained acceptance from him only by claiming to be conducting the research on behalf of the famous Professor Spinelli; something that, in a certain sense, was even true. In any case he had had to swear and swear again that whatever he found was to be submitted for publication only after his approval, which was tantamount to saying that it would not be published ever. Looking up from his phone towards his guest, he could not help but notice her amused expression: "What?" he asked her.

"Nothing."

"Come on, spit it out."

"It's just that you looked so professional, just now," she said, unable to contain her growing smile anymore.

Vinci watched her face light up for a moment and then replied, falsely testy: "I *am* professional. Anyway, thanks to my professionalism that amused you so, we now have an appointment to take a look at the letters."

"Unless they nab me beforehand," said Rebecca, becoming suddenly serious again. "Will it be prudent to return to Florence?"

"Not exactly prudent," Alessandro admitted. "Necessary, yes. Unfortunately, I can't come up with any alternative." The appointment with Professor Rastrini was not until the afternoon of the following day and, until proven otherwise, Vinci's big apartment was the safest place to hide until departure. After dinner, while Alessandro took a shower after the usual evening jog, Rebecca turned on the television, looking among the various networks of digital terrestrial TV for one that was broadcasting the next day's weather forecasts. Her attention was drawn by several images of Padua that cycled across the screen. She recognized the media of the law enforcement and managed to make out the place: Palazzo Liviano. A strike? Another protest in front of the Literature Department? No. It could not be: the recorded images showed the comings and goings of numerous forensics workers, recognizable in their white suits.

Worried, Rebecca read the words that flowed over the footage describing a brutal murder that took place on university premises. Even before she heard the reporter's voice, her blood froze in her veins. They broadcasted photographs of the victim. Rebecca started shaking, cold sweat began to run down her forehead and arms, nausea hit her violently and she almost threw up her whole dinner. She began to breathe faster and faster, until her hands went numb and she could no longer grip the glass jug full of water that she had been holding, causing it to explode on the ground in a thousand pieces. Her vision darkened and her legs no longer supported her. Alessandro's arms grabbed her a second before she fell to the ground. Still wet and wearing only a towel, he picked her up and sat her on the couch while she pointed frantically at the television screen, on which an old passport photo was displayed.

"Vittorio Menin!" Vinci exclaimed.

"It's...my...fault," Rebecca babbled. Vinci turned off the TV with one click, angrily throwing the remote control to the ground. Then he spun towards her. She was sitting on the couch with her arms wrapped around her knees, which were gathered to her chest. She was trembling and weeping. "It's my fault," she repeated. "It's all my fault." Then suddenly she stood up: "I'm going to the police," she proclaimed, but her legs could not manage it and Alessandro was quick to keep her from falling. "It's my fault." She repeated the words like a mantra between sobs. She tried to free herself from Alessandro's grip but he held her tightly to him. "It was me, I killed him!" she shouted finally, venting her anger and pain by covering his chest in blows while he, dumbfounded, let her do it. Then he forcibly laid her down on the ground and immobilized her, but without hurting her.

Their lips came close and it was natural for them to unite in a passionate kiss. Rebecca was about to resist, hesitant, but then welcomed him into her mouth, while his strong arms caressed her shoulders, protecting her. She let herself be lifted off the ground as if she were weightless and be carried into his room, onto his bed. He slipped her shirt off in a fluid motion, returning to kiss her on the neck, and Rebecca let the lovely numbness of excitement overwhelm her mind, separating it from the last few horror- and fear-filled days. Gradually Rebecca felt the pleasure mount, brought higher and higher with each thrust. He moved slowly, perhaps too much so. Rebecca wanted nothing more than for that sweet torture to end, for the anticipated explosion to deliver her from the unbearable tension, but Alessandro did not alter his momentum. Eventually she stopped fighting it and let herself be carried away by his slow, inexorable rhythm. When she reached orgasm, he drove even deeper, wrenching a cry of pleasure from her that seemed to hover over the sheets for entire minutes, until their breathing calmed.

Dr. Mancino, police commissioner of Padua, studied the voluminous binder placed on his desk. It contained dozens, hundreds of sheets printed with the description of the murder scene in Liviano, the status of the preliminary investigation, the partial results from forensics. Before him several officials of various ranking and their subordinates, all crammed into his office, stood waiting. He knew that they were uncomfortable to be packed so tightly together while he watched them from the comfortable chair behind his desk, but he wanted to affirm his position. Behind him, the agent in charge was prompting the digital presentation on a gigantic, electronic, multimedia whiteboard, explaining the investigation's progress to all the task force members. Deputy Commissioner Angeloni, to whom they had been entrusted, was not happy to have been put aside as well, given that the responsibility for the operation was his. On the other hand, he knew the police commissioner's delusions of leadership well, and thus he had let it slide and resigned himself, at least for that afternoon, to the role of mere supporting actor.

The distinguished agent De Marchi watched everything carefully from the back of the room. It was the first time he had been invited to a meeting like this and, true to his moniker, he was not going to pass up the opportunity to shine in such a heinous, high-profile case. Assistant chief Valente, his older patrol partner, as usual had taken advantage of his secluded position to doze off, thanks to the late hour of the night, and the monotonous voice of Mancino, with a strong southern accent, did nothing to keep him awake. It was that same voice, however, that provided the detail that would be a turning point in the investigation: "As mentioned before, access to the laboratory of Liviano is regulated by an electronic lock on the door which opens in both directions only when reading the employees' personal cards. And this is the last person who had access to the lab last night."

A copy of the scanned photo of its owner appeared on the big electronic screen. While the commissioner explained that the image had already been given to the media, Valente jumped in his chair, with a muffled cry, awakened suddenly by an elbow in the ribs received from De Marchi. "What in the hell—" he swore; but his younger colleague did not even respond to him, limiting himself to gesturing excitedly towards the enlarged image of Rebecca De Cardinale.

**

The light of dawn made its way into the room, painting the half-empty and unmade bed. When Rebecca regained consciousness she was alone in bed. She did not even remember falling asleep; she felt just...well. With a little bit of effort, she recalled the details of the previous night, trying to remember how long it had been since she had felt this way. Ah! Who was she kidding? She could not remember such good sex since who knows how long ago...maybe never. Beyond the door, Rebecca heard Alessandro moving, making a lot of noise. She imagined him while exercising, maybe with the punching bag. Her eyes followed the blade of light as it cut through the room, to the spot where it ended. The big black-and-white photograph, the naked woman who had disturbed her the first time she saw it. She looked at it again and an idea latched onto her like a parasite, ruining her awakening.

She groped for the button on the table lamp but, not finding it, she put on the boy's shirt that she used as pajamas and decided to get up to turn on the overhead light. Now she understood why, seeing the journalist, she had seemed a familiar face. She had not seen her on the news; she was immortalized before her, in all her sexy, naked and positively brazen beauty, rendered artistic by the black and white.

Instantly she experienced rage as fiery as it was unreasonable. Rebecca knew that she had no right to be jealous of Vinci. They had hardly exchanged promises of loyalty or similar and yet…If she had had him in her hands in that moment, she would have slapped him. Instead, she gave herself a slap; she would never give him the satisfaction of understanding the extent to which she felt used. As though conjured by her thought, she heard his footsteps behind her. She clenched her fists. *I swear that if he tries to kiss me I'll smash his face,* she thought to herself, but Alessandro displayed no mawkish inclination: "We have to leave," he said instead, entering the room and rummaging through the drawers to retrieve some clothes on the fly.

"What?" Rebecca asked, noticing his alarmed expression. In that moment Alessandro seemed worried about everything but what had happened the night before.

"Your picture's in the news," he explained, "and if it's on the television then it's certainly on the desk of every cop in Padua; and we two were seen together," he said, picking her clothes up off the floor and handing them to her.

"At the supermarket!" Rebecca remembered. With terror, she wondered if Vinci was getting rid of her, now that he might be implicated, but then she saw him put his clothes into a bag. He did not intend to ditch her. At least not yet. Rebecca's few belongings were already all gathered in a suitcase; while she got dressed again, she could not help but look in a mirror to see if Alessandro was taking advantage of it to look at her because in such case, out of spite, she would not have shown herself nude before him. But he did not even think to do so. Once presentable, she wanted to try confronting him, throwing his behavior from the night before back in his face, but when she opened her mouth to speak he silenced her with an imperious gesture.

"The traffic," he said, looking very concentratedly into the street below. It was then that Rebecca noticed it: although the morning was already about to begin, the streets were deserted. Not even the gate to the noisy workshop had been opened, like it had been every weekday morning since Rebecca arrived. The entire street was enveloped in an eerie silence. "Roadblocks," Alessandro explained, grabbing her suitcase, his bag, and rushing out of the room. "They're coming for us."

11

The experienced agent De Marchi distinguished perfectly the silhouette behind the half-closed venetian blinds and did not wait for his superior's order. He had been the one to recognize De Cardinale as the woman with his colleague's friend, who had been introduced to him a few days prior, although she had changed her hair color and cut. He remembered the strange feeling that he had had when she had glimpsed them while they happened to pass by: there was the same guilty expression in her eyes as in those of petty thieves caught in the act. Had it not been for the introductions that followed that encounter, he would certainly have stopped her for questioning, and she would already be in the police station now. Even her partner had given him a strange impression; the way he moved emanated a feeling of alertness, of implied threat. He had immediately classified him as potentially dangerous.

Annoyed at having been duped, he now trembled to get his hands on them. De Marchi adored arresting someone in the moment before awakening; the victim is surprised and stunned, his options for flight or defense limited, and then the agents' work becomes a cakewalk. The roadblocks had been more difficult to arrange than expected and they were late, but otherwise everything was going perfectly. He rushed up the stairs, followed closely by the other policemen. No one answered when they knocked so they broke down the door and the large apartment was invaded by the shouts and ordering of the police. Within seconds the entire area had been explored from top to bottom. "Clear!" the last of his men finally shouted, after they had checked all the rooms. De Marchi was beside himself. He was absolutely certain that he had seen them…Where the fuck had those sons of bitches run off to?

"This way," whispered Alessandro.

They had fled from the attic through a floating panel—which did not appear to be such—in the ceiling, which had allowed them to escape from the roof. Since then Rebecca had not stopped watching his movements and imitating them, forcing herself not to look down as they climbed over the rooftops and went from building to building on a path that, judging by the confidence with which her companion led her, had to have been planned in advance. Once they were far enough out of the sight of their pursuing team, Vinci stopped for a moment to check that she was all right. When she nodded, lying and afraid, he smiled and reassured her: "We're almost there." He forced open a metal door and made way for her down the stairs of a condominium with crumbling walls. The strong scents that permeated the many apartments seemed to come from a number of ethnic cuisines and, at that hour of the morning, were almost as irritating to Rebecca's stomach as they sprint at breakneck speed. They met a prostitute who was evidently coming back from a night of work and passed by without even looking up, with the distracted air of those who are used to not seeing in order to avoid finding trouble.

Finally they reached the ground floor and a rusty, squeaky sliding door which gave access to a garage. Inside Rebecca saw a dark pickup truck with a covered bed. Alessandro threw their luggage in and invited her to climb up with an impatient gesture of the head. Within seconds they were out of the garage, leaving the neighborhood behind them and, as far as Rebecca was able to understand, the roadblocks.

The woman expected that any moment Alessandro would step on the accelerator, giving way to a full-speed flight through the streets of Padua, but instead he proceeded with caution: just another car in the peak hour of city traffic. *The logical thing to do*, Rebecca realized after a few kilometers, fighting the urge to curl up under the seat at every local police patrol they met on the street. Alessandro did not speak, intent on driving and checking that they were not followed. Only when they were almost out of town did he seem to relax. He turned on the radio, but instead of music, segments of conversation in a barely intelligible language, made up of codes and extremely brief dialogues, emitted from the speakers. Intrigued, Rebecca noticed that under the radio another, a more rudimentary-looking device was situated. "A scanner," said Alessandro, anticipating her question. "It's tuned to police frequencies." Rebecca knew exactly what a scanner was: a radio receiver capable of picking up the frequencies of public security services. From what she knew, it was against the law to use it and only journalists and criminals even used it. She prayed that this one had come with the standard equipment of the former of the two categories. Upon that consideration, the thought of that morning's discovery immediately came to her and, along with the recollection, the anger returned.

"Stop!" she said. "Now!"

"What?" Vinci looked at her in shock.

"I said stop! Now!"

"Are you crazy? We need to be as far away from Padua as possible for when they circulate our identikit…"

"Stop or I'll jump out!" she shouted back, fiddling with the car door. Alessandro was just barely able to hold her back while executing a sharp turn onto a side street. He braked in a dusty and desolate clearing and, just as soon as they were stopped, she opened the door and rushed out of the pickup. Coming round the car, Alessandro hardly had time to get himself out when she confronted him: "Tell me what this is!" she yelled at him, pointing to his transportation.

"It's a car…"

"Don't play stupid! No graduate student bookworm knows as many policemen as you, knows how to use a scanner to intercept protected frequencies and has a garage with a hidden car ready to go. Either tell me what's going on or I'm leaving!" Rebecca yelled, scarlet, her voice increasingly shrill. When she quieted, she got a better look at him and only then noticed how he was dressed: the casual clothing of the last few days had given way to a tight black T-shirt, a pair of soft pants with side pockets and combat boots. She took a step back, even more confused.

"I was in the police," he said in one breath. "I got hurt," he continued, indicating the shoulder with the wide scar, "and now I'm a Ph.D. student in Literature." *So much for "slow on the uptake,"* Rebecca thought to herself, remembering the comment she had made to her colleagues the day they had met; if he was still completing his doctorate it was because his second life had begun only after the first had ended. But was it really over? He was not telling her everything, she felt.

"That's not enough for me. I don't think that all policemen on leave have a rooftop escape route just in case!"

"Let's get in the car," Alessandro suggested, conciliatory. "I'll tell you the rest on the road, but if we stay here we risk being reported and caught." Rebecca got back into the car without a reply. When Vinci started them off again she did not even ask where they were heading, registering only that they were leaving the highway. "I was a cop. I was part of a…special escort team for the Spinelli family…" he proceeded in one breath. Rebecca's eyes widened.

"Michele?"

"Yes, although the one who was in danger was his brother, Filippo Spinelli. A judge who was involved in several extremely high-profile cases and who had received serious threats." He caught his breath, as though it were painful for him to tell this story. "There was an attack, Filippo Spinelli and his wife were killed, along with three men in my unit and every member of the killing commando."

"Is that when you were injured?" Rebecca asked, afraid and repentant for the harshness of her behavior earlier.

"Yes, in the shoulder." Again she had the acute feeling that he was not telling her everything, but it was obvious the difficulty with which Alessandro admitted his failure as a bodyguard and she did not seek to push further, preferring to let him speak. "Michele Spinelli was present on the day of the attack as well, but managed to get away," he went on.

"That's why you were shadowing him and had this escape plan ready? Are you afraid that someone will show up to finish the job?

"It's possible," he admitted.

"If you're an ex-cop, why didn't you drag me to the police station the second I knocked on your door?"

"I organized protection for the Spinelli family. Everything that happened was my responsibility…" he confessed, with a mixture of shame and rage.

"And you want to be the one to take care of his kidnapping," Rebecca concluded for him.

"Yeah. This time I want to get to the bottom of it."

"And Silvia? She has something to do with it?" Rebecca pressed, determined to address all her curiosities.

"We were together," he said naturally, seemingly happy to change the subject. The memory of the attack must really hurt him if talking to her about an ex seemed preferable. Or maybe the night before meant nothing to him; nothing more than a conquest to add to the others. Shortly thereafter the car stopped along a side street of a village on the outskirts of Padua, of which the young woman did not have time to make out the name on the street sign. Alessandro got out of the car and fumbled for a moment in the trunk; when he returned, he was wearing a tacky sweatshirt with a construction company name in plain sight and a visored cap. There was an empty backpack on one shoulder. "I have to get something from the bank," he explained laconically, gesturing to a bank's sign a couple hundred meters ahead tilting the visor of his hat over his face to avoid being captured on the bank cameras.

She shuddered, remembering that they were both wanted. She wrapped her scarf around her head, as if she were worried that the wind would ruffle her hair, put on her sunglasses and followed Alessandro. Passing by only a few minutes after opening, they were among the first clients and for this, too, they did not go unobserved; a senior clerk looked up from his bifocals, watching them head for the security boxes. Vinci drew a key from his pocket and, after a quick look around to make sure they were alone, he opened the corresponding box. Inside were several wads of banknotes, two passports and a pistol with two spare magazines, which terrified Rebecca to death. Everything went into the backpack. She followed him wordlessly until they were outside of the bank. No one stopped them; even the employee who had stared at them hard in the entrance did not even bother to shoot them a glance.

"Explain to me your relationship with Silvia again," Rebecca insisted once they had started off again. She was not sure that she wanted to go back to what had happened between them the night before, but she was too curious and needed an excuse to forget the disturbing presence of the gun that was lying at his feet in the front seat.

"We were together, I told you. A lifetime ago. But now it's over."

"I understand," she said doubtfully, thinking back to the strange exchange of words she had witnessed during their meeting at the newspaper headquarters. But he kept her photo, naked, in his bedroom.

"The photo!" he exclaimed. "You saw the photo of Silvia."

He started to add something but Rebecca, furious with herself rather than him for the ease with which he had read her thoughts, cut him off:

"Look, let's not talk about it, okay? Actually, let's not talk about what happened last night, either. We both needed it, but it can't happen again. Never again!" she finished harshly. On Vinci's face there was painted the expression that only an innocent child can have when you take away his favorite toy. Seeing how her words had hurt him, Rebecca was about to take it all back but in the fraction of a second the cold determination that she had now learned to recognize reappeared on his face and she remained silent, bewildered.

It was as though there was not just one, but two men seated next to her, distinct in character and temperament, fighting against each other. One drove a Ford Fiesta, studied Literature and took fascinating and disturbing photos; the other wore military shoes, drove a pickup truck and got shot at by bad guys. Once on the highway, Alessandro shut off the scanner and turned on the radio, tuning to a station that played metal music, remaining silent. Rebecca found herself thinking that the soundtrack was appropriate. As they progressed along their way Rebecca felt increasingly guilty for having directed her anger towards him. Alessandro was the only person who was helping her, not to mention the small detail of having saved her life…She tried to mend fences by seeking to strike up a conversation a couple of times, but he answered her in monosyllables. How could she blame him?

"The last time I traveled this road, Professor Spinelli talked almost the whole time," she provoked him a last time. "Galileo Galilei is truly a passion of his…"

"An obsession, I would say," he corrected her. Rebecca struggled to subdue a smile. *He resumed speaking…* "Did I already tell you that he's also a fan of genealogy? Once he even tried to convince me that his family, the Spinellis, were direct descendants of an illegitimate son of Galileo himself!" They both laughed, and the tension between them finally dissipated.

"When he talks about it, it seems that he almost feels...personal resentment for how Galileo was treated then," the woman observed.

"True. It is one of the points on which we often clashed."

"Why, are you not convinced that Galileo was persecuted by the Catholic Church? That it claims intellectual infallibility? Or that thanks to Galilei's discoveries Western Civilization was awakened from the Middle Ages in order to enter the modern world?"

"Spinelli's conviction that the Middle Ages were exclusively a dark age, from which humanity was resurrected only with Humanism and the Renaissance, is prejudice. A prejudice born in the sixteenth century, with the rediscovery of ancient Greek and Latin. It was the intellectuals of that time who began to denigrate all that was temporally interposed between ancient Rome and themselves. Beyond that, at that time, the majority of the philosophical elite was Protestant. The only genuine philosopher of that period for whom a place in the history of science was secured was Galileo, guess why."

"Because he was tried and condemned by the Catholic Church?"

"Exactly. You need to be objective in regards to both medieval scientific achievements and to the Catholic Church's attitude towards science. Keep in mind that 'science' as we understand it didn't exist until the mid-nineteenth century. Only then did the scientist character get recognized as scholar of natural phenomena, different from the artist and the philosopher. With the conditions passed down from earlier thinkers, scholars of the nineteenth century saw the results of what today is still known as the Scientific Revolution as derived directly from the intellectual achievements of Copernicus and Galileo, who were connected to those of ancient Greece, through the medieval stagnation."

"And this isn't so?"

"Certainly not. The Middle Ages, even with all the death and destruction that characterize it, saw a technological and intellectual advancement fundamental to the furthering of knowledge. The lenses with which Galileo modified the telescope, equipping it to observe the skies, are a medieval invention, and the Catholic Church had a major role in this. Remember that at that time the only cultural institutions were universities, which depended on the Church. Within them all scholars, including natural philosophers, the ancestors of modern scientists, found refuge and protection. If all of nature was designed by God, then medieval thinkers were convinced that they got closer to the Creator through the study of it. To the point that they came to believe that the only way to discover divine laws was through experience and observation."

"Galileo's *'sensate esperienze'*!"

"Correct." Alessandro smiled. "In some of his writings he mentions studies before his own, dating back to medieval thinkers, who certainly helped him reach the right conclusions: Galileo had the ability and intelligence to collect all the good that had been done before him in this field and verify it through the experiments, thus contributing to the genesis of the 'scientific method,' upon which modern and contemporary science is based."

"Now you don't mean to tell me that the Church favored research on the origin of the universe?" Rebecca interrupted, thinking about the stories she knew of the Inquisition, its burnings and its courts.

"In fact I won't tell you; but think about how much happens in your field, medicine; do you really want to make me believe that if an organization or a pharmaceutical company invests millions for research on a drug and the financing of a research project, that it won't be found that their scientific results are closely dovetailed with their own interests? That no effort is made to downplay the data that is not?" Rebecca nodded. As much as she disliked it, Vinci was right. "For every branch of knowledge the Church placed limits beyond which scholars could not go in respect to religious dogmas. The condemnation of

Galileo by the Inquisition was a huge mistake, but one that maybe Galileo didn't know to avoid due to overconfidence. Trusting in his friendship with Pope Urban VIII, a scholar like him and a vocal admirer of his, Galileo published his *Dialogue Concerning the Two Chief World Systems* in the form of a dialogue with three characters: one of these was called Simplicio and, if his name already provoked derision, during the disquisition he played the part of the imbecile, perched on philosophically and scientifically untenable positions that were the same claims of the pope who, incited by the Jesuits, got furious, leaving the field open to the Inquisition…"

"…That forced him to recant," continued Rebecca, because that part of the story she had learned.

"He had no choice; with the smoke still in the air from the burning of Giordano Bruno, burned alive for heresy, at almost seventy years old Galileo had no choice but submit to the mercy of the court. The conclusion was the humiliating sentence of abjuration and confinement to his home, with very little possibility of seeing other people. Fortunately for us, this did not prevent him from writing and publishing in Holland his last, or perhaps second to last, book, *Two New Sciences,* which contains the mature exposition of his theories on motion, for which generations of scholars to come, beginning with Newton, were, are, and will be deeply grateful."

"Indeed," Rebecca approved. Then, infected by Alessandro's passion, she continued: "If we could recover *Stella Novissima,* maybe someone will thank us too…one day."

"Why not?" he said, as a hopeful smile spread across his face.

**

The bank employee had not deliberately watched the man with his dark-haired female companion walking away. Accustomed to scrutinizing those entering to identify potential robbers, he was immediately suspicious when upon entering they had removed neither cap nor scarf, and he was ready to press the emergency button if it was needed. The pair, however, had not approached the teller, heading instead quickly towards the restricted area.

In the corridor a camera was planted which, without taping the contents of safe deposit boxes, allowed surveillance of the hall where they were kept. He knew, even before checking and rechecking the tape, that they would open precisely that box, but only when he was certain did he decide to pick up the phone. The official on the other end received the message in a flat voice, but as soon as he set down the receiver, he began to scroll through the contacts on his own mobile phone and quickly dialed a number: "Get me Colonel Achille," he said nervously.

12

The car stopped in the parking lot of a motel on the outskirts of Florence. One of the bright letters of the sign was broken and, overall, it had a rather shabby feel.

"Why are we stopping here?" asked Rebecca.

"Because it seems like a by-the-hour motel, the kind preferred by clandestine couples." Rebecca immediately adopted an expression of annoyance, wondering if he was alluding to something. "We can't show your identification, you know? And here it's more likely that they'll turn a blind eye…" he explained, and Rebecca had to agree that he was right.

"So you'll get a single room, right?"

"It's the only way to not give your personal details. But don't worry, we won't have to sleep together." She blushed briefly, regretting that her thoughts were so obvious.

"But the police of Padua will have made your personal details public as well," she objected.

"And I won't give them, actually," he said, pulling from his backpack one of the two passports taken out at the bank, and headed for the front desk. The clerk at the counter greeted them casually, immersed as he was in watching a soap opera, and handed them a single form for data collection. He seemed more than accustomed to that kind of situation.

"We do not wish to be disturbed…" said Alessandro, coupling his request with a wink, a prepayment for seven nights and a substantial tip handed over under the counter. The man tore his gaze completely away from the television program, made sure that there was nobody else around and quickly pocketed the banknotes. He handed the room keys to Vinci with a knowing smile, glancing in Rebecca's direction as though to weigh her up; the woman felt almost stripped and left the dingy reception desk, slamming the door. The room was not as small as she believed it would be, with a double bed in the center, a small sofa and a desk that held an LCD screen TV. To her surprise, she even found that it was decently clean. It was not the Savoy, but neither was it the mouse hole that it seemed from outside.

"That's a trick that you learned while a policeman?" asked Rebecca, still seething.

"Actually, while I was on duty I was involved in high-risk situations, not marital high jinks," he said resentfully. She immediately regretted her words; she had seen clearly the mark on his skin that that life had left him—she had no right to mock him.

"Professor Rastrini is expecting us," Alessandro reminded her, as he finished up preparing the backpack. Rebecca wanted to apologize for her words earlier but his glacial expression stopped her. She took what she needed from the suitcase and, in guilty silence, locked herself in the bathroom to change.

Along the narrow streets crowded with the tourists of the Tuscan capital, and even on the bus they caught, Rebecca could not help but notice the admiring glances that the other women directed at her companion, somewhat blatantly. Initially she felt pleased to be his companion, but then she remembered why they were back in Florence and the risk they faced attracting attention in that way and then it pleased her less, much less. The headquarters of the Department of Literature, their destination, was in the downtown area, just behind the

Duomo, surrounded by high buildings that dated back to the seventies. The moving mass of students led them inexorably to the department entrance. They were about to disappear in the crowd of flashy clothes and cultural pipe dreams when they were called by a female voice: "Doctor Vinci! Alessandro!"

From a car parked on a sidewalk at the edge of the square, Silvia Canelli emerged almost running. Rebecca did not at all like seeing Alessandro's ex-lover again but remained silent, determined not to get involved emotionally, limiting herself to expressing genuine surprise at her presence. Alessandro seemed so unamazed that actually, after they had caught up with her, he turned to her with a mischievous smile: "Why aren't I surprised to find you here?" he asked her, climbing in the car together with Rebecca, who sat in the back seat. "Your journalistic instinct picked up something good?" It was impossible not to notice a bitter aftertaste in his words.

"My nose and my ears," she answered promptly, indicating a scanner identical to the one set up in Vinci's car. "You guys know that half the police in Northern Italy are looking for you? Rather, they're looking for you and a certain Rebecca. Certainly not a Marina Gamba who's been resting in her tomb for over three hundred years."

The doctor could not help herself: "How did you know where to find us?" she asked.

"Oh, it wasn't difficult to predict: I who gave you the address of the registered keeper of Galilei's letters, remember? I only had to wait in this parking lot for a few hours..."

"Did you try calling me before you got here?" replied Alessandro, looking worriedly at the clock.

"I tried, but your number is unreachable," she said.

"Did you try on the other phone as well?" he asked.

"No. You had told me I should never use it, except for end-of-the-world emergencies."

Vinci could not suppress a satisfied smile: "Bravo. In any case you wouldn't have found me, I left it in Padua."

Now what the hell are these two talking about? Rebecca thought angrily, feeling excluded.

"So, what's going on?" asked the journalist, turning on a recorder. Alessandro shot her a withering look and she was quick to turn it off, raising her hands in surrender. "I can keep you out of the newspaper for a while," she suggested, avoiding an articulation of what would happen if she did not get the news she sought.

"Spinelli disappeared," Vinci said dryly, heedless of Rebecca's murderous expression behind him. "It is possible that the contents of the letters in Rastrini's possession interest his captors."

"Of the letters from four hundred years ago?" the journalist asked incredulously. "And what do they contain that is so important?"

Rebecca could not hold back any longer. "We have to go," she said, glaring at Vinci and pointing at the clock. *He didn't even ask me if I wanted to share what we know with that woman!*

Silvia looked at her as if seeing her for the first time. She looked her up and down quickly and Rebecca felt upon herself the same cold expression that sometimes iced over Alessandro's countenance. "Who is she?" she asked, still addressing Vinci. "Really, this time."

"Rebecca De Cardinale. Doctor Rebecca De Cardinale," she specified in a defiant tone.

"I know that full well. It's written in every press and police dispatch from here to the border." Then, turning again to Alessandro: "How informed is she?"

"She knows all about my past on the police force as a bodyguard, knows that I took my leave after the injury and the attack in which the Spinelli family lost their lives."

"Night?"

Rebecca distinctly saw the fear painted across her face as she uttered that word, though Rebecca had not the slightest idea of its meaning.

"What do you want, Silvia?" he went on, trying to end the conversation.

The journalist lit a cigarette, ignoring the young woman's disapproving look: "Exclusive coverage on the story, when it's all over."

"Why should we give you the exclusive? I thought we were even when you told us where to find the letters that remain."

"Aside from the fact that you extorted information from me without telling me what it was worth, it could be handy for you to have my newspaper's resources behind you. For starters I can give you a new sim card for making calls without problems."

"I also need money and a safe place to stay in case of need." She nodded. "You could find yourself in serious trouble; and not only with the police," he warned her. Genuine concern was apparent in his voice.

"No one will ever be able to charge me for being robbed of a cell phone," she replied, winking at the two cell phones abandoned on the dashboard. "As for the rest, I know how to look out for myself; I had a good teacher…" Without speaking, Alessandro chose one of the two phones—a smartphone with internet access—then he started out marching towards the building. Rebecca made to follow him, but was held back by the journalist: "My number is in the contact list on that phone," she said. "Call me." Rebecca got out in a hurry and watched the journalist glance one last time in Alessandro's direction as he walked away. Her eyes had abandoned the professional hardness they had taken on until a moment before, and in that instant the doctor confirmed what she had expected from the start: Silvia Canelli was still in love with him.

Professor Rastrini's office was decidedly more sober than Benatti's, but there, too, loomed a refined leather desk, at the moment buried under dozens of different folders and papers. It had to be a luxury reserved for first-class professors, Rebecca thought sarcastically. The musty, dusty smell permeated everything, even the elegant clothes of their host, who welcomed them with a serious and formal expression. The professor was almost shorter than she was and his height must have been a major cause of concern for him, judging by the irregular height of his shoe heels.

"So you two work for Professor Spinelli," he began.

"Indeed," replied Alessandro, assuming the professional-scholarly tone that he had flaunted to him the day before on the phone.

"It's a shame that he is not present himself," objected Rastrini, clearly offended by what seemed a violation of professional courtesy.

"The professor has asked me to convey his apologies," Vinci replied diplomatically, reciting the excuse that they had prepared earlier. "Unfortunately he was detained by very important personal events. Were it not so, I would not be here in his place." Rebecca admired the skill with which he was furnishing the sole justification that could neither be contested nor verified.

"I can give you a scan and a heightened resolution of the letters," Rastrini said dryly.

"That is not what you promised," Vinci replied.

"Certainly you will understand that this is very delicate material," he replied in Tuscan dialect, unable to keep from glancing in the direction of a stack of papers on his right. Following his gaze, Rebecca saw a CD in its plastic case, partially hidden under several papers on top of a stack of books. It was the only technological object in the office, besides an antediluvian computer connected to a scanner.

"We are used to handling sensitive documents." Alessandro began to show signs of impatience.

"Naturally, but they have been entrusted to my care; I, and only I, answer for them."

"Professor Spinelli will not be happy to learn that you had us come so far in vain."

"I'm sure that Professor Spinelli will share my reasoning, as soon as I can speak to him directly," he concluded in a mocking tone. Rebecca watched the muscles of Alessandro's neck contract in anger; she quickly placed her hand on his leg. Keep calm.

"Perhaps we can settle for the CD for now," she said, turning to Rastrini. Vinci looked at her, shocked by her meddling.

"For that I will need a couple of days yes," said the professor, looking at his hands. It was clear as day that he was lying.

"Two days?" this time it was Rebecca who got irritated. "But—"

"In that case," Vinci interrupted her, "we will see each other the day after tomorrow." He concluded, rising and holding out a hand to the scholar, who shook it, happy they were leaving his office.

Later, in that same office, the phone rang.

"Hello?"

"Professor Rastrini?" asked the secretary's voice. "There's someone on the line for you."

"Who is it?" the man asked rudely. If it was that Dr. Vinci again…

"He did not say a name, only that he is calling on behalf of Pegasus Pharmaceutics," said the secretary. Pegasus whom?

"All right. Put him through," said Rastrini, intrigued. The professor listened for a few moments to the strange timbre of the voice—almost feminine—on the other end of the line; then he hurried to close his office door.

13

When they were on the road again, dazzled by the strong, late-morning sun, Rebecca confronted Alessandro: "That bastard! I'm sure the CD was ready, I saw it on the desk."

"I saw it too."

"Then why have we left?"

"What could we have done? Forced him?"

"You're right, but that dwarf with a superiority complex is still a bastard! Someone should teach him a lesson!" In reality, Rebecca knew that the real reason for her anger was not Rastrini. Not just him, at least. "Why did you tell the journalist everything?" she attacked, while they traveled on foot towards the city center.

"We can trust her," he replied. "As long as she's certain of getting her exclusive, she won't say anything to anyone."

"I would've liked to have been consulted!"

"The money is going to run out before long and we'll have to leave the motel sooner or later. As her sources she will provide us with many more resources and the protection of anonymity."

She stepped in front of him, looking him straight in the eye: "It was not your choice!" she said firmly. "No more decisions off the top of your head; there are two of us in this matter and I do not intend to be a...puppet!"

"Okay," he conceded, surprised. They had just come out of an alley and the shadow of the buildings had given way to a colorful ray of sunlight that reflected off Rebecca's tresses, whose original curls had regained the upper hand over the smooth curve obtained with a flat iron. Alessandro saw her tense features gradually relax, and then open up entirely in a loud and liberating laugh.

"Sorry, it's just that it all seems so…surreal; a few weeks ago at the most I had to worry that my techniques for manipulation of a plastic dish were rigorous, now I'm a wanted fugitive in Florence with a journalist wanting to use me as a source. And you…" said Rebecca as he stared at her with wide eyes, struck by her nervous reaction. She had never seen that look on his face. He seemed… stunned and bewildered. Or maybe something else that she could not define. Once she calmed down, she looked around and saw that their little scene was attracting the attention of passersby. She remembered the women who were looking at them on the bus. "You know, I think that it's your turn to change appearance," she suggested.

"I don't think bleaching my hair is a good idea," he said, amused. "I would be ridiculous even before attracting attention."

"That's not what I had in mind," she said, dragging him into the kind of shop that a man like Alessandro would never dream of entering, but she gave him no time to protest: "You're a tourist, you're in Italy," she said, showing him a pair of Bermuda shorts of super-colorful pattern, German-style open sandals and a wide-brimmed hat that resembled those typical of gondoliers. He shook his head in disgust, but Rebecca insisted so much that eventually he put them on. When he came out of the dressing room, even she could not suppress a laugh, but it worked. No police officer, looking at him, would see Alessandro Vinci, just a foreign tourist in a city packed with tourists. But something was still missing.

"We can do better," she said thoughtfully, looking around here and there among the vendors. Then, beaming, she sped towards a wall.

"Voila," she said, laying a couple of thin-rimmed fake glasses on his nose.

"Glasses?" he asked, more annoyed than ever. "With fake lenses, to boot! Are you really sure that these will help me to look less suspicious?"

"They worked for Clark Kent."

"Who?"

"Look it up online!" she teased him, taking a few steps back to admire the ensemble. "And now the final touch: do you have a camera?" he nodded, indicating the backpack on his back. "Good. Put it around your neck, go on. Then I swear we're done." Alessandro snorted, then did as she wanted; he put the single-lens reflex camera around his neck and looked in the mirror dejectedly.

"If you even try to take a photo of me and put it on Facebook I'll throw you into the Arno," he threatened. At those words Rebecca burst out in a silvery laugh. Alessandro was quick to take advantage of it; he rapidly brought the camera to his eyes and, mindful of his artistic passion, snapped a rapid series of shots. Rebecca, however, suddenly stopped laughing when she saw the icy gaze that frightened her so flash in his eyes.

"Let's go," she said, unexpectedly restless, pulling him out of the store.

They returned to the motel on foot, eating a couple of flat breads bought from a baker. As soon as they got back to their room, Alessandro threw his backpack on the couch and pulled out the pistol. He checked the magazine and the safety, then started to put it back but was attacked by the near-hysterical voice of Rebecca: "You kept the gun with you all afternoon!" she accused. He nodded uncomprehendingly while nonchalantly handling the weapon. "I don't want to be walking around armed, and that thing makes me afraid."

"I have a license to carry firearms," he said with an innocent expression.

"I imagine, but I can't think about you starting to shoot all of a sudden."

"I carry it precisely because we may find ourselves in a situation where we might have to use it," he insisted, setting it on a table so that seeing him handling it would not upset her further.

She paused, then shook her head. "Please," she whispered.

"Whatever you like," he conceded, unconvinced, raising his hands in surrender. "Is it okay with you if we leave it in the bag?" he asked, pointing to his luggage bag, which was situated on top of the wardrobe.

"The bag is okay," she yielded, but she did not relax until she saw him put the weapon back where he had promised. "Thank you."

They spent the remaining hours of the afternoon in their room, then decided to go out to look for a place to eat something. When they returned, Alessandro first took a shower and then sat on the couch to work on his computer, deep in thought. Rebecca followed suit shortly thereafter, turning on her laptop—the only thing that she had managed to take away from her Florentine luggage besides money, her cell phone and identification—taking the bed for herself, but it was not long before tiredness took hold of her, despite the disturbing presence of Silvia's portrait in the bedroom.

When daylight flooded the small room, tickling her until she awoke, it had already been morning for an hour. Her computer was lying closed on the table and someone, Alessandro, had put a blanket over her. Grateful for these gestures, she imagined that her companion had gone for a run and in fact, when he returned after half an hour, he was panting and sweating. He barely greeted her and handed her a paper bag with her breakfast inside. She felt guilty for never having reciprocated his thoughtfulness. Then he slipped into the shower.

They ate breakfast on the almost-made bed. Alessandro fiddled absentmindedly with the camera while Rebecca, munching a croissant, finished a few calculations on her computer. When the data she had entered seemed to match, she fixated intently on the monitor, almost wanting to get inside it. She was not even distracted by the sound of the young man's reflex camera as he brandished it in front of her: "We've got it!" she said triumphantly, turning the laptop to him, who returned a questioning look. "I finished connecting the astronomical observations of a bunch of meteor showers with the data on their orbits. In doing so, I've gone back through the centuries to all their previous intersections with the Earth's orbit." Alessandro observed the graphics on the monitor again, beginning to understand.

"So, if we're right…"

"If Galilei's right," she corrected, "the worst epidemics known to the world may have been caused by microorganisms from these meteors. It's a precise cluster that periodically crosses the Earth's trajectory. Always the same. Look here: the plague of the 1300s and 1600s began after the intersection with its orbit; even the Spanish flu epidemic that decimated the population in the early twentieth century and which caused more deaths than the First World War," Rebecca confirmed, a bit distracted by the fragrance of myrrh that emanated from his still-wet body. "Now we just have to prove it."

The rest of the day passed in total monotony. Disguised or not, the two fugitives had decided not to run the risk of being identified wandering aimlessly through the streets of Florence. Rebecca spent hours checking her calculations but Alessandro, having tinkered with the laptop and the camera for some time, began pacing the few square meters of the room like a caged tiger.

In the late afternoon, he could not take it anymore: "Let's go out, let's go to dinner."

Rebecca looked at him uncertainly. "Shouldn't we avoid unnecessary exposure?" she replied, but the imprisonment was overwhelming for her too and it did not take long for her to be convinced. They headed for the outskirts of the city, wrapped in the warm light of the early summer sunset. After a long walk, which had the effect of relaxing the nerves of both, they entered a small eatery which offered traditional Tuscan dishes. Rebecca devoured the Tuscan liver crostini and the excellent Tuscan soup, while Alessandro surprised her again with the speed with which he finished off his steak. When they left the establishment, they were much more content and good-humored, also because of the Chianti. Once evening had fallen, they noticed that the lighting around the area was totally inadequate, so they had to look hard at where they put their feet so as not to stumble on the bumpy cobblestones. It was not long before Rebecca realized that they were moving into a very disreputable neighborhood. She walked on Alessandro's arm and suddenly felt him stiffen: not understanding, she looked up at him. It was too dark to see his face well, but she realized that he was looking towards the alley where they were headed.

Semi-hidden by the shadows there were two men who at first glance seemed occupied in an argument, but by the rapid glances they shot in their direction she realized that they were waiting for them. Alessandro slowed and was about to change course, but a heavily Slavic-accented voice behind them froze them in their tracks: "Money, purse and wallet. Now!" Rebecca blanched and began to tremble, beginning to panic. When she turned she saw a man pointing a knife at her chest at the slightest distance from her shirt. Alessandro raised his hands in a slow, sure gesture, demonstrating that he did not intend to put up a fight. The other two, meanwhile, had come closer. One was tall and thin, the other a bit shorter but much more robust, and he hurried to place another knife to Alessandro's throat. Vinci pulled out his wallet and handed it over along with the camera without ever taking his gaze from the eyes of their aggressors, almost oblivious to the blade held to his throat. She gave up her bag, which was ripped from her hands by the only wrongdoer who was unarmed. *Please, let it be over now!*

"Let us go now," Alessandro said. "We don't have anything else." The brute's blade came even closer to his throat, grazing the skin, and his mouth twisted into a hideous grin. Even in the dim light of the few streetlamps Rebecca could make out the rotten and irregular teeth typical of addicts. People capable of killing for a lot less than what they had. She could not suppress a cry.

"No shouting!" rebuked the first assailant, grabbing her by the waist and starting to drag her away.

"Leave her," said a voice. A deep, guttural voice, whose vibrations were felt by her body even before her ears. Rebecca turned to see who was coming, but behind her there was only Alessandro. But it was not the Alessandro that she knew. He seemed a bit shorter than usual, as though compressed onto his own legs. His chin was lowered, his gaze directed with cold ferocity at the man who held her. "You have the money. Get out of here." An expression of mutual understanding appeared on the faces of the three men as though they had expected that reaction.

What happened next came at the speed of lightning, but to Rebecca it seemed to take place in slow motion: Alessandro spun around, dodging the blow from the stronger aggressor. Simultaneously he grabbed his wrist, twisting it violently, and dealt a kick to the lanky man's genitals. Immediately he launched himself against the man who had grabbed her and struck him full in the chest with one fist, making him sprawl to the ground, before the man could even think of using the knife against her.

But in the meantime the first thug had recovered and lunged with the knife at Alessandro's back. Vinci swerved aside, swooped under the man's tensed arm and shot an open-handed blow at the man's throat.

His assailant gasped and dropped the knife. The thinnest of the three tried to hold Vinci's shoulders, but he swung his head back into his nose so hard that it began pouring blood. A kick in the stomach finally settled him, collapsing him in agony in the alleyway. But the Slav who was struck in the chest had gotten back up and lunged at him with the knife. Vinci dodged and tripped him and, once he was on the ground, disarmed him, grabbed his head and slammed it into the sidewalk twice, three times, until he lost consciousness. With an angry roar, the last one standing, the brute, struck Alessandro from behind, pummeling him with his fists. Alessandro reacted and countered in his turn until the attacker, struck again and again, lost consciousness.

"Enough!" Rebecca shouted, when she saw him grabbing the now-fallen adversary by the neck. Without knowing why, in that instant, one particular of his conversation with the journalist came to mind, something that she had said and which had had a strange effect on him. "Night; stop!" she ordered him. "Stop, please…" she implored. The mortal grip on his attacker's neck loosened and the man fell to the ground; unconscious, but still alive. Little by little, Alessandro's self seemed to reemerge from the homicidal fury that had almost engulfed him. Without speaking, he gave a last look at the other two attackers, passed out and immobile where he had left them, and he hurriedly recuperated the bag, wallet and camera. Then he turned to her.

"Let's get away from here," he said, dragging her out of the alley.

Rebecca had some difficulty moving her legs, near paralyzed by fear. "We have to call the police…" she proposed timidly.

"Certainly, why not? Then tomorrow they'll walk free and we'll be in prison!" The woman quieted and concentrated on keeping up her pace until they reached the motel. Once safe in their room, she leaned against the door and waiting for her shoulders and hands to stop trembling from fear and adrenaline, then she joined Alessandro in the bathroom. He had removed his bloody T-shirt, which he had thrown to the ground, and he was washing his hands of the filth and blood from the fight. Rebecca noticed that he was more vigorous than necessary, as though that mechanical gesture was some cathartic rite, in addition to a normal hygienic precaution. She looked at his face reflected in the mirror and she saw the same yearning of a former drug addict who is offered a dose. She saw his shoulders grow rigid. She witnessed his effort. She remembered that, had he wanted to, he could have fled, leaving her prey to those three animals, but instead he had saved her life in risking his own. For the second time. And she had not even thanked him.

"Thank you. You were..." she said to him, coming nearer and touching his shoulder with one hand. He turned slightly, just enough for the scar on his chest to come right before her eyes. She could not hold herself back and touched it lightly with her fingers. The tangible demonstration of his courage. She looked into his eyes and recognized the same desire that illuminated her own. Suddenly, he lifted her off the ground, carrying her into the bedroom. Before she knew it, Rebecca found her lips on his, with his tongue dancing eagerly in her mouth. She arched her neck and he kissed it and bit her, over and over again, as if to nourish himself with her flesh, tearing a low cry of pain and pleasure from her and he took her furiously, with an erotic violence that lifted her in successive waves of pleasure to the last, explosive orgasm.

**

Deputy Commissioner Angeloni was tearing his hair out. Which was a figure of speech, given that the police officer was completely bald. The task force had been based in the Florence Police Headquarters, where the investigation into the Apennine homicides had begun, and there he was stranded. He could not explain how the woman Rebecca De Cardinale and her alleged accomplice had managed to evade arrest. At

Vinci's home he had not found a single trace of him or the doctor, and had it not been for the testimony of his agents who saw them together in the supermarket, he never would have connected the two to one another. Even in the phone records there was no communication between the two, even if both of their phones were untraceable.

He had studied the statement made in that same police station by the doctor a few days prior. The security cameras from the places where she had told them she had been had confirmed her version: at the time of Zacchia's attack and the massacre at the Centini villa she was in a bookshop or at the bar of Yab, so she could not be the physical executor of those crimes, but she could still be an accomplice, or even the instigator. The third homicide remained, that of Carmela Gerospi. When the policemen, following the doctor's deposition, went to her residence, they had difficulty finding her corpse in the midst of the all-consuming garbage. The woman had been strangled but the heat and the conditions of the body had rendered divination of the exact hour of death quite difficult, and the legal doctor had declared only the day with certainty: the one after the double homicide at the Simoni farmstead. Gerospi too had been completely eviscerated.

In this case it seemed that doctor De Cardinale did not have an alibi; the shots captured by the only camera at the entrance of the underground garage of the Hotel Savoy showed that the night of the homicide Professor Spinelli had come back alone. Where was she at the time of the murder? He still knew nothing of the movements of Alessandro Vinci during the dates in question, though. The fact that he was an ex-policeman worried him a good deal. He had gathered information on him and knew that one so well trained as he would not be captured easily; what was more, the reporters had sniffed something out and he knew that, although he had promised immediate transfer to the nation's prisons for any of his men who let slip even the smallest indiscretion, it was only a matter of time before someone yielded the temptation of accepting a bribe.

He heard a knock on the glass of his door: "Not now!" he yelled, perturbed when he saw that in spite of the lack of invitation to enter, the door was opened just the same. The new arrival entered anyway, not in the least bit intimidated. He wore civilian clothing, but his demeanor classified him immediately in Angeloni's eyes as military: gray hair that seemed cut with a square ruler, a dark jacket over a perfectly ironed light cotton turtleneck despite the heat of mid-June. "Colonel Achille," he introduced himself, without even giving a greeting.

The commissioner deliberately delayed answering, annoyed, and decided not to greet him either: "You have the wrong office. I am not expecting any Colonel."

"No error," the other replied, coming even closer to the desk. "A bank employee informed me that we have perhaps a common problem: Alessandro Vinci."

Angeloni's attitude changed instantly. "Please. I'm all ears," he said, inviting him to sit.

**

Rebecca was awoken by the light that filtered through the blinds. The early morning sun played strange games on the sheets and on her skin. She was lying on her stomach; the place next to hers was empty. She darted her gaze around to search for Alessandro. She saw him seated straddling a broken chair, leaning with his elbows over the seat back while wearing the usual jeans, watching her. Still numb with sleep, Rebecca took a minute to bring into focus the young man's expression. Worry. He was worried he had hurt her, perhaps that he had compelled her to let happen that which she said she no longer wanted, she read it in his eyes. Rebecca covered herself with the sheet, then with a gesture invited him to sit next to her on the bed. He rose from the chair, indulging her, and she recognized the marks of her nails on his back, scarlet testaments that the previous night's pleasure had not been taken forcibly, but was welcomed.

"You overwhelmed me, last night," she murmured. A shadow was suddenly cast over his face. Rebecca bit her lip. She wanted to compliment his virility and instead she had made a half accusation. She smiled, kissing him on the lips and saw that his expression relaxed. "I've never felt like that," she confessed. He stiffened, resuming his earlier expression, as though he thought she was in danger. But why? He wordlessly stood and walked towards the bathroom. Shortly after, Rebecca heard the running water, sure sign that he was taking a shower. Disturbed by her companion's rapid mood swing, she in her turn rose from the bed, more confused than ever and cursing herself for never managing to predict things with him. Being hungry too, she then decided to quiet her doubts by setting into a box of cookies.

Less than an hour later they left the motel to go to the second appointment with Rastrini. The countless Florentine electronic gates prevented them from driving through the city center without being identified, photographed and even stopped by some zealous municipal policeman, so they continued to move in the slow, but anonymous buses towards the headquarters of the Department of Literature, where they were expected by the university professor.

"Good morning," Vinci greeted him, still showing off his professional expression. The professor barely lifted his eyes from the book he was reading, without even inviting them to sit.

There was something different about him, Rebecca felt it as soon as she came in; from his face every trace of professional courtesy had disappeared. She sensed Alessandro's impatience and preempted him:

"We're here for the CD, remember? If it is possible to have the copy we discussed…"

"It has not been mastered." The man's gaze shifted again to the stack of his books on his desk.

"How?" replied Vinci. "Yesterday you promised us that it would be ready for us today. Professor Spinelli—"

"Professor Spinelli appears to be unreachable for a few days," the man interrupted them, standing up. "And they say that his assistant is wanted by the police."

Vinci's movement seemed as fluid as it was rapid; in a single bound he was at the desk, dominating the gray academic with his bulk. "You should not believe everything they say," he threatened, before Rebecca grabbed his arm, dragging him out of the office.

"It's useless," the doctor said as they walked down the building's corridors. "He'll be calling the police right now."

"I don't think so. If he wanted to get us arrested we would have found a welcome committee all over here. If he didn't report us it's because he's afraid of losing something, perhaps control of the letters, if we get arrested in connection to the meeting with him."

"Or maybe they promised him something!" Rebecca explained, as though thunderstruck. "Pegasus! If they found out about the recovered Galilean letters, they will definitely be interested. Maybe they were the ones to warn him and make him a proposal, in exchange for his promise not to advertise it."

"That's very likely," he admitted, slowing down as soon as they arrived in the street. Rebecca stopped in a corner, leaning against the wall.

"And now? Without those letters we can't prove anything."

"Perhaps all is not lost. I think I know where the CD is."

"Still in the stack of books on his desk?"

"You noticed that too, didn't you?"

"Yes, but...you mean to steal it?" she asked with apprehension.

Alessandro smiled, winking at her. "After all, he prepared it for us."

14

Alessandro was happy when Rebecca gladly agreed not to accompany him.

"You would slow me down and I would have to look after you too," he had explained to her roughly, leaving the motel late at night and trying not to let on that, at least on his part, the interest in her well-being was gaining priority that went well beyond the danger connected with their quest. But it was not the moment to think about that. That afternoon he had observed the area surrounding the university and had not noticed any security cameras. It was almost certain that the windows of the department were not protected by alarm systems.

Once he had arrived at the department armed only with a crowbar, he took advantage of a moment in which no one was passing by to force the inner courtyard door. After ensuring that no one had noticed his intrusion, he did the same with the front door, slipping quickly inside the building. The darkness was almost total, softened only by a few emergency lights. The lock on the professor's office door was the easiest to spring. When he entered he closed the door behind him and turned on a small flashlight. He used a dark rag to filter the bright beam and directed it down, so that it was not visible from the outside.

He found the CD in seconds. Fortunately for him, it was right where he had last seen it, barely concealed on a stack of books. He made to pocket it and leave the building, but then he had a doubt: what if it was not what they sought? He did not want to even consider the idea of going back empty-handed, so he sat down at the desk and turned on Rastrini's computer, counting on it not being password-protected, given the age of its owner. He prayed that he was not mistaken. When he recognized the familiar screen of an old version of Windows on the monitor, he could not suppress a smile. He cursed how slow it was to boot up until the hard drive's little light stopped blinking, indicating that he could access the system. He inserted the CD and checked the contents. Eureka! The last letters of Galileo Galilei, in high resolution and carefully catalogued, were there before his eyes.

The academic in him emerged, overcoming the policeman, and he began to read. He perused one after the other, impatient, until he heard screeching tires. He strained his ears. No, he was not mistaken. A car had slowed just below his window, making him suddenly remember where he was and how dangerous it was for him to stay there any longer. He took the disc out and turned off the computer as fast as he could, then peered through the blinds in the direction of the noise, hoping with all his heart that it was not what he thought; unfortunately for him, it was: the security vehicle.

He saw the watchman, who held a massive flashlight, get out and head purposefully towards the entrance. With dismay he caught sight of his hand resting on the gate, which he had only drawn closed, opening it with a creak. The man pulled out a walkie-talkie and communicated something to his operations center. Vinci hoped it was a warning, otherwise before long the place would be swarmed with police officers. He cursed his own incompetence and began evaluating his options: if he started running, he could make it to the opposite wing of the building and get out through a window before the guard noticed him.

While patrolling the room and the hallway, his eyes fell upon the document scanner placed in the awkward position behind the comput-er. What if it was the tool used to scan the letters? Following that thought he fought back the instinct to escape and lingered to peek under the scanner cover where, in the dim light of his flashlight, he saw the corner of a yellowed paper. He lifted the lid and his heart skipped a beat with excitement: his fingers were clutched nothing less than a long letter written by Galileo Galilei. The academic in him emerged violently but the cop fought back, outright forbidding him from stopping to examine it, so he gently put it in a PVC folder that he found in a desk drawer and hid it under his shirt. *Menin must be turning in his grave,* he thought, considering the total lack of respect with which those documents of priceless historical value were forgotten and lamenting the veneration with which the expert, on the other hand, had handled every single relic. *Is he normal?* The academic and the policeman wondered together.

His ears brought him back to the present. He heard the gate creak and imagined that in the end, the security guard had decided to check it out for himself before calling in reinforcements. He turned slightly towards the blinds and saw that the man had entered the building. Good; had he sent up the alarm he would have stayed outside, waiting for backup. Nevertheless, the situation had not improved much; the guard, entering, had blocked his access to the stairs. Vinci smiled to see that the man had not turned on the lights, preferring to use the long flashlight; he must have seen too many television dramas.

Alessandro waited silently for the security guard to enter the office to check it and slipped out of the study towards the bathroom. The wall behind the door had a small indentation and he took the opportunity to flatten into it as much as possible. Just in time: the man, continuing his inspection, was headed directly for it. Vinci did not even breathe, holding his breath and muscular tension: the guard's neck was centimeters from him. *Now,* said the third voice in his head: the voice of the killer, never truly silenced. With just a single, silent move, there would be nothing left of that man except his lifeless body. One move. *Now.* A drop of sweat beaded on his forehead. Not from the fear of being discovered, but from all the effort required to control that instinct.

The guard opened the stall doors one by one and left the room, without even casting a glance towards his hideout. Vinci slowly resumed breathing, listening to the footsteps moving away down the hall. The man was walking noisily, from side to side, uncertain. Alessandro could see the reflection of his flashlight's beam which drew a confused to-and-fro motion on the ceiling and the floor. Fifteen minutes, maybe more, passed like this. He did not understand what the man had in mind; if he had discovered his infraction, he should have called for backup. If he had not, then his determination to stick around there was unjustifiable. Maybe he just wanted to be sure of not making a mistake. At one time he was more than used to infinite periods of waiting, but that had been years ago, a prior life. He felt the tension grow; he had to do something or he would inevitably make an error and be discovered or worse.

The guard passed by the bathroom another time, heading towards the faculty offices. Alessandro spun out behind him like a shadow, concealing himself in another corner of the hall without losing sight of him. Another step...The guard reached Rastrini's office and stopped at the door he had just forced open. He heard him mutter something on the radio. He did not recognize the words, but the tone was calm. Perhaps he had not understood that the door had been broken into. Then he saw him go inside. Vinci seized the opportunity, slipped behind his back unseen towards the main doorway. The door creaked slightly, but now he was out of the building and disappeared into the night, plunging quickly into the labyrinth of dark alleys. He made a big circle to ensure that he was not followed. He had turned his coat inside out so that the light-colored lining was visible instead of the dark color he had sported until then in more-than-likely case that some surveillance camera had caught him near the institute and he fell in with a party of oblivious foreign students who dragged their cheerful clamor from one brewery to another. Only when he was certain of not being identified did he decide to get on a bus. As a precaution, he got off a few stops from the motel.

When he knocked at the door of the room he shared with Rebecca, he received no response. An anxiety he had rarely experienced in his life swept over him. He went to the deserted reception and retrieved the key, fearing that she was ill or…worse. The room was empty. Instinctively, he thought that she had been arrested, but he corrected himself immediately. No, if she had been arrested he would have found agents in the room and he would now be in prison as well. Law enforcement, however, was not the only thing to look for. If Rebecca was right, there was Pegasus. A multinational big enough to afford private killers who, perhaps, were the perpetrators of all the murders. In his past, Alessandro had dealt with people like that. He imagined Rebecca in their hands. He began to shiver.

She's dead. Gather everything and leave. The killer's voice still rang in his head, and he knew that it spoke to him like this because he himself, in those people's shoes, would never have left her alive after obtaining the letters. One minute…the letters! Rebecca's computer was still on the desk, and his own was there, too. He opened up his laptop and checked the contents. The letters were still there. No one had erased them and no one had used the computer in his absence. He relaxed. No, Pegasus was not involved, they would have made everything disappear. So where the hell…The door's lock clicked behind him, and when Rebecca, entering, met Vinci's gaze, she literally jumped back yelling with fright.

"Where have you been?"

The doctor heard the same guttural voice that she had heard during the attack coming from him. Terrified, she dropped her bag on the ground and looked at him wide-eyed, silent and pale. Then she suddenly lunged at him shouting and began beating his arms and chest: "Do you want to give me a heart attack?" she accused. "Don't ever do that again!" Alessandro wanted to be angry because it was he who had reason to be, but Rebecca was so comical in that moment of hysteria that, in spite of himself, he began laughing. She noticed this and became even angrier, hitting him more vigorously.

"Stop, stop!" he demurred, pinning her. "Please, tell me where you've been. I was scared to death," he asked again, sounding more conciliatory.

"You weren't coming back, I was worried! I was afraid that something had happened. I went out to the car and turned on the scanner. At one point I heard that a police patrol was called to the Department of Literature for a suspected intrusion and I feared that they had gotten you, but then, after a long time, I heard they were going back and they didn't have your description so I realized that you had made it…and I came back here. Where you almost made me die of fear," she confessed, freeing herself ungracefully from his embrace.

"It's me that nearly died when I didn't find you in the room. Don't ever pull that on me again, I beg you!" Rebecca looked at him and saw no trace of anger in his eyes, only relief and gratitude, which embarrassed her a lot since she, far from showing joy for his having returned safely, had just begun beating him.

"Did you find the disc?" she said, changing the subject, as if remembering only then the purpose of their separation. Alessandro waved it triumphantly in front of her nose. She grabbed it like a predator and hurried to insert it in her computer's reader. Then she looked to him quizzically. Alessandro settled beside her and started to examine the screen: "Yes, they seem authentic to me. They're letters from Galilei. I cannot be certain without an expert, but I'm ready to bet. Paper, handwriting, color…they're very similar to Spinelli's letter. Too much to be fake," he said, his deep professional excitement ill-concealed.

"But there are…dozens," she replied, disconsolate.

"A real treasure," confirmed the academic in him, trying vainly to tear his eyes from the monitor.

"A very bulky treasure," Rebecca observed. "Do we have to read all of them?"

"Yes, if necessary. Welcome to my world. Did you really think we would find what we're looking for on the first try?" he asked wryly. "In any case, don't worry. Tomorrow morning we'll examine them calmly; right now I'm too tired." Rebecca had not realized it, but she was too. They fell asleep as soon as they touched the bed.

The next morning, their minds fresh, they began analyzing documents and established a working method: Alessandro read the letters and transcribed them into standard Italian, Rebecca examined them and organized them, in search of the information they needed. They proceeded like this for many hours; as Alessandro finished rending a letter more intelligible, she transferred the text to her computer. When they were little more than a third of the way through, however, both had burning eyes and a bad headache. "Let's take them to be printed," she suggested. "I think I saw a copy shop right on the bus route."

"Okay," Alessandro accepted, stretching his back and preparing to exit. He refused to wear the police-proof combination of clothes that Rebecca had chosen for him, opting instead for practical clothing. His dignity deserved the risk. He grabbed his backpack with the emergency stockpile and situated the laptop inside. He reached for the gun, but one eloquent look from Rebecca compelled him to reluctantly yield to this at least and he put it back in the big bag on the armoire. *Strange,* he thought touching it; it did not seem to be in the same position in which he had placed it the day before. Perhaps it had shifted with the movement of the bag.

She slipped in her bag her own lifeless cell phone as well as Silvia's, and they left. Once at the copy shop, Rebecca handed over a flash drive containing the authentic letters and those that had already been converted and distracted the clerk with some banality so that he did not pay too much attention to what he was printing. Finally, after a time that seemed endless, the clerk handed them a parcel of their prints and let them go, but not before getting Rebecca to leave him her (fake) phone number. Both laughing about the ease with which she had seduced the copy shop employee, they climbed on the bus and waited for their stop in silence.

Absorbed in her own thoughts, Rebecca considered her situation. For the second time in the course of a week she was in Florence, for the second time on a quest; but while on the first trip she felt like a privileged woman who was living the cinematographic dream of her life, now she was a potential killer on the run and that sooner or later, she would be captured; it was just a matter of time. Rather, she would turn herself in willingly to the police, but not before having some more assurance to strengthen her position, or she would not even be sufficiently evaluated.

She was torn from her thoughts by the annoying ring of a blaring cell phone. She was about to lapse into her usual judgment of impolite people who keep their cell phones on maximum volume in a bus, when she realized that the sound was coming from her purse. But it was not her phone's ringtone; and anyway that would have been impossible, she had removed the sim card. So what? she wondered, rummaging in the shoulder bag. The journalist's mobile phone! Rebecca pulled it out of her pocket while it was still ringing, and glanced at the number on the display: obviously she did not recognize it. She glanced uncertainly at Alessandro. "Answer it," he urged her.

She pressed the green button: "Christ, pick up!" snapped the voice on the other end of the line even before she brought the phone to her ear. It was Silvia. "Didn't you hear about Rastrini?"

"Mmm…no. What happened?"

"He was killed last night." Alessandro saw Rebecca whiten as her fingers almost lost their grip on the phone. He took it from her and continued to listen. "…there are several patrols hunting for you that are directed towards a motel; I suppose it's yours. But don't you listen to the scanner?" Vinci cursed through his clenched teeth, ending the conversation fast, and Rebecca saw his face turn into a mask of ice.

"We have to get off this bus," he ordered peremptorily. Rebecca wiped away the tears that were stinging her eyes and tried to compose herself. They got off one stop before the one closest to the motel and he led her in a slightly different direction, through a side alley. Zig-zagging a bit through the streets, they arrived at the pickup truck, parked in a small square at some distance from the hotel.

"The motel is done for; but we have a bit of money, the computers and the letters. We're still in the race," he said confidently.

"And the clothes? The gun?"

"We'll buy what we need for a few days more. As for the gun, it's not registered."

"But your fingerprints are on it."

"Just like the rest of the motel room. Another small crime to be added to the list. Now let's think about getting out of Florence." He started the engine and they vanished unseen, driving at medium speed towards the Apennines.

**

Special agent De Marchi moved along the cobbled street at a crawl. Finally, his insistence on being part of the task force on the trail of the

Killer of the Apennines, as he had been called, was paying off. In Padua, even though he was the one who suggested the link between Alessandro Vinci and Dr. De Cardinale, no one had given any credit to his intuition. He had been set aside by that pompous Deputy Commissioner Angeloni. Nevertheless, he had wanted to be among the first to examine the material elements in the doctor's room at the Hotel Savoy and, when they checked the testimony given at the Tuscan police station a few nights before, no one had believed the doctor's version—which involved Pegasus Pharmaceutics—and he did not believe it either. It was more probable that she herself had devised Spinelli's kidnapping and probably both massacres in the Tuscan hills, with the help of her accomplice. He did not know why they continued to refer to the disappearance of the professor as a kidnapping; he could have bet that no one would ever see him again. The woman must have eliminated him too, probably to take credit for some literary or scientific discovery.

But his luck would change. That same evening. Relegated to the paperwork, reviewing for the umpteenth time the elements of the case, he—and only he—had noticed what no one else had paid attention to, taken as they all were with chasing down the two fugitives. Unseen, he had pocketed the white-and-blue calling card and he had moved away from the barracks to dial, away from prying ears, the number shown on the card.

"Krupp," said someone on the other side. The voice seemed strange, camouflaged. After presenting himself, De Marchi demanded a meeting and was surprised not so much by the speed with which the other accepted, but more by the fact that for the meeting he had chosen a secluded spot; he probably did not want anyone to know of his involvement with the wanted woman. He played along. He did not want to share his idea with the others, either; he would not let the credit for another breakthrough in the investigation be snatched away a second time.

An hour later he stopped the car precisely where he had been told to. He did not even notice the broken lamppost in the corner. It was he who lit the way; two quick flashes of the high beams, followed by a third. The agreed upon signal. After a few minutes of waiting, a figure in a dust coat appeared out of nowhere from the darkness and approached the car from the passenger side. The officer looked at him, concentrating on his appearance. His face was clearly disguised. Evidently the person deceived himself in thinking that he would be excluded from the investigation. In the low light of the courtesy car, De Marchi could not help but notice something strange. Some facial feature that his expert identikit eye spotted as…abnormal, fake.

"You are sure it is my business card?" the androgynous voice of the figure asked, skipping pleasantries and leaning towards him, with one hand behind the headrest of the driver's seat. Holding out the sealed envelope containing the calling card as case evidence, the policeman nodded, determined to lead the game from that point on. He started to ask his first question, but he did not have the time. An electric shock shot him in the back of the neck.

Writhing in pain, he could not move a single muscle. For a few seconds he could not breathe either from the surprise, pain, or the electric paralysis caused by the taser. Fighting to stay awake, he first sensed the flash of the blade, then an excruciating pain in the abdomen while the knife was pushed in deep, over and over again. As life left him, he was illuminated by an insight: he could remember the person to whom those features belonged, which his murderer had failed to conceal.

15

Alessandro turned off the engine and parked in an unfrequented side street, immersed in the vegetation of the Apennines and quite distant from the closest inhabited area. For the whole journey which had brought them there, about a hundred kilometers from the Tuscan capital, they had hardly spoken. Alessandro raised the volume of the scanner and reassured Rebecca. The police were still looking for them at the motel and this gave them some advantage, maybe a few hours. There, the thick vegetation would protect them even if the police decided to use helicopters to look for them.

"We need to proceed with the letters," she said, to avoid thinking about their situation, "but I can't work with that gizmo working at full volume. It makes me anxious." Rebecca pointed to the scanner.

"Why don't you go back there?" Vinci encouraged her, indicating the truck bed of the pickup, which had been modified to be one with the cabin. "I'll stay here in front to see if they come closer."

"What do we do about the computers?" she asked, while trying to take a seat in the back, moving the bags around, without wondering what was inside them. "The batteries won't last forever." He fumbled about in the glove compartment and took out a transformer, which he inserted in the lighter socket. Connecting it to his PC's plug, Rebecca wondered whether there was anything he was not prepared to face. Maybe the situation they were in was amusing him, as much as it was terrorizing her...She went back to work, but the night arrived soon, and with it her weariness. They had only had some energy bars for dinner and had freshened up with the water from one of the two tanks in the side pockets of the pickup. Rebecca made an effort to continue, but her eyes were burning and she was not able to do much anymore. "That's enough for today," she begged, closing the screen after having saved everything on a USB flash drive, just to make sure. Alessandro agreed; he reclined the seats and laid down two rolled up mats and a blanket, to make some sort of improvised bed. He looked away while she took her clothes off, keeping only her underwear and a top. He kept only his boxer shorts.

"I'm sorry, but this is all I can offer," he told her, laying down beside her. Then, trying to read her expression, he changed his mind and standing up a little he suggested: "I could sleep on the front seats."

Rebecca studied him hard and smiled: he was not joking. He was...embarrassed. Before he could react, she pushed him down with her hand: "Come here, you fool." She straddled him and leaned down, gently kissing his lips, and she soon felt his response under her. He sat up, embracing and kissing her. She let herself go in his embrace, but then she resolutely pushed him down again, while she took her last pieces of clothing off. Alessandro tried to gain back control over the situation, but she did not give up. She stayed firmly on top of him, and almost exhausted him, until she decided to satisfy him, accepting him inside her, until they both collapsed, sweaty and breathless. She curled up beside him and her last thought before falling asleep in his arms was that being hunted by police, lost in the woods and having to sleep in a pickup, well...that was probably the happiest moment of her whole life.

For the first time since this madness had begun, Rebecca woke up the following day beside Alessandro: he had not gone running, he had not slipped out of bed in silence. He was there, already awake, and he was watching her in silence. Their silence was interrupted by the crackling of the scanner. Alessandro turned towards the device, straining his ears. Rebecca gave in. He would surely never turn it off. After a fast breakfast of more energy bars, they went back to work and they continued for the whole day, eating more energy bars for lunch and consuming the water provisions in the tank.

At times Rebecca relaxed with some games on her cell phone, on mute, but always able to give her a feeling of familiar safety. Even the telephone they had borrowed from the journalist could not be of any use: there was no network in those woods. In the late afternoon, Alessandro got out of the pickup to stretch his muscles and Rebecca did the same. Her neck hurt and her eyes were burning from the many hours she had spent on her laptop. While he exercised to loosen his joints, she looked at him, unable to hold back a pleased smile. "What's up?" he asked her in return. She approached him, with hope in her look.

"There's no way we could eat in a restaurant tonight? If I see another energy bar..."

"Don't worry. We also have to refuel and move the pickup. The restaurant is okay, but only if you don't make me dress up like Clark Kent!" he replied.

"Deal, Superman!" she answered, offering him her best smile. When they got to the closest village they found a small restaurant. With a juicy steak and a tasty mixed bean soup in front of them, for a while they forgot about the letters, the police and the murders.

Then, together with the symbol of network availability on their phones, their concerns reappeared. Once they were back in the pickup, he decided to take stock of the situation: "Is there really something in those letters?"

She shook her head, desolate. "Nothing which could justify the murders or the interest of a pharmaceutical company like Pegasus."

He remained silent. They both knew that was their last option: if nothing came out of the examination of those documents, the only alternative left would be to surrender, with everything that implied. "We're not over yet," he concluded, but his tone did not convince her. They went back to the woods shortly thereafter; the silence between them was only interrupted by the syncopated crackling of the radio frequency scanner. Alessandro and Rebecca went back to their respective tasks, but with no enthusiasm, aware that the closer they got to finishing their study of the documents, the dimmer their hopes of finding something in the documents grew. As the hours passed, Alessandro started paying less attention to the letters to focus more on what came from the scanner. The messages were apparently the usual ones, but the tone of voice had changed, it seemed more agitated…

"There's something here," Rebecca said all of a sudden, without turning her eyes away from her screen, examining the last transcription he had passed her.

"Where?"

"This letter to Giovanni Sagredo. He must have been somebody important to him. The tone is different from that of the other letters."

"Giovanfrancesco, one of the dearest friends of Galileo since when he was in Padua," Alessandro confirmed, turning back into a Ph.D. student in Literature. "They were partners in scientific speculations, and in revelry. They probably planned the prank on the Jesuits together."

"What prank?"

Alessandro smiled, trying to remember the details. "The Jesuits represented the established powers, they were the most erudite, self-righteous and intransigent members of the Catholic Church. The two wrote letters, pretending to be a sanctimonious noblewoman devoted to the Jesuits, a certain Angela Colomba, who was seeking moral advice on how to leave a very important amount of money to the order. Apparently, the response was prompt and swift, and was joined by a testamentary form, easing any difficulty she may had. The prank continued for several months, after which Sagredo had to leave Venice to take on the role of ambassador in Aleppo, Syria. From that moment on, he and Galileo never saw each other again."

"Angela Colomba? Isn't that the name you used to introduce me to the policemen at the supermarket?"

"Exactly," Alessandro confirmed. "You know, these letters are a priceless treasure: nobody ever found any trace of Galilei's replies to his friend."

Carried away by their enthusiasm, they neglected a double reading, poring over letter after letter: "Did I get this right?" she asked.

"Sagredo is informing Galilei that there's a rumor in Syria about several cases of plague in a village within proximity of the place where a meteorite had fallen. Over many letters the two scientists discuss the possibility that the disease came from the meteorite itself. Initially Galileo resists this idea, which he brands as a myth," Vinci continued. "But Sagredo insists, talking about some travelers who visited the region for business and never came back because of the plague."

"All but one," Rebecca continued, passing from one letter to another with a few mouse clicks. "An Ottoman soldier who actually bought a fragment of the rock that had fallen from the sky and had it mounted in a piece of jewelry. They said that amulet was so cursed that his whole family, not only him, died in the space of a few days after he came into possession of it."

"That makes sense, because nobody knew the origin of infectious diseases yet; but Galilei, at some point, senses a possible correlation between the meteorite and the epidemic," Alessandro continued, still browsing through the letters. "By then, though, the scientist is busy defining his theory of the universe and Sagredo is already dead. The plague problem shifts to the back burner. Galileo comes back to it only after the Inquisition's sentencing, when the possibility of actively carrying on with his studies on celestial matters is forbidden."

"And in fact the dialogue gets interrupted," Rebecca remarked, increasingly excited, scrolling through the subsequent letters on the screen.

"Sagredo is dead, but one of his pages, who remained in Aleppo, discovers a new fact: he personally met a man who wore the cursed jewel, the fragment of meteorite mounted on glass, and saw him boarding a ship directed to Italy, to Genoa. He was a merchant from a Swiss family, Virgilio Donati. It seems he had acquired the jewel with the intention of giving it as a gift to his wife."

"And in those exact years Italy gets decimated by a new plague!" she replied.

Vinci nodded: "The plague of 1630, the one described by Alessandro Manzoni in *The Betrothed*. The page, treasuring the correspondence with his old master, informs his scientist friend. The documents allow him to trace the movements of Donati upon his arrival in Italy. He moves to Susa first, to purchase fabric. Then he heads for Turin, then later to Lyon."

"My God!" Rebecca cried out, frenetically clicking on her laptop. Once she reached the page she was interested in, she turned the screen to let her companion see it: "Susa, Turin, Lyon. These are exactly the first cities the epidemic hit! It could be true, that man could have really been the plague-spreader!"

Alessandro could not believe it: "This is pure superstition. He should have died as well before spreading the infection, shouldn't he?"

"Maybe not," she explained to him. "He could have been immune to that pathogen."

"What do you mean?"

"A pathogen is a microorganism which is able to cause a disease. Some individuals can be naturally immune to it, by a genetic predisposition or from previous contact. For this reason, it can happen that all the members of a family but one are hit by a flu strain. There are even individuals who are inexplicably resistant to the HIV virus, and who will never contract AIDS in their life. If the account is true, this person was immune to the plague, but he could spread it, through this mysterious cursed amulet, the meteorite fragment."

"Which contains the bacterium responsible for all this," Alessandro replied.

"It's more likely a virus," she specified. "According to some theories, asteroids can carry viruses."

"But the plague is transmitted through a bacterium, or am I wrong?" Vinci objected.

"The Yersinia pestis," Rebecca confirmed remembering what Krupp had told her during their encounter. She had continued her research, and now she had elaborated a new theory, which was even worse than the initial one. "We can't forget that before pathogens were discovered, all epidemics were considered 'plague.' We don't actually know what it was. Concerning the last plague pandemics, two forms were known: bubonic plague, which was revealed through the swelling of lymph nodes, also called buboes, and pulmonary plague. While the first one was only spread through direct contact and had a much longer incubation period, pulmonary plague was transmitted through the air and became lethal in two or three days: there were cases in which a person felt well in the evening and was found dead in the morning."

"So you suppose the bubonic form was actually the plague, while the pulmonary form was a viral disease caused by an unknown virus?" Alessandro tried to follow her.

"Yes, and a much stronger and easily transmissible one, of extraterrestrial origin. But I'm not the one proposing this: it's Galileo Galilei!"

"Right. Facing this suspicion, Galileo comes up with a new theory, which contains the correction of his initial ideas about comets, hazarding the possibility that some plagues are transmitted by these phenomena coming from space, and he writes *Stella Novissima*," he continued, infected with excitement.

"But he realizes he can't consider printing it here in Italy; so he sends his disciple Maffini to the Protestant Northern European countries, more tolerant and open to new scientific ideas," Rebecca continued.

"And...?"

"Nothing. The letters end here." Alessandro, in dismay, checked the contents of the CD once more. There was nothing else. The tracks were lost in Lyon, from which Maffini had sent his last letter. Then, enlightened by new hope, he began to fumble about in his travel bag, until he found a small plastic folder.

"In Rastrini's studio, there was this folio abandoned in the scanner. I thought whoever had scanned them forgot to put them back, but maybe..." he explained to Rebecca, who was hanging off his every word.

"I don't think I ever read these letters. Actually, I'm sure about it: they were not on the CD!" she said after examining the sheet. Their lips moved together, as if they were reciting a silent prayer, reading those centuries-old words. When she interrupted, lost because of the handwriting or the archaic language, Alessandro helped her, until they had finished their traveling through time.

"Galileo guides his disciple and sends him towards Switzerland, with the manuscript of *Stella Novissima*. He has to bring the book abroad to have it published," Rebecca said, resuming the narration. "But he has to do another fundamental thing: Virgilio Donati is buried in Switzerland, where he died in the meantime from a fall, and he is buried with his wife, who died of plague soon after her husband came back home."

"Infected by him, by the jewel he wears."

"That's exactly what Maffini has to find. But, as soon as he gets to Switzerland, he finds out that Galileo is dead. He doesn't have the ability or the audacity to carry on the scientist's work, and therefore he buries his manuscript with Donati and sends the maestro's entourage a farewell as well as information on his movements up to that point. Then he disappears from history."

"In the meantime, in Florence, the Inquisition does not loosen its grip on Galileo, not even after his death; the *longa manus* of the Jesuits is still powerful and Vincenzo Viviani, erring on the side of caution, collects and hides the letters exchanged with Sagredo and the correspondence with Maffini. That's how the last, visionary intuition of Galilei is forgotten until, in the twenty-first century, some construction projects brought everything back to light." Alessandro took a deep breath to digest everything that had come out of their findings. "What I still don't understand is the interest of a pharmaceutical company like Pegasus in Galilei's book," he objected.

"Are you kidding?" she replied in shock. "Here we have the evidence that an extraterrestrial virus is able to unleash a lethal epidemic! And that could happen nowadays as well! If a pathogen like the black plague could be spread in the seventeenth century, just imagine what it could cause in these times, when intercontinental flights are available to everybody. Remember this," she said showing him her calculations on the orbits of the comets.

"But the cluster you pointed out intercepts the Earth's orbit much more often than epidemics," he remarked.

"You're right, but one or more meteorites do not always fall down in inhabited places, and the virus may not survive the overheating from entrance through the atmosphere. It's always a living organism. And don't forget that seven tenths of the planet are covered by oceans and the virus may die in the water. Who knows?"

"So what Pegasus wants is the virus. The jewelry with the meteorite fragment."

"The native virus before anything else, but not only. Wherever the book is hidden, the merchant is buried too. Virgilio Donati was immune to the plague, but his wife died of it. If they can put their hands on the two bodies, they will have a specimen of the virus, and even the DNA of an individual who is resistant to it and one who isn't: more than enough material to elaborate an antiviral drug or a vaccine. With the drug, money would follow. A heap of money, because in the case of a new epidemic they would be the only ones to have a medication to treat it."

"But even admitting they are behind all these deaths and that the motive is financial, why did they have to kill Zacchia, Maddalena Centini and Carmela Gerospi? They had nothing but imitations in their hands: scrap paper."

"Not for them. The letters interested them for the information they contained, not for their historical value. Authentic or fake, they probably considered it necessary to verify the information contained in those as well."

"Yes, it's plausible. A fake letter might very well be the faithful transcription of an authentic one, which is maybe lost. I guess it was still worth it for them to verify that. At any cost."

"But Spinelli had the best of the merchandise, and since he would never ever sell them, they kidnapped him and killed the previous proprietors to set me up and prevent me from proceeding with our research, after I refused their offer!" Rebecca concluded, thinking back to Krupp again, growing more fearful.

"It's possible; but this means they haven't got all the letters." Vinci grabbed Rebecca's hands and looked her straight in the eye. They both knew that was a crucial moment. "Let's recap: the letters are found during the construction works and are immediately divided: the majority are given to the Inspectorate, that is—to Rastrini. One letter gets to Spinelli, God knows how, and one or so to Pegasus, maybe through the same provider. Now we have those that Rastrini and Spinelli had, thanks to which we were able to reconstruct the whole sequence of events."

"But we're still missing their letters," Rebecca remarked. "The name of the Swiss city where Maffini stopped is likely right there. We have no clue where the tombs are. Unless you can trace it back by examining some old land registry…"

Alessandro shook his head: "Even if we were extremely fortunate, such research takes months, if not years. The civil registry of the time was not as well organized as it is today."

"Then we're stuck. Pegasus got us, if they're really behind all this."

"It's not over yet. Even if they were the ones to reach Rastrini's place and they killed him to take possession of the letters, they can't know where Maffini hid the manuscript, because we have that information." He pointed at the last yellowed paper, the one forgotten by the professor in the scanner. "They're also stuck: they're missing the X on the map!" She had a bright smile, and her impulse was to hug him, but before she got close, she saw him stiffen. His expression was petrified, erasing any trace of sweetness on his face.

"What's wrong?" she whispered, confused.

He did not reply, beckoning to her with his hand. "The scanner." Alessandro pointed at the device.

"It's not saying anything," she replied, after listening for a few seconds.

"Exactly. No noise. No message. They found out we have a scanner and they've ordered radio silence. We've been discovered!" he concluded, rushing to the wheel. Rebecca hurried to secure the laptops, before slipping into the front seat. She had just the time to latch her seat belt, then the pickup left the trail they had come from and flew along the ridge, through the woods. A second later she heard the blades of the helicopter lower in the wood. Out of the corner of her eye, she caught a glimpse of some police cars turn up on the trail they had just left.

Rebecca screamed while the vehicle jolted, grateful for having worn her seat belt. In terror, she watched the ridge becoming steeper and steeper as they gained speed. Alessandro continued the desperate descent, avoiding the bigger shrubs and risking slamming into a tree or a rock every meter. Above them they heard the constant noise of the helicopter chasing them from above like an angered hornet. Rebecca thought she was doomed: she and Alessandro would end up crashing into a tree or at the bottom of a cliff. She closed her eyes, overcome by the shrieking of the wheels and the racket of the helicopter which tailgated them blindly, piercing the night with the light under its metallic belly. Suddenly the car turned to the left, unexpectedly, and it was so abrupt that Rebecca felt her face violently slam against the window. Then, darkness.

16

"Rebecca! Rebecca! Breathe…" Alessandro shouted loudly. She regained consciousness with difficulty, realizing that her hands were still holding tight to the seat belt, bloodless from the huge effort. He opened them gently. "It's over, we've stopped," he told her once more, worried. She obliged herself to react to the numbness, and she looked around. In the semi-darkness, she could recognize some boards and some bricks. They had broken down the wooden door of a shack in ruins. The dust and the hay were still lingering in the air after the impact, slowly covering their car. She did not hear any noise around. Only silence. When she recovered, Alessandro turned off the lights, leaving only the parking lights on, to avoid stumbling; then he tried to put the broken door back together, to hide any trace of their passage. Once he came back to the car, he made sure that Rebecca had come out of it as well.

"I'm good," she lied. She still showed the signs of the shock she had gone through. "I'm just cold." All of a sudden, the scanner began to crackle again, startling them both. "Turn it off!" she begged, close to becoming hysterical. "Please, turn that thing off!" Alessandro was about to answer back, but Rebecca was so terrified that he gave up on arguing with her and decided to humor her. He embraced her, to warm her up and comfort her at the same time. She had not stopped shaking yet.

"You know what we'll do?" he suggested. "We'll light a fire."

"Won't they see us?"

"No, not if we keep the flame low and far from the door," he reassured her, convinced that this would distract her. He assembled some underbrush to ignite the wood boards left here and there in the shack. Curled up close to him, hypnotized by the fire and reassured by its coziness, she seemed to calm down. She didn't like the idea of remaining alone at all: even the iPhone was out of battery, and she would not have anything to kill the time. Even though she had that look, Vinci left the shack anyway, after a last glance at the partially broken door which hardly stood on its hinges. It did not seem stable at all, but it could probably resist for the night.

In spite of Rebecca's anxiety, he could not keep still. The helicopter would certainly not leave the ground in the darkness. With all that vegetation, it would have risked getting caught in cables or in the branches of a tall tree, but he knew the hunt would certainly not stop. He tried to put himself in their chasers' shoes, trying to get his bearings as well as possible in a wood and with complete darkness all around. He wanted to try and make out what direction they could arrive from, to anticipate them and avoid getting trapped.

**

The two policemen were almost at the end of their shift, and they were exhausted. Nobody liked to wander at night in a wood, on foot, even less so to hunt down a dangerous murderer. That morning they were informed about the finding of De Marchi's corpse. There was no doubt that the murderer was the Killer of the Apennines. Their colleague had not just been killed: he had been dismembered and suffocated with his own innards. The autopsy had obviously not been made public, but there were people who swore they had heard he was still alive while he was being butchered. They had every reason to be furious. Furious and frightened.

It was the younger of the two to notice recent tire tracks on the grass, just above the undergrowth. Before informing the headquarters, they decided to make a last attempt on their own and they followed them. They saw them disappear into a grassless patch before the wood declined, but a little further away they glimpsed some branches broken by the passage of a car, and easily noticeable. They followed those as well.

At a certain point the older of the two tugged the other by the sleeve: there was a light glow between the branches. A smell of fire reached their nostrils. They pulled out their flashlights and approached in silence. They reached closer to what seemed to be a ruin, a hovel abandoned long ago, but somebody was surely camping there, and had lit the fire. They brandished their guns and proceeded slowly, concentrating on their task. They parted and went around each side of the shack, to make sure nobody was around. When they met again, they waited in ambush on the front corner of the dilapidated building, leaning on a girder in precarious balance, which would allow them to peek inside without being seen. Or at least, so they hoped.

"It's them," proclaimed the older one, indicating the pickup. "I'll tell central, then we go in."

"Wait," ordered the other. He stretched out along the supporting girder of the shack, almost demolished by the pickup's devastating entrance, which had made it sway dangerously. The silhouette of the woman was the only one that could be made out, illuminated by a small fire. Maybe he was sleeping in the car, in darkness. The younger one aimed.

"What are you doing?" the other one asked, alarmed, lowering the weapon's barrel.

"You saw what they did to De Marchi!"

165

"Exactly. Don't you want to wait for backup?" he asked his partner in a whisper, thinking it would not be wise to face them both by themselves.

"No, I don't want them to get away with it!"

"Are you nuts?"

"You know how this'll go," the other hissed through his teeth, careful to keep the level of his voice as quiet as possible. "Some asshole of a lawyer will find some trick to save them by copping them an insanity plea. Two years in jail and then they'll be out to make millions in talk shows!"

"And you want to—"

"We'll say we were taken by surprise," the younger one insisted, taking aim again.

**

Vinci was startled when he saw the police car. Very rapidly, he crouched down in the undergrowth, with his ears wide open. The car was empty. That meant the two men had left it to look for them. He calculated the direction that separated them from the shack and he understood they would have quickly found the pickup's tracks through the woods and followed them. Rebecca! He started to run trying to make as little noise as possible, as they had taught him to do during his training. In a moment he was back in the vicinity of the shack. He saw the silhouettes of the two men in uniform crouching down by the unstable entrance of the ruin, lying in ambush between the fallen bricks. He approached slowly, unsure of what he could do. Until that moment, he and Rebecca had never committed a crime. They had never even been stopped and, maybe, a good lawyer could still ward off the accusations against them. But anything he would have done against those two policemen would inevitably make them guilty. He tried to think of a subterfuge to distract them and allow Rebecca to get away, but how could he warn her of his intentions? The light of the weak bonfire was seeping in above the two crouching men. The heavy wooden girder, which supported the entrance and impeded its complete collapse, was hanging on one side.

Suddenly Alessandro realized that the fluctuating dim light coming from inside the shanty was not due to the unsteady light of the flames, but the girder, which was moving, maybe because the two men were leaning with all their weight on its shaky pillars. It could collapse at any moment. Alessandro widened his view to include the whole unstable construction. If the girder fell, most of the ceiling would probably follow...and Rebecca was still inside! The risk was too great: he stood up and decided to call the policemen's attention to himself. He was not ready to risk his companion's life, prosecution or no. In the same moment, from the profile of one of the two men, he saw the barrel of a gun. Vinci saw him point the gun towards Rebecca and aim.

"No!" he screamed, jumping forward. The shot echoed in the night anyway, but his intervention had frightened the shooter, making him raise his gun. Alessandro also heard Rebecca scream, but he could not do anything, since the second man had already pulled his gun out of its holster and had pointed it towards him, shooting. Luckily for him, the bullet missed its target. Alessandro pounced on him with all his weight before he could pull the trigger again, knocking him down and disarming him. He was about to jump on the second policeman, when the girder above them finally ceded, bringing down not only the structure of the doorway but the wall it supported.

The two policemen were hit by the plaster, and he was hardly able to keep at a distance, rolling to the side. He stood up immediately, with his mouth full of cement dust, just in time to see the whole shack collapse. "Rebecca!" he shouted, throwing himself among the ruins. He did not care anymore if other policemen were around and could hear him. He continued to call her with all his might, digging with his bare hands among the plaster and the girders, in darkness, his nails and his knuckles welling with blood.

After what seemed like an eternity, he was able to reach the place where she was a moment before the collapse. Even the pickup's nose emerged from the ruins. He found the doctor curled up under a girder that had fallen down diagonally but that did not touch her, leaning instead on the corner of a wall which still stood. Her body did not seem to be hurt. He rushed to free her face from the dust of wood and bricks, hoping he was in time, hoping he did not...he heard her breathe; shortly thereafter, she regained consciousness. *Thank you, God*, Alessandro thought. "Rebecca!" he called her. "Can you move your legs?" She moved her feet and nodded, unable to speak. He felt her neck going limp in his hands. "No, don't leave me. Rebecca!" he encouraged her, gently slapping her.

Rebecca came to: "I wasn't...I wasn't hit," she whispered, before she slipped back into the numbness caused by the shock. "I curled up under the girder. I wasn't hit..." Only partially reassured, Vinci looked up. The darkness was almost complete, disturbed only by the pickup's lights. They looked like two survivors of an attack. In fact, he considered angrily, they actually were. He took off his shirt, to use it as a pillow for her, then he climbed over the rubble to reach the car. Dents aside, it looked undamaged. What was left of the ruin's ceiling was too light to damage it for real. He could enter the cabin by slipping through an open window; he turned the key and, when the engine answered with a roar, he could not withhold a smile. They had been very lucky.

He went back to Rebecca and made sure her breathing was regular; then he lifted her up in his arms and, trying to find an unlikely balance among the ruins, now fully illuminated by the pickup, remembered the two men still lying buried under the plaster. The men who had just tried to kill them. He ran towards them, principally to ensure that they could pose no further threat, and then to see how they were. Both unconscious, but they both breathed regularly. *Do it*, the voice in his head told him. Alessandro stopped for a second, maybe even more than he had to. He did what he had to do, then he got back in the pickup and turned on the engine.

The car's lights illuminated everything that was left of the shack. Rebecca had been very lucky: almost the whole construction had collapsed towards the corner where they had lit the fire, and if it had not been for that providential girder, she would not have had a chance. The rear of the pickup was relatively free from the ruins and Vinci rapidly cleared the few that were left, then shifted into reverse. With some difficulty, he was able to drive the pickup out of what remained of the building; he loaded Rebecca into the truck while she was still alternating between moments of wakefulness and temporary blackouts. Then he left with the lights off in the night. His first thought was to carry the doctor to the first ER to verify her condition. Then he realized their arrival would promptly be alerted because their photos had surely been sent to all the hospitals in the region. He wasn't only worried. He was angry. The two policemen had shot at Rebecca from behind. There was only one explanation for such conduct: they were not trying to catch them alive. He only had one option left. He blatantly cursed and kept moving. Destination: Florence.

He called her on her cell phone when he was in front of her house and just told her to open the door, with the peremptory tone of someone who is ordering something, not just asking. That's why, when Silvia did what she was told to do, she had nothing but a top and her underwear on. Though she was alarmed by the ringtone that had surprised her in the middle of the night, and even more when she had read the name on the display, she was not fully awake yet when she went to open the door; but she regained her lucidity when she saw on his face the expression she had learned to hate, while she let Alessandro enter the apartment she had rented in the name of the newspaper in Florence. She could not hold back a curse when she saw the body he was holding in his hands. She stepped aside, rushing to close the door behind her, before overwhelming him with questions to which he did not even respond, as occupied as he was finding a place to lay the semiconscious doctor.

"This way," she said, indicating her unmade bed. While he was laying Rebecca on the blankets, she saw on his face the signs of an unprecedented worry, which was finding a way into his petrified gaze. Worry and maybe something else.

"What happened?"

"Nothing serious, at least that's what I think. The ceiling of a barn fell on her."

"What?" the journalist asked, even more alarmed, approaching the other woman. "And that's 'nothing serious' to you? We need to take her to the hospital, idiot!"

"They shot at her, Silvia. The police. They shot at her back: we can't go anywhere." The woman was stunned, furious and frightened.

"No hospital," said a feeble voice under them. Rebecca's eyes were partly open. "I'm good…I just have to…just give me a few minutes," she whispered, before falling asleep again.

Silvia stood there looking at him covering her up with a blanket, then she dragged him out of the room: "Let her rest," she suggested. Then, looking at him, he could not avoid noticing the signs of weariness on his face. "And why don't you sleep a bit as well?"

"I can't," the young man replied, still loaded with adrenaline.

"Listen, if they knew where you were, from what you say, they would have already broken down the door. You're devastated and you can't think logically. Lie down on the sofa for a bit, relax."

"And you?"

Only in that moment Silvia realized she was still almost naked in front of him and that the young man did not even seem to have noticed it. She was about to cover up, by crossing her arms in front of her breasts, but she understood it was useless. If he was looking at her in that moment, he surely did not do so with desire.

"There's another armchair in my room," she answered laconically. "So I can keep an eye on the doctor." Convinced, Alessandro sat on the sofa in the living room and finally laid his head on the armrest, closing his eyes.

**

Police Deputy Commissioner Angeloni was fuming with anger in his office, irritated by the man who sat calmly in the chair on the other side of his desk. "Great job, you trained a perfect killer!" Colonel Achille just raised his eyebrow. "Who is going to explain it to the wives and the mothers of my two men, now?"

"I thought you had found them alive and in a safe position," the man replied quietly.

"With a concussion, and with both arms and pelvis fractured! They will be lucky if they recover in three months."

"I didn't quite understand what they dictated in their preliminary report," Achille answered, putting the folder with the two accounts on the desk. "They declared they were surprised by Vinci coming from the rear, and that they did not have time to defend themselves. But both guns fired a bullet. If it was not towards Vinci, who were they shooting at?" Angeloni did not reply, as he had not been convinced either by the story the two men had given.

"Anyway, now he's accused of attempted murder of a police officer. He won't do with less than ten years in jail!"

"If you catch him. It's time for my squad to step in."

"I don't even want to hear about your squad! I bet I won't even hear about Vinci anymore if you intervene. I want that asshole in jail, together with his bacteriologist girlfriend!"

"He put them in a safe position," Achille continued undismayed, showing the pictures of the two policemen, as the rescuers found them, "and he communicated to the radio their position to let us find them rapidly. There was no plaster on them, just a bit of detritus. It means he extracted them from the ruins. He probably saved their lives."

"I don't care if he's a fucking boy scout!" Angeloni growled. "I want that bastard caught and not necessarily alive. I'm going to call the SWAT team."

The colonel raised his eyebrow again: "If you want to avoid being accountable for too much blood, let my squad intervene. You know my team says about the SWAT? They call them twats, rather than SWAT..." he insisted.

"Bullshit! You just want to put your hands on your agent's neck. You think the SWAT isn't able to deal with your little soldier?"

"I think my team is more...fit for this operation. But that's true, I do have something to settle with Alessandro Vinci."

"Too late!" Angeloni exclaimed triumphantly, leaning back on the armchair. "I already called the SWAT. One unit will get to Florence in two hours."

"That's a mistake." Achille sighed, standing up and going towards the door. Then he stepped back, bending over the desk: "You know how to get in touch with me...when you'll need to." Angeloni could not avoid swearing loudly at him while the door closed behind the colonel.

172

17

When Rebecca woke up, she found herself in an unknown room, in which darkness was partially attenuated by the blades of light seeping in through the shutters. She sat up on her arms, still confused, but a stab of headache brought her back to reality in a second.

"How are you?" a female voice in front of her asked. Even in the darkness, she realized it was Silvia. She silently cursed in her head.

"Very bad, thank you," she answered sincerely. She was able to sit in the bed, so she tried to stand up, but a feeling of dizziness almost made her fall down. The other woman supported her by taking her arm until she felt secure, and distanced herself from her, with a kind but firm gesture. "Where is Alessandro?" she asked, looking around and opening the windows. She needed air. The strong luminosity of the late morning obliged her to close her eyes for a few seconds; her temples pulsated with the pain.

"He's out," Silvia replied. "He said he needed to clear his head. He's like that." That reference to an intimacy she thought was forgotten, irritated her: she had no right, however. She turned towards Silvia and looked at her for a moment, before concluding she could never compete with the journalist. The same captivating sensuality that had been immortalized in the photo hanging in Alessandro's room seem to emanate from that person in front of her, perhaps even more so than in the photo, though now she was bare-faced and wearing a revealing top and panties. She was furious thinking that he had seen her like that as well, and only a few hours before. Her thoughts were probably quite manifest, because Silvia could not withhold a malicious smile. Then, with a careless gesture, she took her top off and threw it on the bed, revealing firm breasts, much bigger than her own. She took a bra out from a drawer, and put it on together with a dark T-shirt. "He's not like that," she said, as if she were reading Rebecca's thoughts. "I could do a naked lap dance in front of him and he would not even look at me, if he was with another woman."

"Yeah," Rebecca replied sarcastically. "Sure, because he's Mister Goody-goody. I saw the souvenirs he keeps in his room," she said before she could regret her words. Silvia laughed, but there was no trace of mockery in her laugh. This made Rebecca even more furious.

"My photo in the room! That's why you can't stand me!" Rebecca did not reply, blushing violently. "Don't you want to take a shower, before you dress?" Silvia asked, looking at her. Rebecca looked at herself in the mirror and she realized the journalist was right. "I can lend you something," she said guessing that Rebecca had nothing to change into. She opened the drawers and prepared some clean underwear and a T-shirt for her. "This should fit you." Rebecca took her pants and her T-shirt off in front of her, letting them fall on the floor. They were still full of dust and plaster. Then, without taking her eyes off of Silvia's, she took her bra off as well.

"The photo surprised me, it's true," she said collecting her clothes and going towards the bathroom. "But I thought it was a thing of the past," she lied, passing naked in front of Silvia.

"He would never do that," Silvia repeated from the room. "He would never do anything behind your back. Trust is everything for him." Rebecca retraced her steps, covering herself with the clean clothes she had given her.

"Really? Listen, I know it's not my business, but I need to know. What happened between you and him?"

Silvia waited for a few seconds, before she answered: "We were together, then something happened…"

"You slept with somebody else?"

"He wouldn't be as mad with me if it was just that."

"You did something worse?" Silvia bit her lip. "Come on, I have the right to know! Someone just shot at me, and he's the only one who's helping me. It's not fair that I don't know anything about what happened between the two of you!"

"You had sex, didn't you?" she finally asked.

"It's none of your business," Rebecca burst out, with an expression that left no doubts. "What does this have to do with anything?"

"Did you have sex or not?"

"Yes, we did," Rebecca answered almost cruelly in answer to the other's insistence, taking her revenge for that cursed photo. "Actually, I had sex with many different versions of Alessandro: once he was slow and sweet. Another time he overpowered me, almost hurting me. Once more, I went on top of him…" Rebecca realized she felt really good in articulating those words, as if saying it aloud made the whole thing feel more real.

"Alright, alright, I got that," Silvia stopped her. "I asked you that because Alessandro would never sleep with a woman he didn't trust or didn't care about," she said, raising her hands as if in surrender.

"Let's do this: go take a shower, and I'll prepare something to eat. Then we'll chat a bit."

"Good idea," the doctor agreed, smiling about the whole situation and her own embarrassment. The lukewarm water washed out what was left of her hair dye, and of the dust. Rebecca touched her head: on the spot that was sideswiped by the girder there was a small bump, but it only hurt if she touched it. Otherwise, apart from some weariness, she did not feel any other aching. She dried rapidly, and she wore the

175

clothes Silvia had lent her, impatient to know something more about her mysterious companion.

"I was sure you were not dark-haired," Silvia received her when she returned to the kitchen. The temporary dye had definitely washed off, and the doctor had not even bothered to restore it: the disguise had not protected her from the bullets, and she loved her natural hair color. "You start," Silvia suggested, handing her a cup of peach tea. "Tell me how the two of you ended up in this mess." Rebecca told her everything, even the details they had neglected in the previous meeting. After all, if Alessandro trusted her, she could do so as well. She even told her about the virus-bearing comets.

"Now it's your turn," she concluded, looking at the amazed journalist. "What does 'Night' mean?" Rebecca understood she had asked the right question. Silvia held her breath, astonished.

"What...what do you know about Night?" she shot back.

"I don't know anything apart the fact that when I called Alessandro by that name he almost broke the neck of some ugly mug who was trying to stab me, and only because when he heard me call him that, he hit harder than his three aggressors." Silvia nodded, trying to gain some time. "You know, I think he's gone precisely to give us time to talk to each other," the doctor insinuated. "So that you can tell me everything."

Rebecca understood immediately that Silvia did not believe that, though the journalist smiled maliciously: "He can choose his women well." Rebecca accepted the compliment, continuing to stare at her. If she thought she would get by with that...

"Alright. I already got hell for doing it once. It can't go much worse." Silvia sat at the corner of the table, sipping her own cup of tea. "Alessandro was an orphan quite early in his life, when he was about fifteen or sixteen years old. He finished high school when he could, then he enrolled in the army. He was immediately noticed by a recruiter who was looking for outstanding men for a special squad. His initial assignment was as a sniper, but he rapidly became the leading figure of his squad. Night was his code name.

"I met him by chance: I was coming back from Padua from one of my first assignments. Alessandro saved me when he saw me slide down into a river in my car. He dove into the frozen water and got me out of the cabin before it was too late. We started to hang out with each other, for a while we lived together. At the time he only told me he was a policeman and he always tried to keep me away from his work, but one evening I was able to intercept a service call and I thought he was a terrorist. At that point Alessandro had to tell me the truth: his squad was not a simple assault squad. And not only that. It was a unit established at the end of the seventies, during the 'Years of Lead' and it was intended to be an antiterrorism unit. But it turned out to be a squad of murderers. When anybody else failed, they were sent to solve the problem, once and for all.

"Alessandro was the best; at times he let out some horrifying details about his missions, which he justified on the principle of the lesser evil. If it were necessary, he could kill a man with a paper clip. The more time passed, though, the more I saw him insecure about his choice, about that life. Little by little, he was sinking into an abyss of darkness from which I was never able to save him. Until the last mission."

"The one in which the judge was killed, Professor Spinelli's brother?" Rebecca was hanging off her words.

"Exactly. They had received many threats, so his squad was ordered to escort the magistrate and his family. Alessandro was the one to organize it, with all the necessary precision, but during a transfer they were attacked, the judge was killed together with his wife, and since he defended the judge until the very last moment, fighting like a lion, he was also severely wounded…in his back."

"And they made him responsible for what happened?"

"That's right. But that wasn't the worst thing. What still gets at him is that he did not agree to that last transfer, because he had been suspecting for a while that somebody from the inside was informing the attackers. But his superiors didn't believe him, or they pretended they didn't; for them it was much easier to fault a single man's failure, rather than risking a huge fuss and unleashing a witch hunt."

At that point, Silvia stopped, unsure, sipping her tea. Rebecca urged her. "And so?"

"As a journalist I rushed to the shooting scene without knowing who was involved, and I was able to shoot some photos: some caught Alessandro's unconscious body while he was being transferred in an ambulance. With his face exposed. I remember the camera fell out of my hands when I recognized him. I went to visit him in the intensive care unit, after they had just hardly saved his life, and the first thing he asked me was where his gun was: he wanted to finish the job. I understood he was at the bottom of that abyss. He would have never left that life, not before he was completely lost. I thought I had only one thing left to do: I published the photos with his face. I got the first page of the newspaper, and two days later they hired me at the *Corriere*."

"But he lost his job."

Silvia nodded. "Once his identity had been revealed, he could not go back to the squad and his superiors didn't miss the opportunity to kill two birds with one stone: they got rid of a troublemaker, and they could relieve their consciences by blaming him for the failure of the mission. I think he didn't end up in jail only because there was not enough evidence."

"How did he react?"

Silvia smiled bitterly. "Once the photos came out in the newspaper, he refused to see me in the hospital, and as soon as he was able to walk, he turned up at my house immediately, with the coldest, most merciless expression I've ever seen on his face. Maybe only his targets had seen that before me. He didn't even speak; for a second I thought he would kill me...but it was almost worse. I had committed the worst crime for him: I had betrayed him. He disappeared from my life like that, in silence. I think I still have some of his stuff in my garage." She remained silent for a while, then she resumed, with a tougher tone of voice: "My choice had its merits: I know that after he was forced to abandon the squad, he gave himself over to literature, to photography, and this makes me happy, but the choice of studying for his Ph.D. with Professor Spinelli makes me think he never turned his back on his previous life." Rebecca nodded, remembering that Alessandro had said the same thing a few days before. "I think he still despises me," the journalist confessed, bitterly.

"Well, I don't think so. After all, he still had your picture in his room."

Silvia smiled. "If I know him well, that serves as a memento to remember he can't trust anybody." The doctor did not know if she should feel relieved by that new angle or sad, in a sign of solidarity. She was saved from that moment of embarrassment by the noise of the door opening.

Alessandro came into the kitchen and his somber expression brightened up when he saw Rebecca standing and in good physical condition, but then it became once more dark and deep, like it had been over the last few hours: "I brought you the newspaper," he said, putting it on the table in front of Silvia. Rebecca knew—without needing to ask—that he had profited from the time he had spent outside to consider all the alternative options of escape from that apartment. After speaking with Silvia she felt almost...relieved. Knowing, finally, about Alessandro's traumatic experience, troubled her less than she had feared: his past still appeared less ugly than their prospective future. She met his eyes inspecting her, to see if she was really as well as she said. Then she saw him look at her hair.

"Don't even think about it!" she shouted, with her finger high, to threaten him, fearing he wanted her to dye her hair again, or worse, to cut it more. He burst out in a loud laugh, raising his hands to surrender and Silvia, raising her eyes from the newspaper for a while, caught that knowing look, Alessandro's rapid change of mood and she understood. Her heart tightened, but she gave up, going back to her newspaper.

"I think this might interest you," she told them opening the newspaper on the table and indicating a paid ad:

Important pharmaceutical company desires to contact anyone who has news regarding the book Stella Novissima *or authentic letters of G.G.*

An adequate reward is guaranteed.

Pegasus' logo and a cell phone number closed the ad. "It's certainly a trap," Silvia concluded.

"Yes, I think so too," Rebecca replied, disconcerted. "They're trying to smoke us out."

"Could you ask about who bought the ad?" Alessandro suggested, talking to the journalist. Silvia hesitated at first, but then she got on her phone.

"What do we do?" Rebecca asked, nervously touching her hair.

"We're at a standoff," Vinci remarked after a few seconds. "There's two possibilities: either the ad is real and we try to find out what the people at Pegasus have in their hands, or it's a trap and we find the police waiting for us, or worse."

Rebecca did not ask what he meant by "worse" and objected: "Or we could simply not show up."

"You mean run away, vanish without leaving a trace, even though our faces are on every news bulletin? Even if we succeeded in moving, we would have to go abroad and erase our whole lives. Dangerous, but possible."

"Never!" she exclaimed resolutely. "We didn't commit any crime. No, I have no intention of spending my whole life in hiding; and then there is the risk of a pandemic!"

"In that case we could only surrender and hope the truth comes out by itself." Rebecca thought about the short chat she had had at the police headquarters in Florence a while before, when she just wanted to report Professor Spinelli missing, and she almost moaned at the thought of what could happen this time when she was wanted for abduction and murder.

"Meeting," she decided. "I definitely vote to meet with Pegasus."

"The ad seems authentic," Silvia interrupted them, closing her phone call in anger. "It has been paid for by an account in the name of Pegasus Pharmaceutics."

Alessandro could hardly withhold an amused smile: "So it's decided? We'll go to the meeting!" Rebecca nodded reluctantly, looking in vain for some comfort in her lifeless iPhone. "Can you lend us your car?" Vinci asked Silvia. "They're certainly looking for the pickup."

"Lend you? I'm coming with you!" she replied.

"No way," he answered abruptly. "You will stay here and you will be our ears and our backup in case we need it. I don't even want Rebecca to come, but I think no agreement will be possible without her; they only know her face, until now."

"But—"

"That's it. I can't ensure your safety as well. Will you lend us your car, yes or no?"

Silvia cursed, but nodded.

They spent the following hours planning all the details, the place and time of the meeting, then they contacted Pegasus from a telephone booth. When it was time to move, Silvia stopped Vinci by the door: "Alessandro?" she asked.

"Yes," he assured her, turning back. "You will have the exclusive on this story. Only you."

Hearing that answer, the words she was about to pronounce dried up on her lips.

When Silvia heard the building gate close, she rapidly took her cell phone out from her pocket and dialed the first number in the contact list. She told her name to the indifferent secretary and she waited. "I don't care if he's in a meeting!" she shouted, when she reported the message. "I need to talk to him right now!"

A few seconds later, she heard at the other end of the receiver the annoyed voice of Riccardo Patrioti: "Canelli, I'm in a meeting with the sales manager: it's not a good time—"

"I have no time, Patrioti. I'm about to write a piece which will make our sales and our web contacts go sky-high. I'm not exaggerating, and I want to be the reporter streaming the news live. I want my name on this piece."

"What are you talking about?" her editor asked, sensing the news with the instinct of an expert journalist, which had earned him the nickname Shark. "Where are you?"

"No questions now, I told you there's no time," Silvia rebutted, looking back at the scanner crackling beside her. "I want you to assure me we will be streaming on the web as soon as I tell you and I want the minimum delay the technicians can give me; and I want them to be ready as soon as I need them."

"If you don't give me any hints about what it is about I can't promise you anything. Can't we talk about it after the meeting?" Silvia held back, torn. She did not want to run the risk of having somebody steal her story, but she had to at least bait the hook.

"The murder of Rastrini and the ones in the Tuscan hills, and that's only the tip of the iceberg," she said in a single breath. She waited a few seconds, then she heard Patrioti's voice ordering the secretary to excuse him from the meeting. *Good*, Silvia thought. *The news Shark has taken the bait. Now I just have to be careful not to get bitten by him.*

18

Alessandro turned up at the place where the meeting was planned about two hours early, and walked around the whole area, examining every street. It was on the outskirts, in a decaying area, filled with abandoned buildings and inhabited exclusively only by rats, junkies and homeless people of several ethnicities. With one glance only, Vinci made them all understand they had to keep away from him, and he completed his stroll undisturbed. There was no sniper on the roofs, no unmarked car around. He was satisfied, and waited there. A few minutes before the agreed time, he saw a black Mercedes with tinted windows stopping in the square they had chosen to meet in, which was enclosed by four buildings in slightly better condition than the others.

One man only came out of the car, from the driver's side. Vinci could not be sure of it, but it looked like nobody else was in the car, as he had requested on the phone. The man looked at his watch several times, probably uncomfortable with the situation or the place, or both. As they had agreed, a few minutes later Rebecca appeared out of the neighborhood's main street. With his hand on the butt of his gun, which he had left in the pickup until that moment, Vinci checked that the Pegasus emissary did not venture in any risky move and only then he decided to come out into the open and to reach him, just before her. The man saw him appear all of a sudden, but he immediately regained his composure. Rebecca thought she would meet Dr. Krupp, but when she got closer, she realized it was somebody else.

"Good evening...Doctor De Cardinale, I suppose?" the man began, holding out his hand which neither of the two shook. Rebecca nodded. "And you must be Doctor Vinci," he continued.

"Who are you?" Alessandro replied, intimidating.

The man tried to insert his hand in his jacket pocket, but he found Vinci's gun pointed at him together with his ice-cold look. He raised both hands: "I'm...I'm unarmed," he said almost stammering, but without losing his calm. Alessandro rapidly searched him, then, reassured, he put his gun away. Rebecca also sighed in relief: she did not know he had another gun, apart from the one he had left in the motel, and she was absolutely not happy about it. She took the business card the man was finally able to take out of his pocket. It was identical to the one Krupp had given him, only the name changed: A. Torre.

"I'm happy you replied to the ad in the newspaper," he began cordially, as if that was just a transaction like any other. The man looked around, nervous, trying not to have his eyes fall on the gun on Alessandro's hip. "You have something we need, Doctor. The company I represent is able to make a very generous offer—"

"And if I didn't accept, they would get tired of waiting, right?" she attacked him, quoting Krupp's own words.

Being a criminal, Torre was very good at pretending, because his bewildered expression seemed very authentic. "I think we both want the research in this field to continue without further delay," Torre pressed her, still talking to Rebecca only, "and we are willing to purchase the letters Professor Spinelli talked to us about, since he is unreachable. In our last contact, he told us he was working with you."

Unreachable, Rebecca though with disdain. As if they did not know exactly where he was, dead or alive. As if they were not the ones responsible for his disappearance. With an unnatural slowness, timorously looking at her partner, Torre extracted a check from his pocket. "You write the amount," he offered, handing it out to the woman.

185

"For Spinelli's letters?" Rebecca asked, confused.

"No, for all of Galileo's letters. Including the ones that were removed from Professor Rastrini's home. We were about to make another generous donation for the second part of the documents, when he was killed. But I doubt the first transaction made the university rich, if I am permitted to say so." Vinci's jaw got even more tense. Now he understood why the professor did not appreciate any questions being asked about those letters: he had sold a part of them under the table. That dwarf jerk!

"We have nothing to do with that happened at Rastrini's place!" she objected, doubly indignant. The man's hand was fast to withdraw the check and make it disappear into the same pocket it had come out of.

"Of course I did not mean to accuse you of murder," he conceded. "But…what about the letters?"

"We didn't take them," Vinci roared. "What we have is a CD with the scans of those letters, that Professor Rastrini himself gave us."

Rebecca extracted the CD from the bag Silvia had lent her, after hers had been destroyed, along with everything it contained, in the shack's collapse. Only the iPhone had been saved because it was in the pickup. Thinking about it she shivered, but she obliged herself to focus on the man in front of her, who was bringing his hand back to the pocket in which he kept the check. She stopped him: "We want a copy of the letters you own, in exchange for these."

The man smiled and for the first time he looked at ease. It didn't take much to understand why. "I don't think that's a fair exchange. After all, there could be anything on that CD. And then, why would I have the letters with me? They are findings of inestimable value, of course it wouldn't have been prudent to carry them in this…charming neighborhood," the man said, indicating the sordid square.

"We don't need the originals either," Rebecca replied, while Alessandro silenced the objections of the academic that was in him. "I'm sure you made a copy of the letters, and I'm sure you have a laptop in your car to examine this CD."

"I thought that in the…situation you're in, you would prefer a check," he said. "In these letters there could be the clue to recovering a lost book by Galileo Galilei. The company I represent would have nothing against attributing its possible finding to you. Or to pretend it never happened, if you prefer," he said, with a mellifluous tone of voice.

A mediator, Rebecca thought with relief, studying the affected manners of the man. Always better than the gangster she was expecting. "What will happen if we refuse?"

"During the Cold War, the United States commissioned research to understand the effects of a nuclear bombing on an entire continent. They elaborated the simulation of a holocaust, but they realized the worst conjectures had been overcome by something that had actually happened: the plague epidemic of 1348." Rebecca looked at him questioningly. "If we can't find an agreement, I think we will both lose an important opportunity; and the heaviest losses will hit the world's population, which will be hit by the worst pandemic humankind can remember."

"Very altruistic of you."

"Altruism has nothing to do with this, Doctor. It's about business."

"No threats, this time?"

"I don't know what you're talking about, Doctor," Torre said, continuing to play the deaf, blind, mute. "I was charged by my company with offering you a solution which could prove…satisfying to all of us. Certain methods are not part of our business policy," he concluded.

"That's not what your predecessor, Doctor Krupp, used to maintain."

"Krupp? When did you meet him? And where?" the man asked, opening his eyes widely.

"Not more than ten days ago, here in Florence," she replied.

"That's not possible! Krupp—"

Vinci, who had lost his patience, interrupted the conversation. They were wasting too much time. "Your letters for ours," he ordered. Rebecca, with ostentation, put the CD back in her bag. Torre stepped aside and invited her to sit in the back seat of his car, opening the door for her. Before entering, she looked at Alessandro, who nodded his head and remained outside to monitor the situation.

In the cabin, with the doors open, Torre took out a laptop from his briefcase and turned it on. He looked at her, impatient, but she did not cede to him. "Yours first." Smiling, Torre pulled out from one of the briefcase's pockets a CD and inserted it into the reader. Rebecca looked at the images, and she understood she had made a mistake: the dates on the letters seemed to correspond to those of the exchanges between Galilei and Maffini, but she could not tell if they were authentic or well-done imitations. She could not even make out a city's name, any kind of indication which allowed them to narrow their search. Vinci should have been in the car, not her. When she called him, he showed up immediately, alarmed. "We should switch," she suggested, indicating the images on the screen. In that moment, though, the cell phone in Alessandro's pocket rang. He stiffened and extracted it rapidly. Silvia. They had agreed that she would call them in one case only: the police had found them.

"Come out of there. Right now!" he told Rebecca, who hesitated. Then they heard the helicopter's blades. "Go back to our car!" he shouted at her, running out in the open to attract the helicopter, which immediately turned towards him. Rebecca heard the siren, rapidly approaching. Terrified, she saw Alessandro run towards a three-story building in ruins and with walled-up windows. She was about to step out of the Mercedes and walk towards Silvia's car, but she was pulled back, almost falling on her seat. Torre. The man had grabbed her bag with both hands, agitated and struggling on his seat, with a ravenous expression which had nothing in common with that of the seraphic spokesperson of shortly before. She resisted with all her strength and she finally managed to tear her bag from his hands, but when she turned to get out of the car, she had a gun pointed at her face.

"Get out of the car, slowly," a policeman ordered while another two, armed with machine guns, positioned themselves on the other side of the Mercedes. Pale, shocked and shaking, Rebecca did what was ordered, while strong hands were taking Torre out of the opposite door.

"Doctor De Cardinale?" asked the man who had taken her out, lowering his gun, while he was turning her around and searching her, with rapid and expert moves. Another policeman did the same with Torre, while another one, with his machine gun in his hands, took aim at them. "I'm Deputy Commissioner Angeloni," the man continued when he was done with the search. Rebecca's attention, however, was focused on what was happening a little further down, in the decrepit apartment block in which Vinci had sought refuge. He saw the SWAT unit headed there and her heart stopped. She saw the first floor of the apartment building invaded by the dense and acrid smoke of smoke bombs; their smell reached even their car.

"It's over, Doctor. Now you're safe," the commissioner said, also observing the scene. Colonel Achille positioned himself not too far from them. He would not have missed that show for anything in the world. "You should be grateful to us, Doctor," the hoarse voice of the commissioner continued. "We're saving you from a crazed killer." Rebecca was startled. What was he talking about? "We know you can't be responsible for the murders: we've seen the videos of the places you were in while the victims were being killed." Rebecca was overwhelmed by relief, but she continued to keep her eyes straight on the building in which the manhunt had begun.

"Then stop! Stop those men, before they hurt Alessandro!"

"You mean Vinci? But he's the murderer!"

The SWAT team broke into the apartment building, barging into the lobby. They separated in small squads of three or four men, positioning themselves one on each floor. They were all equipped with a Kriss Super V machine gun and 45 mm ammunition: a weapon characterized by little recoil and great shooting precision, perfect for raids like that. Without saying a word, the agents moved to explore the area, covering each other. That place for them was a real nightmare, as it was filled with ledges and blind corners, difficult to clear. Out of tension, one of them accidentally shot a series of gunshots, which hit the wall and alarmed some of his companions. When they understood it was nothing but a false alarm, they resumed their exploration, trying to hunt down their target in the fog caused by the smoke bombs.

The agent who had shot involuntarily stayed behind. He knew he would be reprimanded, and probably disciplined once they were back. He cursed that bastard who was their target and let the rest of the patrol proceed forward, remaining in the small lobby to watch his comrades' backs. He raised his finger from the trigger. He could not make any other mistake. No more false alarms. The squad leader waved with his hand and two men followed him on the sides of a pile of fallen bricks from a half-demolished wall. Under them, even in the smoke, they could discern a dark boot. A tactical boot. Their target was armed and extremely dangerous.

Slowly, they approached, ready to neutralize him. The orders were to catch him alive, if possible, but everybody knew that only a miracle could have got Alessandro Vinci out of there breathing. The men held their breath in their gas masks. When they finally burst from behind the ruins, shooting blindly, the boot rolled on the floor, empty. Behind them two shots were fired. They ran towards the noise and in the small landing behind their shoulders they found a dead comrade. His blood had stained the tactical uniform from the neck down to his shoulder.

While the others covered him, the squad leader saw that the man on the floor was still moving. He signaled on the radio that an agent had been wounded and with the help of another soldier he hurried to transfer him out of the building. "I want him dead!" he shouted at the men remaining on the upper floors, who immediately resumed their search, even more combative than before, praying that the military ambulance parked nearby would hurry.

"It's impossible!" Rebecca objected, desperately trying to convince the commissioner. "Vinci was in Padua while the victims were being killed."

"Who says that, Doctor? You were in Florence: how can you know where your friend was? And what about the murders committed in Padua?"

"But he was with me the whole time!"

"The whole time?" the man insisted, while nervously staring at the SWAT's movement.

"Yes, always…" she answered, thinking once more about what had happened in the previous days, and trying to remember everything, second by second. "He didn't kill anybody!" Rebecca screamed, wriggling away from his hands.

"Oh, really?" Angeloni sarcastically replied. "Why don't you ask Colonel Achille here? Ask him what kind of psychopathic murderer he cultivated." Angeloni indicated the soldier with a gesture, then he continued: "The gun that killed Rastrini is the same one we found in your love nest at the motel and his fingerprints are on it. Only his fingerprints, and nobody else's." Rebecca was about to faint, but luckily Angeloni did not realize that, more worried about the continuous silence of his transceiver. He brusquely turned to the other two policemen: "They're taking too long. Come closer and tell me what is happening," he ordered, while an astounded Torre was brought in front of him. The two rushed to obey. In that moment the ambulance was proceeding extremely fast and with sirens wailing towards the apartment block while two men came out of it, transporting a third. Angeloni could not restrain himself: "Shit, did you see that? He shot a policeman!"

"He surely defended himself," Rebecca replied.

"I would check that ambulance," Colonel Achille suggested with a dry tone, rapidly walking immediately after it towards the scene. Angeloni interrupted his resounding curses and remained speechless for a second. Then he grabbed his cell phone and cursed even more when nobody replied to the call. The ambulance moved. The commissioner roared. "Stay here. Don't move," he told Rebecca and Torre, tearing the keys off the Mercedes' dashboard.

"I won't go anywhere," the man assured him, pale and frightened. Then, after staring eloquently at the doctor, the commissioner started to run towards the ambulance driving away with the sirens wailing, waving in every possible way to attract the other policemens' attention. As soon as he turned his back on her, Rebecca jumped into the Mercedes and took the CD out of Torre's laptop. When she had it in her hands, she tried to come out of the opposite door, but the man blocked her again, holding her by a sleeve: "Let me go!" she screamed, but he squeezed even more, holding on to her shoulder strap with all his might.

Rebecca understood she would not be able to wriggle away, and that she did not have the time to play tug-of-war. She put her hand in her bag, grabbed her own CD and threw it at the man. Satisfied, Torre let go of her and rushed to pick it up, with his disgusting, sweaty, chubby hands. She abandoned him, foaming at the mouth in his car, and she started to run breathlessly through the alleys she had come from, with the vision of seeing Angeloni or another policeman aiming his gun at her. She was lucky. The police had other things to think about in that moment. She reached Silvia's car unharmed. The car was parked and concealed behind a dumpster. She had problems finding the keys. She grabbed them with shaking hands and they fell. She picked them up. She pushed the button and the door opened. She turned on the car and sped away, screeching, along the roads, careless of Alessandro's advice of trying not to get noticed.

Alessandro…

The ambulance was not moving, the flashing lights still on. When it reached a side alley by Angeloni's car, the driver and the nurse were handcuffed in the back, chained to a metallic lock. Their guns were on the back seat. They were incredulous and furious, but unharmed. The nurse had no shoes on.

"He drew us into a pile of ruins," the SWAT's squad leader later explained to his superior, on the phone. Furious and humiliated, he stared at the building, the scene of their defeat. Angeloni and Achille were beside him. "He stunned one of our men. He removed his helmet and his body armor, and he wore them, then he shot in the air twice. He dirtied himself with some pitch to give the impression of blood. With the gas mask glasses on, they have the same color." He remained silent for a second, then he sighed: "Yes, sir. I put him in that ambulance." Angeloni left, furious and incredulous, leaving the squad leader to his confession on the phone. When he turned back again towards the many police cars still lined up, Colonel Achille was in front of him. He was chewing on some boxed nuts. He offered him some, with a mocking smile. "Peanuts?"

"Alright!" he shouted in his face, at the peak of his rage. "Call your squad. I want Vinci's head on my desk!"

19

Rebecca reached the apartment still upset, not caring about the restricted traffic area and the cameras taking pictures of the transgressor's license plates. Once she reached the small apartment building, she knocked on the door with her fists.

"Let me in!" she hysterically screamed to Silvia, when she asked who it was. The journalist opened the door for her, with a face marked by worry. She was smoking. On the table Rebecca saw an ashtray full of cigarette butts. The scanner was still crackling in the background, but it was not saying anything comprehensible.

"Are you good? Where's Alessandro? How did it go?" The doctor threw the CD on the table, then she took a glass of water and tried to bring it to her lips, but her hands shook so hard that she dropped most of it on herself.

"They found us."

"I know." Silvia indicated the scanner. "I warned you. Who informed them? Pegasus?" the journalist pressed her.

"No, I don't think so. Torre…their man seemed as surprised as we were." *It was a negotiator*, Rebecca remembered. To run away she was obliged to give him the CD with their letters: luckily, they had copied them on both their laptops, to be sure. "He ruined your bag," she told her, showing her a little unstitching. She was still shocked by what had happened, and by the policeman's words. Had Alessandro's gun really been used to kill Rastrini?

"Who cares about the bag. Where is Alessandro? Is he okay? Did they catch him?"

"I don't know! I don't know! There were some shots, I saw an ambulance…then I ran. I ran away…" Rebecca was about to cry. Silvia approached her, taking her hands in her own, trying to calm her down. Somebody knocked on the door. The women were startled. Two knocks, then one more. It was the agreed-upon signal. Rebecca jumped to the door and opened it wide: "Alessandro!" she screamed, embracing him tightly. He was sweaty, he was coughing and his eyes were red and swollen because of the smoke bombs. But he was alive. Silvia, unseen, dumped the ashtray out of the window.

Vinci told the two women how he was able to escape from the SWAT and how, pretending he was wounded, he had succeeded in escaping in the ambulance. Once he was in the vehicle, he had easily overpowered the astounded rescuers, forcing them to deviate from the path towards the hospital while the police cars were still assisting the manhunt out of the abandoned building. Then, once he had immobilized and muffled the driver and the nurse, he walked back to the apartment.

"Are you wounded?" Rebecca asked, worried, watching his swollen eyes and his efforts to eliminate from his lungs the rests of the irritating gas.

"No," he replied, with an ease which bothered the doctor, still reeling from what had happened.

"You should put something in those eyes, they're swelling more and more."

"True," Silvia confirmed. Then, talking to the doctor. "I can go and buy something in the pharmacy before they close. Tell me what you need," she suggested.

"He should apply some antibiotic and some cortisone; but the pharmacist usually requires a prescription for that," she said.

"Write the name of that stuff down for me," Silvia replied, self-assured. "I'll take care of the pharmacist." The doctor scribbled the name of the eyewash on a piece of paper adding some more things that she said would be useful in the following days. The woman took it and ran out. As soon as she was gone, Rebecca's attention went back to Alessandro. She was still out of breath and on the edge of a breakdown.

Alessandro, however, seemed very calm, even after everything he had been through, and in spite of his cough and the eye irritation. He was always on his guard, of course: his irritated eyes constantly inspected the lights coming in from the window, and his ears did not miss a single noise coming from the street, but otherwise he behaved like escaping a SWAT raid alive was a daily occurrence. Vinci took of his pitch-dirty T-shirt. On his sweating skin, his old scars stood out even more. His muscles, still swollen from the effort of the fight and the escape, defined his chest and his abdomen.

"You scared me to death!" She finally burst out crying, jumping into his massive chest. "I can't take this anymore, I can't…" Then she threw her arms over his neck, letting her worries and her fear vanish in a kiss, while her tears were mixing up with the sweat. When their lips met, their bodies burnt up with desire. They let the adrenaline and excitement overcome them, and only after they had reached their climax together did they calm down, embracing on the floor.

"We need to take a shower," he suggested after a few minutes. "Silvia could come back."

Even better, Rebecca thought maliciously. "You're right," she said instead, letting him take her in his arms and bring her to the bathroom. They got in the shower together, and instead of cooling them down, the water, the soap and the caresses excited them and they became entwined again. Only when they were satisfied did they come out of the stall and allow themselves to relax on the bed, wrapped up in their towels. Alessandro's eyes were not as irritated as before, thanks to the cool water, but when he closed them he could not hide a small grimace of pain.

"Keep them closed," the doctor whispered, gently touching his eyelids with her hand. "They won't bother you as much." He obeyed and she kept staring at him while his breath grew calmer and a refreshing sleep relaxed his facial features.

"So, Patrioti, did you decide? Everything ready for the live streaming?" As soon as she was out of the door and she had walked around the corner, Silvia had wasted no time and had got on the phone.

"I don't know," he answered, with a tone of voice which was much more self-assured than the one he had in their previous conversation. "The live covering is dangerous, a minimum delay cannot be avoided and the image quality could be awful if we don't organize it carefully. I'm saying it for your benefit: if you screw up now, you'll write filler pieces for the rest of your life."

Silvia decided to force his hand. She had to make him smell blood, but without allowing him to follow its trail, or he would have snatched the prey. "Listen, my sources assure me that this story is linked with what happened in Florence this afternoon."

"You mean the SWAT raid?" Patrioti let slip, excited.

"Exactly. Now, either you give me the story, or I go and sell it to our competitors. I already have two TV stations interested," she lied, praying her voice did not betray her bluff.

Patrioti's answer turned into a growl: "Alright, but I want to know the details of the story before it's broadcasted and if it's bullshit, I swear you'll never have another chance!" he concluded, ending the call. More excited than she had ever been before, Silvia had to stop to catch her breath again. She had put all her cards on the table: after that phone call, her career would have come to a new level or collapsed down into an abyss. She took a deep breath and headed for the pharmacy.

Rebecca knew perfectly well that adrenaline was powerful and deceiving, and that it was able to bewitch people who were thrust into exciting events, like Alessandro and herself. She also knew that the passion borne from the hormone known as "the fight or flight hormone" was destined to diminish when the conditions which caused its production disappeared, but in that moment she could not care less, because she felt she was in love. It was not only physical attraction, no, but only God knew that that muscled, quick-moving body ignited her desire as no man had ever been able to. No, she was really in love with Alessandro Vinci. She could not find any words to describe what she felt. In light of that feeling, all the dangerous things that were happening around her were nothing but background noise: dark and terrible background noise, but not enough to cloud the light that obscured what was in the foreground. The two of them.

Her eyes fell on his arm muscles, on his strong hands, on his torn knuckles and then, unexpectedly and suddenly, Angeloni's words came back to her mind. She shook her head. Alessandro a murderer? Impossible! In that instant, his eyes opened wide, frightening her.

"The CD," he said. "Torre's CD!"

"I've got it," she said, laying a hand on his chest to reassure him. "It's down there, in the kitchen."

"Really? Great! We need to look for the letters that can tell us where to find the book," he continued, trying to stand up.

She took his arm and threw it around her own body, inviting him to curl up with her. "A few more minutes, please," she whispered. His arm wrapped her waist. "I was good too, wasn't I? I didn't fend off a SWAT team, but I got by, this time."

"Yeah, not too bad for somebody who was born in Cittadella."

"I was born in Padua," she replied, pretending to be offended. A shadow appeared in her mind, an unidentified alarm signal coming from her subconscious; but in that moment she was too happy to give it priority. About ten minutes later, Silvia came back.

"Where are you?"

"We're here," she answered from the bedroom, rushing to get dressed. Silvia did not show she had sensed what had happened in the apartment in her absence; she gave the eyewash to Rebecca, who used it to medicate Vinci's reddened eyes. The doctor looked at the journalist: he wanted her partner to see her as well, but he had to keep his eyelids closed for a few minutes. Her expression was more elusive, almost on pins and needles. *Trust no one.* The last warning she had received from Spinelli before his disappearance came back to her mind, making her growing sense of anxiety even worse. More calmly, Silvia asked Rebecca to tell her once more how the meeting had gone. She was listening carefully, as if she was taking mental notes, and asking her to repeat in order the events of that morning. Vinci, laying on the sofa with his eyes closed, seemed to be carefully listening to the two women's words as well.

"You were lucky that there was no other man to restrain you, while Angeloni ran to the scene of the fight against the SWAT team," Silvia remarked, abandoning for a second her professional tone of voice. "What did you say his name was?"

"I told you I don't remember!" Rebecca burst out, uneasy with the interrogation. "But I don't think he was a policeman. Maybe someone from the military. Angeloni called him Colonel..." Vinci stiffened, but without opening his eyes. "You should have seen how Torre jumped at my bag. He almost seemed...transformed. From white collar to a tiger—or better yet, a rhinoceros, seeing how big he is. He was literally holding down my bag with all his weight," she concluded, with half a smile. Then, suddenly, her face lit up triumphantly: "Achille! Colonel Achille. That's what he called him."

Vinci stood up with a jump, frightening Rebecca. "Are you sure?"

"Yes," she confirmed, thinking about it once more. "Why?"

"This changes the situation," Vinci concluded, going to his room to change. "This changes everything."

"What changes?" Rebecca asked, reading on Silvia's face the same worry. "Who's this Achille?" she asked.

"It's the former commander of the unit Alessandro was part of. If he's in this, the squad is in this."

"I need to go out, I need to think," he said, running out and almost slamming the door behind him. Had he not been Vinci the invincible, Alessandro Vinci, the man "ready for anything," Rebecca could have sworn his nervous expression was of ill-concealed fear.

**

"There's no need to keep me here," Torre said, adjusting his elegant suit with his hands.

"I'm the one who decides what's needed and what's not," Angeloni replied, to make him understand who was in control.

"I want to know what you were doing in that alley with Doctor De Cardinale and her accomplice, Alessandro Vinci, and I want to know it right now."

"Accomplice?" the man gained time, without loosing his composure. "I don't know what you're talking about. The two came in response to an ad my company published in a newspaper. They looked like…psychos to me. Especially the doctor."

Angeloni became blue in the face. "Really? You know what I think? I think if Pegasus had informed us of this meeting, we could have had the time to organize better and catch them safely. But they ran away again, Goddamn it! Either you explain to me what the fuck your company wants from them, or I'll charge you all for obstruction of justice and I'll bury you under so much shit that the heaps you'll have to pay to your lawyers to clear it will be so massive that they'll become the main factor in your fucking budget!" Torre was left speechless, scandalized by this sudden explosion of vulgarity. The possibility of clarifying the whole matter without taking legal action and making it public was growing fainter. "Tell me. What do those two have which is of so much interest for the company?"

"Letters."

"Letters?!"

"Ancient letters," Torre rapidly explained. "They were owned by Professor Spinelli and Professor Rastrini. They are...of inestimable value." A huge question mark was still branded on the commissioner's face. "They're authentics of Galileo Galilei. They're priceless."

"What does a pharmaceutical company have to do with old letters?"

"We're interested in purchasing them. The *Code Leicester* by Leonardo da Vinci was bought for about thirty-one million euros in 1994. By Bill Gates."

"So it's a monetary matter?"

"An investment," Torre corrected him.

Angeloni stared at his eyes, then he snorted, unconvinced: "I don't know what you're hiding from me. But you're at our disposal until you spit it out!" he concluded, standing up from the chair.

The man in the brown suit stayed calm, convinced he could still manage not to reveal his company's plans. He tamely let one of the policemen take him by his arm. Once he was by the door, though, he turned toward Angeloni: "You know, I just realized that Doctor De Cardinale thought I was my colleague Krupp. She said she met him a few days ago."

"So what?" Angeloni replied rudely.

"Krupp died four months ago in an accident."

20

The news bulletins the following day did not focus much on the impressive police operation that had taken place in the outskirts of the city. No hint was made at the special forces being employed, almost as if it had been a simple roundup of a few minor malefactors. That same morning, Colonel Achille's cell phone rang its monotonous tone. The official, who was in a meeting with other members of the squad, looked at the screen, annoyed, trying to identify the number of the person calling. He recognized the area code of Florence, but not the number.

"Achille," he said brusquely, sure that the call had been made as a mistake.

"Alessandro Vinci."

The colonel's expression loosened into what was supposed to be a smile, but to the eyes of everybody else in the room it looked like what it actually was: a growl. With a gesture, the other people in the room jumped up to track down the call. "You're quite difficult to find," the colonel said, trying to gain some time. "Even for some old friends like us. Difficult, but not impossible," he concluded, turning the dialogue into a threat.

"I'd like to meet you, colonel," Vinci cut in.

"You can come to the headquarters whenever you want. They're waiting for you with open arms," Achille suggested sarcastically.

"I'd prefer something more intimate," Vinci replied, checking on his watch how many seconds had passed. "Me and you, colonel: in Arcetri, Via Pian dei Giullari 42, in an hour."

"In an hour," Achille confirmed, but on the other side of the receiver the call had already been ended.

"In an hour?" the man sitting in front of him asked, with a deep voice. "Your pet lost some of his brilliance," he commented wryly, standing up and zooming in on the cartographic image of Florence on the big screen around which they were elaborating the plan. He immediately identified the area from which the call originated and the area indicated by Vinci for the meeting. His mind instantly started to elaborate the strategy to secure it. "An hour is also enough time to get bored."

A sneer reappeared on the colonel's face: "Vinci doesn't know we now have a mobile operating unit. When he left our command it was in Pisa: for all he knows, one hour is the right time to get from there to here."

"Good for us, then. Operating code confirmed?"

"Confirmed," Achille replied, emotionless.

In Via Pian dei Giullari 42, in Arcetri, is the gate of a villa called Il Gioiello—The Jewel; it was the residence where Galileo Galilei spent the last years of his life. When the squad got there, Achille understood why Vinci had chosen that place: it was relatively far, crowded with visiting tourists and with trees obstructing sight lines and creating many blind corners. There were two members of the squad for both entrances to the uphill lane and from the cobblestone pavement, and some plainclothes soldiers were in the small bar offering cheap local specialties.

The only ones wearing the tactical uniforms were the two snipers on the roofs. They had had some difficulties climbing up to their post without being seen: Arcetri is a very tiny village, up on the hills about ten kilometers from the city center of Florence, in which all inhabitants know each other by name. Managing to pass unnoticed, for the colonel's men, was the most difficult part, and their target surely knew this as well. Colonel Achille was sat in the middle of the street in front of the gate, in plain view. He did not even pretend to be interested in the marble bust of Galileo Galilei or in the plate describing the historical significance of the place. All his attention was on the cell phone in his hand, which rang right on time.

"You're here, finally. But I can't see you."

"Get on the scooter," Vinci ordered. The colonel saw a Piaggio scooter approaching, slowly driven by a black man wearing a helmet. Achille waved no, and out of the corner of his eye he saw his men, ready to spring into action, resume their positions. The guy beckoned him to take a seat behind him. "Wait," Vinci's voice stopped him, before he could climb on. "Leave your cell phone on the ground. One of your men will pick it up."

"Why should I? You said you wanted to meet me."

"Only you, Colonel. Not the whole squad. Not yet. The guy on the scooter is a taxi driver, paid in advance. If you don't get on the seat in the next three minutes, he will leave." Reluctantly, Achille obeyed and the scooter started to drive down the very tiny one-way streets of the hamlet going the wrong way. The scooter could easily move through them, while the unit's heavy vehicles could hardly pass by. The colonel immediately understood that the guy had been paid to follow a prearranged route that was thought to impede pursuit by the other components of the squad. His driver eventually stopped under the shadow of Palazzo della Signoria's tower, in the very center of Florence. He let his passenger come down and left without a word.

Achille knew that he would be reached by his squad in a few minutes, anyway, thanks to the signal system he had on himself, but his target's move had compromised their preparation for a "silent" operation. There, under the eyes of thousands of civilians, it would be complex, or even impossible, to move as his unit was trained to do. Vinci knew perfectly that, according to procedure, the normal units had not been warned of the intervention. He looked around and spotted him: the target was sitting at a café on the square, surrounded by tourists sipping their beers or cappuccinos. He beckoned him. The colonel approached and sat in the chair in front of him.

"I took the liberty of ordering a tonic water for you as well," Alessandro welcomed him. Achille sipped his drink, taking as much time as he could, to give his men the time to reach him.

"You need to come with me. You know it is the only way this can end."

"They're setting me up," Vinci said.

"I've already heard this," the colonel harshly replied.

"You're still convinced I'm dirty, aren't you? That I was responsible for the attack on the judge. I was cleared. They almost killed me," he reminded him.

"That's true, the Court of Enquiry absolved you; but you're the only survivor. And what about this mess? Only coincidence? You know what I think about coincidence."

Alessandro wished he could reply, but he knew he only had a few minutes left before the rest of the squad reached them. "This time there's more to it than just me, something more important. I'm talking about a pandemic that could hit thousands, maybe millions of people. If you don't give me a few days of freedom, we could lose the opportunity of preventing it before it explodes. I only ask you for a week of truce; then I'll give myself up to the police or to the squad, as you prefer."

Achille's sneering smile came back on his face. "Sorry, son. You're under arrest. You have a gun pointed at you under the table. Now we'll move from here, like two friends, and we'll wait for the van. Then you'll explain everything to the police, to a psychiatrist, or to whomever you want. Get up," he ordered, hitting the young man's thigh with his weapon.

"We're going nowhere," Vinci hissed. Achille recognized the behavior; it was the behavior all of his best men had: an ice-cool calm which masked the most lethal intents. He knew something was about to happen and he got ready to pull the trigger. "Do you see that reflection on the roof?" he asked, indicating a spot behind his shoulders. "No trick," he insisted, raising his hands to show he was unarmed.

Achille turned for a fraction of second, then he turned back to stare at Vinci. "I could shoot you now, before he has time to hit me," the colonel replied, glimpsing a reflection of the sun on what could be a rifle pointed at him.

"And who said you're the target?" Vinci replied with a gelid smile, while a waitress approached the table.

"Do you need anything?" she asked, talking to the older man. Achille shook his head in refusal. Vinci distractedly took the receipt that the waitress handed out to him and did not stop staring at the colonel.

"Would you shoot at civilians?" the man asked, making the gun disappear under his jacket so rapidly that none of the other customers seemed to have noticed him.

"Not if I stand up and leave this place by myself in ten seconds from now."

"It could be a bluff," Achille replied. "A metallic reflection on the table."

"In that case, you should wonder if I'm really as dangerous as you think," Vinci concluded, slowly standing up from the table and signing the credit card receipt he had left as a payment.

"If you leave I won't be able to guarantee your safety," Achille told him, taking a quick look towards Via dei Calzaiuoli. "A policeman was killed. You know what that means."

"Code Omega?" Vinci asked.

"Affirmative," Achille concluded.

Vinci slightly looked up, towards the roof behind the colonel's shoulders: "If you keep sitting here for five minutes, and nobody follows me, everything will be all right," he said, rapidly leaving the bar and disappearing in the crowd.

Less than a minute later, Achille was reached by the first two men. They exchanged a few words with the colonel and the first one received a communication on the radio: "Negative, sir. There's no sniper on the roof. Just a piece of metal." Then he turned towards Achille: "It's a real shame to let him go like that, Colonel. Angelo could have shot him at any moment."

The fake waitress, freeing herself from the café uniform, smiled back. "I was ready, but the colonel didn't give the order," she said defensively. Then her eyes fell to the receipt. "Colonel," she said, handing out to her what she initially thought was just a signature on the credit card payment. Achille read the receipt and handed it to the other man. It said: "Great disguise. Almost perfect." The young man smiled, with the same sneer Achille had.

**

It's not good. It's not good at all, Vinci thought as he sneaked off, making sure he was not being followed. A code Omega was on his head: his squad would not stop until he was killed. He had no time to waste. Weaving among the tourists and changing direction and pace several times, he finally reached the rented apartment. He and Rebecca had to leave Florence as soon as possible. They would examine Pegasus' letters along the way, and if they discovered Maffini's last destination, they had to try to recover what they were looking for; otherwise, he would have to separate Rebecca from him. With a code Omega on his head, she was in danger as well; then he remembered about the two policemen who attacked her, in the wood. *The squad would never hit somebody who's not a target*, he thought. Rebecca had better stay with him until the end; it was the safest option. Maybe.

Before going back into the apartment, he went to the pickup. He had parked it in a side alley, with other cars, covering it up with a large plastic tarp he had found in a garage in Silvia's apartment building; one of those tarps people use to cover their cars from the sun. To make it more plausible, he had written a license plate number with a marker. It was an expedient many car owners used to avoid the blanket being stolen from other people to cover their own cars: with the license plate written in plain view, they would have been discovered. Obviously, Vinci had written a different license plate number. As soon as he entered the narrow alley, though, a bad surprise was waiting for him: right behind his pickup there was a car from the local police. A traffic policeman had lifted the cover up and was checking the real license plate, while the other in the car was communicating with the headquarters through the radio. He kept walking without stopping: the police had probably spread the order to check all the vehicles which could correspond to the description of his own and the move had paid off. One more obstacle. He reached the apartment and jumped up the stairs, knocking loudly on the door.

"We need to go," he began without a big preamble when he walked in.

"We know where the grave is!" the two women said as a reply, almost in unison. They waved Pegasus' CD in front of him; they had been studying it up until that moment. "It's in Switzerland! In Lausanne!" He did not bat an eye.

208

"The squad is hunting me," he only said. Silvia's face looked dismayed, and Rebecca was able to understand how bad the situation was. "We'll proceed to Switzerland," Vinci said, arranging his bag. He counted some banknotes, and handed them to the doctor, keeping only a few. "There's not much left, since they found us in the motel, but it should be enough to end our search. Do you want to come with me, Rebecca? I'd rather have you come with me, but you need to tell me what you want to do. I know now that the squad has targeted me, and they won't stop until they catch me. Dead or alive."

"Dead, you mean," Silvia intervened. "We know very well that they won't risk a public trail to reveal the existence of the unit." The silence she obtained from Vinci was a very significant reply.

"The last time we separated they shot at me. I'm coming with you," Rebecca decided, as confused as she was from the last events, and especially by the commissioner's words.

"The squad will never miss their target, I can grant you that," Vinci reassured her, worried and happy at the same time by her choice.

"Then they won't kill an innocent. Angeloni doesn't believe the charges against me and while we're together you will be safer. They won't be able to kill you with me so close to you...right?" Vinci smiled, to reassure her. Of course they could, but he did not see any reason to tell her.

"We'll use my car," Silvia suggested.

"No, Silvia, you're not coming. There's no reason to expose you to this risk, and the less you're involved, the more useful you'll be to us."

"Less involved than this, you mean?" she asked, indicating with a gesture the apartment she had rented for them in her name.

"You understand very well what I mean." His expression was very serious and Silvia recognized it; it was the same expression with which he had left her once already. And once more, she had to step back. She looked at Rebecca and him leaving the apartment in a rush, with the few bags they had.

She smiled in annoyance when he bid her farewell with a kiss on her forehead: "Be careful," she whispered to him while he went down the stairs. She looked out the window and watched her car leave and turn the corner. Immediately she grabbed her cell phone and dialed a number. On the other end of the receiver, the other person picked up on the first ring: "Patrioti?"

The car with Rebecca and Vinci in it left Florence and got on the highway towards Milan. From here, deviating to the east, they would proceed towards Aosta and the Gotthard Tunnel, to reach Switzerland. Along the curvy development of the A1 highway in the Apennines, the constant and almost monotonous rhythm of the car made Rebecca fall asleep in spite of the excitement of recent events. Alessandro knew he had to keep as much distance as possible between him and the squad, and he drove for the couple hundred kilometers with his eyes glued to the odometer, trying to speed as much as possible whilst trying to avoid exceeding the speed limit and attracting the attention of the local police. He continually checked the rearview mirror, to make sure they were not being followed. After driving by Milan and Novara, the darkness and the weariness added to the burning feeling which had not left his eyes after he was exposed to the teargas the day before, in spite of Rebecca's treatment. Vinci realized he was blinking more and more, and that it was getting more difficult for him to keep them open. He almost dozed off, but he immediately regained control of his car.

Roused by adrenaline, he watched Rebecca, still sleeping beside him, and cursed himself for the unnecessary risk he had put both of them through. He reduced the speed and resigned himself to stop at a service station. He looked for a spot far away from the obvious security cameras and, after a last glance around to make sure the area was reasonably safe, he laid his head on the seat and allowed himself some restless sleep.

21

When Alessandro woke up, the sun was rising and Rebecca was still
sleeping beside him. He could feel her regular breath, and this calmed
him down. He left the car and headed towards the café. The crisp air
and the wonderful sight of the Alps, which towered above them, had
the effect of clearing his mind for a moment of the escape strategies, of
the constant tension, of the responsibility that was gripping him. For
the first time in days, what he was missing was not the weight of his
gun in his trousers, but the weight of his camera. At that time, rays of
sunlight were peeking out over the background of the highest mountain
range in Europe, which stood out in the clear sky, magnificent and
vivid. He found himself studying the possible framing of the picture,
the most effective composition, and he regretted having left his reflex
camera in Florence. It was one of the very few times he was not carrying
it since he had developed a passion for photography.

Thinking about his hobby for a moment, Alessandro thought about
himself and went through his whole life until that moment as if he were
the main character of a movie: the years in the military, the hard climb
which had allowed him to re-emerge after the abyss of violence his life
had turned into, the daily fight to free himself from that darkness, until
the day he had fallen back into it when Rebecca had knocked at his
apartment door. He felt like a heroin addict, for which a single dose
had sufficed to wipe out years and years of improvement, to let him fall
back into his addiction. He clenched his fists energetically, looking at

that sunrise through the eyes he had promised himself he would use to look at his new life: the eyes of the academic and the photographer searching for beauty, not the eyes of a killer. He swore to himself that he would not fall back into it. And Rebecca...What had he made her endure, with his recent silences, his harshness. He did not want to lose her. She was special: another possibility for a future without loneliness. He swore to himself he would not give up the opportunity this time.

A growing sunray through the window woke her up. A little in pain from the awkward position she had slept in, she tried to stretch her muscles and figure out where they were, but she only understood that it was a service station. Alessandro had left the cabin so silently that, if it had not been for the closing of the door, she would not even have noticed it. The usual ninja. So she woke up alone, dealing with something that had bothered her thoughts since the day before, but that she had not been able to completely focus on until then. Then she suddenly got it: she remembered Alessandro's words, after they had made love at Silvia's place, happy to still be alive: "Not too bad for somebody who was born in Cittadella." But she was born in Padua. That was what her ID said, that is what was written on her Facebook profile. The only place where he could have read about Cittadella was the university website; but she had asked to correct that months before their first encounter in Professor Benatti's office.

Trust no one. Spinelli's words were digging into her and they were adding to Angeloni's words. What if the commissioner was telling the truth about the gun? Was it really the one that had killed Rastrini? And why would Angeloni feel the need to lie to her, in the moment in which he was sure he had caught them both? An interrogation strategy to weaken their mutual trust? Maybe. But what if it was not like that? Rebecca focused to recall to her mind all the details of the conversation with the commissioner.

213

He had asked her if she was sure that he had always been with her while the murders were being committed. Initially she could have sworn it was like that, but thinking about it once more she realized she was wrong: for the murders committed after she had knocked on his door, she could not swear Alessandro was with her. In Padua he had gone out to get pizzas, when Menin was killed, and he was also quite late! They were not together in Florence either, the evening Professor Rastrini was shot; he had insisted on going out alone to look for the CD. Nonetheless, it seemed just as impossible to her to think that Alessandro was able to kill, or better, to be a cool-headed killer. Both Alessandro and his journalist friend had told her about his secret past and she had no doubts he would be more than ready to get blood on his hands, but with a uniform on, and for the public good.

Alessandro. But…what about Night? The mercenary, fanatical about the metal music that had deafened her during their first journey in the pickup? The one who had bitten and taken her almost to the point of hurting her? In that moment, she had found it exciting, but now it did not look like a game anymore, a spicy addiction to their already stimulating research. To her it looked almost like…schizophrenia. More and more anxious, Rebecca wondered if the shock he had endured after the attack had not created the personality of Vinci the academic. Even though she had not specialized in psychiatry, she knew that strong traumas could cause a splitting of personality. If that was the case, in theory it was possible that Spinelli's kidnapping had brought back up his main personality: the military man, the murderer, and maybe this one had taken control of the other. She could testify to the academic's innocence by staking her life on it, but what about the other? While she ruminated, she saw Vinci approach the car with two paper cups and a white-and-red bag. He did not seem like the same man from the night before: he was walking in a different way, much more relaxed, and he almost smiled, something she had not seen him do for about two days. Her anxiety increased even more with that new change.

"Breakfast," Alessandro said jovially, handing her a smoking hot cappuccino and a croissant in the paper bag. She took them and sipped her hot drink, hardly thanking him. "You know," he said, "I'm happy to be with you through all this…"

"I need to go to the toilet," she said turning pale, and rapidly opening the door wide. She left the car, her breakfast and her astounded interlocutor behind.

"Deputy Commissioner Angeloni?" The commissioner turned towards his secretary peeking in from the door and he snorted, annoyed. She mimed the gesture of a phone call. "It's a certain Doctor De Cardinale. She says it's important."

"De Cardinale?! Pass me the call, right now!" he screamed almost falling down from his chair to run to the telephone. "Hello?"

"Was that gun really used to kill Professor Rastrini?" Rebecca asked without any preamble.

"I swear it on my mother," the commissioner assured her, with a hand on the receiver, while he frenetically ordered his collaborators to track down the call. "Where are you?" he asked, trying to make her talk.

"I don't want him to be hurt," she said.

"Then you need to give yourselves up to the police and as soon as possible. You have no clue who is chasing you." *I do know, very well,* she though, thinking about Achille's squad. "Tell me where you are and in fifteen minutes everything will be over," the policeman assured her. "Nobody will be hurt." Rebecca was about to reply, but then she though once more about the moment he had opened his door to her, helping her in the worst moment of her life; she thought about all the times he had protected and loved her, she thought about the way he had made her feel through those days. *My God, what am I doing?* she asked herself, hanging up the phone. "Hello? Hello? Damn it! Tell me you tracked her down!" Angeloni begged his technicians.

"It's a public phone at the service station near Aosta," a subordinate triumphantly replied.

At that news, the commissioner growled, rather than smiled: "I want checkpoints at every toll booth and a helicopter ready to leave in ten minutes!"

Almost three quarters of an hour later, the coffee had got cold, just like the cappuccino he had brought Rebecca. Alessandro was left astounded, waiting for her to come back. He did not expect a reaction like that, not after he had bared himself to her as much as he had. Wounded and disconcerted, he focused back on the situation they were in. His trained eye started to examine their surroundings, looking for possible threats. As if he had perceived it in advance, a helicopter stood out in the distance. Backlit like that, he could not make out if it was a police helicopter or not, but his senses were alerted. He watched an older couple heading towards him with suspicion. The man was probably over sixty-five years old, and he was walking arm in arm with a smiling ruddy old lady, probably his wife. To his surprise, he realized Rebecca was walking with him.

"Here, dear, we finally found a ride," she said, with an unnaturally relieved tone of voice. Alessandro looked at her with a questioning glance. He was about to talk, but she cut him off: "We can leave the car here and call the tow truck to come for the car," she said, winking at him. "I met this very kind couple in the bathroom and they're also heading to Lausanne; we'll be able to get there in time for my sister's wedding!" Then she approached him close enough for the older couple not to hear them, and she whispered, "I heard the radio inside the bar. They announced some checkpoints." Alessandro was surprised and alarmed by the news, but if he had noticed her blushing, he did not show it.

He laid his gaze on the radiant expression of the two elderly people who were getting into the car parked beside them: a gray station wagon with a Swiss license plate. He considered them harmless and he thanked the fact that they were foreigners and old enough not to know that hitchhiking is forbidden on Italian highways. He pulled out his best smile, grabbed the bags from the trunk and sat in the back seat of the car beside Rebecca, warmly thanking their two hosts. Once he was in the car, he watched the man pull out of the service station and sighed in relief when he saw him access the ramp bringing them back to the highway a few seconds before the police helicopter came to examine the whole service station from above, without noting his presence at all. They traveled the following kilometers with relative ease; the man was driving calmly, almost making them falling asleep. The woman at times struck up conversation, to which Rebecca replied with a jovial tone: if the old woman had sensed the hidden tension in her words, she did not show it. Alessandro was continuously looking at the street and the rearview mirrors. All of a sudden the car slowed down, almost stopping, a couple of kilometers before the exit of Aosta East.

"It's probably an accident," the man said, unaware.

"Or a checkpoint," Vinci replied. The sight off the sirens' lights confirmed his suspicions. An impressive deployment of police cars and trucks framed the military roadblocks, which had channeled the traffic so vehicles could proceed only after being inspected by agents armed with machine guns and protected by body armor.

"What happened?" the woman asked, curious and worried. The two did not reply, stiffening in their seats. When the motionless car was reached by an agent, Vinci lay himself across the seat, pretending to be relaxed. Rebecca's fingers frenetically tightened on his fingers, and he kept her hand in his, forcing her to relax against the seat as well, so as not to give the impression of fearing the checkpoint and rouse suspicions. If they were identified, they could never escape. With that huge deployment of forces, the only solution was to surrender.

The policeman who approached them had his service weapon on his arm, a machine gun Beretta M12, well aware of its weight. He had been informed, as had all his colleagues, that the male suspect was armed and very dangerous and the close contact with his weapon made him feel safer. He approached the car with the Swiss license plate and stared at the old driver: he saw his wife beside him and probably his daughter with her boyfriend in the backseats. He only gave them a second of his attention, then he examined the following car, in which he saw what looked like a young couple, signaling them to move on.

22

They crossed the artificial border between Italy and Switzerland without even being checked at customs, luckily, and the Great St. Bernard Tunnel swallowed them into its almost seventeen kilometers dug through the bowels of the Alps. The tunnel was spacious and well-lit, but Rebecca could not avoid a growing sense of claustrophobia. She felt confused, furious with herself and guilty. She had been an idiot to let Angeloni's words spoil her trust in Alessandro. Or maybe she was an idiot for being there, still sitting beside a schizophrenic murderer. Nonetheless, a few moments before, she had squeezed his hand like a frightened little boy does with his mother. In other words, she was an idiot. With one impulsive telephone call, she had put all their efforts up to that moment at risk, compromising their quest and what they hoped to obtain in order to save millions of people.

The worst thing, though, was the knowledge that when Alessandro found out about what she had done, he would lose all faith in her, and Silvia had explained to her very well what the consequences would be. And how could she blame him? Even she did not trust herself anymore. Once they were out of the tunnel, Alessandro offered to take his shift driving, and the old man gratefully accepted. They reached Lausanne that way: from the distance, the serene Lake Geneva reflected the sky and the higher mountaintops still covered with snow. They went through the outskirts of the city and Alessandro pulled over by a car rental. They greeted and thanked the kind old couple, but not before

219

they had exchanged their respective addresses. A fake one, on the young couple's part.

"We need a car," Alessandro said, watching the old couple leave and raising his worried gaze towards the sign of the rental car agency.

"We...did you spend the money?"

"It's not just that," he replied, considering the little amount of money that was left in his pocket. "They'll surely ask to hold onto a credit card," he concluded, taking a Visa out of his wallet.

"And that one's not covered?"

"It is covered, but it will activate a signal which the squad will see. We'll have them close in on us way before we know it."

"But we're abroad!" Rebecca objected. "Won't they have jurisdiction problems?"

"Only if they get caught," Vinci replied. "On the other hand, we can't walk," he concluded, resolutely stepping into the agency. They came out of it shortly after, driving a Chrysler Cruiser of an indefinite green color: the best compromise they could reach between their needs and the car rental's immediate availability. Soon after, they passed by the shop of a mobile operator.

"Stop," Rebecca said indicating it. He slowed down, pulling over beside the sidewalk, with a questioning look. "We could buy a SIM card for my phone," she continued.

"You don't even have an ID."

"But you do; and we could pay cash, withdrawing it with your credit card, since it's blown anyway. Think about it, we could get separated and need to communicate."

Alessandro agreed and, a few minutes later, Rebecca put the box containing her new SIM card in the spacious bag Silvia had lent her, the same one she had at the meeting with Torre. She did not insert the card immediately: she would wait for a moment of quiet, but in the meantime she anticipated the moment her iPhone would be brought back to life.

"How do we find the merchant's tomb?" she asked, once they were back in the car. "Maybe at the cemetery? Will there be some kind of registry?"

"The cemeteries as we know them are quite a recent custom," Alessandro replied, following the GPS through the ordered streets of the Swiss city. "If I remember well, from after the French Revolution. Before then, the dead were buried in churches, or immediately around them."

"My God," she let go. "It will be impossible to find the merchant's tomb. We don't even know exactly when he died…"

"We don't," he tried to reassure her. "But maybe somebody does."

The car climbed the steep Rue Louis-Auguste Curtat, till it reached one of the highest points of the city, right beside the Lausanne Cathedral. The awe-inspiring Gothic cathedral loomed over them and over the city sprawled at its feet. The southern-facing side, where they were in that moment, was partly covered with scaffolding; there were renovations in progress, probably. Alessandro parked in a pay parking area, then he took out his cell phone, and once he found the number he was looking for he dialed it. A voice replied in French and Alessandro, with some difficulties, was able to get the person he was looking for on the line: Grégoire Toso, the curator of the cathedral. Alessandro introduced himself with his real name and some small talk followed. Luckily the curator spoke Italian very well. When Alessandro expressed his request, he replied with great willingness: "Of course you can consult our register. What day are you intending to come to Lausanne?"

"Well, actually, I'd be grateful to you if I could consult them…this afternoon?" Then, before the other man could reply, he added: "My fiancée torments me because I'm always working: I had to make up a vacation in Switzerland to avoid trouble…I don't know if you can

221

understand. I'm already risking a fight with her, if I spend a few hours consulting the registers; it will cost me a fortune with her shopping…We'll be leaving for Geneva tomorrow." He held his breath, while on the other end of the receiver the curator considered the situation and Rebecca gave him a dirty look for his chauvinist lie.

"It's quite an unusual request…but I'll try to help you, for the good of your marriage. We could meet around five in my office?"

"That would be perfect, thank you so much," Alessandro replied, looking for a pen to note down the address the curator gave him. According to their smartphone, the office was on their right. They decided not to stay there, though, and continued their descent, which distanced them from the cathedral and brought them inside the city.

"All right, now you can explain to your insensitive fiancée what the hell you think you're doing," Rebecca attacked him, serious and amused at the same time.

"Male solidarity always works, as you can see, and it just granted us an appointment," he justified.

"For what?" she insisted.

"To consult the parish registers."

"The…parish registers? Don't we have anything better?"

"Not for the seventeenth century, unfortunately. Until after the French Revolution, the only institution that kept records of births, deaths, marriages, children and everything else was the Church. Those registers are a treasure trove of information for historians. Without them, we would lose a large share of European memory."

"We'll waste a lot of time among dusty papers, though," the doctor moaned.

"Maybe not. We could narrow the field: we know the plague stormed Europe starting in about 1630. At that time, Virgilio Donati had to be alive, if he is the one who introduced it in Europe. And Galileo died in 1642. We only have to deal with twelve years."

"That's definitely a less terrifying prospect. In a city like this one, in twelve years, with about two deaths per week, we will have to leaf through…about one thousand five hundred names," she calculated, relieved. "And by the way…I'll save that afternoon of shopping for another day!" They found a modest hotel in the outskirts and, after eating something, they tried to kill the hours separating them from the meeting. Alessandro stretched out on the sofa, still unsure of how to behave with Rebecca after her reaction that morning. She walked up and down the length of the room, checking and rechecking her own calculations with her laptop, trying to elude his gaze as much as possible.

Grégoire Toso was a sixty-year-old lively but very elegant man—almost affected, and with friendly manners. He spoke Italian perfectly, with only a slight French inflection. He received them in his office and offered the young scholar and his suffocating fiancée a small refreshment, with exquisite chocolates and thirst-quenching fruit juices. Alessandro tried to accelerate the procedure by showing his university ID.

"Usually we display the antique records only after an official request by the university," Toso objected, still perplexed.

"It's still personal research," Alessandro justified himself. "I'm in the preparatory phase of my study on the commercial movements of the sixteenth and seventeenth centuries. If I find enough data, I'll be able to officially start my research."

"I understand," the man said hesitantly, examining the ID. "I'll have to make a copy of this."

"Sure."

Toso stood up, showing the way to the archives in the basement of the big building. He turned on the weak lights, which illuminated a huge room. Right at the center stood a large number of volumes, more or less antique, on big metal shelving units. Some faded writing indicated bibliographical or temporal references. When the eyes of the two guests adjusted to the dim light, they were able to glimpse on the walls some indicators of temperature and humidity: they were in a controlled environment, to ensure the survival of the documents kept there. The curator approached a computer, located in a corner of the library, almost invisible.

"I'd like to start with the mortuary registers from 1600 to 1650," Alessandro explained.

Typing on the keyboard, the curator raised his eyebrow and said, "I'm afraid an afternoon of shopping won't be enough," printing the bibliographical references. Then he walked along the corridors, looking for the corresponding section.

"What does that mean?" Rebecca asked, whispering.

"It's the years of the plague," Alessandro replied. "There were tens of thousands of deaths all around Europe."

"You knew that!" she accused him, frightened by the enormity of the task, while they reached a shelf and Grégoire Toso, with a gesture, indicated the mountain of volumes containing the registers concerning the period they were interested in. He gave them some cotton gloves and made sure Alessandro would handle the first volume correctly, the register for the year 1630. He invited them to sit down at a close-by big desk in hardwood. He passed a second chair to the woman, who seemed increasingly embittered, and he left to copy Alessandro's ID. The dusty and stained pages opened creaking at Vinci's expert touch, revealing a series of names handwritten in antique ink, with an almost unintelligible handwriting for the inexpert eyes of Rebecca. Each recorded death had the first name and family name of the deceased, his birth date, and the date of his death, followed by a cross. Struggling to understand the writings and trying to avoid the depression caused by the huge amount of work awaiting them, Rebecca asked: "What are those figures beside the name?"

"It's the donation the deceased have left to the Church, in exchange for prayers and intercessions," Alessandro replied, not frightened at all, and even excited for that research. "Money and lands are listed, and even castles. The critics of the Church call these 'fire insurances,' meaning insurance against the flames of Hell. Back then, priests were the only ones who could perform the task of notaries, and this facilitated the passage of earthly possessions to the Church. In some cases it functioned as a protection of the capital: the ecclesiastical possessions were the only ones safe from the arbitrary acts of the aristocracy, and protected from the looting of soldiers during their military campaigns. The owners transferred their possessions to the Church, limiting themselves to benefitting from their revenues until their deaths. Something similar to a bare ownership."

"What do the last letters in the row mean?"

"That's what we're interested in: the place where the remains of these people rest after their burial. In the apses of the churches the relics of the saints are kept and venerated, and the richest people battled to be buried beside them, or at least, according to their means, inside the church or in the immediate proximity, convinced that the prayers recited there every day would grant them a step forward towards the salvation of their souls. The majority of them, who could not dispose of huge means, were buried in mass graves, but always around the church. Vincenzo Donati was a rich merchant: that's why it's logical to suppose that he wanted to ensure for himself a burial inside the cathedral."

"I don't even want to think about the smell of those mass graves," Rebecca remarked, horrified. "And think about how the diseases could spread..." Then a sudden thought hit her: "During the plague, there were dozens of deaths per day and the corpses were all thrown in huge mass graves. What if the merchant and his wife were also buried like that? We would never find them!"

"No, that's not how it went, don't you remember? Maffini, the man sent from Galileo to print the book abroad wrote he left it in Donati's grave. He found it, therefore the merchant was not buried in a mass grave. Let's go on looking for him." After a time which seemed infinite to Rebecca, they had only finished the first tome. Rebecca put it back and picked up the second one, which she passed on to Alessandro. She took one for herself, sat in front of Alessandro and started to read, reluctantly. "I found it!" Alessandro screamed all of a sudden, startling her. Rebecca immediately rushed to his side, full of hope.

"The merchant?"

"No," he replied, with his expression of triumph rapidly turning into a depressed sneer. "His wife, Henrietta Bermann. You see?" he said, pointing at the faded words with which her death and her marriage with the merchant had been recorded. Beside her name there was a big P.

"It stands for *pestilentia*, plague," Alessandro confirmed, "and since there is no indication about her burial, it means she was buried in a mass grave." Rebecca slowly understood the meaning of his words: without the amulet, which must have been buried together with the person to which it had been given as a gift, without the woman's body, or any biological specimen deriving from the contact with the extraterrestrial microorganism, their whole quest meant nothing anymore. It was impossible, unthinkable to find it anywhere else; nobody could have granted it was really the virus they were looking for. End of their mission. End of everything; even of the hope of finding a vaccine. She swallowed dryly, seeing her astonished expression mirrored in Alessandro's.

"Wait!" he shouted out. "Maffini wrote he left the manuscript in Virgilio Donati's grave, beside his wife's grave. The wife's grave must be somewhere! Let's find Donati's grave and we'll find both." Alessandro resumed reading with even more zeal. Rebecca did the same, and a little while later, they were lucky: choosing by chance a volume from 1641; her eyes fell on a name. She read it once, twice, ten times to make sure she was not wrong: "Alessandro, here it is!" she said out loud. "Virgilio Donati! It's quite readable, he's here…"

Vinci almost fell from his chair from the haste of standing up to check. "Yes, that's him! Deceased on September 15, 1641. Falling from a staircase," he confirmed. "We have to call the curator."

"I'm happy you were so fortunate," Toso congratulated them, seeing their radiant expressions and taking a look to the register himself.

"Could you explain to us what these letters mean? It's the localization of his burial, right?" Alessandro asked.

The curator dwelled on the faded writing for a few seconds, then he confirmed: "Yes, he's buried in our cathedral, more or less…yes, he's actually exactly in the area under renovation right now," he concluded, lowering his reading glasses. "A generous merchant," he commented. "He left all of his belongings to the Church. Including a salt mine."

"Salt?" Rebecca asked.

"Yes, around here it was as precious as gold, back then. Switzerland is far away from the sea and the salt had to be transferred in a caravan by merchants, who sold it at a very high price, or it had to be extracted from the rare salt mines, like this one." He remained silent for a moment, thoughtful. "You know what? I think I've heard about this mine in particular. Actually, I'm sure I have. It's a few kilometers away from the city, once they held religious ceremonies there. Now I understand why," he concluded, continuing his reading of the register. "It's a specific request by the donator, Virgilio Donati. That's strange, usually the moribund person would request the mass to be celebrated in his name in the cathedral. Anyway, the mine now belongs to a secular institution and it became a tourist attraction," he informed them, preceding them up the stairs which would bring them out of the archive.

The light of the sunset had almost disappeared and the scaffolding which clashed with the Gothic profile of the cathedral, on the southern side, was well visible, illuminated by safety lights. The Gothic building was impressive: the nave and the two aisles were beautified by the colorful stained-glass windows on which the lives of saints were depicted, and the few reddish lights that still reflected on the rose window behind the altar increased its charm. The curator turned on some electric lights, which ruthlessly lit up the part of the aisle covered by the scaffolding, internally and externally. On the whole flooring, brightened by a flashlight Toso had brought with him, they could glimpse the epitaphs of the rich and lucky people who could afford a front-row seat on Judgment Day. "There it is." He pointed, after raising the cloth concealing the renovation work from sight. "The area you're looking for is just around here." Rebecca and Alessandro were expecting to see graves in full view, but their expectations were disappointed. A pile of detritus was covering the flooring, hiding everything. Careless of the dejection on their faces, the curator added: "If you can convince your fiancée, tomorrow morning you can come here and continue your research. Even though I really don't understand of what use discovering an epitaph could be for you."

Rebecca was about to reply, but Alessandro held her back by gently grabbing her arm, understanding on the fly the insinuation in their host's behavior. "Thank you, you've been really kind," he ceded, pulling out his most charming manners, which irritated the woman beside him a great deal. "If we decide to conclude our research, could we contact you at your number tomorrow?"

"Of course," the man kindly said, accompanying them outside and closing the cathedral's gate behind them.

Once they were back in the car, Rebecca attacked him: "We can't wait for tomorrow, we have no time! The Italian police are surely in touch with the Swiss police already. We'll be fugitives here too, before long."

"Probably; but what did you want to do? Violate a grave in front of its curator?"

"What will we do, then?"

"Let's eat something, rest for a couple of hours and come back when nobody's here anymore."

23

Late into the night, the air was much cooler than what they had breathed during those humid weeks in Italy. Several stage lights illuminated the cathedral, and their hopes of moving unnoticed, protected by darkness, vanished. Rebecca was tired, but excited. Unlike Vinci, she had not slept in the previous hours. She feared the success of their nighttime challenge, even more than she feared its failure. If they really found the book, what would Alessandro do? Since she had dragged him into this madness, he said he was able to collaborate in exchange for a part of the revenues of the discovery. Until two days before she had never thought about it, but now she was wondering what he would do; what if he decided he was satisfied with that half-success and vanished without a trace? And how could she blame him, if he decided to take advantage of the fact that they had expatriated to escape from the squad that was chasing after him to kill him?

That evening, after greeting the curator, they had pretended to take a walk around the cathedral, arm in arm, like two lovers on their holiday, but their aim was actually to locate all the security cameras: there were two of them, but Alessandro was not particularly worried about them. They parked the car at a short distance from the cathedral, and they climbed up a side street to reach the Gothic monument. Alessandro looked for the camera on that side and took Rebecca by the hand, guiding her laterally at first, towards the corner which turned over to the facade, almost crawling against the wall, until they reached the scaffolding. An illustrated sign warned that the scaffolding was alarmed, but Vinci handled the wires and was able to deactivate the security system in a very short time.

Then, covered by the cloth that protected the scaffolding, they climbed as silently as possible, until they reached one of the stained-glass windows. That afternoon they had both noticed that it had been partially removed, probably to be restored. The hole in the wall was protected by another layer of plastic material, but for the young man it was extremely easy to remove it enough to pass through. He swiftly sneaked in the opening and beckoned Rebecca to follow him. She obeyed, slowed down by the capacious shoulder bag Silvia had lent her and by its necessary contents. Once they had passed onto the scaffolding on the other side of the stained-glass window, they climbed down with caution, helped by the weak light of a flashlight.

Once on the ground, they started to remove the detritus hiding the flooring with the tools they found in the renovation site inside. The writings on the tombs appeared faded, eroded by the footsteps of thousands of feet over the centuries. Their work continued silently, in spite of the echo produced by the ancient walls, which amplified even the smallest noise. Then, some writing materialized in front of their eyes, the inscription with the name they were looking for: VIRGILIO DONATI. They both held their breath at that discovery. They looked at each other, triumphantly. That was the end of their quest, because right beside the gravestone lay another one, this too in pink marble, on which the name Henrietta Bermann was inscribed.

"You choose," Alessandro said, recovering from the shock caused by the discovery. "Where do we start from?"

Rebecca replied faster than he expected. "From Donati's grave…" and she stopped before finishing her sentence. Alessandro stared at her without understanding the reason for her weird behavior, once more. In the last two days, she seemed distracted, tense, as if she wanted to distance herself from him. Around them, there certainly were more than enough tools to open the grave: he found a heavy hammer and a long scalpel, and he started by removing the concrete framing the merchant's gravestone. The stone crumbled easily, crumbling over his hands and on Rebecca's, who was trying to remove the detritus to make the procedure faster. Sweeping the dust and the rubble with a broom and with her hands, she cleaned the gravestone beside the merchant's, the one housing the remains of his wife. She asked herself if the man ever imagined he was the involuntary cause of her death, and of the death of so many thousands of people. She pictured him offering her the necklace as a gift, with the fragment of meteorite mounted on it, literally delivering her the instrument of her death.

She shook her head, carrying on cleaning the dust, until she discovered a moving dedication, the last thought of affection her husband had consecrated to her and which had outlived the centuries: SALE AD COELUM. A new slam of the hammer brought her back to reality. Her heart pounded and not only from the excitement of the discovery. While their efforts were barely perceptible until then, Alessandro's blows were now louder and louder, echoing and resounding in her head and in the whole nave. There was no alternative, but they had to hurry up, because the more the time passed, the more likely it was for a passerby, a priest or a patrolling policeman to hear them.

"Finally," Alessandro said, dripping with sweat, after the last hammer blow. "The gravestone should be open." He still used the shovel and a long bar, leveraging on the surrounding stone, until the marble covering slid down, in a precarious balance, opening the entrance of the tomb, then he pointed the flashlight down at the bottom. They held their breath again, excited. Inside, the darkened wood coffin had surprisingly remained intact, with just a few signs of buckling on the bottom.

"Wait," Rebecca said, before the young man could step forward towards the coffin. She looked inside the bag and took out two face masks with FFP3 filters, the ones used when handling toxic or carcinogenic substances. The most effective protection they could find in a pharmacy, which Silvia had procured for them at her behest the day before. Rebecca wore one, showing Alessandro how to secure his own to allow correct adherence to his face: "In the abdomen there are germs which can be pathogenic if they're breathed in and once the host has died, they proliferate and overcome the defensive barriers of the intestinal mucosa. They're the ones to cause the putrefaction of the corpse," she explained.

"And they can survive for years?"

"Even for centuries, as spores," she replied, wearing latex gloves and handing a package to him as well. He wore them and jumped down into the grave, closely followed by Rebecca. Then, he prepared to examine the coffin, assisted by the flashlight.

"It's not sealed," he told her.

"What does that mean?"

"All coffins were sealed, to avoid the smell of the decomposing corpse to cause the 'mala aria,' or bad air, which could infect the living. Nonetheless, the faithful often lamented a terrible smell coming from the flooring of the churches and from their cloisters. That shouldn't have been surprising, since they were walking around on a cemetery. The fact that the seal is missing, confirms Maffini's version. The tomb was opened. Maybe even by him." He looked at it once more, not happy at all about what he expected to find, as he removed the top and broke it with a shovel. When he breathed again, he was surprised to realize he smelled nothing of what he feared, no terrible stink of putrefaction, only an unpleasant and sweetish stuffy smell. Probably that was due to the lack of the seal. He pointed the flashlight at the inside again and withheld a grimace of disgust, just like Rebecca.

Virgilio Donati's corpse lay there, mummified, grotesquely covered by what probably was his best attire. Now that the death had shrunken the tissues, the outfit drooped on the gaunt limbs. Even the rings were dangling from fingers which could not fill them anymore. For just a moment, he imagined how happy a scholar of renaissance fashion would have been to have the opportunity to see that grave. The flashlight illuminated the whole coffin, until it focused on a bundle at the deceased's feet. Alessandro stretched to grab it and realized his hand was almost trembling. And what his fingers perceived only increased his excitement. The scholar in him exulted. He could not resist, and decided to open it before stepping back from the tomb. A manuscript, actually, *the* manuscript: the one every scholar, every collector, and probably every human being with at least a little discernment yearned for. His fingers trembled while they felt the antique letters composing its title.

DE STELLA NOVISSIMA
DEL SIGNOR
GALILEO GALILEI, LINCEO FILOSOFO E MATEMATICO

Alessandro continued to hold the volume in his fingers, forgetting the condition they were in, the squad, everything but those wonderful pages, which for so many centuries had waited to be read. The dream of any researcher had become reality in his own hands. He could not think about anything else. Rebecca looked at his transfigured expression. In that moment, he looked like somebody else and the seeds of doubt rooted deeper in her mind. *This is it*, she thought. *Now it's really over. Now he'll take his prize and I'll never hear anything from him again.*

"Listen," he told her factually, holding the volume tight. "This book…" Rebecca thought she knew what the following words would be, and she started to panic. "…It's better if you keep it," he concluded, separating himself reluctantly from the literary treasure his fingers craved so much. "I don't know what will happen, if they'll be able to get me or not, but it's fundamental for this book not to be damaged." Those words made Rebecca's jaw drop. She had prepared and resigned herself to the fact that he would keep the book, that he would disappear from her life and that he would abandon her in that moment, just a step away from the end of their true mission, the research on the extraterrestrial virus. She was disoriented, feeling doubly guilty for doubting his intentions. "Rebecca?" he asked, worried, pointing the flashlight at her face. She shook her body, trying to hide her uneasiness and slipping the volume, still covered by a fabric shell, in the large bag.

"I…I have to talk to you," she whispered.

"Later, there's no time now," Alessandro replied, resurfacing from the tomb and resuming his work with the scalpel and the hammer, this time on the wife's grave.

"Stop!" she commanded, almost tearing the tools away from his hands.

"What?"

Rebecca descended once more into the tomb, leaning on the marble plate that had sealed it for centuries, without realizing she had moved it enough to make it sway, dangerously, towards the interior. "Give me some light," she told him, handing out the flashlight. He watched her rummage in her bag and pull out a sterile container, the kind used for urinalysis. He saw her remove it from the package and open it by unscrewing the red cap. He went along with her, curious, and followed her with the flashlight, while she approached the corpse. He could not withhold another frown of disgust when she easily used the same cap to tear off a finger from his hand, dropping it into the container. She rapidly closed it and put it back into the package and then in the bag. Then she searched the corpse's clothes, especially around the neck, but there was no trace of the necklace with the meteorite. He must have really given it to his wife as a present.

"The immune carrier," Rebecca explained. "From a study of his tissues, we could probably receive some information about his resistance to the virus or even develop a vaccine."

Alessandro nodded. "Now let's think about his wife," he suggested, thinking he had understood her intentions.

"No!" She blocked him again, still at the bottom of the tomb. "Now we have to stop."

"What?" he asked, incredulous.

"If we demolish this wall," she said knocking with her knuckles on the thin diaphragm of stone separating the side wall of the merchant's grave from his wife's grave, "we could release the virus."

Alessandro was horrified: "From the wife's grave?"

"Exactly," she confirmed. "These protections are not sufficient," she said indicating the mask. "We can't make it by ourselves. It's the moment to give up, call the authorities and maybe the World Health Organization. Their seat is here in Switzerland, we need to convince them to listen to us."

"And how would we sign the letter? 'Doctors wanted for multiple homicide?'"

Rebecca insisted: "We need to stop, Alessandro. Help me get out." Then she looked at the wall, curious about a shadow created by the light of the flashlight and she blanched. It was not a shadow: on the concrete wall there were thin cracks she had not noticed before. She was not able to say if they were already there before, or if their blows had caused them. But she surely could not swear they would guarantee the other tomb's seal was intact. The one containing the corpse of someone who died from an extraterrestrial virus. A virus which was transmitted through the air. And now she was breathing that air...

"Get me out of here!" she screamed, panicking. She was so nervous that she leaned on the marble cover of the tombs, already unstable. The heavy cover swayed perilously and then fell down inside the grave, moving in slow motion in front of their eyes. The flashlight was leaning on it and it fell as well, and the plate hit the wall separating the two graves, causing a considerable breach in the partition and a tremendous uproar which resounded through the whole cathedral. Speechless and unable to move, like fawns surprised on a street by car headlights, Henrietta's grave suddenly opened in front of their terrified eyes, illuminated by the fallen flashlight. The grave was empty.

Grégoire Toso was tossing and turning in his bed, victim of his recurrent insomnia. He had been the curator of Lausanne's cathedral for fifteen years; he had worked with literates and researchers coming from everywhere in the world. He had always tried to be as helpful as possible, in the interest of culture and knowledge. That is why he had not hesitated that afternoon, in spite of the unusual request. He had felt uneasy when the Italian Ph.D. student could not provide any official request, but after the call to the administrative office of the University of Padua, who had confirmed his credentials, he had felt a little relieved. It was the secretary's tone of voice which had upset him, now that he though about it; as if there was something that woman did not want to tell him, or could not tell him. And he did not understand why she had asked how she could contact him the following day. There was no solution, even the old remedy of the lukewarm glass of milk could not help: he could not fall asleep. He decided to take a short walk in the cool night.

He had covered the usual itinerary, when his attention was drawn by some noises in the distance. It seemed like…they were coming from the cathedral! It could not be the workers. While he rapidly approached the cathedral, he realized the noises were getting louder: they were surely coming from inside the church. Panting from the hard climb and the fast run, he reached the cathedral and entered from the side opposite the one under renovation. Totally careless of his own safety, he opened the gate wide and rushed to look for the light switch. When the lamps turned on, he had just the time to see two figures vanishing through the cloths on the scaffolding.

"Stop!" he shouted. "Police, help! Come back!" But, in the time it took him to run through the cathedral, the two figures had already disappeared. He tried to run after them, forgetting about his own safety, but he was distracted by what he saw at his feet: the flooring had been torn up, and at the bottom of a violated grave, he saw the corpse of a man, partially exhumed. Blanching at the terrifying image, he crossed himself and took out his cell phone to dial the emergency number.

If Alessandro's hand had not been there to drag her, Rebecca would not have been able to walk. They had run down the scaffolding, careless of the curator's screams. She hardly remembered the moment he had pushed her into the car or their return to the small hotel on the outskirts. They heard thunder coming from the sky: the first warnings of a storm approaching. Rebecca was shocked, sitting on the bed with her face in her hands.

"It's all over," she whispered to Alessandro, who felt just as beaten down as she did. "Why don't you take the book? That's what you were looking for, isn't it?" she provoked him, blaming him but more angry with herself than with anybody else. Vinci did not answer. "Isn't that what you wanted? Credit for the discovery of the book?" she insisted. "I'm sorry, but there won't be any revenue from the development of the vaccine. Thanks to us, there will be no vaccine at all!"

"If I hadn't told you I wanted something material in exchange for my help, would you have trusted me?" he asked her, offended. "Would you have let me help you?" Rebecca would have loved to jump at his neck, to kiss him, to hold him tight. But she restrained herself. She knew Alessandro would have chased her away. From his world, maybe even from that room. And she completely deserved it.

"I need to tell you something," she said, hoping he would not notice her fingers trembling.

"Can't that wait tomorrow morning?" Vinci asked, tired and disconcerted. He needed to gather his thoughts.

"I was the one to warn Deputy Commissioner Angeloni, at the service station," she confessed, all at once. Her tears were wetting her tired eyes.

"What?" Alessandro jumped up, immediately awake.

"I was afraid. Afraid that the squad would find you…would find us, that they would hurt us. And then he made me think about so many things—"

"About what?" Alessandro was furious.

"The gun," Rebecca answered, frightened. "The one that killed Rastrini. Angeloni swore the bullets that had killed the professor had come out of the gun that we had…that you had in the room in Florence."

"And you believed him?" he asked, remembering he had noticed the weapon was not in the place where he had left it. At that moment he had not thought about it too much, but now…

"I was afraid they would hurt you. The squad. Angeloni assured me that if we surrendered, nobody would be hurt. But at the last moment I couldn't do it. I didn't tell them where we were. I hung up."

"But they traced your call immediately," he said, talking to himself more than to her. Now he understood how they were able to find them. Rebecca expected him to leave the room in that very moment, slamming the door and disappearing from her life forever. She would have done it. "They want us to turn on each other, don't you realize that?"

he said instead, crouching down in front of her and staring at her in the eyes. "Tell me: do you really think I'm a psycho?"

She tried to approach him, gently reaching for his wrists, but he held back, waiting for her answer: "When did you hear about me for the first time?"

"What does that matter now?" he said, the signs of rage reappearing on his face.

"Please, tell me, then I will understand if you want to erase me from your life forever, you would have every right to want that. But I'm begging you, answer this."

Thrown off by that question, completely out of context, Alessandro reflected for a few seconds, then he answered: "A few days before we came to look for you in the office, at the institute where you work," he said. Rebecca knew that was not possible, but before that thought became a sentence in her head, he added: "No, wait. A few months before…in February, maybe. Professor Spinelli asked me to check the personal data of a few people. He was…he is a fanatic of genealogical research; I told you already, remember? It wasn't the first time he asked me to do that. Now that I think about it, I believe…yes, I'm sure your name was there as well."

"Is there any foolishness in my family tree?" she asked, unable to withhold the tears any further. They ran down from her eyes, from the relief and her sense of guilt. She explained everything: her doubts and her fears, hoping she was not too late in uprooting the seeds that had polluted her trust in him. "What will you do now? Will you leave?" His silence echoed inside her like a cannonball.

"You didn't leave. Even when you thought I was a crazy murderer."

"I didn't have much choice…" Rebecca threw her arms around him and embraced him deeply, unable to restrain herself, pressing herself against his chest. Only when she felt his arms hug her did she start to breathe again…and she finally felt happy. The reality of their condition, though, soon came back to inhabit their thoughts. They looked each other in the eyes, both speechless because both knew there were no words to say. Nothing that could change things. They had followed each and every possible trail, they had put all the cards on the table and they had no hidden ace up their sleeve.

"You need to leave," she said eventually. "You need to disappear and hold out until the real murderer is caught. Maybe now that we have found the book they'll be convinced that it's not just my imagination. Maybe they'll begin to investigate Pegasus…"

"And what about the super-virus? Should we wait for the next world epidemic? For more millions of victims?" Rebecca stretched out her arms, unarmed. "No, this can't happen," he said. "We'll give them what they want. Tomorrow I'll give myself up to the Swiss police and I'll assume all responsibility for the murders. This should restore your credibility and the opportunity to continue looking for the virus…"

She gently caressed his face with her hand, moved: "There's no place where we can look for the virus anymore. We have no more evidence and if we don't have that, Pegasus doesn't either; nobody does. Our hope was all in that grave, and it went right up to the heavens with its corpse, as the epigraph said."

"There was an epigraph?"

"Yes. Maybe you were too busy digging to notice it. It was quite moving, the words of a man who wishes the wife he was forced to leave behind a blessed journey to the afterworld: it read *sale ad coelum*."

Alessandro remained silent for a few seconds. "Can you repeat that?"

"*Sale ad coelum*. 'Rise to the heavens.' These are the words on Henrietta's epigraph…"

"Are you sure these are the exact words? Are you absolutely sure?" Vinci's eyes lit up.

Rebecca thought about it for a while, then she confirmed: "Yes, exactly these words. I'm sure. Why?"

Her companion's lips opened in the broadest smile she had ever seen on him. "Because I know where Henrietta Bermann is buried."

24

Rebecca looked at Alessandro in the same way she would have looked at somebody lost in hallucinations and delirium and she followed him, while he rushed to the laptop, cursing the slowness of his operating system. When he was able to connect to the Internet through the hotel's Wi-Fi network, he finally spoke: "Think about what happened: Virgilio Donati gives the cursed jewel to his wife and he sees her dying from the plague, maybe the extraterrestrial kind. Like many rich people at the time, he probably had bought a place in the cathedral for himself and his wife, or he bought it only when she died, that doesn't make any difference. She cannot benefit from it, though, because like all the people who died for the plague, she has to be thrown in a mass grave, like many hundreds of poor people. Far away from the church and from the prayers which should have paved her way to Heaven."

Rebecca was trying to follow him, but she still did not understand what he was getting at with his conclusions. "So? She's lost forever for our research…"

"No, that's not true, because her husband, who is so in love with her, cannot tolerate her being abandoned, not even because of her death by plague, and he buries her in another place, owned by him, making sure that after he's dead they would celebrate at least one mass a day in that place. A providential fact, because in a few years a fall would terminate his life as well."

"But how do you…"

"*Sale ad coelum* doesn't mean 'Rise to the heavens.' *Sale* in Latin is the ablative of the noun *sal*: 'salt.' The epigraph means 'To the sky through salt.'"

"The salt mine!"

"The salt mine. Exactly," he concluded, showing her on the laptop's screen the website of the tourist attraction the salt mine had become.

She was now as excited as he was. "We'll call the World Health Organization tomorrow. Even if we have to stage a sit-in at their door, we won't leave until they listen to us…"

"There's even a blueprint of the mine. God bless Swiss efficiency, look here!" he added.

"Waterfall Cave," Rebecca translated from the French. "Abyss Cave…" Beside each tunnel, indicated by picturesque nicknames, the respective explanations: from Waterfall Cave you can admire the point at which an underground river has a twenty-meter drop, and then reemerges right before Abyss Cave, where it sinks back down into a never-explored abyss, which drops into the bowels of the Earth. "Tabernacle Cave…" Translating the lines which explained the origin of that name, Rebecca had goose bumps: "Situated between Waterfall Cave and Abyss Cave. So called because tradition holds that until the mine was transferred from the church to the present management, a mass was celebrated here every day."

"I told you! We found the X where we have to dig!" Alessandro was excited, but his smile faded when he saw Rebecca's expression turn wan. "What's wrong?" Unable to speak, she indicated a red blinking banner on the top right corner of the webpage. Alessandro's French was poor, so he asked for a confirmation: "Please, tell me I'm reading it wrong."

"No," she confirmed instead. "Tomorrow will be the last day the mine is open. Then it will be closed indefinitely to ensure the structural safety of some tunnels. It says here that the underground river has weakened the ground of the whole area closed to the public, and they have decided to blow everything up, to make sure it won't threaten the tourist path. They will explode a stone diaphragm, to connect the Waterfall Cave with Abyss Cave, passing through Tabernacle Cave."

"We don't have any time for the WHO sit-in." Alessandro's voice had lost any trace of excitement.

"We don't have any time for anything. We only have one possibility, and a very small one."

They rested for a few hours only, but when they woke up they were readier than ever. Vinci was wearing his tight T-shirt, the cargo pants and his boots. You could see from the way he moved that he felt at ease with those clothes on, like a warrior in his armor. Rebecca checked once again the few tools she had for biological sample taking, unplugged her phone from the charger and inserted the new SIM card, even though she was not sure at all that it would work, since they had to go underground and there would probably be no network there. They ate something, got in the car and left towards the mine, just a few kilometers away. The expected storm had finally arrived and the pouring rain showed no sign of stopping.

Once they reached their destination, the first disappointment of the day was there for them: even though they had planned to reach the ticket shop before it opened, to make sure they were among the first to enter, a long line was awaiting them: the news of the site's closing had apparently attracted an unusual multitude of enthusiastic people. They lined up, resigned and careless of the rain, under the umbrella they found in the rented car. All of a sudden, Alessandro's cell phone ringing had the effect of a blaring trumpet. They expected no call to that number. Vinci looked at the display without recognizing the number, but he decided to reply anyway. "Thank God you're alive!" Even from the distance, Rebecca recognized Silvia's vocal timbre. "Where are you, did you find the graves? Tell me something, please!"

245

"We're in Switzerland, in a salt mine close to Lausanne," Vinci confessed, trying to cover the deafening noise of a jet speeding above them. "Don't worry, you'll be the first one to know when we come back." He promised her the exclusive once more and rapidly ended the conversation.

"Are you sure this is a good idea? How much do you trust her?" Rebecca reproached him with ill-concealed disappointment.

"What do you mean?"

"I'm thinking about all the times we were surprised by the police. Don't you think it's strange they always found us? In Florence, in the Apennines, at the meeting with Torre. She was the only one to know our position and we were never traced when we were with her."

"She wouldn't gain anything by doing that."

"Are you sure? You were the one to tell me she would do anything for a good story and you asked her to pledge that she would not write anything until everything is over."

"Exactly, and it's not over yet."

"But it would be if we were arrested; and she would have the exclusive for a front-page story in her hands." He remained silent, annoyed. "But you know her better than me," Rebecca softened her tone of voice. "If you think you can trust her, I will as well."

"Silvia would never hurt me. I trust her."

And you're wrong. You have no idea the things a rejected woman can do, Rebecca thought, but she did not speak. She knew there were only a few things more dangerous than a love turned into resentment and she felt that their relationship was not in the past for Silvia, whatever she tried to show. How could Alessandro not realize that? Undisturbed by that conversation, Vinci turned towards the parking lot, noticing a movement. Maybe, if he had not rushed that call so much, he would have noticed the noise of the jet which had temporarily deafened them could be heard at the other end of the receiver as well.

**

Deputy Commissioner Angeloni hung up, perplexed.

"Did you trace the call?" he asked, though he already knew the answer.

"Negative," the technician confirmed. Once more, an unknown voice altered with some electronic contraption, had informed him about the position of the two runaways. The first time they were sent to the motel in the outskirts of Florence, the second time in the woods on the Apennines. In Florence he thought it was somebody alarmed by the mug shots they had spread all over the media. The second call had begun to arouse his suspicion, but the third call, the one which allowed them to turn up at the meeting with the man Pegasus had sent, excluded any coincidence. There was another player in that game. Who could be interesting in having those two arrested? Ruminating on it, he dialed Colonel Achille's number. "They're at a salt mine twenty kilometers south east of Lausanne."

"That's good news," the official commented. "Out."

"No, wait," the policeman stopped him. "The more I think about it, the less this story convinces me. I need you to catch Vinci alive."

"Too late, Commissioner. They're already in Lausanne. They followed a credit card and I just communicated the position of their code Omega."

"Call them off, I'm telling you!"

"I can't. From now on they're on radio silence. Standard operating procedure." Right after, Angeloni heard the familiar *click* which indicated the other man had hung up.

"Son of a bitch!" the commissioner shouted, violently throwing the cordless phone against the wall and wrecking it, under the technician's astounded scrutiny. He knew very well that Achille had just fed him a lot of bullshit, but he could do nothing about it; he could not cross the border so easily, and resorting to the Interpol would have required many hours, if not days. Then he thought about the last point of that triangle, who was still sleeping in the commissioner's cell with a drunkard from Congo who was twice as big as him. Angeloni knew he was forcing his hand and he would have to answer for some violation of rights, but he was convinced that that kind of pressure, on a guy like that, would bear fruit.

When he opened the cell door, in fact, Torre was wide awake and almost threw himself at the commissioner. He did not even look like himself anymore; his eyes were red and his clothes rumpled. Angeloni smiled and ordered the two corporals following him to accompany him into the interrogation room. During the short itinerary from the cell to the room, Torre did not stop begging for more decent treatment, and he continued threatening the commissioner with legal action. They made him sit on an uncomfortable chair behind a desk. He was given a sealed bottle of water and a glass, and he drank it eagerly. It was clear he did not think it was healthy to quench his thirst using the same sink that his cellmate used to urinate. The chair on the other side of the desk was intentionally about two inches higher than the one he was sitting in, they had been selected expressly to increase the impression of psychological superiority of the person conducting the interrogation, but the commissioner stood up at the other side of the desk, leaning on it with his hands, as if he was about to jump on him: "Switzerland. Lausanne. What are Vinci and Doctor De Cardinale looking for there?" The commissioner obtained much more than the man's simple attention: Torre suddenly sat upright, folded his hands in front of himself and rested them on the desk as if he had all the time in the world.

"I told you already. Some letters…which lead to a book. A book by Galileo Galilei," Torre replied, hoping the policeman would be convinced that that was the last secret he wanted to protect.

"You don't kill so many people for a book!" Angeloni shouted. The more the policeman lost his control, the more the other man seemed to recover his own.

"It depends on the book. This one is of inestimable value."

"Bullshit! And why would they look for it in a mine?"

"A...mine?"

"Yes. A salt mine! If you don't tell me what I want to know, I'll throw you back in jail with your little friend and I'm sure you'll be engaged to marry by the end of the evening..." But Torre was not listening to him anymore. From the letters Pegasus had, Donati's name had come out several times, just like his residence, Lausanne, but the experts had not been able to specify his importance. From their research he knew that a salt mine had been mentioned among the past possessions of the Swiss merchant's family, along with some land and buildings. The lawyers had traced the present owners of all of them, but it would have been useless and expensive to blindly acquire everything that had belonged to Virgilio Donati without being sure they would have actually gained something from it. And now here was the information they had been waiting for, handed over on a silver platter. If the doctor and her partner were there, that surely was not a coincidence. Now he knew what to do.

"I want to speak to my lawyer," he said.

"What?"

"You know perfectly well that anything I say cannot and will not be used against me, if I'm not in the presence of my lawyer. I could even claim to be the perpetrator of all the murders you told me about, but you still could not use my declarations." Angeloni, still standing up and mad with rage, was left speechless. "If I'm not allowed to speak to my lawyer immediately I will make sure that you lose your job and that you will be charged. You know, my company has...extensive media and economic resources. I guess you don't want to be accused of abuses on the front-page of every newspaper, do you?" The commissioner blanched, then he kicked the chair, which slammed against the metal door. The sentry immediately appeared at the threshold with a questioning expression. After having verified that neither of the two people in the room were showing evident traces of violence he was about to leave, but his superior blocked him, opening the door wide and leaving the room.

"Give him a phone. One call. Then bring him back to his cell until his lawyer arrives."

"The other prisoner has just thrown up everywhere. It's a mess," the policeman objected. Angeloni smiled.

**

After more than one hour in line, they still had to cover half of the initial distance separating them from the ticket shop. Alessandro was frantic, impatient, until something alarmed him and he started to look around himself. Rebecca recognized the signs of tension on his face, the cold look she feared so much. She followed his look and met some tourist attraction employees, recognizable by their uniform, who were idly smoking under a canopy, before disappearing in different directions when their break was over.

"What's wrong?" she asked, alarmed.

"Nothing," he replied, unable to locate what had disturbed his unconscious radar.

"Stay in line," he told her, quickly abandoning it and disappearing behind the prefabricated ticket shop. Rebecca remained for a few minutes under the umbrella, struggling to keep her purse out of the rain, and trembling from the cold. They had wrapped up the book in a triple plastic cover, and brought it with them: Alessandro was the one to insist. He could not even imagine losing it, now that he had it in his

250

hands. The cell phone ring startled her. Only one number was registered on the phone, Alessandro's, and he was the one calling her.

"Come behind the ticket shop," he told her peremptorily. "You will find a door with a sign that says STAFF: when I ring your phone again, enter with nonchalance."

"But…" she objected, but he had already hung up. Red with embarrassment and trying not to hurt anybody's eyes with the umbrella, she walked back through part of the line, excusing herself in every language she could think of, until she was able to find a passage in the barriers and she rapidly disappeared where the tourists' eyes could not reach her. She located the prefab building Vinci had talked about. She followed the instructions and, when she touched the handle, he almost dragged her inside. "Alessandro!" she reproached him vigorously.

"Take this, put it on." He handed her coveralls like the ones the people working in the tourist department of the mine were wearing. The institution's logo stood out on the back. Rebecca was happy to free herself from her wet clothes and wear something dry and definitely warmer. "Here is the path," Alessandro said, with the blueprint of the mine they had printed in high definition that morning in the hotel. "The cave we're interested in is this one," he indicated. She nodded, as if only the strength of her conviction could overcome all the obstacles they still had to face. She knew she could not expect any comprehension from her partner from then on: Alessandro the academic was vanishing to make room for Vinci the ninja. She hoped it would not make room for Night. They were lucky, because the storm was getting steadily worse, and the ticket inspector did not even look out to recognize the two colleagues in uniform and let them pass without a word.

Once they had entered the mine, Rebecca started to envy Alessandro's boots: even though her shoes had rubber soles, at every step she risked slipping in what looked like a stream of rainwater, which from the outside, even from the walls, seemed to come in and descend towards the bottom of the mine. The tourist path was a little higher up, so tourists' feet would soon be on dry ground, but their destination was downhill, in front of them. Once they abandoned the visitors' path, proceeding with caution because the artificial light was reduced to the minimum, they eventually reached a right-angle deviation, whose entrance was forbidden. After making sure nobody was following them, they decided to follow that direction. Shortly after, on their slippery road they found a wooden door blocking the way. A sign in several languages clearly stated: DANGER. ACCESS FORBIDDEN TO ALL EMPLOYEES. Vinci consulted the map and handed it to Rebecca, who confirmed that was the right direction.

"We can't continue," she said, trying to open the lock. Vinci did not reply: he pulled a picklock out of one of his side pockets and he tried to handle the lock. It was a terrible idea: the mechanism had become rusty because of the water and his intervention got it stuck, instead of unlocking it. "Damn it, we're stuck!" she moaned, frustrated.

"Why stuck?"

"What do you mean why? The path is blocked, and even you can't pass through the doors…"

He stared at her for a second, as if he was accepting a challenge. "I don't see any barrier." Immediately after, he broke down the door with a powerful back kick which made Rebecca jump, since she was not expecting that at all. Then he turned to her again, with a beaming smile.

"You fool!" she reprimanded him. He continued to smile, amused. *How I'd like to smash his head when he's like that*, Rebecca thought, preceding him in the darkness. Once they had passed through the gate, Vinci put an empty metal can right on the top corner, in precarious balance, to ensure that if anybody opened it, it would create a lot of noise, warning them. Guided by their flashlight, they continued walking through the tunnels carved in the rock. They were not part of the tourist path, and thus were still steep and had no lights. Rebecca slipped several times, almost falling. Under their feet, frozen water ran rapidly and vigorously: much of it came from above, probably from the pouring rain, but they soon realized it was running along the walls as well.

With growing anxiety, Rebecca thought about the underground river and the possible danger of flooding that the mine website had talked about. After passing a sharp turn, the tunnel enlarged to become a broader room, with a stony vault about three meters above the ground. From there, according to the map, other tunnels started in each direction; the Tabernacle Cave could not be too far. They went forward, lighting up the way with their flashlight and with the growing background noise of the water running under them. The waterfall had to be close by, but before they could reach the place where the roar of the falling water would have drowned out any other noise, a metallic clang behind them shook them like a gun shot. The can had fallen down. Vinci turned and she saw his nostrils were dilated and his jaw clamped: "Don't stop," he told her, handing her the flashlight and the map. "The Tabernacle Cave is a little further down. If I don't come back in ten minutes, get out of here and look for the police. Repeat."

"But…"

"Repeat!"

Rebecca realized with horror that she was talking to Night. "If you don't come back in ten minutes I'll get out of here and give myself up to the police."

"Good," he said, walking back the way they had come.

"Alessandro!" she called him back. "Be careful, please…" But he had already vanished.

The four agents had got to the mine in a disguised van right after it opened and the first thing they had done was to use their eyes and cameras to inspect all the people waiting in line. Unfortunately, it had been almost useless, since almost everyone was protecting their faces under umbrellas or hoods because of the storm. The squad leader had then ordered his men to monitor the entrance turnstiles and every single door which looked like it could lead somewhere underground. When he saw two employees pass the barriers, one of the agents reported those two were wearing civilian clothes when they had entered the door, but they had not used the staff entrance to get there; they were a man and a woman. The squad leader did not need to hear anything else and started the operation, following them into the mine. His intention was to get as close as possible to them, then to attack them from the rear before they could even realize they were there. Right after the tourist area, though, they had fallen for the old can trick and that was a farewell to the element of surprise.

Ever alert, the squad leader was walking in front of everybody, with a HK P2000 in his hands, with 9mm bullets; a smaller gun which could be easily hidden under clothing. It was also partially made of polymeric, which made it lighter and perfect for aiming in tight spaces, but he could not carry any more gear on him apart from the body armor they were wearing under their coats. No goggles with light amplification, no tactical guns: too bulky and hard to conceal for their unauthorized mission abroad. He missed them, but he still had confidence in the success of the operation.

The other three followed him silently, with their weapons in their hands, locked and loaded. The silencer would prevent attracting the attention of the staff or the tourists with their firing, but the squad leader still hoped he would not have to shoot more than once. In a place like that, you could not predict the trajectories of ricochet bullets and they had to face an extremely dangerous armed man. Maybe a traitor; surely a threat to eliminate. If he was not lucky with the first shot, it would be harder, but still doable. He still was mad at himself for not catching him in Florence, and even more so because Achille continued to think he was the best. In about an hour he would not be anymore.

The tunnel enlarged a little and then it narrowed again, dividing in several directions. The noise of the water blocked out all sound, making it difficult to identify any possible movement. A thought popped into his head, distracting him for a moment: what had the target and the woman come to do down there? The final man closed the formation and was the last one to leave the widening section. The water ran everywhere, dripping down from the ceiling and bouncing on his dark uniform. As instructed by the squad leader, he deviated to explore one of the side tunnels. Then he was hit by something which did not seem to be a drop, too solid…a rock fragment? He looked up, but the last thing his flashlight illuminated was a dark figure pouncing on him.

Vinci hit his enemy and he grabbed his neck from behind, impeding him from shouting to alert his companions, and he blocked the oxygen supply to his brain at the same time. *Do it!* the killer's voice screamed in his head, but while his hands were holding tight he saw Rebecca's face in his mind, and when the man stopped fighting him, he let him collapse to the ground, knocked out but alive. He did not want to kill anymore. No more. That was why he had left his gun in the hotel, to avoid the temptation to use it. He took his body armor, disarmed the gun by throwing the magazine far away and then continued, behind the other soldiers' backs.

The second man was just as easy to overpower: seeing him come from behind, in the dark and wearing the body armor, he did not suspect the threat until he was already on him, and Vinci was able to stun him with a clean blow under the chin, taking hold of him by the mouth and nose. This impeded him from breathing until he passed out as well. At that point Vinci's luck was over: preceded by a hiss, a bullet penetrated the rock just a few inches from his ear and he was hit in the face by an explosion of rock splinters which scratched his skin and filled his eyes with dust and fragments.

He escaped entering the tunnel he had come from, while two more muffled shots chipped the rock beside him. *Silencer*, he had the time to think before a terrible pain shot through his back, making him fall backwards. No shout, no warning: code Omega. The body armor had protected him, but he had to stand up as soon as possible. The man entered the larger cave a few moments after him, with his gun in his hand. Crouching down there, he was indistinguishable from the dark rocks and he was able to direct a kick up at the hand holding the weapon, causing the gun to fall.

Before he could stand back up, a kick in his face clouded his vision even more. His mouth filled with the metallic taste of blood. His enemy was good, his blows were not too strong, but they were quick and they could hurt him even though he was blindly trying to protect the vital points: his eyes, his throat, his solar plexus, his groin. He was better, though: as soon as he could see again, he was able to effectively dodge a punch, and while his enemy was out of balance, he kneed him in the groin. His enemy reacted immediately and answered with a blow to his throat which would have left him winded or even dead if it had hit him. Vinci dodged it by a hair's breadth, jumping to the side and trapping him in a neck hold. He felt him struggling. He almost felt his bones cracking under his weight. Then he was horrified. His enemy was too light. He let go and the body fell on him like a dead weight. He illuminated it weakly with his flashlight: it was the woman, the same one who was in Florence, disguised as a waitress.

"Get away from her. Now!" the squad leader's growl resounded in the small cave. He had his gun pointed at Vinci, and he would have surely shot him had his companion's body not been covering him.

"The gun," Vinci ordered, with a deep voice. The squad leader threw his weapon a few steps behind him. Only then did Vinci let the woman's body fall down. He had temporarily lost his vision from the dust, which he had not succeeded in washing away with tears, and one of his shoulders could not move anymore because of the blows it had taken and the shot fired a few minutes before.

"The famous Night," the squad leader provoked him, realizing his enemy was unarmed and his colleague, maybe, was still alive. "Infamous, I should say," he continued, trying to distract him. "Let's see if you can handle a man as well."

"I wasn't the one to bring her here, and she's still breathing anyway."

"A real gentleman," the other man snarled. Then he threw himself at Vinci and there was no space left for words anymore. The two began to hit each other with lethal moves and countermoves: quick blows, which would have caused significant damage to less experienced enemies, but from which both of them were able to escape at the last second. A few minutes later, they were both bleeding and in pain, both breathless. In the dark, Vinci did not notice the man had pulled out a knife from his belt and threw himself back in for another attack. If he had not had his body armor, he would have been disemboweled. He escaped the second attack by sliding on the ground and rolling onto his side. On the ground his hands touched something familiar: the woman's gun. Before the squad leader could hit again, he pointed the HK a few inches from his face. Both were motionless. "Come on, shoot," the man provoked him. "You know I'm not going to stop anyway."

"Throw the knife down," Vinci ordered moving the gun's barrel from the squad leader's head to aim it at the unconscious woman. He hoped with all his heart the bluff would work. He felt his strength leaving him. The only eye he could see from was clouding over. He was the only one left between Rebecca and them. The thought of her in danger instilled a new strength in his vision. The knife fell down and the soldier gritted his teeth, waiting for the bullet that would shatter his skull. Vinci lowered the gun, though. "We just want to leave. There's something at stake which is worth the life of thousands of people. Give me twenty-four hours. Tomorrow I'll give myself up to the police," he almost whispered to him. The squad leader opened his eyes wide. Out of the corner of his eye, Vinci saw at the same time a movement behind his shoulders and a nod of the man he had in front of him, but before he could react he felt a strong pain in his head. Then nothing.

25

While she walked on towards their target, Rebecca felt she was lonelier than ever. She hoped, she prayed that her worries were unfounded, that the can had fallen because of the airstream and that nobody was following their tracks, especially Alessandro's former colleagues. Extremely anxious, she gave another look at the map and in doing so she slipped another time. At that point, an actual stream was running under her feet, with the rainwater joining the seepage from the walls. It was colder and colder and the deafening noise of the underground river was growing step after step. She continued to look behind her, hoping to see Alessandro reappear, but she did not stop. Tomorrow it would be too late. She finally reached Waterfall Cave and with the weak beam of her flashlight, she enjoyed the view of the impressive cataract. She knew the Tabernacle Cave was between that spectacular volume of water and the following Abyss Cave, into which the water would be channeled. Trying to hold onto the wet wall to avoid slipping again, she looked at the map once more and tried to orient herself. At her right there should have been a wall dug into the stone, and a little further on, access to Tabernacle Cave. She only saw some detritus instead, and the underground river that was furiously washing around a rocky spur.

Disoriented, she forced herself to reexamine the map they had printed. After a few seconds she understood and she was so surprised that she lost her grip on the map, and had to see it swallowed by the swirling water. The geologists were wrong, or maybe the torrential rain had made the situation collapse; in any case, the underground river had swamped the wall of the Tabernacle Cave and the river was growing still; very soon, it would fill it completely. Desperate, she looked behind her once more. *Alessandro, where are you? I need you!* How much time had passed since he had left her? A minute? An hour? A century? Rebecca felt close to panicking, but she resisted and approached the wall, panting. There was still a part of the flooring that seemed to be sound. She leaned on it and turned towards the rocky spur.

The Tabernacle Cave, or what was left of it, was around her. It had to be a little larger than the two neighboring walls; originally it had probably been a collection center, when the mine was still active. Some cavities and some holes in the wall formed a cross, a crucifix probably hung there when it was used as an altar and she finally was definitively certain that she was in the right place. *Lord, help me.* She instinctively prayed, while she struggled to calculate how long she could last inside there, before the fear, the river or even the ground under her feet would overcome her.

She looked around, using the flashlight. No sign of a tomb. She did not expect to find it in full sight: if anybody had known the body of a person who died of plague was there, nobody would have risked going, and that would have meant no redeeming prayers anymore. Then, at the bottom, on the opposite wall, the one facing Abyss Cave, she saw something that looked like it was moving, shaken by the airstream which blew ever stronger from the river towards the abyss. Overcoming her terror she approached, pointing her flashlight in that direction. *Oh my God.* Standing up, in the wall of rock and salt, Rebecca saw a mummy, half-revealed by the violence of the water. Originally, it was probably covered by blankets of cloth, which were by now decomposed, and from the corpse she understood the deceased had to be a woman: Henrietta.

Rebecca put on her mask with the protection filter immediately, praying it was not too late already. Her professional instinct suggested that the powerful airstream that was blowing over her, going towards the abyss, would carry any aerial virus down with it, even better than any extractor fan in her lab, but she was not so dumb as to bet on it. *Yes, continue to fool yourself,* she thought while she put on two sets of gloves. A sudden wave flooded the cave, devastating most of the flooring the doctor had walked on. She held on to the walls, miraculously succeeding in keeping her balance. Even the mummy was hit: the lower part of it was almost dragged away by water, while the upper one remained partially trapped in the rock covering it. *That was so close,* Rebecca thought, looking at the remains with horror.

Trying to keep her balance among the waves of frozen water and the rock brought by its force, she got closer and finally saw it: the medallion! A circular-shaped jewel was hanging from the mummy's neck. It was shining with yellow reflections in the flashlight's beam: it was surely gold, but the necklace was mounted on something she could not see, almost completely consumed by salt and water. Another wave suddenly flooded the cave and part of the flooring collapsed in the abyss, displacing the corpse. That medallion was probably the only possibility of isolating the virus. She could not allow it to be lost forever. Rebecca drew on the little courage she had left in her; she opened the container and kept it open with her right hand, moving it towards the corpse, while she held to the wall with the left hand, as fast as she could.

Using the container's rim as a lever, after a couple of failed tries, the medallion was finally detached from the worn-out metal chain and fell inside the plastic jar. Rebecca felt the rock crumbling under her feet. She struggled to avoid looking down towards where the river disappeared into darkness, and to avoid wondering what would happen to her if she fell inside it, because she knew she was not done yet. She sealed the container with the medallion, and opened another one right after. With a last effort, a superhuman effort for her, she leaned over and tried to recuperate a piece of the corpse's face tissue, which was by then uncovered. A part of the nose was left, probably conserved by the cave's salt or by the strong cold. It broke up easily into little pieces with the pressure of the container and fell inside it. Unable to hold her breath, Rebecca gained her balance back and hermetically sealed that jar as well.

A moment later a large segment of the wall, the one she had leaned on until a moment before, collapsed with a deafening racket, plummeting into the abyss together with a large part of the remaining flooring and the body of Henrietta Bermann, swept out of Rebecca's sight and from the world forever. Rebecca was panting, hyperventilating to compensate for the hypoxia and the fear. Without letting go of the containers, she wrapped the glove she was handling them with around them, slipping it off inside out. Then she did the same with the first glove of the other hand and she repeated the operation with the last two gloves, sealing it all with a knot. Then she put everything inside the thick bag carrying the other container, the one with Virgilio Donati's remains, and she sealed it: the closest thing to a hermetically sealed container she had.

She slipped it into her bag and rushed towards the narrow rocky spur she had passed on the way there, and she was stunned to discover it was even smaller now. She feared she would not be able to get through, but she had to try in any possible way: she tucked the flashlight in her belt and she held onto the wall with both hands, squeezing it so hard that she broke her nails. She was hardly able to fend off the rushing water, which threatened to carry her down. When she felt solid ground under her feet, she started to run, falling down repeatedly on the wet rock. When she had no breath left and was obliged to slow down, she heard the roar of the river much further away and she understood she was safe. Now she would just need to follow the path up to avoid losing herself in the tunnels and go back to the entrance. She craved the sunlight and she wanted to be rid as soon as possible of the terrible prize that was making her bag much heavier. A flashlight's beam hit her. Alessandro?

**

The newspaper van was stationed in the parking lot of the mine, double parked. Cursing the wind and the rain which were doing damage to her coiffure and makeup, Silvia had given up trying to recognize Alessandro's and Rebecca's faces among the cold tourists in line. Like them, she knew from what she had read in the letters that they were in Lausanne, and careless of Alessandro's recommendations, she had followed him and Rebecca to Switzerland as soon as she could. After the last call, she soon had the confirmation that the only mine around was the one in front of her. She had found out about the profanation of the tombs in the cathedral from the newsflash in the morning, and she knew the curator had implicated an Italian Ph.D. student and his partner as the most likely culprits. The journalist could not help wondering how Vinci could not avoid being noticed, with all his training as a raider. Maybe it was because of Rebecca. If that was the reason, she had to do something to solve the problem.

Using her press pass, she was able to avoid the line and she placed herself right under the large entrance to the main cave, protected from the rain, though not from the wind. She had been able to get a recording crew from her boss, but because of the short amount of time she had not succeeded in having him sign her promotion. Actually, she had put all of her credibility at stake: if this did not prove to be the story she had promised, her career would plummet like a diving jet. She dialed Alessandro's number for the last time. Still unreachable. Frustrated, she was about to throw it against the rock in front of her, but then she restrained herself and put it back in her pocket. Maybe that was a sign that he was inside the mine, right in front of her. So close, yet so far. She could only wait.

Her attention was drawn by four employees in coveralls, three men and a woman, who were carrying a heavy dark bag. She saw them leave the cave, passing through a side exit, a little far from their position. At least one of them seemed to walk with a limp and his face was bruised. She recognized the feeling she had when she sensed news and she continued to follow them with her eyes. When they stopped behind a traditional foods van, her feeling of being after something increased. She ordered the cameraman to film them as well as possible while they climbed into the van and she tried to reach them, but suddenly stopped when she heard sirens approaching. Two Swiss police cars, followed by a dark sedan and a van rushed into the open space, almost breaking through the queue. The van bore the logo of Pegasus Pharmaceutics.

"Film, film everything!" Silvia screamed to the cameraman. She ordered an assistant to hold her tablet, connected to their website: "Patrioti, why am I not broadcasting yet?" she began.

"Canelli, you did not give me a single reason to do that, and you have to answer when I call you on the phone, you got that?" he replied, alluding to the many calls she had ignored that morning.

"The situation is about to explode here right now, and we're the only newspaper on the field," she answered. She knew the director could watch the images from his own screen. She let the cameraman focus on the police, starting the evacuation of the tourists in line and commanding the evacuation of those who were still inside the mine. One of the policemen tried to stop them, but with a nod from her, one of the crew furiously advocated the right to information, speaking in French. Taking advantage of the hole created in the crowd, while other police cars reached the area with their sirens wailing, the Pegasus van approached the entrance. From the side hidden from the crowd three

264

people in sealed white coveralls came out, but Silvia saw them anyway. Their protective suits allowed them to see only through a transparent Plexiglas visor. On their back they carried oxygen tanks connected to a respirator. They proceeded into the cave, without hesitating, causing some alarmed cries. "Patrioti!" Silvia screamed into her cell phone, turning her anxiety into rage: Rebecca? Alessandro?

In Italy, the director's voice resounded, trembling: "Talk to me, Canelli. What's going on? I can give you the live broadcast in five minutes..." But she was not listening to him anymore. Behind the men in white uniforms, two policemen were walking with their machine guns in their hands, together with a man who had come out of the sedan. He had an upset expression, an unshaven face, and red eyes. He looked like somebody who had not slept for two days. Even his expensive suit was all wrinkled, but she could still swear he was a Pegasus man as well.

**

Rebecca passed the door Vinci had broken open and she was almost out in the tourist corridor, but she still had not reached the well-lit area. Soon the glare was brighter, so bright that Rebecca had to look away from it. It could not be Alessandro, their flashlights were not so powerful...when she was able to reopen her eyelids, she saw three white figures headed towards her. Behind them she could perceive other men, some with high-visibility uniforms. Further up another light, even stronger. Maybe even...a camera?

"Doctor De Cardinale?" She recognized that voice. Torre. How could that unctuous accountant reach her there? "Can we speak to the doctor for a moment, agent?" the bureaucrat asked the policeman in French. The police officer had not been informed of any details, he only knew there was a biologic alarm in the area of the mine and he was quite relieved about the idea of getting away from that place. Going back towards the cave, he let even a journalist with her crew pass him. His superiors could very well take his place down there if they had anything to say about him leaving! "Doctor, I think you have something that belongs to my company," Torre said to her, with his smarmy voice. One of the three men in white, the one who was closer to her, handed her a metal container with symbols of biologic risk printed all over it.

"It doesn't belong to your company," Rebecca replied, pulling the plastic container with the precious contents out of her bag and keeping it behind her, as if she wanted to throw it in the water running on the ground, towards darkness.

"I'm afraid you're wrong, Doctor," he replied, introducing a hand in his pocket. Rebecca stepped back. She knew there was no escape behind her, but Torre did not. "Easy," he told her, slowly extracting a piece of paper from his jacket. "It's the contract regarding the ownership of this mine." The satisfaction the man enjoyed in Rebecca's astounded look paid him back for everything: the sleepless nights in the cell, the SWAT's attack and the obliged proximity to pseudo-human people. "You know, Doctor, Deputy Commissioner Angeloni was so kind as to inform me about your position while I was in the cell and the previous CEO of the company who ran this place was really happy to sell the mine to Pegasus when he heard our offer. Oh, yes. He was so happy that he signed the agreement on the spot, less than three hours ago. Of course, I don't expect you to trust my word," Torre wheedled her. "That's why I brought a copy of the contract with me."

"That's quite a dramatic turn of events! I guess you won't have anything against showing that to the press…and explaining the situation to our audience!"

Torre turned suddenly, surprised by the journalist who had approached him with her cameraman, but he was quite fast in regaining his composure. "Of course…I have nothing against that," he said in the most affable tone of voice, handing it over to Silvia, who took advantage of the situation to get even closer. The journalist briefly read the purchase agreement, then she screamed to let the woman recognize her, since she was still blinded by the flashlights: "It's true, Doctor De Cardinale."

"Silvia!" Rebecca shouted, happy to feel a friendly presence. Then she remained uncertain and anxious when she did not hear any response.

"Yes, Doctor. I'm a journalist," she finally said in the most professional tone of voice she could use, to make sure the others would not suspect that they knew each other. "Your venture must have been immensely difficult…are you alone? Is somebody else there with you?" She wanted to know about Alessandro. But if she had not met him either, where was he? A feeling of imminent failure hit Rebecca, even more than when she had run away from the flooded cave.

"I was with another person," she played along, "but I don't know where he is."

"I think the Swiss police want to talk to you regarding a theft in the cathedral, Doctor," Torre insisted, to keep her under pressure. "And the Italian police as well. Are you not tired of running away?" Then he added: "Do you know my company is able to prepare a vaccine, and that this is the only way to make it available in case of an epidemic? Actually, to prevent it."

Rebecca lowered her hand, apparently defeated, then she sprung forward, bursting through the men in white and avoiding Torre's chubby hands. A few steps later, though, because of her urge to get out, of her terror and of the slippery ground, the doctor stumbled and fell down. To protect the precious package she had in her hands, she let go of the bag. Behind her, she felt the nervous steps of her pursuers. She had no time to pick it up. She stood back up and ran some more, in pain. As soon as the bright lights of the exit penetrated the darkness of the cave, Rebecca realized her mad dash was hopeless. In front of the entrance a safety cordon had been deployed: on the other side, the policemen were awaiting her, aiming with their guns and machine guns. Nobody would have come out of the cave without their permission. Panting, Rebecca stopped, defeated. Behind her arrived the journalists and the Pegasus scientists, impeded by their coveralls. Torre came last: "That's enough now!" he ordered. "Or I'll have them shoot you."

"You won't shoot anybody," Silvia interrupted him, with her cameraman continuously filming the scene. Surprised, Rebecca regained her breath. She saw that the bag containing *Stella Novissima* was still in its waterproof cover, at the journalist's feet. What game was she playing?

"You can't impede that, you have no authority here," Torre answered to Silvia. "Actually, I think I could sue you for filming on my propriety without any authorization."

Silvia ignored him and picked up the phone, still staring at the tablet: "Patrioti, you saw what this is about: you have five seconds to broadcast it live," she said. "And I want my name as owner of the story in the subtitles. Five seconds!" Rebecca did not jump at her only because she feared the police would shoot. She knew that woman would betray them at the first opportunity, she had always known that. And now that they were in the most difficult position they had ever been in, she did not only give them the cold shoulder, but she even sold them out for her fifteen minutes of fame, allowing Pegasus to run away with their loot. What a bastard!

Torre was about to reply, but Silvia turned the tablet towards him, showing him his image on the screen, surrounded by the cave's walls. They were by then in the tourist area and the network was perfect. She kept her finger pointed at the men in white and at Torre, to indicate her cameraman what to film. The man was left speechless. When Silvia had read the words she was expecting, her expression immediately changed and she turned to her audience with a charming smile. The same smile Rebecca could not stand on Alessandro's lips, and now she knew why. Then she began her show.

"Good morning everybody, we're here today for an exceptional discovery in the salt mine on the outskirts of Lausanne..." Her voice was explaining how and why they were there, but Rebecca was not even listening to her. She saw the policemen lowering their weapons in front of the camera, but without freeing up the safety cordon. Following the journalist's look, though, the expert cameraman was not filming them, keeping the camera on her and on the Pegasus staff. "It's only thanks to the generosity of Pegasus Pharmaceutics that we could achieve this success," Silvia's confident voice continued. Then, with an elegant gesture of her hands, she let the operator film the astounded Rebecca. "Here is Doctor De Cardinale, an expert biologist who, acting as a consultant for Pegasus, just recovered a biological specimen indispensable to creating a vaccine against a terrible pandemic which was threatening the human race, and now hands it to the squad who has come here to transport and analyze it."

Rebecca could only acquiesce, abandoning the result of all her efforts, all her research in the sterile container of the pharmaceutical company. She wanted to strangle Silvia! Torre, instead, was smiling, surprised but satisfied. He looked like a cat who had just trapped a mouse. "And now let's talk to Pegasus' representative." The cameraman focused on him. "It's the moment to announce your company's donation, isn't it?" The smile on his face weakened. "Pegasus has in fact announced that the vaccine will be developed and distributed for free all over the world. Isn't that right, Doctor Torre?"

In front of the cameras, the man gulped, temporizing and struggling to breathe. Then he replied with the largest smile he could fake: "Of course...my company has always been attentive to the population's well-being. This is a tremendous gift Pegasus offers to humankind."

"And we want to thank you for your commitment to the renovation of Lausanne's cathedral, which was damaged during the investigation," Silvia continued unperturbedly. The cameraman kept filming the man until he was forced to give a sign of silent consent with a growl. Then he turned his back to the camera and headed towards the van with his men, and they left escorted by the police, sirens wailing. Rebecca did not even care anymore where they were going.

Silvia concluded the broadcast and her crew headed to the mobile broadcasting station. They had to check the figures and the quality of the images. "Is this bag yours?" one of the policemen asked her, in faltering Italian, in the only police car left. The doctor looked at the bag the man had picked up and she knew she soon would have to relinquish the precious manuscript, because they would confiscate everything she had before any new orders were issued. Another inestimable find would be forever lost for her country.

"It's mine," Silvia interrupted him.

"Are you sure?" the policeman asked, since he had seen the woman wearing that bag, shortly before.

"Yes, I am. Check the label," he said, pointing at it.

"Are you Silvia Canelli?" the man asked, raising an eyebrow, still unconvinced.

"Sure I am. Check, if you don't trust me," she said, pulling her ID out of her pocket.

The policeman checked and reluctantly handed her the bag. Then he turned towards Rebecca. "You will have to come with us, we need to ask you some questions."

"I'm sure the curator will retract his report after Torre's declarations," Silvia whispered to her, accompanying her to the car.

Rebecca found the energy to smile: "He can choose his women well," she said, repeating her words from a few days before. The thoughts of both women went to the only one who was still missing.

"Alessandro?" the journalist asked. Rebecca shook her head and her smile died on her lips. They both thought about the same thing: the squad. Even Silvia looked confused at the beginning, but then she remembered the four people who were carrying a heavy bag, right before the police arrived. Their vehicle had an Italian license plate, and she had filmed it. She watched Rebecca enter the police car and leave, then she took out her cell phone and dialed Deputy Commissioner Angeloni's number.

"We're looking for you, Miss Canelli," the man welcomed her, when she said her name.

"Where is Alessandro Vinci?" the journalist asked.

"Where are you now? Obstruction of justice is a serious crime, and housing two wanted people and offering them a car is as well."

"Did you find my car already? I didn't even have the time to report it missing."

"Don't try to mess with me. We traced you from the license plate we found in the service station. You want to tell me that it's a coincidence that your car was in the last place where your former boyfriend—"

"No, you don't mess with me," she interrupted him harshly. "I have the license plate of the squad's van. I filmed them. I have their faces, and they have been recorded executing an operation abroad. I bet the cantonal government will be very happy about this."

"What squad are you talking about? We did not send anybody," he replied seraphically, but Silvia did not fall for it.

"I want Alessandro Vinci, and I want him alive! If you don't tell me that he's alive and where he is in the next ten minutes, you'll see the videos on the internet. And the whole world will see them." And she hung up.

**

Colonel Achille was enraged. He did not care that he had been neutralized. The order had not been carried out, the code Omega had not been respected.

"Why did you not complete the mission?" he asked his squad leader over the radio. That idiot would not get by with just a scolding.

"You were right about him, you know? He really was the best. He could have killed me. He could have killed all of us, he had the chance to do it; but he didn't."

"And since when are you the one to decide who deserves to die and who doesn't?"

"Colonel, with all due respect, you know just as well as me that code Omega has to be carried out only when an alternative is lacking. I did have an alternate option, and I did my duty."

The colonel was furious and he was about to reply when his cell phone rang. He recognized the number on the screen; Deputy Commissioner Angeloni. That incompetent fool was the last person he needed at that time. He rapidly dismissed the squad leader, intending to personally execute the code Omega, and answered the phone.

"You need to give me Vinci. Alive," the commissioner ordered before he could even say, "Achille."

"That's not an option," the colonel replied, dilating his nostrils.

"If I don't call a journalist in seven minutes, the details of the operation will be shown worldwide. Together with the license plate of your van."

He liked Angeloni's relaxed tone of voice even less than his words. "We'll bury everything in the sand, like we always do," the officer replied, with arrogance. "And the van's license plate obviously doesn't exist."

"They filmed your men's faces. All four. If we don't tell her where Vinci is and that he's alive and well, we'll see them online on the *Corriere*'s website. I'm sure the minister will be pleased about having to give explanations on your squad and its unauthorized operations abroad."

Now Achille was sure the other one was ecstatic.

"Goddamn it!" were the last words Angeloni heard before the other man hung up.

26

The Swiss police did not take long at all to hand her over to the Italian police. As Silvia had predicted, the curator withdrew his report as soon as he found out Pegasus had officially declared they would cover the cost of the renovation of the cathedral, so they had no reason to keep her there. The police truck waited for her to be accompanied to the border, then brought her back, escorted, to Padua as fast as possible. They got there at the first light of dawn. In Padua, Rebecca found Deputy Commissioner Angeloni waiting for her in the headquarters and he was almost kind to her, considering everything. He questioned her for more than three hours, but then he let her go, ordering her to remain in the city. The officer watched her walk out, wait for the journalist and then leave with her.

"You're assuming a great responsibility, Commissioner," his boss told him. "You could have freed a murderer."

"No, I'm convinced she was framed. I'm not sure about it yet, but all evidence against her could have been made up. Even the badge used to enter the Department of Literature to kill Menin could have been smuggled from her home: we found signs of forced entry."

"I know that, we examined this hypothesis together, but according to your theory we just let the doctor leave with a murderer who was ready to do anything she could to get her lover back." The commissioner lit up another cigarette, heedless of the sign in the room: he had watched the recording of the journalist's scoop as well. Silvia Canelli had been too clever, as though she could predict what would happen way before anybody else…as though she had planned everything. She was the only one to know the doctor and Vinci's movements in real time, the only one who could warn the police at any time. Angeloni would bet she was behind all that. Maybe the whole story was a pretext to let Alessandro Vinci's dark personality reemerge, to get back the agent, the lover who had abandoned her. A way to have him back, or maybe, to get her revenge. That was why he had carried out a fake interrogation of her and the doctor: if he was right, Dr. De Cardinale would be his bait.

**

A little later, after stopping by Silvia's house, the two women rushed to the hospital, and rapidly walked towards the ward where Vinci was hospitalized. The embarrassed head nurse was not able to slow them down and the patrolling policeman blocked them from entering the room.

"I want to see him!" Silvia said, trying to peek into the room, behind the man's shoulders, but he rejected her, with a threatening expression. "I'm his wife!" Silvia intimidated him. At those words, everybody froze, including Rebecca. "You don't want to prevent a wife from seeing her husband, do you? I don't even know how he is!" The policeman looked around himself, unsure of what he should do, then he stared at the two women and decided they were no threat, not more than being accused of violation of rights by a fierce journalist.

"Five minutes," he conceded, "and I'll be inside the room with you." Rebecca was the first one to cut past him. When she entered the room she felt sick. Vinci was lying on the hospital bed, with his face black and blue from the infinite number of blows he had received.

"Alessandro?" she tried to call him.

"He was sedated," the policeman explained, indicating the infusion pump connected to his left arm. The right arm was instead secured to the bed with handcuffs.

"This is torture!" Silvia attacked him, hurling abuse at him with all the might of her journalistic eloquence. Too occupied by defending himself from her protesting, the agent did not realize that Rebecca was approaching the almost motionless body of Vinci, and she was bending down over him as if she wanted to kiss his forehead and caress him.

"He's already lucky to be here and not in a cell!" Pressed by Silvia, the policeman continued to defend himself, overheating more and more. "Once the medical checkup is over he'll go back there; he's considered extremely dangerous!"

"Are handcuffs not enough? Did you also have to drug him?" Silvia persisted.

"From what I've heard, it's necessary," the man justified, obviously unaware of the details of the operation. Then he lifted up his watch with ostentation. "The five minutes have passed," he said firmly, escorting them to the door.

When they were out in the street, far from indiscreet ears, Rebecca asked: "His wife?"

"I improvised. Did you succeed in giving him the keys?" Silvia replied, still furious over her argument with the policeman. The doctor confirmed. Silvia had found in her apartment some old handcuffs Vinci had left there, and they had planned the visit to the hospital together to sneak them to him. Trying not to ask why she had them, Rebecca had listened to her explain that all service handcuffs had the same keys, and that it was very likely that those keys could open the handcuffs trapping him in that moment. They only had to hope those were service handcuffs, otherwise the keys would be completely useless.

"I did more. I changed the levels of the pump sedating him," Rebecca replied proudly. When they had entered the room, the benzodiazepines were injected at 1.0 milligram per minute. After her quick intervention, the injection speed marked on the indicator was at 0.1 milligrams per minute: ten times less. She was sure the policeman would not realize that and the dosage would be reduced at least until the next doctor or nurse passed to check on him.

"Good job. Now we just have to wait." Silvia smiled, pleased, leaving her to return to her newsroom.

The numbness induced by the medication slowly and gradually abandoned Vinci's mind. His dreams and his nightmares gave way to a progressively clearer image of the room and of the policeman watching him, sitting in a corner, reading a magazine. Reacquiring his clarity of mind little by little, he kept his eyelids closed to mislead the agent. He was still able by then to distinguish the bed's outline and the handcuffs, and he heard the television perfectly, with the news bulletin playing. The man on duty did not realize anything. Real memories and hallucinations still mixed up in his mind, clouded by the sedative, though less so. Until a few minutes before he felt like he had gone back to the times around the attack on the judge: his worst nightmare.

He had seen that scene hundreds of times in his dreams: the tension in the air, the feeling of something being wrong...then the explosion: flames and incandescent detritus everywhere, three of his men on the ground...then that burning pain in his shoulder, the judge and his wife falling, riddled with bullets...the rage...the pain...the darkness. However, in dreams, unlike in reality, he was able to turn back and see the enemy's face one second before the gun behind him could explode the shot which had finished his career, at least, if not his life. Every time he was able to recognize that face, but unfortunately, when he woke up, the betrayer's features got confused in his memory until they completely vanished, becoming unrecognizable and he could only feel a sense of consuming impotence, frustration…and a returning desire for revenge, the same that he could never put at ease, in spite of the years gone by.

This time his mind showed him another face, two actually. He was not sure it was a dream, because it was too vivid, but how could he be sure of it? Silvia's face at first, and Rebecca's right after, bent over him. Maybe it was a trick of his mind, bringing back to his conscience the only forms of affection he had felt since his lonely adolescence, and both were maybe lost, but…he really felt like it was real. So real that the words whispered by Rebecca, before she left the bed and his dreams, resounded in his head: "The keys for the handcuffs. They're in your gown." In that moment he woke up completely. He remembered seeing the doctor approach the electronic pump controlling the injection of the sedative.

While Silvia was distracting the policeman, Rebecca had probably reduced the rate of injection, rendering the medication useless. That was why he had woken up. Pretending to be sleeping still, he curled up on one side; the policeman watched him with suspicion, but then he relaxed and went back to his reading, when he realized he was motionless again. Vinci rummaged in the light cotton gown he had been clothed with, after they took off his clothes in the hospital, where he was brought by the police. He found the key, slowly exploring the folds to avoid attracting his guard's attention.

The policeman, occupied by his magazine, did not even move when Vinci's skillful hands unlocked the handcuffs. Alessandro did not remove them yet, to avoid messing up the plan he had excogitated. Usually, during the last hour of service, any security guard is less efficient, and he decided to wait for that moment. He looked at the television to find an indication of time: the change of shift usually happened at 2 p.m. His attention was attracted by the news scrolling in the lower part of the screen, under the TV bulletin's host. Professor Rastrini, agent De Marchi, maybe even Professor Benatti. The investigators were sure the death of Carmela Gerospi could also be blamed on the same person, just like the murders of Gianfranco Zacchia, Antonio Simoni and his wife Maddalena Centini.

Vinci had never heard the name of the woman murdered before: she had always been called by her husband's name up to that point. That sequence of names brought a thought back to his mind, a dark and imposing one, like the betrayer's face in his dream. Gerospi, Zacchia, Centini…in less time than it takes for a lightning bolt to illuminate a stormy night, he found the missing piece in the story and everything finally fit together, like the pieces of a puzzle. The series of murders had a meaning and he was now able to see it, clearly and unquestionably, like the murderer's face. After the awareness came the terror.

Rebecca! He slipped out of his handcuffs. To hell with caution! The policeman saw him fidgeting and approached. Vinci surprised him and hit him as hard as he could with a punch, and before he could stand back up he got rid of the I.V. and jumped on him to knock him out. Then he removed the policeman's clothes. He put on his shoes, his T-shirt and his trousers the other way around, to hide the colorful side stripes, leaving the shirt there: it was too easily recognizable. He rang the emergency bell off a nearby room and he took advantage of the confusion engendered by the fake emergency and by the staff coming and going to leave the ward; within a few minutes, he was already far from the hospital. He had been in such a rush that he had not thought to take the policeman's cell phone, and now he regretted that mistake. He had no money on him to call a taxi and somebody might notice him if he used public transportation. He could only walk fast, praying he was not too late.

**

Rebecca did not know why she was there and not in her apartment. Alessandro's attic had seemed like the best choice when she had left Silvia. She had lied to the policemen, who had let her go reluctantly, making sure that she would go back home after the hospital visit. She should have been glad. Thanks to Silvia, Pegasus was forced to credit the discovery to her and now her career would surely take off and soar to new heights. She should have been even happier that thanks to her an incredible amount of human beings would be saved, and she had confirmed the theory of panspermia.

On the radio, somebody was talking about books, films. And she remembered that the recovered book by Galileo Galilei was still in her bag. That volume would wait for Alessandro Vinci, she had decided. That discovery would have been credited to him and her, whatever happened after. He would be the one to make it available to the whole world. He deserved it. Rebecca pulled the manuscript out of the bag, released it from all the covers wrapping it, and put it on the kitchen table, taking just a quick look at it. Everything she felt was a sensation of emptiness.

When she had passed the attic's door, careless of the fact that police had prohibited access to the house, she had met a disastrous sight: the apartment had been violated and searched by the police, and they had not thought about returning the apartment to a normal state. Without even realizing it, she started to reorganize the things that had fallen, and to set the photos hanging on the walls upright.

In Alessandro's office she saw several binders, once well-ordered on the library shelves, and now on the ground with their contents all over the place. She remembered that it was from one of those that he had pulled out the short article which had brought them to Silvia. She kneeled down to pick all the papers up: there were documents, photos, newspaper cuttings, everything linked to Filippo Spinelli, the magistrate brother of the professor. Vinci was really obsessed with that old story.

Full of sadness, she thought about calling Silvia, the only one she could talk to in that moment, but when she got to the room, in front of her picture, she hung up the phone without waiting for her to pick up. Looking at that portrait once more, she could finally understand what troubled her so much about it. It was not just a naked picture of his previous girlfriend. It was a picture of Silvia in a special moment: the exact moment of orgasm. But more than the eye of the photographer staring at her, immortal, it looked like...the eye of the murderer.

Rebecca's blood ran cold. She left the bedroom and ran to look at all the other pictures around the house and she realized why those pictures, which were undoubtedly beautiful, had always made her uneasy and anxious: every man, woman or child pictured had been immortalized in the exact moment in which they were expressing something, maybe their best moment. The artisan working the wood, the child shooting a penalty, the dancer doing her best pirouette, even the woman in her most intimate moment. The person who had frozen them in time was not an artist; it was the sniper, shooting with his camera as if it were a gun. Rebecca tried to escape from the apartment as fast as she could: but she had to hang on to the semi-closed door: she was short of breath. She had to go out, she had to leave...As soon as she was out of the door, a figure blocked her path, startling her. When she recognized the person, her breath failed her entirely.

27

Vinci ran, careless of the curious looks of the passersby. He had searched for Rebecca at her place first—he remembered her address from when he had done research on her—but he had found the apartment locked and a gossipy neighbor had assured him she had not seen her for many days. He decided to go back to his attic then. When he could see it in the distance, convinced that it would be under surveillance, he stopped running and moved with caution.

His trained eye was able to easily locate the unmarked car with the two patrolling policemen and he tried to avoid them by taking a side alley, when he realized the two agents were not in the car. Caught by a bad presentiment, he carefully approached and had his suspicions confirmed: the cabin seemed empty, but there were traces of blood in the car, and one of the windows had been broken and then rolled down to avoid it being noticed. He heard a buzz while he looked into the car, and when he turned around he saw a fly on a blanket on the backseat. He moved it and, horrified, he discovered the two men's corpses. Both agents had been shot.

Before rushing into his apartment, Vinci used the car radio to alert the police station to what had happened, then he ran up the stairs, his anxiety mounting. The door was open and he rapidly overstepped it, without paying attention to the mess caused by the search. He felt he could perceive Rebecca's scent, but he forced himself to erase that idea from his mind. If he wanted to keep a hope of tracking her down, of saving her, his mind had to be cold, focused. He rapidly changed, putting the few things which could be of use in the following hours in a bag, then he went down to the workshop. It was past 7 p.m., and he did not find anybody, as he expected. He opened the shutter with a backup key and lifted up a greasy blanket. His motorbike was still where he had left it; the police had not thought about looking for his stuff in the workshop as well. He started the bike and sped away while he heard the first sirens arriving.

The gray clouds of an approaching storm had obscured what seemed a quiet afternoon. Silvia walked around in her office, at the newspaper, like a trapped animal. She was torn, tormented: she should be moving to Milan in the first few days of the following week, to the headquarters of the national newspaper. She was supposed to be in the office to organize her relocation, but she was actually there because she did not know where else to go: her place was an empty apartment; the few people she could see as friends worked with her, and now they were either intimidated or jealous of her promotion in the field, and they avoided her. God, how she wished she had a cigarette! The long-awaited storm finally arrived and a sudden lightning revealed a shadow at her window.

She was terrified, but she could still recognize who it was. "Alessandro!" she screamed, before taking a step back to let him come in from the windowsill. He must have climbed up the drainpipe to avoid passing the reception. "Jesus Christ, do you want to give me a heart attack?" she shouted at him, running to hug him immediately after. "Are you okay?" Vinci did not embrace her and he did not answer: he remained there, speechless, like a steel statue, until she detached herself from him. Meeting his gaze, Silvia was also rendered speechless: that was not Alessandro, the man she had loved and for whose safety she had sacrificed so much: she had Night in front of her. "Why did you not come in through the main entrance?" she asked, trying to stay calm and to figure out what was going on.

"It's being surveyed by the police," he communicated, and before she could ask any more questions, he told her why he was there: "Rebecca. She's been kidnapped. By the same person who's responsible for all the murders."

"Who?" asked Silvia with a firm and resolute voice, in response to that news.

"Michele Spinelli."

"Professor Spinelli?" she asked, mouth gaping.

"Yes. He's obsessed with Galileo Galilei, and he thinks he's one of his descendants. I always thought he only said that to make an impression, but now I'm convinced that it's a real obsession. You need to give me a list of all of his family's properties."

"Wait, I don't understand anything at all. Explain." The journalist in her would not move a finger without any further explanation, Vinci knew that.

"Zacchia, Gerospi, Centini. These are all names of the cardinals involved in the trial of Galileo Galilei by the Inquisition, the one which condemned him to recantation and imprisonment. Zacchia was in the court, but he did not sign the condemnation. That's why Spinelli humiliated him, but did not kill him: he died by accident. The other two…"

"My God!" Silvia uttered, remembering the few images that had been made public and the descriptions of the two massacres.

"He has Rebecca," he insisted. "We need to find out where he could be hiding her." Upset, Silvia ran to her computer and then to the phone, trying to trace everything that could lead to Spinelli's properties. After a few endless minutes, she had not discovered anything important. Vinci could not withhold an annoyed gesture. "Extend to his whole family," he suggested. "After his brother's murder I think he's the only heir left." Silvia went back to the keyboard but she stopped almost immediately, struck by an idea.

"The construction worker!" She typed even faster than before and, in the online archive of the newspaper, she finally found what she was looking for. Leaving the webpage open, she got on the phone and prayed that somebody would answer the company phone, despite the hour. She was lucky, and as soon as she heard somebody at the other end of the receiver, she immediately changed her tone of voice into a more formal one. She introduced herself and, resorting to all her human and professional gifts, and she was able to have the owner of the construction company tell her what she needed to know. She wrote it down on a piece of paper and hung up.

"You're a genius," she said talking to Alessandro. "The company that was doing the renovation works in Florence, do you remember? The one that found Galileo's papers in the plaster of the house under renovation. Well, they're now working on a villa which belonged to judge Spinelli and which is now property of his brother Michele. It wasn't mentioned among his possessions before, because formally it was a property of the judge's wife, but as she was killed in the attack, Michele is the only heir." She handed him the piece of paper with the address of the villa. The name of the company stood out: Terenzi brothers, the same name which had rung a bell in Silvia's memory. "Here is the link we were missing," the journalist continued. "That's how the letters got to Spinelli…Jesus Christ!" With a gesture she invited Vinci to read the article on the screen. Alessandro did it, but without understanding. "This construction worker was found hanged a few months ago, and he was working for the Terenzi brothers. They initially considered it a suicide, but the investigator later believed he had been killed. Now we know by whom."

"He knew Spinelli because he had worked in his house during the renovation and he approached him to sell him some letters he had smuggled at work. He took the letters and killed him," Vinci continued. Silvia saw the rage in his eyes, that the revelations had only made worse. Then she understood and felt bad for him. Vinci did not move an inch, his fury hardly restrained: "It was always him. The plant." His voice was strangely deep, almost a growl. Silvia had never seen him like that and she got scared. "The attack. I knew there had to be somebody inside. I always knew it." He grabbed the paper with the address and he was about to leave.

Silvia held his arm. "What does Rebecca have to do with this?"

"Think about her family name," he answered laconically, looking out the window. A moment later, he was not there anymore.

Once in the street, Vinci looked for the address on his smart phone's GPS: it was a villa by the sea, a few kilometers south of Ancona. The most logical place, the furthest away from all the murder scenes; uninhabited, even. He sped down the highway, heedless of any speed limit. When he reached his destination, he parked at a safe distance from the house, a cliff-side building, half covered by scaffolding. After a rapid inspection, he understood there was only one way to enter without sending off the alarm system: the most dangerous way possible. He checked his emergency equipment once more and made a last call. Then he left, more determined than ever to stay alive until the end of the operation.

**

Rebecca did not know if she had been awoken by the rumbling thunder or by the throbbing pain she felt in her head. She felt numb and she could not move her arms. What the hell was happening? Then, just as terrifying as the last clap thunder, came the memory of what had happened: Michele Spinelli appearing in front of her all of a sudden while she was rushing to leave Alessandro's apartment. Uncombed, unshaven and wearing wrinkly clothing. The exact opposite of the well-groomed person she knew. He had come into the apartment while she stepped back, astonished. He had told her that he had been kidnapped by Pegasus and that he had succeeded in escaping. He had come there to look for his old bodyguard, Vinci.

Before she could dial the number of the police, he had asked her for a glass of water. She had drunk one as well, trying to calm down; then she felt numb and sleepy…where the heck was she now? It was all dark around here, she could only make out the contours of the objects thanks to the forks of lightning that pierced the blackness. She tried to move, but she found out her wrists were tied up and she was chained to…a wooden beam? While she gradually recovered, her mind was able to remember the last time she had felt such a headache: the night she found herself in bed with Spinelli. The base of the beam immobilizing her was buried under a pile of shapeless materials. She tried to move her legs, to force the block with her bare feet, until she was sure about it. It was wood. A huge pile of wood.

"You're up," a voice behind her said, while a construction light turned on, blinding her. When her eyes adjusted to the light, she saw she was inside a villa under renovation; the high ceiling of the glass walls was protecting her from the stormy sky, but without hiding it. Michele Spinelli was sitting not too far away, close to a large table where a computer and some electronic equipment stood out. Rebecca, terrorized, tried to chase away the idea that was forming in her mind, and tried to move again, panicking. "Don't try to free yourself, it's useless," the man said, without taking his eyes off of his laptop. Rebecca was able to glimpse at a part of the images on the screen and she realized the man was watching security camera footage. On the same table she could easily distinguish Galileo's book, *Stella Novissima*. "Don't you want to know why you're here?" Spinelli stood up and walked closer to her. He held a knife in his hands. Rebecca felt her legs buckle with fear, and she would have fallen if the chains securing her wrists to the beam were not supporting her.

"No. I want you to free me! Have you gone mad?" she screamed.

"Yes, shout. Feel the fear. Feel what your lineage has inflicted for centuries to hundreds, thousands of other people!"

The doctor remained silent; she was very pale. In the eyes of the man in front of her she could see no light, only madness. She understood what she was bound to: a pyre. "You're crazy!" she screamed in terror. "I didn't do anything at all, I was born thirty-five years ago!"

"Your blood is what counts: the same of the cardinals who condemned my blood to imprisonment and the humiliation of recantation."

Rebecca desperately looked for arguments to make him see reason: "My name is Rebecca De Cardinale. My father was an engineer, my grandfather a lawyer. Michele, it's me, we traveled together, do you remember? We looked for Galileo's letters together!"

The man burst into thunderous laughter. "The letters? You still don't understand? The letters were a pretext, an excuse to bring you to your accomplices."

"My…accomplices?"

"The last descendants of the conspirers who condemned my ancestor, Galileo. The last ones alive." Alessandro had spoken the truth: Spinelli thought he was a relative of Galilei and now he wanted to take his revenge on his accusers, attacking their descendants, as if the last four centuries had not passed. She understood she had no way out, but she still tried to distract him, to make him speak, in the hope of delaying his schemes as much as possible.

"So you were the one to kill them…"

"I only did what was fair. I did justice to the memory of my relative."

"But why did you bring me to the victims' houses?"

"My initial plan was to blame you for everything. At every meeting I didn't touch anything, if not with my gloves on. Nobody had seen me, so everybody would have thought I was missing, or another victim. You would be the only one blamed for all the murders, unjustly, and you would have felt for yourself the taste of imprisonment for a crime you did not commit."

"You killed Zacchia, the Simonis, even the hoarder?"

"I only wanted to humiliate Zacchia: his ancestor did not sign the condemnation. His death was accidental: I put too much GHB in his fruit juice during our visit and when I went back to his place that night he was already in a coma. Carmela Gerospi descended from Fabrizio Gerospi, who signed Galileo's condemnation and Maddalena Centini is a descendant of Felice Centini."

"I have nothing to do with Galileo and the Inquisition!" Rebecca screamed, bringing back to her mind the descriptions she had read of Maddalena Centini's massacre.

"You're the worst," Spinelli hissed, approaching her with his knife. "Your blood is the blackest and your family name says that. De Cardinale: the family name attributed in the past to the illegitimate son of a cardinal. You carry your shame with you: you descend from cardinal Guido Bentivoglio. My genealogical research is very accurate and I can't be wrong. Your ancestor was a betrayer, he had even been in Galileo's house! My ancestor had hosted him, he had been his master and he...and you betrayed him, condemned him!" he roared. Rebecca did not even struggle to hold back her tears anymore, while she uselessly clawed at her chains. Pleased by her suffering, he continued his monologue: "I had organized everything. I brought you to the houses of your accomplices; I made you believe we were persecuted by a mysterious criminal organization..."

"But Pegasus did chase us!"

"You're really stupid! You saw what I wanted you to see! The dark cars we always had behind us? Pure suggestion. Do you have any idea how many dark cars there are around? I just had to point a couple of them to you to have your imagination give them a name. Maybe you thought you were living in an adventure story."

Rebecca felt ashamed for how naïve she had been, and she found her fighting spirit back. "Bullshit! I spoke to Pegasus, I gave them the biologic material and they'll make a vaccine with it!"

"Yes, I saw your nice scene, and I should compliment you. Maybe I should visit that journalist as well. What's her name? Silvia Canelli?"

"She has nothing to do with this! Pegasus is real. The rest is just made up by your imagination…"

"Of course Pegasus is real! Who do you think called them? Who told them about the virus, the asteroids?"

"Professor Benatti," she replied, remembering the copy of the emails in Krupp's hands, the first emissary of the pharmaceutical company who contacted her in Florence.

Spinelli laughed again. "You're so easy to deceive. I sent that email. This email." Michele pulled out of his jacket a piece of paper and held it under her eyes. "Don't you remember what happened the morning we met, in Benatti's office? How I helped him to open the e-mail I had just sent him with Galilei's letter? A trick I excogitated on purpose to watch that fossil type his email credentials."

"You saw his password," she replied.

"You're starting to understand, good. Then I sent this e-mail from his address and I erased any trace of it."

"But that e-mail would still be in Krupp's computer!" Rebecca objected, holding on to that last weak hope.

"I don't think so. Krupp's email address did not exist. Krupp himself did not exist."

Rebecca remembered when Deputy Commissioner Angeloni had told her during the last interrogation that Torre had confirmed the existence of Krupp, but he has also said he had died a long time before. "But Pegasus said Krupp did work for them. Before he died...Oh my God, did you kill him as well? But...according to the police he died in a car crash before we met. I saw him, though, I met him in Florence!"

"Or maybe you just met a tall man with glasses, a scar on his face and a strong German accent, didn't you?" he said, imitating Krupp's voice perfectly. Or better, what she had thought was Krupp's voice. "It's incredible how a detail can make you forget about everything else, isn't it? A mask and a fake scar were enough to mislead you; and it takes a minute to print a fake business card. The real Krupp was a greedy and slimy betrayer who would have sold his mother if he could. Mankind has not lost much with his death: I had talked to him about the letters, and about the possibility of finding Galilei's posthumous book, but instead of financing my efforts, he immediately understood the potential of the discovery. He bought some of the letters from my greedy colleague Rastrini and he made me understand quite clearly that he would keep the profits of the discovery all for himself. I had to silence him, but I brought him back to life for you, to keep you under pressure and in Florence when you wanted to leave, you remember that? It was essential that the police pinned you at the crime scenes in the period in which they were committed and when police questioned you, you would declare you had just met a man who had died months before: in the best case, they would have thought you were crazy."

"You thought about everything," Rebecca growled, more furious than desperate.

"Yes, but I did not consider the Rebecca variable." The knife was moving again between his fingers. "I couldn't know that, while I was doing justice..."

"While you were massacring innocents, you mean," she interrupted him.

He jumped forward and laid the knife's blade on her lips, forcing her to silence. "The evening we ate in the restaurant together, the evening of the red dress, do you remember?" Rebecca became red with rage and shame. "That evening I poured some GHB into your glass. It's surprising how easy it is to buy that in any club." GHB, a rape drug! That's why she did not remember anything: once ingested, it subdued the victims, erasing all their memories. She was not drunk, when she ended up in bed with him: she had been drugged! Her rage increased even more, but she could only go on listening to him. "I put you in the car and as soon as we were out of the restaurant, I moved you to the trunk. When I gave the valet the car, he did not see you. It wasn't easy after, but I went back to the garage and I brought you to my room. You couldn't be spotted in the hotel that evening, to avoid giving you an alibi for Carmela Gerospi's death. I couldn't know that while I was doing justice in the previous evenings, instead of remaining in the room, you went out around Florence in places with security cameras. And especially I could not imagine that after I went missing, you would go into my room to take the letters and you would be able to escape the police."

"They'll find the letters, we brought them to Menin, and he made copies of them…" the woman tried to temporize.

"They'll find the copies I created. Zacchia, Centini and Gerospi only had useless papers, which did not say anything about *Stella Novissima*: the ones you found in my room were fake, I had prepared them in case you insisted on seeing the documents I had bought, to convince you they concerned the book. I immediately hid the letters I had really bought, because I thought you would be too ignorant to see the difference, and in fact you didn't see it. I had even called Zacchia and Centini a few days before our visits, offering them very high amounts of money. I became my own competition, and that worked: you thought somebody was really chasing us for those letters. When you ran away to Padua you surprised me, I have to admit that. I tried to wait for you at your place, but you didn't even stop by there, not even today. Really smart, but I found your old ID instead."

"To access the Department of Literature and kill Doctor Menin."

"From the records, you were the last one to enter." The man nodded with satisfaction. "If everything had gone the way it was supposed to go, you would have been arrested and charged with all the murders. I would remain hidden for some time and then I would remerge when everything quieted down. I would have said I had been kidnapped and kept in a secret place by your accomplices, before escaping. Who would have believed the words of a visionary murderer, at that point?"

"I'm happy I made your house of cards crumble."

"Oh…we'll see how happy you'll be in a second." His tone of voice lost all of its condescendence to become threatening. "Keep in mind that it was your fault alone I had to take care of Benatti as well, and even Menin. I wanted to impede them from revealing my fake letters, but I came too late: he had already sent you an email…And even Rastrini, but I have to admit that was almost a pleasure: less competition for the remaining letters of Galilei, he was the only one who could have stolen them from me. I regained his trust first, revealing to him that the two of you were wanted."

"That's why he refused to give us the documents he had, the second day!"

"Exactly. It's a shame that he refused to give me those documents as well, that evening. I had to take care of him as well."

"With the gun you found in our motel," Rebecca realized.

"A skillful move, wasn't it? I entered when you both were not there. I used the gun and put it back where it was without you even realizing it. I eliminated a rival while blaming another rival for it. Brilliant, don't you think?"

"Why Benatti?" Rebecca asked, ever more surprised by her own naïvety.

"Because he would have denied that he had sent me the emails and he could have confirmed your version of the events."

The more she listened to him, the more she realized something was not right. "How did you know I would go back to Padua? I could have fled anywhere."

"Oh, I had taken my precautions," Spinelli said, pulling out of his pocket the doctor's cell phone. With a very thin screwdriver, he opened it up without any care for its delicate components and he showed her the circuits inside, proud of himself. "It's a locator. I always knew where you were, at any time. Just in case anything went wrong and I needed to know where you were."

"But the cell phone had no SIM card!" she objected, remembering the exact moment in which her phone had mysteriously fallen out of its case outside at the Hotel Savoy. She had not thought too much about it in that moment, and why should she have?

"There's no need for a SIM card: the transistor works independently of that; it's charged by the phone battery."

"That's the reason the police could always find us: you were the one to inform them!" Rebecca also understood why they had not been followed at other times. When her cell phone was out of charge, the bud did not work. "And you were the one who tried to run us over in Padua, weren't you?"

Spinelli giggled. "That evening I had parked my car in the parking lot of Torre Molino; I was tracing you and then you suddenly appeared in front of me, reading the inscription on the tower. I couldn't risk you seeing me, so I ran away, at the risk of killing you both in advance."

Rebecca trembled from the implied menace. Her only hope was having him keep talking: "The car was not your Mercedes."

"No. Unfortunately that was taken into custody. I used a friend's car. The one I used to move around in Florence, leaving my 'official' car in the hotel's parking lot: the police would think I had remained in the hotel, while I was actually carrying out my fair sentences. When you escaped you messed up my plans and you forced me to improvise, to follow your movements: I couldn't imagine you would turn to that boy scout, Vinci. I even tried to recruit those three incompetents to kidnap you, but he knocked them out. Fortunately, they will never be able to tell the police anything that can lead them to me: the only one I had contact with thinks he has been paid by a German man with a scar on his face…the same face that policeman, De Marchi, saw before dying. He had found Krupp's fake business card. But he was too ambitious and too stupid to share what he had found out with his colleagues, so I had to take care of him as well."

"And you found me in the same way last night," she realized. "Following my cell phone. You're a psychotic murderer. A bastard and a maniac!"

"That's not what you said a few weeks ago," he mocked her. "You should have seen the doe-eyed expression you had while I gave you lectures on the Middle Ages. You really believed you were the heroine of a novel."

If Rebecca could have blushed, she would have, but her face was too pale with fear. "I thought you were different," she whispered, in her defense.

"Oh, I did as well, you know. I didn't think you would be that difficult…" With his knife's blade he entered her shirt, slowly, sadistically. Rebecca prepared to feel the pain, but the steel only brushed against her skin. The blade made the first button fall off, and she trembled. She saw the man's evil expression, while he made another button fall off.

"No!" she screamed, trying to hold back, but Spinelli did not stop until he had completely opened her shirt. The blade entered under her bra and cut it, leaving her naked, exposed to Spinelli's gaze. Unable to stand the humiliation, she raised her face again, in a last defying move. "You don't have your blue pills with you this time, do you?" Blinded by fury, the man punched her face. Rebecca saw his armed fist rise up and then down on her. She closed her eyes, expecting the worst, but nothing happened. She opened her eyelids again and saw the knife's blade hanging a few centimeters from her breast.

"You're good, I almost fell for it," he said, smiling. "You'd like to die rapidly, wouldn't you?" He lowered his knife and stepped back. He came down from the pyre of wood and picked up a jug from the ground. He unscrewed the top and started to spread its contents on the heap. Rebecca understood what it was from the smell: gasoline. "You know, there were several ways to burn somebody at the stake," Spinelli said sadistically to his prisoner. "Some had green wood bundles just around the condemned person, who would then die choking on the smoke caused by the combustion, even before the flames could burn him. Those were the most compassionate." He ignited the lighter and shut up, enjoying the terrorized expression on the woman's face. "Then there were the worst heretics, those who had to become a show. In that case, they prepared a pyre of large beams, which burned slowly, letting the heat lightly brush the condemned's body. Very slowly. They say that some people could watch their own belly explode from the heat before dying. We'll soon discover if that's just a myth."

"They'll find you!" she said, in tears.

"That's possible," he admitted. "I'm afraid I'll have to leave the country. Brazil, then maybe India. I think I won't have many problems hiding my tracks. I'll be one of the many who can get away with murder…"

"Alessandro will find you, even if you hide in the Antarctic!"

"I don't think so," he sneered. "Even without counting his record, which isn't the best at all, he still is the only suspect for all of the murders. He'll be stuck in jail for years, decades, before they reach a verdict and maybe…who knows? Something might happen to him in jail…"

"I wouldn't count on that," a voice behind him growled, hardly covered by a new rumble of thunder. Rebecca and Spinelli looked at the same time. The professor turned pale. The gasoline jerry can fell from his hands, spurting on him. Out of the corner of his eye, Spinelli looked at his laptop. The alarms had not gone off. "Don't try to figure out how I could get in. You always underrated me, always. Just like I always underrated you; but this will be the last time, you can bet on that." Rebecca watched Vinci come forward from the window, with his gun aimed at the professor. He looked awful: he was soaking wet. His face, his hands and his knees were covered in scratches; he was dirty, bleeding and in his eyes was the look of a murderer. Even she was scared of him. That was not Alessandro, and not even Vinci the ninja, that was Night.

Spinelli did not even seem to realize that. He stared at Vinci's gun and challenged him: "If you shoot me, the lighter falls down and everything will explode," he explained, showing the flame in his left hand. Night was aware of that, and that was why he had not shot him yet. "But I have to admit you're right. I did underrate you. You did not only escape the arrest, but you were even able to find me and climb up the cliff twenty meters to reach me, on a stormy night like this one! You should have died only from thinking of such madness. The worst mistake of my life was the day I didn't manage to kill you. You're too fucking lucky!"

"It was always you, wasn't it? All the murders: Zacchia, Gerospi, Centini, like the cardinals of the Galilei trial."

"You're shrewder than I thought," his enemy replied wryly.

"Your brother as well. You were the plant. I had checked the scene before letting you come down from the armored car. It couldn't have been anybody else. You were the only one behind me."

"Is that why you wanted me to be your Ph.D. supervisor? To check up on me?"

"Keep your friends close and your enemies closer," he mocked him.

"Why?" Night looked at the tied-up girl and at the man with the flame in his hands, analyzing his options. He saw the table beside him, and perceived the ancient book.

"I found out Filippo was about to interdict me. He did not share my passion for the Maestro. He thought I was crazy. And I needed money. My…lifestyle was quite expensive, surely more than the salary of a full professor allowed, and my brother's wife was rich, very rich, and she liked to throw her wealth in my face! But now," Spinelli said, satisfied with a wide gesture indicating the whole environment, "now it's all mine."

"You won't get out of here alive," Night growled.

"I think I will," he said, giggling, raising the gasoline jerry can. Vinci moved his gun, but Spinelli showed him the lighter's flame again. He began to slowly walk away from the pyre, without turning, continuing to pour the gasoline on the ground. "You see, now I'll build a gasoline trail. When I'm behind that door I'll light it up. You will be too busy extinguishing the flames before they reach your beauty to stop me. You'll never see me again."

"And you'll never see this anymore!" Night jumped to the table and grabbed the book, still aiming at the man with his gun. Spinelli blanched. "You don't want the last writings by your ancestor to disappear among the flames…his revenge against the Inquisition!" Spinelli raised the gasoline jerry can and walked a few paces towards him. Exactly what he was expecting. Vinci saw his resoluteness cede for a moment and immediately took advantage of it: he threw the book up and Spinelli let go of the jerry can to catch the book, losing at the same time his grip on the lighter. The flame did not touch the ground but fell on Spinelli himself, and he caught fire immediately, since he had gasoline on himself as well. He did not even realize it at the beginning, as he was too busy trying to protect the ancient pages from the flames, but he was soon seized by a luminous spiral and his bestial screams filled the air.

Night raised his gun, but then, after a last cold look, he let him burn in the hell he had procured himself. His empty eyes remained there to watch him contort in agony. He slowly put his weapon back in his belt and looked away, then he ran towards Rebecca, who was luckily not menaced by the fire. "Are you okay?" he rapidly asked, while she nodded, relieved but in tears. Night tried to test the chains, they were sound, so he absolutely had to find a tool. The thunder partially covered the terrible screams of the man who was burning alive, their pitch higher and higher. Closer and closer. Rebecca looked at Spinelli in terror; he was by then completely covered by fire and he was dragging his body to the gasoline trail, to throw himself on it with his last breath.

"Alessandro!" she screamed, impotent, while the fire trail ran towards the pyre, creating a wall of flames around them. "My God! Help me! I don't want to die like that!" Rebecca screamed with all the breath she had left. The flames reached the gasoline-covered pyre, and unlike what his jailor intended to happen, they approached her too fast. Night realized that he did not have the time to look for any tools. He tried to move the beam to which Rebecca was tied, but that hardly moved; the bastard had done a great job, wedging it in at the bottom. It would take time to force it out. Time he did not have. The heat was soon unbearable; the chains were getting warmer, almost scorching. Rebecca heard the noise of the flesh of his hands sizzling while he grabbed them and tried with all his energy to break them, though with no success. "Alessandro! Alessandro!" she screamed, desperate. "You need to leave. Go away, or we'll both die!" she said with tears running down her cheeks. "Use your gun," she begged him. "Hurry up, I don't want to suffer."

He lifted up his gun and stared at her in the eyes. "We'll either leave together or neither of us will leave," he said, then he shot first at the chain behind Rebecca's shoulders, breaking it, and then exploded the following shots above their head, towards the large window on the room's roof. The bullets made the glass collapse, letting the pouring rain fall down on them. Night shielded her with his own body, protecting her from the heavy glass falling on them. The torrential rain gave her some relief and extinguished the flames closest to her, those burning the wood that was not touched by the gasoline. The pyre was infernal, though, and it did not yield to the bad weather. All they had gained was some more time, and that was what Night was looking for. He removed his T-shirt and used it to protect his already burnt hands. He tried to unfasten the chain but even though it was broken, it was still trapped by the central beam; without any alternative, he started to move it back and forth, until he was able to bend it.

Then he grabbed it as fast as he could, and pushed it down from the pyre with all his force, on the only side that had not been set on fire yet. Rebecca saw the muscle fibers in his chest and in his arms stretch so much that she feared they would break, but it was the wood beam to break, stripped from its base. With all the force he had left, he dragged it towards himself, allowing Rebecca to get away from the fire and untying the chains that kept her imprisoned. When she was free, he used the beam as a bridge between two shores in flame. He placed it over the pyre, on the coolest side and he climbed onto it, taking the woman in his arms. They fell on the floor, burnt, but alive. Night rushed to attend to Rebecca, who was coughing from the inhaled smoke, to the point that her throat was bleeding.

"I'm okay. I'm okay," she said. She saw him give a last look at Spinelli's consumed body, and then pulled out of his belt buckle an object slightly bigger than a pen.

He turned it towards himself and then said, "I hope you recorded everything, Colonel."

"Great! You filmed his confession." Rebecca coughed, looking at her partner. Night did not hide his malicious smile, while he helped her stand up, to walk towards the first sirens arriving in the villa's garden. "Standard operative tactic." He nodded, laying her down and lifting up his hands when the police arrived. The last thing Rebecca saw was him, immobilized by the SWAT. *They didn't shoot him*, she thought, while a doctor placed an oxygen mask on her face. *They didn't shoot him.*

EPILOGUE

"I don't think I've ever spent so much time in a hospital," Silvia said, handing Rebecca a fruit juice. She smiled, but she did not answer, trying to spare her voice. Her larynx was still swollen, but she would heal. The doctor had reassured her. For her convalescence, she was in a single room paid by the newspaper, as the journalist had told her the first time she visited her, a couple of days before.

"How will this end?" Rebecca asked, immediately regretting having spoken. Her throat burned as if she had swallowed acid.

"The police received the video. There will be some details to clarify, but I'm sure you will be acquitted of all charges."

"Even from the charges of assault and attempted murder of a police officer?" the doctor asked again, without regretting it this time.

"I don't really think anybody wants the story about two policemen shooting an unarmed woman from behind to come out…those charges will be dismissed as well, I'm sure about that." Silvia smiled and placed a pillow under Rebecca's head.

"Oh, I forgot, I think Achille 'spontaneously' retired. The squad leader testified about his obsession with Alessandro. And he did not believe Alessandro when he was convinced the attack on Judge Spinelli had been organized by an insider. If he had acted earlier, he would have avoided a good number of corpses." An embarrassed silence descended in the room, and could not hide the unasked question. Eventually,

Silvia could not restrain herself: "And about the two of you? What do you plan to do?"

Rebecca sighed, not sure about what to answer. "I haven't decided yet. A part of me loves him to death. I think a large part of me loves him to death…"

"But?" Silvia insisted.

"But another part of me can't forget about his dark side. You didn't see him kill; I did. He watched Spinelli die in an atrocious way, and he stared at him without any emotion, deciding his fate with an ice-cold expression. That was not Alessandro; there was only darkness. The deepest darkness. Now I understand why they called him Night."

"You're telling me you're sorry he let Spinelli—the man who was burning you alive, after having caused so many deaths—die?"

Rebecca smiled bitterly. "I'm not saying he didn't deserve his death, or that I wouldn't have done the same in that moment. I'm saying that in situations like that, I see a side of him that I'm not sure I am ready to handle, and I'm not even sure I want to. It feels like Alessandro vanishes to be replaced by a demon."

"It's true, there's a demon inside him, one he might never be rid of. It's his personal Hell. I saw it and was burnt by it, but for you that man threw away the life he had struggled so much to reconstruct: he faced the abyss again to save you. I don't think many women can say the same about the men they have beside them."

"I'm an ungrateful bitch, right?" she replied, contrite. "I should build a monument to him; he saved my life so many times. Actually, the whole of humankind should build a monument to him; without him, we would never even get close to a vaccine."

"But?"

"But I could not face Night again. I could not spend my life beside him. Not even if I owe him that life."

"You know, I think I get what he found in you. I saw it clearly one day, while he was looking at you." Rebecca did not reply, curious, while Silvia took a packet from her bag. She handed it to her. Rebecca took out three photographs. Three close-ups of her, printed in black and white. She remembered that day in Florence, right after meeting professor Rastrini, when she had asked Alessandro to dress like an American tourist. His expression had made her smile and he had been quick to take pictures of her. "I found these in his reflex camera, he had left it in the apartment he rented," Silvia continued. "You understand what I mean? I realized this in Florence. You had just been wounded by the ruins of the barn, after they had tried to kill you, you remember? He was dangerously close to his abyss, I recognized the signs of it, but then something magical happened: you smiled."

"What?"

"Yes, you smiled over a banality, but when you did I saw his expression change, I saw him reemerge from his darkness. It's something I was never able to do. You're his ray of sunshine." They both shut up, with their eyes wet. Then they burst out in a great peal of laughter, hugging each other and telling one another they were being silly. "So, what will you do?" Silvia asked her, standing up to bid her farewell.

"I don't know. I think I'll wait to find out who will come in that door: Alessandro or Night."

Later on, Rebecca was alone in the hospital room. When he heard their code knocked on the door outside visiting hours, she sat up on the bed with her heart in her throat. She was tempted not to answer; then she mustered all her courage and whispered as loud as she could: "Come in."

He came in and she was immediately struck with anxiety: he had one arm hanging in a sling, both hands were bandaged, his forehead was full of excoriations and his cheekbone was still blue from the last scuffle. She was tempted to climb out of the bed and run to embrace him, but his tough expression stopped her. He looked petrified. Lost. One moment later she saw his face brightened by the same bewildered expression, filled with vulnerable sweetness which had made her fall in love more than any of his courageous feats. She saw he was afraid. Afraid to lose her. When he approached, she threw her arms around him, sighing with relief against his chest.

"Hi...Alessandro."

ABOUT THE AUTHOR

Aristide Bergamasco was born in 1970 in Padua. He graduated in medicine and specialized in general surgery, and lives in the Euganean Hills where he works as an emergency doctor. He is passionate about photography and mythology, and his stories have been awarded in numerous national competitions.

CPSIA information can be obtained
at www.ICGtesting.com
Printed in the USA
LVHW021554220321
682097LV00031B/1112